Gail Roughton

ISBN: 978-1-77145-258-8

Books We Love Ltd.
Chestermere, Alberta
Canada

Copyright 2014 by Gail Roughton

Cover art by Michelle Lee Copyright 2014

All rights reserved. Without limiting the rights under copyright reserved above, no part of this publication may be reproduced, stored in or introduced into a retrieval system, or transmitted, in any form, or by any means (electronic, mechanical, photocopying, recording, or otherwise) without the prior written permission of both the copyright owner and the publisher of this book

SLATER PUBLIC LIBRARY
105 N TAMA, BOX 598
SLATER, IA 50244

Dedication:

For my son-in-law, Sgt. Jason Smith, K-9 Officer, Cobra Crime Suppression Unit, and his fellow officers of the Twiggs County Sheriff's Department.

I couldn't have done it without you, Twiggs 19!

Chapter One

Clayton Chapel loomed out of the darkness, caught in the spear of the patrol cruiser's headlights. Deputy Alec Wimberly left the engine running per protocol and got out to do his obligatory night check walk-around, eyes open for stray teenagers. Clayton Chapel's reputation drew them like magnets. He ran the flashlight's beam around the dark windows of the second floor. And froze. For just a moment.

He raced hell bent for leather back to the car and scrambled in. The cruiser careened down the country road in a flurry of squealing wheels and flying gravel. He didn't look back. If he looked back, he'd see it. He knew he would. The silhouette of a little girl in banana curls, backlit in the window. Pounding organ music still rang in his ears.

He slowed just enough to negotiate a wide turn onto Highway 96. Back on the asphalt, he could pretend it never happened. He checked the speedometer and eased off the gas. Or tried to. For a moment his foot, lead on the pedal, wouldn't obey. He reached to his shoulder and hit the send button on his radio phone.

"Rockland 19, back on patrol from property check at Clayton Chapel."

"Ten-four Rockland 19." Dispatcher Aileen Sanders hesitated. "You okay, Nineteen? You sound kinda funny."

"Fine. Nineteen out." His heart rate slowed. *I didn't see anything. I didn't see anything, I didn't hear anything, and I'm never gonna see it again. Because I ain't goin' back there alone. Ever.*

* * * *

On the other side of the county, in a big house off Highway 80, a hand reached for the ringing phone.

"Tonight's delivery's made. It's done."

"Went all right? No problems?"

Slight hesitation. "No problems."

"What went wrong?"

Damn. The caller cringed. *Should have known better.*

"Nothing went wrong. Somebody unexpected showed up. Didn't see anything, though."

"Who?"

"One of the deputies. Out on night patrol. Ran like a scared rabbit, no big deal."

"You better hope so. What the hell happened? We're supposed to know the schedules."

"We do. Mostly. Can't always call it down to the minute."

"S'posed to be able to. Why else we spend the money, for Chrissakes?"

"Wasn't no problem," the caller reiterated. "He didn't see anything."

"You know which deputy?"

"Yeah."

"Well?"

"Well, what?" The caller had a soft spot for all the young Rockland deputies.

"Who the hell was it, and don't you ever make me ask you something twice."

"Alec Wimberly."

"Not one of ours. Could he be, though?"

"Wellll, I don't know, sir."

"Keep an eye on him."

"Yes sir."

Dial tone. The caller sighed in relief. Damn, he hated being on the Boss Man's bad side. He wasn't real fond of being on the Boss Man's good side. Had to be an easier way to make a living. Well, hell, he knew there was. Just not this good a living.

Chapter Two

A gray Mustang, traveling at a speed just shy of the speed law enforcement noticed, ran out of Macon and onto Emory Highway, up Riggins Mill Road. Billy Brayton smiled when he crossed the railroad tracks. Now came the fun part, the sharp curves and steep hills that made this back country road a mini-rollercoaster for folks who knew how to drive it. Billy knew how to drive it. A good start to this homecoming twenty-five years in the making.

He didn't expect a homecoming parade. Being railroaded out of town at eighteen with a trumped-up armed robbery charge hanging over your head didn't leave the town folk with many fond memories of you.

He closed his eyes for a second and shook his head. Even eighteen-year-olds should've had more sense, and he'd been a very old eighteen. What the hell was he thinking when he fell in love with Big John Kincaid's daughter Maggie? Public high school and private academy. Poor white trash and county gentry. Why had he ever imagined Big John Kincaid, owner of mineral rights to acres of land in a county rich with kaolin, majority shareholder in two local banks, owner of the county's biggest farm—why had he ever thought Big John would just stand back and see his daughter paired with the town bad boy?

He'd known Big John ran the county. Any fool knew that. But the absolute ruthlessness of that power? Well, the night the Sheriff hauled him out of his salvaged Mustang at the stop sign off of Highway 80 and Gilead Road and arrested him for armed robbery—that'd get anybody's attention. He could still see the blue swirls of the sirens and feel the bite of the metal handcuffs. He could still hear the sneers of the Sheriff and his deputies.

"Bit off more'n you could chew this time, boy. What happens when you get too far above yourself, son, you always gon' fall."

"I don't know what you're talking about, I didn't do anything!"

"Jim Ellis over at the Chevron, he says different."

"Ask Maggie! I just took her home!"

"Son, you got no business with Maggie Kincaid. You shoulda been listening those times Big John tried to warn you off."

Well, too late, too bad, so sad. Big John's long reach had him squarely by the balls. He'd listened to the strong suggestions of the local Judge and the circuit DA (both of whom just happened to be Kincaid's cousins). Move on out, GI Joe. It beat the hell out of the pen. He hadn't expected to see Maggie before he left town. She was under virtual house arrest, for sure. But he had expected, in the end, that everything would turn out okay. Ah, sweet innocence of youth.

Real life seldom works the same way fantasies do. Four weeks into his six weeks of basic training at Ft. Benning, mail call brought a newspaper clipping from the Turkey Creek weekly, announcing Maggie's engagement to Dean Albright, her third or possibly fourth cousin, probably once or twice removed. Private academy boy, county gentry. Just like Maggie. And currently attending the Walter F. George School of Law in Macon. Big John would like that, having a lawyer in the family.

Two weeks after the first clipping, immediately prior to the end of basic, another newspaper clipping arrived at mail call, announcing Maggie's wedding. Flipping the cutting over, he noted the Turkey Creek Garden Club was meeting at Wanda Thompson's house that week.

He shoved the memories out of his mind and put his attention back on the road. He was approaching the biggest and baddest of the local Deadman's Curves. He knew this road like the back of his hand, but it'd been a long time since he'd driven it. He slowed the Mustang enough to drop it into fourth gear for the steep hill bearing sharply to the left. This road didn't get a lot of traffic, but what traffic it did get usually took their half out of the middle on this curve.

Then he cursed, loud and fluent, at a fool in a white Civic barrelling around the curve. In the middle of the road, of course. It flew past a black Eclipse fighting to keep control and edging toward the shoulder. Billy swerved to his right and dropped into third as the Civic slipped through the gap between the Mustang and the Eclipse. Horn blaring, it raced down and over the next hill, disappearing from sight. Billy ran onto his shoulder and jerked his head around to check on the Eclipse. That driver had to be out of road room, and there wasn't any shoulder on that side of the road. It just dropped off sharply into free-fall.

The struggling front tires made a valiant, futile effort to regain traction. The car was going over. Billy cut his engine and hit the ground running.

He peered through the swirls of dust over the drop-off. The hood looked like an accordion, crumpled against a fair-sized oak tree. The smell of gas hung heavy in the air. Billy half-ran, half-slid down to the Eclipse, grabbing onto tree trunks for balance and swinging off them for speed and leverage as he moved. Judging by the steady stream of profanity flowing out from the cracked windshield, the driver was probably okay.

"Shit, damn, hell! *Son-of-a-bitch*! If I ever get my hands on that mother—"

Billy grinned and yanked on the door handle. A good-looking boy in his late teens beat shaking hands against the air bag. Beads of sweat stood out from his hairline. Nothing wrong with his voice, though. His vocabulary was superb. He'd been trained by a master. Billy shrugged off a niggling trace of déjà-vu and gave the kid a brief once over.

"I'll teach you a few more when we get you out of here, son, but right now we need to move. Gas is leaking somewhere, let's go, let's go!" Billy shoved his arm between the air bag and the boy's body and snagged the seatbelt release.

The boy, no fool, wiggled and shrugged the harness off his shoulder as he scrambled out. Billy positioned the boy in front of him going back up the hill, boosting him with a hand in the small of his back as they grabbed tree trunks and moved toward the pavement.

"Here, get in and sit down." Billy opened the driver's door of the Mustang and settled the kid in. He reached across to the console and grabbed for his cellphone, dialing 911. He reported the accident, requested an officer, no ambulance, and turned his attention back to the boy.

"You okay, son? Here, let's have a look. Not trying to frisk you or feel you up now, just checking," he said as he ran his hands down the boy's arms and legs.

"You're pretty cool under pressure, man, that was some good driving to miss me and that asshole in the Civic both. I'm okay, really, just shook."

Billy stepped back. The boy was a natural athlete by his build, muscular and toned. He worked out hard. Football, Billy guessed, maybe some baseball. Not basketball.

"Anybody'd be shook, and that was some pretty good driving you did, too. Good thing you weren't speeding yourself, or you sure wouldn't have come out this good." Billy reached for the console's cup holder and grabbed the bottle of Coke he'd been drinking. "Here. Not a good habit, I know, but I don't have anything catching at the moment, and you need the sugar. Helps with shock. And anybody coming out of that's a little shocky."

The boy took the bottle and chugged. "Thanks. Jake Rubin," the boy said, and stuck out his right hand.

"Well, pleased to meet you, Jake. Though the circumstances sure could have been better. Billy Brayton."

Jake, who had the Coke half-way back to his mouth, dropped his arm and glared. His expression hardened, his eyes narrowed.

"Excuse me?" he said.

What the hell? This kid was way too young to have any idea who Billy was or heard any tales of his less than sterling reputation.

"Billy Brayton," he repeated. "I grew up in Turkey Creek. Just retired from the army. I decided to come back home."

The boy kept glaring.

"You know something about me to put that look on your face, son?"

"I know you look pretty good for a dead man. Better than you're going to look after my mother gets her hands on you, for sure."

"Excuse me?"

"My mother's changed the flowers on your grave four times a year for the past twenty-five years. Glad you were comin' along and all, but how the hell could you do that to her? Let her think you were dead?"

Chapter Three

Billy's stomach did a slow roll. "And your mother would be?"

"Maggie Kincaid."

"You mean Maggie Albright. Or—didn't you just tell me your name was Rubin?"

"I mean Maggie Kincaid, my mother's never been married." Jake threw back another swig of the Coke and realized what he'd said. "I guess that sounds funny. I'm adopted. So you've been where all this time and didn't try to see Mom why?"

"She thinks I'm dead?"

"Man, everybody thinks you're dead. You've got a *headstone*. I've seen your *obituary*. Freak accident in boot camp. It's in her high school scrapbook. It ends with that obituary."

Billy struggled to get his bearings. The kid was relentless. And enraged on his mother's behalf.

"I'm gonna ask till you answer, you know. You've been where doing what while my mother's been tendin' your grave?"

Billy reached for his wallet, opened it, and pulled out the two small laminated clippings announcing Maggie's engagement and marriage. He'd never really understood why he'd kept them. For years now, he'd only looked at them when he was drunk and he didn't get drunk very often.

"Do you know how I left here?"

"Yeah. Not from Mom, she doesn't talk about it much, but I've pieced stuff together. Folks talk. I mean, this is Turkey Creek, you know?"

Billy gave a short laugh. "Oh, hell, yeah, I know."

"Framed you like a picture and pretty much put Mom under lock and key, took her phone and car and everything, didn't let up 'til you were buried. Which was pretty damn quick, as I recall, three, four weeks, something like that. Mom left home for the University of Georgia that fall and never lived in his house again."

"Hate to admit it, but it's damn near brilliant. Me being dead, that simplified things a lot for Big John, much cleaner. And he did own the newspaper."

Billy handed the clippings over to Jake, who gave a soft whistle as his eyes moved over the words.

"Yeah. Sick brilliant. She thought you were dead and you thought she'd forgotten all about you."

"I got the first one four weeks into basic training and the second one two weeks after that. You don't get leave during basic training. By the time I did, didn't seem like a lot left to go back to."

"So why are you back now?"

Billy shrugged.

"Don't really know. Guess the closest I can come is, I wanted to show everybody. You know?"

"Yeah," the boy said slowly, considering all implications. "Yeah, I think I know."

"But Maggie. Why stay? There's nothing keeping her here."

"I asked her that once. She said this was her town, her woods, her people, her heritage. And that he'd taken somebody she loved very much away from her but he wasn't taking anything else. Didn't call a name, but I'm not stupid." Jake swallowed. "Man, I am so, so sorry."

"For what, getting pissed off for your mother? Don't worry about it."

"No, not that. I mean, yeah, sorry I jumped you, but what I mean is—I'm sorry for all the lost time. For both of you."

Sympathy darkened Jake's eyes. The boy was older than his years.

"Yeah, me too."

"So start thinking. We've got to keep Mom calm enough not to kill you on sight before we can explain what happened. Once she knows you're alive, of course. We got maybe a ten second window of opportunity to grab her attention."

"And what makes you think it'll matter to her?"

Jake snorted. "What part of she's changed the flowers on your grave four times a year for twenty-five years didn't you get?"

"We were kids, Jake. We're not the same people. It's been a long time."

"Mom's never been a kid," Jake said. Somehow the statement was a compliment, not a complaint. "And I don't much think you ever were, either. And people, they don't change much. Not at their center."

This kid would bear watching.

Shifting gears announced the approach of a big truck.

"T-bone," Jake said. "Damn, I hope he didn't call Mom already."

"I didn't have any names to give at the time. T-bone? You mean Jack Jones?"

Jake looked at him in surprise. "Yeah. You know T-bone?"

"Grew up here, remember? He took over from his Dad, huh? Still has the junkyard and towing?"

"That's him. And I know his name's really Jack but nobody ever calls him that except Mom now and then and I don't even know where T-bone came from."

"Tell you later."

"When I'm older?" Jake grinned.

"It's not dirty, smart-ass. The football team always ran the T-formation, the coach called him the team backbone. So he's T-bone. And he's sure goin' to know who I am, so brace yourself."

The driver pulled in front of the Mustang. Wrong side of the road, but there wasn't much room to maneuver. He started toward them.

"*Billy?*" He stopped dead-still. Then he shouted. "*Billy! Billy Brayton!* Well, I will just be *damned*, boy, you're supposed to be *dead*, where the *hell* have you been?" He moved forward, enveloping the much taller, much broader, much less plump Billy in a bear hug that almost lifted him off the ground.

"Down, man, down!" Billy laughed. "The reports of my death have been greatly exaggerated." Jake choked a laugh into a strangled cough.

T-bone looked around Billy and saw Jake.

"Oh, shit, Jake, are you all right? I didn't know it was you, where's your wheels?"

Jake pointed to the other side of the road.

"Over there. And *down* there. Can't see it from here. Yeah, I'm okay. Other than some asshole running me off the side. Just glad Billy was there."

T-bone walked over and looked down.

"Damn, boy, that's luck. Well, thank the Lord you're okay. Damn good thing you were coming along, Billy, Maggie'd go nuts anything happened to that boy –" T-bone broke off his sentence and looked at Billy. "Maggie's going to freakin' *kill* you, man. You ain't gonna be alive for long."

"Seems to be the general consensus around here, yeah," Billy said ruefully.

"That girl's never gotten over you, you asshole! How could you—"

"Hey! You didn't even *like* her when we started dating, remember? What was that you said? Why'd I want to get involved with a spoiled private school sorority bitch was gonna treat me like trash and break my heart?"

"Well, that was before I knew her! Maggie's the best friend I've ever had, except for you! I thought! Didn't even care enough to let us know where you were —"

"Guys!" Jake broke in as referee. "Can it!" He passed the laminated clippings over. T-bone's eyes widened as he scanned them.

"That low-down, conniving, manipulating, high-falutin' bastard! That—"

"Don't sugar coat it, T-bone, tell us what you really think," said Jake.

"If this ain't a mess! Well, how you plan on fixin' it, hotshot?"

"You don't have to sound like it's my fault! Hell, I didn't know! And why both of you are assumin' there's anything left to fix, I don't know!"

T-bone snorted. Then his face changed. "Why you coming back and are you coming back alone?"

"I look alone, don't I?"

"Don't get smart with me, boy, you know what I mean. Are you married, 'cause if you are, showing up after all these years'd be pure damn mean and low-down, you need to turn your ass around and go back where you came from. I ain't playing with you, now. Maggie's special to folks 'round this town."

"No."

"You ever been married?"

"No."

"All right then. And you're back here now because why?"

"Because—"

Billy broke off at the sound of the approaching siren. The driver turned the patrol car and parked squarely in the middle of the road, blue lights flashing. Alec Wimberly got out and walked up to the small group.

"Damn, Alec!" said T-Bone. "Saw you on patrol last night when I was out on a job. Drivin' like a bat outta hell down Ninety-Six, matter of fact. What the hell you doing still on duty?"

"Short a man today, I was closest to here when the call came in. Looks like it ain't too bad, y'all standing around in a group chit-chatting. Jake, you all right? Where's your car, buddy?" He turned to Billy, the only unknown face in the group. "Hello, sir, Alec Wimberly. You the Good Samaritan calling in? 'Preciate you looking out for the kid, he's a lot of trouble but lots of folks 'round town like him. Not me, o'course, but a lot of folks."

He reached back into the cruiser and pulled out a hand-held traffic Stop and Go sign.

"T-Bone, get Jim out of that truck and send him around the curve with the sign 'til I get there in case somebody thinks those blue lights are just for show. I need to talk to Jake and then I'll come take over while y'all get his car up."

Billy looked the deputy over. He was dog-tired from pulling the double-shift, but he'd still responded with sirens and lights blaring. He'd made an immediate assessment of the situation, handled it with proper safety concerns, and treated Jake with perfect big-brother rough concern impossible in a larger law enforcement territory where the deputies didn't know their people personally. And he'd introduced himself politely to the only stranger in the group. Law enforcement at its finest.

"What about it, buddy? You recognize the car, get a partial plate?"

"No, no license number, no way. It was just a white Civic and the faces were a blur."

Alec looked at Billy. "And you, sir? Anything?"

Billy shook his head. "No, I was too busy trying to track where the Eclipse was going to go. Didn't figure it could stay on the road, not on that curve."

Alec sighed. "Well. Didn't hit either of you anywhere, did it? Chance of paint chips?"

"No."

"Go ahead and say hell, Alec," urged Jake. "You know you want to."

Alec grinned slightly and shook his head. "Civilian stranger on the premises, buddy. Can't give the wrong impression. My luck, he's the new preacher at Mt. Gilead or something."

T-Bone walked back toward them.

"No, I'm pretty sure he ain't no new local preacher. But you never did answer my last question. Where you been and why you back now?"

Well, hell. Everybody'd know within the next five minutes anyway. This was Turkey Creek. He'd rather introduce himself to the sheriff first, but Alec probably wouldn't trust him later if he didn't come clean. He didn't need that on the force.

"Army, Military Police. Retired. Sheriff hired me as a County Investigator. That suit your hinny?" Billy reverted to their childhood slang for the cross between 'highness' and 'hind-end.'

"Oh, hell!" Alec groaned in spite of himself. "My uniform –"

"Your uniform looks like you've been on duty for a double-shift, you look dog-tired, and you're doing a helluva job. Go call in, sign out, and get some sleep, for God's sake. Rest of the boys like you, I'm goin' to like it here."

T-bone waited for Alec to leave before he lit into Billy again.

"'Bout damn time you showed your face. You coulda called somebody, come back to see us, something!"

"But—"

"But what? 'Cause whatever 'buts' you got, they ain't enough! I think what Maggie went through 'cause of you, I could just—"

"Guys!" Jake interjected again. "Focus here. T-bone, just get my car back to the junkyard. It's totaled, right?"

T-bone gave an appraising glance. "Oh, yeah."

"Okay. Hell. I loved that car. Com'on, Billy, you're taking me home. T-bone, don't you *dare* call Mom before I talk to her. We ain't got but one shot at this. Otherwise, Billy really will be dead so it won't matter."

Billy shook his head and followed orders.

"Are you *sure* Maggie's not really your mother?" He settled behind the wheel.

"I'm sure she really *is* my mother. But not my birth mother. Why?"

"'Cause you damn sure couldn't act any more like her if you were blood. Bossy as hell."

"Natural talent and good raisin'." Jake slid into the passenger seat. "Hey, wait a minute!"

He opened his door and stood up to look over the roof. "T-bone!" "Yo?"

"I never knew where T-bone came from 'til Billy told me. If you were T-bone, what was Billy?"

T-bone laughed. "He was *Greazzzzzeeeed Lightninnnng!*"

Chapter Four

Billy pulled out and headed into Turkey Creek. Not with the same attitude he'd had before meeting Jake. Maggie thought he was dead. She'd always thought he was dead.

"So." He shifted gears. "What does Maggie do? I'm assumin' she doesn't take money from Big John."

Jake laughed. "God, that's funny! She's never even spoken to him but once since she left home for college and that was when she got me. See, my mother was her best friend in college, my parents were killed in a car crash when I was a baby. Don't know if you noticed, but Rubin's a—"

"Jewish name. Yeah, I'm sure Big John loved that."

"Oh, yeah! It's one of the town legends, the day Big John came over and started raisin' hell she'd disgraced him with the county white trash—no offense—"

"None taken."

"And now she wanted to raise a mongrel stray. Between the two of 'em, folks say the whole town damn near burned up."

Billy laughed. "But she still lives in Turkey Creek? He didn't try to sabotage her?"

"Well, she's still his blood, you know, so basically he just ignores her. Just wouldn't look good or sit right with folks for him to come right out and threaten or anything, beneath his notice, sort of, like using a sledge hammer to swat a fly. Besides, I think he thought sooner or later his money would win and she'd cave in and come running to him for help. I'm not sure what would have happened if he'd really tried to run her out of town. Particularly then. I don't think he could do it now. Mom's made her own place with folks, has a lot of pull around town, but not the same way or for the same reason. She's not Big John's daughter to them, she's Maggie Kincaid. But back then—I just don't know."

"So what does she do?"

Jake laughed shortly. "Works her ass off. She owns Clean Class—that's a combination sort of building up on Highway 80 — one side's the Laundromat and one side's a combination deal—"

"Floyd's Laundry and Dry Cleaning."

"Yeah, used to be. Now one side's a clothes shop, coffee and snack shop, tanning beds, lady's stuff in general. And she put a pool table in one of the side rooms so a bunch of kids hang out in the evenings. The laundry side she unlocks at seven in the morning and the store side opens up at two-thirty or three and she closes the whole shooting match at ten. *And* she owns the Scales of Justice Café, that's across from the Courthouse—"

"Little wood building next to the grocery store?"

"Yeah."

"Man, that thing's had nine lives. Barb's Barbecue in my day. How the *hell* does she do all that by herself?"

"I help a lot. Not as much as I think I should or as much as I'd like to, but she won't let me. Says you're only young once."

"Didn't think you just sat around on your ass with your hand out, Jake, you ain't got that look. It's just—I'm pissed off as hell she's been handling all that and raisin' a kid by herself without— well, go on, I want to hear it all."

"Well, that's about it. Mostly she lets me and a few other kids handle Clean Class. At least in the late afternoons till closing. The restaurant does breakfast and lunch, not supper, so she runs up there in the morning, usually by six or six-thirty, helps out with the breakfast crowd. Her cooks are great, though. Junie Bug and Leola. And she sticks around and works the cash register at lunch— except I do it when I'm out of school—but when lunch tapers on down, she leaves it with Junie Bug and goes up to the Clean Class to open about two-thirty or three, depends on the lunch crowd that day. That's when the little ole ladies start coming in, they got a real afternoon coffee ritual thing going on. And after that she leaves it to me or whoever's working that day. Sometimes I think she mostly leaves it open after six just so all us kids'll have somewhere safe to hang. And, of course, she may or may not go back to the café, depends on the day, heavy cleaning, inventory, like that."

"Lord, my God. Does she ever sleep?"

"Not enough, trust me."

Billy groaned. Way too much work for one woman. If the plans they'd made when they were eighteen had worked out, she wouldn't have lived a life of luxury. But she damn sure wouldn't have been working three businesses and raising a kid by herself, either. How the hell did things get so screwed up?

"Just out of curiosity—where am I buried? And who buried me? My ol' man didn't have the money and wouldn't have spent it on my funeral if he did. Can't say there was a lot of love lost there."

Jake laughed again, a happier laugh. "Yeah, well, now that I know you're not dead—that's really kinda funny."

"Because?"

"Because Big John buried you. Well, no, that's not right, really. Mom actually did the planning thing. What's the word for that? Arrangements? He just paid for it. Not because he wanted to, of course, because Mom threw a bitch fit, threatened to run away the minute she got let out of her room and never speak to him again if he didn't. She sort of kept it to herself that she didn't intend to ever speak to him again anyway until she actually got to UGA."

"She told you this?"

"Oh hell no. You remember Miss Luellen? Big John's housekeeper, helped raise Mom?"

"Sure."

"Well, when Mom came back to town, Aunt Lulu—that's what I've always called her—she left Big John flat. She actually moved in with Mom for a long time after I came along, helped raise me, too. Loves to tell me 'Mom' stories. Though I might should warn you, she thinks you really weren't near good enough for Mom. Don't take it real personal, though, she doesn't think anybody is."

"And she's right."

Jake gave him an assessing look.

"Freudian slip much?"

"A well-read teenager, whaddaya know."

"Anyhow, that's how you got buried. Out in—"

"Oh, I know where. If Maggie had anything to do with it, I know where I'm buried. Mt. Olive."

Chapter Five

One Saturday afternoon in October of 1985, Billy Brayton turned his rusty old pick-up to the right and drove into the opening between the two overgrown hedges that pretty much hid the entrance to the old cemetery adjacent to abandoned Mt. Olive Primitive Missionary Baptist Church. And his life changed forever. He didn't know at the time, though.

He cussed out loud. Shit. Just shit. Of all damn people. Maggie Kincaid. What the hell was *she* doing here? And what the hell did she think she was *doing*? Well, that much was obvious, anyway. She *thought* she was about to change a tire, but from the looks of that jack, she was about to crash the low, mean, brand-spankin' new, black Pontiac Trans Am right back down on the flat tire she was trying to change. And would probably hurt herself badly in the process. What a waste! A car like that needed a driver who knew what they were doing, not a spoiled rich bitch who had to have an automatic because they couldn't drive a stick-shift. Trans Ams should be sticks. It was an insult to put an automatic transmission in a Trans Am.

She straightened up at the sound of his truck. If he didn't stay and help, she'd go running straight to Daddy complaining about the mere ordinary mortal who hadn't rushed up to offer the county princess assistance. Billy'd never get another part-time job in Turkey Creek again. He needed those jobs just to live, and he needed anything extra he could get if he was ever going to resurrect the Mustang he'd pulled from T-bone's Daddy's junkyard and send his rattling truck to the junkyard in its place.

Besides, his mama'd always said being a gentleman had nothing to do with money and didn't cost a cent. She'd tried like hell to raise one. Wasn't her fault it hadn't taken as well as she'd like. And you couldn't leave a girl to change a flat tire. You just couldn't do it.

Shit! He settled the transmission into first gear and pulled what passed as the emergency brake. He got out and slammed the truck door.

"What the hell do you think you're doin'?"

"Well, hey to you, too! Are you that blind or that dumb? I'm changing a flat tire."

"No, you're fixin' to kill yourself is what you're fixin' to do! That jack's not going to hold, gonna come down and tear the bumper off. Now get out of the way."

Maggie raised a dirty hand to her sweating forehead and pushed back her hair, tossing her head. October didn't always feel like fall in the Deep South, but it did today. It was sunny though, and getting the car jacked up had taken a lot of exertion. She'd been proud of herself for getting it up as far as she had.

"I'm doing just fine, don't need help from somebody doesn't want to give it. What'd I ever do to you to put that look on your face anyway, Billy Lee Brayton?"

Billy started. "You know who I am?"

"In case you've never noticed, there's not a lot of folks live in this county. You know who I am, don't you?"

"Yeah, but everybody knows you. You're Big John's little girl."

Her eyes widened and shot fire. "I am *not* just Big John's *anything*. And I'm *not* a little girl."

Billy snorted. "Well, excuse me, Princess Bitch. Now, get out of the way and let me get the jack right." He moved forward and nudged her out of the way with his shoulder.

She didn't want to move, but didn't have much choice. Besides, she wasn't doing so hot on the tire.

"What the hell are you doing out here in the middle of nowhere, anyway?" Billy lowered the car down and adjusted the jack. Miracle she hadn't torn the damn bumper completely off.

"Taking pictures. Of the old country churches. It's a history project."

"And you didn't think maybe you ought to take somebody with you instead of driving around in the back of beyond by yourself?"

"Why?"

Billy snorted again. "Flat tires, maybe? Why the hell you even try this by yourself?"

"I believe you just pointed out this is the middle of nowhere. Five miles maybe to the nearest house. Think I should just sit here 'til somebody noticed I was missing?"

Well, she had a point. And she had spunk. And okay, she hadn't done all that bad for somebody who'd obviously never changed a tire.

"Better to walk five miles than have the car fall down on you while you're trying to tighten a lug nut."

"Okay, so it wasn't as good a job as I thought it was. Here, move, you've got it lined up right now. I'll just finish up and you can get on about your business."

She tried the shoulder maneuver on him but it didn't work nearly as well in reverse. "*Give it up* and stay out of the way!"

"I can't go on about my business while you're sitting here."

"Why not? I'll be fine." She stamped her foot. Then her expression changed. "Oh. Okay."

"Okay what?"

"Okay, when you get it fixed, I'll leave you alone so you can go visit."

"Huh?"

"*You* give it up. You pulled in here to visit a grave. Of course you want to do it by yourself. Okay, I'll stay out of your way."

"Maybe I just pulled in when I saw you stranded."

"Bullshit. You wouldn't have *seen* me if you hadn't already pulled in. The trees? The bushes? Hello?"

"You wouldn't understand."

Her whole body stiffened.

"You are *such* a *snob!*"

"I'm a *what*?"

"*Snob. S-n-o-b. Snob.*"

"You're calling *me* that? When you're a Rockland Academy spoiled brat's always had everything she ever wanted before she even knew she wanted it?"

"You think you know all about me just because my last name's Kincaid and I go to Rockland Academy? You think I don't think other people—whoever they are—have feelings? Or you just think *I* don't have any feelings so other folks' feeling' don't mean anything to me? You think I gotta know how much money a person's got before I'll speak to 'em?"

"Easy to say money ain't important when you always had it!"

"Maybe so. Still don't mean I don't understand why you're visiting a grave. You act like you think I'd make fun or something. Or ruin that bad boy image you work so hard on."

"How the hell you know what my image is?"

"How you know mine, Mr. Front Page Rockland Raiders star running back?"

Okay, so they'd reached—there was a word for this, Billy thought, searching. They'd reached an impasse. He didn't know her world and she damn sure didn't know his. On further thought though, which one of them was the snob? Hell, she was right. He was. He was the one who'd walked up with the chip on his shoulder. She'd only responded in kind. She'd even given every indication that she didn't consider him the dirt beneath her feet. He'd just assumed she did. Damn. He probably owed her an apology.

"Okay. Truce, all right?" Well, that wasn't exactly an apology, but it was as close as he was going to come.

The fire went out of her. She had to be tired. It wouldn't have been all that easy getting the Trans Am up on that jack as far as she had, especially since it hadn't been lined up.

"All right. Whatever. Just—if you'll please get my tire changed, I'll get out of here and leave you alone."

Billy squatted back down, grabbed the lug wrench, and returned his attention to the tire. Without the sparring, he lowered the jack back down in ten minutes and started replacing the tools in the trunk along with the flat tire.

"Thanks," she said, as he slammed the trunk down. "I appreciate it, really. I'd still be fighting the first lug nut, probably."

"No problem."

"Yeah, it was. For you it was a big problem. I'm sorry about that, but I'll get out of your hair now."

It was her expression that did it. As she got in the driver's seat, he caught her expression. It was tired and not very happy. Hurt. He'd hurt her feelings and she didn't want him to know it. His mama would throw a fit at him if she knew just how *not* like a gentleman he'd acted. And considering the location, she probably did.

"Wait!" He grabbed the car door at the top.

"Why? Got another insult you didn't think of?"

"I'm sorry. I had no business acting like that, or saying any of that to you. You're right. I don't know you. I just know your last name's Kincaid and you go to Rockland Academy. And you're right again. All that was snobby. Plain ugly, in fact. And I'm sorry."

She smiled. "That hurt much?"

"Yeah, it did, actually. But it feels all better now."

The smile morphed to a grin. "You got possibilities. See you aroun'."

"No, wait. Would you—would you like to walk over and visit my mother with me?"

"For real? Your mother? And you wouldn't mind?"

"No. No, I wouldn't mind."

She got back out of the car.

"Your mother's buried here? I thought the cemetery hadn't been used in a while."

"It hasn't, but there's a lot of family plots here. My grandmother's buried here, and Mama always kept her grave up, best she could anyway. And being a family plot with the space was already here, my ol' man—"

Billy broke off. No point in parading his whole life-story. Besides, his ol' man was about as useless as tits on a boar hog though he sure as hell wouldn't say anything that crude to Maggie. She knew it anyway. The whole damn town did. His father claimed to be a plumber, did odd jobs here and there. He drank like a fish, smoked a few joints when he could get 'em, passed out in public places. In general, made his mother's life a total misery. And he sure as hell wasn't going to fork out any more money to bury her than he had to. Billy knew his mother was in Heaven, 'cause she'd sure lived in Hell long enough.

"Family plots are nice," Maggie said. "A connection, generation to generation."

"Yeah. Mama used to make me come out here with her to clean off the graves. When I was big enough to cut grass, she made me cut the whole damn cemetery a couple of times every summer. I hated it, always put up a fight about it, but she always won. And now—"

Maggie laughed softly. "And now you regret fussin' with her about it, and she's definitely won because now you keep it clean on your own. That's why you're here, last cut for the year, right?"

"How'd you figure that?"

"There's a lawn mower in the back of the pick-up, Billy."

"Oh," he said. "Yeah, I guess there is."

"And it's not nearly as grown up as it would be if nobody ever did anything. I noticed that when I was taking pictures. And these graves—"

Maggie veered over to the right, directly in front of his mother's grave without him pointing it out to her.

"These are your mother's and grandmother's. Tended right often. I like the azaleas. You planted them, didn't you?"

"Why'd you think that?"

"The bushes are pretty young. Not old enough that I'd think your mother put 'em out. Let's see, she died two years ago. Of what? Unless you don't want to talk about it."

"You're pretty sharp, you know that?"

"Yeah, I know that."

Billy didn't comment on the cause of his mother's death and she didn't ask again. Yeah, she was pretty sharp. The death certificate said heart attack. Billy knew it should really read, "*Cause of Death: Stopped Living.*" The bank foreclosed on the house three years before her actual death. She didn't know his father hadn't made the house payments with the money she brought home from working the one to nine shift at Barb's Barbecue. House hadn't been much, but she'd kept it spotless and was proud of it. She hadn't much cared about anything else since then, except Billy. He missed his mother a lot, even after two years, but he was still mad at her for just giving up and leaving him. He thought he always would be.

"I'm glad you have memories of your mother that make you want to come visit. And keep the graves up. I don't visit my mother."

"You don't?"

"You know my mother killed herself when I was two. Don't you? I mean, the whole county does."

"Well, yeah, I guess I've heard that."

"I was *two*, for God's sake. I don't remember her, not at all, but what kind of mother is that? Who *chooses* to leave a two-year-old baby? She didn't even care enough to see me grow up. So I'm glad you have real memories of your mother. And that they're good ones."

Billy nodded slowly. "Yeah. Yeah, I am, too."

"Well. I should get going. You came to tend to business. Thanks again for my tire. And thank you for lettin' me visit your mother with you. I'm honored."

Billy laughed at her phrasing. "Honored?"

"Don't laugh. It's the closest I can come. It's a private thing for anybody, especially for you. And you shared it with me. That's an honor. So don't try to make it less than that by poking fun."

"Yes, ma'am. C'mon, I'll walk you back to your car."

"And open my door?"

"Well, Mama tried to make me a gentleman. Just didn't take real well."

"Better than you think, maybe."

"Really?"

"Really."

Billy reached for the door handle and swung the heavy door wide in a courtly bow.

Maggie laughed. "Thank you. Again. For everything. I'll see you aroun'."

"You don't have to speak to me if you see me around town, Maggie. It's all right, really."

"You are just *determined* to ruin it, aren't you?"

"What?"

"A nice moment of being human. Why would you think I wouldn't want to speak to you around town? Or be seen with you? Anywhere?"

"Does that mean you would?"

"Of course it does."

"Prove it." Holy Lord, what the hell was he thinking?

"How?"

"Never mind. Guess you're one of the Rockland Rebel cheerleaders, aren't you? So you'd be busy on Friday nights." Thank God, he'd thought of an out before he put his foot up his ass.

"Been there, done that. My Sophomore and Junior years. Never again, thank you. So I'm footloose and fancy free on Friday nights."

She would be. Well, nothing ventured, nothing gained.

"We play at home Friday night. There's a dance afterwards."

"And?"

"And what?"

"That means what to me?"

"Would you like to come to the game? And then go to the dance? With me?"

"Yes, I would, thank you."

"Really?"

"Really." She smiled. "Don't want to interfere with Greased Lightning's game prep, though. Coach might kick me out of the stadium. I'll meet you there."

"You know—"

"That you're Greased Lightnin'? Sure. Everybody does. Don't you read the papers?"

She reached for the door and he closed it firmly. The engine turned, the car backed up, and Maggie gave a quick wave. He gazed after her, listening to the powerful engine moving up through its gears. Unmistakably a stick-shift. Not an automatic. Driven by someone who knew how to drive. Damn.

Chapter Six

In the six days between Saturday afternoon and Friday night, Billy Brayton drove himself half crazy. Would she come or would she change her mind? He stood in the field Friday night, fully suited and warming up. He scanned the home side of the stadium after every windmill.

"Billy, who the hell you lookin' for?" his buddy T-bone asked.

"Got a friend said she might come to the game, that's all."

"She? You mean you got a date after the game and it ain't with Angie? Jeez Louise, man, you got a death wish?"

Angie Malone. She hadn't crossed Billy's mind. They weren't an item or a couple and they'd never been on a real date, but they did end up together frequently. As in *together*. Not that Angie hadn't ended up *together* with the whole team at one time or another. But after the last few games, Billy had been her specific target.

"Crap."

"You can say that again."

"Well, I'm not sure she'll make it, anyway."

"*Who?*"

Ah! There she was. Country class in blue jeans, white tank top, and high-heeled black boots. A soft white sweater draped her shoulders and a leather jacket lay across her arm, proper layering for a football game in October in Rockland County. She waved. Billy waved back. T-bone almost choked.

"Billy! That's *Maggie Kincaid!*"

"Yeah."

"Are you *fuckin' crazy*, man?"

"Probably."

It was the feel-good kind of crazy, though, and it carried on over into a crazy-good winning football night.

He stopped long enough as he came off the field to coordinate with Maggie, purposely positioned so he'd see her.

"Dance is in the gym. Wait for me near the locker room entrance?"

"See ya there."

T-bone shook his head mournfully.

"Man, you'd better hurry it up. Angie's gonna eat her alive you don't get out there pretty damn quick."

"Angie don't know she's with me."

"Yeah? She was right behind her in the stands, caught every bit of that waving the two of you kept doin', you didn't notice?"

"Oh hell. No, I didn't."

"*And* she was right behind her right then, too, buddy, when you were giving meetin' instructions. You really didn't see her?"

"No."

"Jeez, man, you must be far gone. What the *hell* you want to do that to yourself for? Maggie Kincaid's just slummin', man, she's gonna break your heart."

"T-bone, shut up! Would you just *shut up*?"

Billy moved with fever-speed. He had to get showered and out of the locker room. T-bone was right, Angie'd be looking for trouble. She didn't have any claim on Billy, not any more than she did on any other male member of Rockland County High, but that didn't matter. Maggie didn't have any experience with girls like Angie, they were from different worlds. She'd eat Maggie alive just because she could. And she'd enjoy it.

He tore out of the locker room and into the main gym just in time to catch the chant.

"Bitch fight! Bitch fight!"

"...and you can just take your upper-class little ass out of here right now and go back to your own kind. Don't you ever even think of looking at Billy Brayton again, you hear me?"

Billy pushed half-way through the crowd. Angie stepped closer to Maggie and pushed her shoulder.

"Oh, yeah? Show me your brand, honey, you wearing enough jewelry. Which piece came from him? The necklace? The rings? The bracelets? 'Cause if none of 'em did, you ain't got much of a claim! And *don't. Push. Me. Again!*"

"Or *what*?"

"Or I will *take you down*. You don't believe me, you try me!"

Holy hell, was that Maggie Kincaid talking? Did she have a death wish?

Billy broke through the front line just as Angie pushed Maggie's shoulder again, harder this time. He froze in his tracks. Maggie moved forward, dipped, and grabbed Angie's arm. Angie flipped over through the air and landed on her back. *Thump.*

"*Maggie! What the*—? *You just*—*what did you just*—"

Maggie smiled. Not a hair out of place. Lipstick still perfect.

"Self-defense101. Ninth grade gym. All us Rockland Academy girls can do that."

The whole crowd stared. T-bone was bug-eyed.

Billy tried to speak again. "I don't *believe* you just—"

Maggie tucked her arm over his and led him away.

"Just call me Princess Bitch."

Chapter Seven

Jake's ringing cellphone brought Billy back to the present in a red-hot hurry.

"Oh crap! I wanted to brainstorm, still haven't figured out the best way to break it to her yet!"

"Maggie?" Billy asked.

"Who else?" Jake groaned. He stabbed at his phone and hit speaker so Billy could hear.

"Hey, Mom! What's happenin'?"

"You tell me!" The sound of her voice hit Billy in the chest. A tad richer, a bit deeper, a little older. Still as expressive as ever. He'd recognize that voice if he was dead. He shook his head and focused.

"Are you *hurt*? *Where* in the *hell* are you? Agnes Peters just called me and said she'd seen T-bone out the window of Hair Essentials pulling your smashed up car down 80 headed to the 96 intersection! *Did* she? Said she only saw Jim in the truck with T-bone, the car was smashed to smithereens, and she doesn't know how anybody came out of that *alive*! Are you with T-bone? And neither one of you bothered to *call* me?"

"Mom!" Jake leaned forward and banged his head softly against the dashboard a few times. Billy sympathized. No secrets in Turkey Creek. "I'm fine! Calm down! Some asshole ran me off the road on Riggins Mill, car went down one of the gullies—"

"One of the *gullies*! My God, Jake, I can't believe you didn't *call* me—"

"Mom! I'm *fine*! I'm sorry I didn't call, and I'm sorry Agnes Peters called you before I did and scared you to death! Things were happening kinda fast there, but don't worry, I'm with a Good Samaritan who was coming along and went down the gully after me. I wasn't in the car two minutes after it hit the tree—"

"*Tree*! How big a tree, are you sure you're all right, that *kills* people—"

"Mom! Do I *sound* dead?"

"No, you sound like you're just as big a smartass as you always are!"

Billy grinned. Terror was giving way to exasperation. She'd been scared to death for no reason. Trust the Biddy Brigade of Rockland County. He had to admit though, Jake's car did look like hell.

"I'm *sorry*! But I'm fine! My Good Samaritan's bringing me back to town, where you at?"

"Well, put him on, I want to thank him!"

Jake's eyes widened and he looked at Billy in panic. Billy shook his head emphatically. No way Maggie wouldn't recognize his voice. Not even believing him dead.

"Mom, he's driving! You know it's not safe to talk on a cellphone and drive at the same time! You can thank him when we get to town. Now, where are you? Not the laundry, I hope, you'll make a fuss over me in front of the whole damn town."

"The whole damn town is seldom in here at the same time and I'll make a fuss if I want to! But no, I'm at the café. Big lunch crowd today, I told Junie Bug and Leola to leave the big pans soaking and I'd come back and finish up. And when did you get so safety-conscious?"

"Mom, you're not gonna be satisfied till you freakin' work yourself to *death*, are you?" Now Jake's voice was exasperated. The two of them were a pair for sure. And for sure, a pair who worried over each other a lot.

"Don't start fussin' at me, little boy! I've had a traumatic afternoon! How'd *you* feel somebody called you and said they'd seen *my* car wrecked to hell and back on T-bone's wrecker and you hadn't heard from me? Think that might put a ding in *your* afternoon?"

Jake winced. "Sorry. Point taken. Stay at the café, we'll be there in about five minutes."

"Oh, don't worry about that! One of the pans of dressing burned a side, stuck like crazy glue. I'll be here a while. Seein' as how I don't need to rush to the emergency room. Love."

"Love."

The ending exchange hit Billy in the stomach. Private shorthand between them since the first month they started dating. The town bad-ass couldn't be overheard telling his girlfriend "I love you", now could he? Now it was family shorthand it seemed, in a family that should have been his but wasn't.

Jake expelled a loud breath. "Man, that was *close!* Damn it, can't take a leak in this town without everybody knowing how long you peed! I should have known!"

"Yeah, me too, but I'd forgotten. You did real good, son, quick on your feet."

"Thanks. And that's probably the best place for her to be. I need—oh hell!"

Jake flipped his phone back open.

"T-bone? Mom's gonna be callin' you. *Don't* answer!"

"Why she gon' be callin' me? And why don't I answer?"

"Because Agnes Peters saw my car out the window of the beauty shop and called Mom, and she's mad as hell at you and me both for not calling her! And don't answer 'cause she'll know something's screwy from your voice and because you can't keep your mouth shut, that's why! Okay? We're on the way to the café now, that's where she is. So *don't answer!* Got it?"

"Okay, okay, I got it. Gettin' bossed around by kids now, I swear, perfect end to a perfect day, my best friend lettin' me think he was dead all this time, my other best friend's snot-nose kid givin' me orders—"

"Yeah, I know, but we love ya man." Billy grinned. Not a bad Elvis imitation.

Jake turned back to Billy. "Boy, that was close, too. He can't keep *nothing* from Mom, she'd milk him like a cow. Now give me the clipping things, I'll have to go in armed. You park up near the front, the kitchen's back—"

"Know the place well, Jake. Too damn well. Maggie and T-bone really that close?"

"Yeah. Weird combo, I know, but it was kind of a bonding thing, I think. Because of you. He's got a real white knight guardian angel thing going on for Mom. And Mom checks all his business stuff for him and makes sure he's straight with all the regs, she worries he's got the good heart bad business sense thing. And mostly she worries he's got no sense at all. "

Billy laughed. "I can relate to that."

"Now, the kitchen door'll be open, too hot in there for anything but the screen door on a day like this when you're working. I'll go on in, you hang back and hide. I'll stick the clippings in front of her nose and when I'm sure she's read 'em, I'll call you in. How's that sound?"

"Best we got, I guess."

"Yeah, that's what I figure. You nervous?"

"I been in armed combat, buddy. Stand-offs, stand-downs, and hostage situations. Nothing compared to this. Hell, yeah, I'm nervous. You?"

"Oh, yeah. I'd hate for her to kill you right in front of me and have to testify against my own mother at trial."

The Courthouse loomed large in front of the 96 and 80 Four Way Stop. The IGA grocery store stood on the right with the café peeping out past it. He parked in front at the top of the little drive running down the side of the café into the back. He took a deep breath. Jake opened his door and closed it quietly. Billy did the same.

"You ready for this?"

Not really, but he wasn't going to get any readier.

"Mark and move." Billy waved Jake on and watched him disappear into the back. He followed and stopped at the corner of the building.

* * *

She stood on the left-hand side of the kitchen at the double sink designated for dishwashing, ruthlessly attacking the burned-on side crust. Jake figured the ruthlessness was in part directed at him. He should have known somebody'd get to her about his wrecked car before he did. God knows, he'd stopped trying to sneak anything past her by the time he was fourteen. Never worked anyway, somebody always told her everything he was doing.

"Hey, Mom!"

"Hey, buddy!" Maggie dropped the pan back into the water and checked him over. "Well, you do look alive. Sore?"

"No, probably will be later. Speaking of alive, got something you need to read."

The voices carried clearly from the kitchen over the small space separating them from Billy's position on the corner.

"Good Lord, son, right now? Where's your Good Samaritan, I need to thank him—"

"Uh, he's parking his car. No, Mom, you need to read these. Please, it's important."

Jake picked up a dishtowel and handed it to her as she finished shaking water off her hands. The he pushed the old clippings, protected by the laminate covering, in front of her nose.

She frowned but reached to take them, seeing as how he wasn't giving her much choice. Color drained from her face as she read.

"Where'd you get this?"

"Read the next one."

Her hands shook while she read.

"Jake. Where the hell did you get this?"

"From my Good Samaritan. He's from Rockland County, but he's been in the army for a while—"

"Jake. I'm not playin' with you, son. Don't do this to me."

"Mom, you know where I got them. I know you do. I can see it in your face. There's only one person in the world'd laminate these clippings and keep 'em all these years, just like you keep everything about him. And before you really do kill him, don't you *see*—you thought he was dead and he thought you'd forgotten him as soon as he left town. It's not his fault any more than it is yours!"

"Your Good Samaritan is—"

Billy walked through the door.

"Hello, Maggie."

Chapter Eight

Even Maggie's lips were white. And her knees were buckling, too. Before Jake could grab her, Billy was there. He reached out and pulled her close. She tried to speak and choked, and then her arms locked around Billy's neck. The muscles in her arms tightened as though she'd never let him go.

"But there was a *body* in that casket! They told me not to look, that you didn't have a *face*, but I did, I looked, I didn't believe 'em, I looked and you didn't have a *face*—"

"Shhh. Shhh. I'm sorry, Maggie, I'm so damn sorry."

Jake backed away from them. She'd never told him that and neither had Aunt Lulu. He wondered if she knew. Her voice was a bigger heartbreaker than the words. He thought he'd heard his mother's voice in all its variations, but this lost, bewildered wail so full of long-ago anguish—he'd never heard it before and had no business hearing it now. And Billy's voice, so full of emotion as he stroked Maggie's hair—it sounded like it was filtering through coarse gravel. Nobody on earth had any right to hear or see them right now. This was private.

He slipped out the door and reached for his keys. He'd take Mom's car, go home, grab some clothes, and crash at his best friend Ben Clayton's house for a couple of days. He reached in his pocket. Damn! His keys were in his wrecked car. Mom always threw her keys down on the kitchen table, he could probably slip in and out without them noticing. They certainly hadn't noticed his first departure. And it was a sure bet they wouldn't be needing two cars.

He slipped back through the screen just as Maggie pulled back from Billy and slapped him. Hard.

"And you *believed* that shit? Without *calling,* without *checking,* you *believed* that shit!"

"Maggie, I—"

Jake didn't wait for the rest of Billy's attempted explanation. He grabbed Maggie's keys from the table and bolted back out the door, pausing only long enough to work her car key off the ring. His mother didn't hold back when she was mad, so he didn't miss anything.

"And T-bone! How you could possibly believe that shit about me I don't know but even so, you never *once* got in touch with T-bone! He loved you like a *brother*, Billy, how could you *do* that to him?"

"Maggie, I—"

"Don't you Maggie me, Billy Brayton! You—"

Jake cracked the door just wide enough and tossed the key ring back onto the kitchen table. He didn't worry about the noise. God knows they weren't going to hear it.

"To hell with this!" Billy'd finally had enough. About time. He pulled Maggie back against him and kissed her like he hadn't kissed her in twenty-five years. Go, Billy! Okay, this was just as personal as the first anguished wail and the choking gravel voice, but it was a lot more fun to watch. Maggie's hands beat a tattoo on Billy's back for a few seconds—Mom wasn't giving in on a good mad without a struggle—and then her arms relaxed and wound themselves around Billy's neck. She kissed him back. Like she hadn't kissed him in twenty-five years. Jake smiled. All would be right with the world. Pretty damn quick, he'd bet. He'd send her a text in a little while, let her know where he was. He pulled out of the back parking lot, whistling.

* * *

Maggie and Billy were breathless when they finally separated.

"Are you through now?" Billy asked cautiously.

"I guess. For right now, anyway. I'm—drained."

"I'm so damn sorry, Maggie." He glanced around the kitchen and grabbed one of the seen-better-days chairs culled from the dining room. He pulled it out and sat, tugging her down with him to sit on his lap, circling her with his arms. "Here, this is better. We need to be sittin' down when I tell you this, I've got a better hold on you."

"You need to have a *hold* on me? If you're going to tell me you're married after kissing me like that—"

"Good God, woman! What kind of idiot do you take me for? I just got resurrected, don't want to get buried again already. No, I'm not married! Never have been. But when you hear this—well, I guess first I better ask. What kind of shape is T-bone's father in?"

"Jonesy? What kind of shape is *Jonesy* in?"

"He's older now. Good health, bad health, senile, what?"

"Dead, actually. Ten years ago. What the hell does Jonesy have to do with anything?"

"I did call, Maggie. As soon as I could. Basic's not a luxury spa, you know. Limited phone privileges. But as soon as I could call, I did. And of course that's who I called. T-bone. Sure as hell couldn't call your house. The engagement announcement had just come in the mail. Almost went AWOL, but what good would that have done either of us? And Jonesy told me not to call back. Ever."

"*Jonesy* told you that? Billy, that's crazy, you practically *lived* over there, all the Rockland High kids did! And they adopted me right along with you when we started dating! That man loved you like another son!"

"Yeah, well, a man'll do a lot of things when—well, here's the thing. I tried calling back whenever I could—and it wasn't often, I wasn't on vacation, remember—hoping T-bone or his mother would answer, but they never did. It was always Jonesy."

"When? The first time you called. When was it?"

"Right after the first one came. Four weeks into basic."

Billy felt the tension running through Maggie's body and braced himself for the impending explosion.

"*But you were already buried!* Had been for almost a week. You mean to tell me he *knew* you were alive and didn't tell me?"

"Yeah, I knew I'd better have a good grip. The man's dead, Maggie. You can't kill him. And you don't need to go punching the wall, you'll break a bone. So—you want the rest or what?"

"You think?"

"So, I couldn't get anybody on the phone. And the wedding announcement came two weeks after the first one. Right at the end of basic. And I—well, at first I thought maybe you'd done it because it was the only way you could think of to get out from under Big John long enough to get away."

"You really think I'm *that* devious and twisted?"

"Hell, yeah."

"*Hell*, yeah, of course I am. But since you were already dead and buried, I never had to come up with anything. Where would I want to go? But if you hadn't been dead and I wasn't already out of lock-up, that would've worked. Dean would've been perfect, too, great partner in crime, he'd have thought it was a trip."

"Really? Never struck me as having that much personality."

"You never met him but once and that was early on when you still thought having money automatically made people snobs."

"True. Anyway, just in case you were having trouble finding me, I wrote T-bone and told him exactly how to get me. Even had somebody else address it and mailed it in town, regular mail, not military. I knew if it got to him, it'd get to you. And you'd be there. Any day. But he never got any of 'em, I knew that as soon as he saw me, when he came out to get Jake's car. You can't fake that reaction."

"Any of 'em? How many did you send?"

"One from Benning, while I was still there. One from Fort Bliss, my first base. One from Fort Carson. After that—" Billy shrugged. "I'd tried calling again, of course. Home phone number'd been changed to an unlisted one. No point in calling the business phone, Jonesy was sure goin' to answer that. So, for whatever reason you'd gotten married, you'd obviously decided you liked it after all. I didn't know I was dead, Maggie. Just like you didn't know you were married. So I let you go."

"And did I go far?"

"Never."

She reached up and touched his cheek, still red from the force of her slap.

"Damn, that was a hard hit."

"You're tellin' me."

"Did you tell T-bone?"

"No. No point at all in him knowing. Figured that'd be between me and Jonesy. If he was still alive."

"I'm glad you could think that fast. It'd upset him a lot and for no reason. He didn't handle Jonesy's death real well. But I'm still mind-boggled, I don't know how Jonesy—"

"I understand why he did it, Maggie. I think."

"Well, I'm glad. 'Cause I sure as hell don't."

"Princess. Com'on. He ran a business in Rockland County. A man'll do a lot when his family's livelihood's at stake. How many banks are there in Rockland County?"

"Two."

"At which he did all his business and probably had more than one outstanding loan. And who owns those banks?"

"Daddy Dearest."

"Exactly."

"That wasn't all of it, Billy. I don't think he'd have done that to you—and to me—just for money."

"Well, I've got a few ideas about that, too, now that I find out I'm dead, but I haven't thought it through yet. But we're never telling T-bone."

"You didn't tell Jake all that either, did you?"

"No. He seemed fine with the surface explanation." Billy glanced around the kitchen of the Scales of Justice Café, Barb's Barbecue in another life. His mother'd stood in front of that grill and stove many an hour.

"You're remembering your mother in here, aren't you?"

"Yeah. Funny, you buyin' it. But fittin' somehow. Both the women in my life in the same place. Sort of."

"And where else do you want *this* woman in your life?"

"Where she's supposed to be. So how soon you think you might be ready to marry me?"

"Well, I'd have to check my calendar to be certain, but I'm pretty sure I'm not doing anything special tomorrow."

"Tomorrow?"

"Yeah, it's too late today, we can't get a marriage license, courthouse's already closed."

Billy laughed. He was still hers and she was still his. Always had been, always would be.

"Well, then, why don't you just pencil me in? *Can* we get married the same day we get a license?"

"Oh, yeah, much simpler than it used to be. Streamlined the process considerable. Not Vegas, but pretty close."

"Know that on the off-chance you might get married someday?"

"*Excuse you*, when in the hell you think I'd have time with three businesses and a teenage son to think about gettin' married?"

Maggie slipped out of his lap and grabbed a sheet of paper and a marker. She held up the impromptu notice announcing the café was closed Friday.

"I've waited twenty-five years to get married, not gonna work the day I do."

She walked to the single sink on the back wall and picked up the wrapped meat she'd set out not an hour before to thaw for tomorrow.

"Okay, let me put this back in the freezer, it ain't getting used tomorrow. And call Junie Bug—no, I'll get Jake to do that—he's not still here, is he?"

"No, he's anywhere but here, I imagine. Especially after the slappin' and shoutin' started."

Maggie's phone dinged. She laughed and passed it to Billy.

Mom took ur car @ Bens house 4 few days don't get married tomorrow wo me!

"Does that kid know his mom or what?" She hit Jake's number and punched the speaker button.

"Please tell me you're not callin' for help disposing of a body. I've waited a long time to call somebody Dad."

"It's cool, Jake, I'm still alive. Barely."

"And I need help, please," Maggie joined the three-way conversation.

"Today, Mom—whatever you need. No smartass comebacks, even."

"Good Lord! Did you hit your head in that accident?"

"It'd be nice if you reciprocated. That means no smartass comebacks from you either, please. Whatcha' need me to do?"

"I'm leaving a sign on the café door we're closed tomorrow. Call Junie Bug for me, tell her to pass that along to the other girls. And run up to the laundry and put a sign on both sides of the store—*Closed Till Monday*. And pass that down to Katie and whoever's s'posed to work tomorrow night and Saturday night, I can't even think."

"Got it."

"And I don't like you away from home right after crashing down a gully. You need to come home."

"No can do. I'm fine, just ask Billy. Besides, the gang's got plans tonight. You two will just have to entertain each other."

"What was that about not being a smartass?"

"Com'on, Mom, *that* was irresistible."

"Okay, but come back home tomorrow morning, don't go to school."

"Because?"

"We're gettin' married and I need somebody to give the bride away."

"*Freakin' awesome!* Can I call T-bone?"

"You can call the world as far we're concerned," Billy said. "And tell T-bone I need a best man."

"And be careful with my car!"

"Mom, that accident wasn't my fault!"

"I didn't say it was. I said be careful. Love."

"Love."

Maggie turned back to Billy. "We're a package deal, you know."

"Duh."

"Well, just wanted you to know what you're gettin' into. Though he's only gonna be home another year, damn it."

"You did a great job with him, Maggie."

"He saved my life. I don't know what I'd have done without him. Well, yeah, I do. Turned into a bitter old woman at a very young age. Give me your keys."

"Excuse you?"

"Keys. I'm drivin'."

"Some things never change." Billy reached in his pocket and came up empty-handed. "Still in the car. Can't imagine why I'd forget 'em."

"Then let's get locked up. We're going for a little ride."

"To?"

"Just a little ride." She looked around the kitchen floor and picked up the ancient laminated clippings. "Before we go home. Our home. Yours, mine, Jake's. In spite of everything Big John Kincaid's ever done to make sure that never happened."

Chapter Nine

Jake tossed his phone back over into the passenger seat and whooped aloud. A fairy tale ending out of a story book. Jake knew the whole story from Aunt Lulu. His mother didn't talk about it. She'd never even shown him her high school scrapbook. He'd snooped into that on his own, bored out of his head one fevered afternoon in December when he was home sick.

A fairy tale complete with dark, swirling evil. That wail from his mother—just thinking about it made his spine shiver.

But there was a body in that casket! They told me not to look, that you didn't have a face, but I did, I looked, I didn't believe 'em, I looked and you didn't have a face—

Caskets were sealed when the deceased were disfigured in death, weren't they? And why would it ever be unsealed? Oh, sure, he joked his mom could do anything—but a bunch of grown men would stop an eighteen-year-old girl from opening a casket, sealed or unsealed. Wouldn't they?

He hadn't stopped in at Aunt Lulu's in a while. Who probably had some fresh-baked sugar cookies to boot. Jake had wedding plans to make. His mother just intended a quick service at the Courthouse, probably, and that wasn't happening. This was Turkey Creek, plenty of folks beside him would make sure of that when this news spread, which might take all of ten minutes. But he had time to stop at Aunt Lulu's first.

He turned down Cedar Circle and pulled into circular driveway in front of Aunt Lulu's little house.

"Well, well! Look what the cat drug in!" Aunt Lulu flung the door wide. "'Bout time you stopped in to see your Aunt Lulu! Thought you done forgot where I live, son!"

She held her arms open for her hug.

"Yeah, been too long. I'm sorry 'bout that, Aunt Lulu."

"Come on in! Guess what I got in the kitchen?"

Jake lifted his head and sniffed. "Now, see, I can't be that bad, or fresh sugar cookies wouldn't be waitin' on me!" Jake settled at her kitchen table. Aunt Lulu transferred warm cookies to a plate and poured milk.

"So. Why you stop in all of a sudden? Not that I ain't glad to see you, but you got something on your mind. Go ahead, tell your Aunt Lulu what's the matter."

"Nothing's the *matter*, exactly, something great's happened. But Aunt Lulu, did you know—do you know if—back when Mom was eighteen—"

"Son, that was an awful, awful time for yo' mama. I probably never shoulda tol' you all them stories."

"Yeah, but—" Jake paused before plunging on. "She looked in Billy Brayton's casket. She saw the body. The body without a face. Did you know about that?"

"Never forget. I'm the one held her all that night while she cried. Wouldn't lay down, wouldn't try to sleep. We sat in the living room, curled up in a corner of a big sofa. All night long. She cried and cried. Cried herself sick, more than once. Absolutely, pure-de sick. An' when mornin' come, an' I seen her face, I knew—she wasn't my girl no more, that girl was dead, just as dead as that boy in that coffin. And the woman who's yo' mama, she was there in her place. And she been there ever since. And over the years, 'specially after she got you, bits and pieces of that girl came back a little bit and then a little bit more 'til at least the woman could get some joy out of life. But not like the girl. The world was a place of wonder to that girl. Sometime I think if she'd hadn't had you, she wouldn't even laugh at all by now. That's what you did for her, son. You her salvation. Why you askin' 'bout all this *now*? Yo' mama never tol' you that story. Know she wouldn't."

"He's not dead."

"Who's not dead?"

"Billy Brayton's not dead."

* * *

Aunt Lulu shook her head in disbelief when Jake finished the tale of his close encounter with a dead man.

"Lord, Lord! Son, are you *sure* it was Billy Brayton?"

"Well, Mom seemed pretty damn sure it was. Sure enough to marry him tomorrow."

"That boy wasn't near good enough for yo' mama. But I always suspicioned the man would be. Is he? What you think?"

"Oh, yeah. Pair of matched bookends. But when Mom first saw him—I can't even describe her voice. She just *wailed*—how she'd looked and he didn't have a face. I don't *want* to describe it, it was so—I don't know the word, Aunt Lulu. Agonized, maybe. And on the way over here, I got to thinkin'. Don't they *seal* coffins when the dead person's disfigured, like in an accident, things like that? I mean, they wouldn't let anybody view a person from a really bad accident, would they?"

"Son. 'Course they wouldn't. And I have harbored so much hate in my heart for John Kincaid since that day, not that there wasn't enough there anyway—you just don't know. And *he* don't know how lucky he is I'm a Christian, God-fearing woman, or I'd have fed him rat poison for the vermin he is."

"Why'd you stay with him after Mom left town?"

Aunt Lulu snorted. "Jobs ain't that plentiful in this town, son. Not honest jobs. Got to live. My children just gettin' started themselves, couldn't be a burden. Left that house soon as I could though. Just as soon as my girl come back to town." Aunt Lulu shook her head. "I always knew that man be the devil, but this—he just pure outdid himself with this."

"Yeah, but the sealed coffin thing. *Why* wasn't it sealed, didn't he know Mom would look?"

"You smarter than that, Jake. Sure, he knew she'd look. He *wanted* her to look. Wanted her to see. Take the last bit o' fight out of her, he figured. He *intended* her to see, he didn't want to just break her, he wanted to take her soul. Almos' did, too."

"But that's just—that's just—"

"Evil, son. Satan walks among us."

"How does he always know, Aunt Lulu? It's like he goes straight for everybody's jugular, even though he doesn't understand anything about Mom, never has."

"Jake. They just alike, he knows her to the bone."

"They are *nothing* alike, Aunt Lulu, how can you say that?"

"Yeah, they are, son. They got the same exact gifts, they just use 'em different. They both so much smarter than most folks, can't hardly nobody keep up with 'em. But mostly, they can *read* people. They can figure out real quick what's makes 'em tick, what makes 'em happy, what scares 'em, what their weak link is. If you can *read* people, son, you can control 'em. If you want to. And Big John, that's how he works. He *controls* people. Yo' mama, she uses it to *know* people. But she use that to make 'em happy, make 'em feel good about theirselves, 'cause that makes *her* feel good. But iff'n she wants to, somebody give her a reason, she can take 'em down just as hard as Big John ever did. You just ain't seen her do it much, 'cause most folks just plain loves her and she loves 'em back. You think about it, though, you seen it once or twice."

"I never thought of it like that."

"Well, it's like a doctor. If he want to, who better to kill you, son? Ain't never anybody's gift that's good or bad by itself. It's how the person use it. And you think about this, too, son. If Billy Brayton ain't dead, where'd John Kincaid get that body so close to the right build and hair color it make yo' mama believe it was that boy she love so much? That body that just happen not to have a face?"

"Holy. Fuck." Jake realized what he'd said and who he'd said it to the minute the words cleared his throat. "Sorry, Aunt Lulu, I didn't mean to say that."

She laughed.

"Yeah, I think that about covers it."

Chapter Ten

Maggie whistled and opened the door of the steel gray Mustang.

"Yeah, some things never change all right." She settled into the driver's seat, turned the ignition and shifted into first. "You always were a Ford man."

Maggie cleared the parking lot almost before Billy's door clicked shut.

"Nice of you to let me get in the car before you tear off."

"Places to go, things to do." She turned left at the four way stop and headed up Highway 80 out of town. "Sweet car."

"Thanks. We have to fit in a trip to Macon or Dublin tomorrow morning, throw that in the places to go and things to do list."

"Why?"

"Rings. I am *not* marrying you without putting a ring on your finger."

Maggie took her left hand off the wheel and waved it at him. "You put one there a long time ago. The wedding band's still in my jewelry box. Right by yours. Yours probably needs sizing, but I'll use your little finger if it's too tight on your ring finger. Just be damn sure you don't lose it if it's too loose. Or I will be *pissed*."

Billy caught the glimmer of gold and faint flicker of the almost microscopic diamond. Maggie's Christmas present, 1985.

"You still wear that?"

"Never take it off."

"I'd still like for you to have something nicer."

"You haven't changed *one damn bit*, have you, Billy Brayton? If you bought me the Hope diamond, it wouldn't mean as much to me as these rings do. After all, you gave up the Mustang's Hurst shifter *and* the custom paint job to buy 'em. Not to mention the dual exhaust."

"How'd you know that? Never mind. T-bone."

"He's been wonderful to me and Jake over the years."

"I'm glad."

"Maybe he's got a car he's redone Jake can use till I can get with the insurance company, have to check with him. I think he sold all the last batch he was re-doing already, though."

"We can take him car shopping Saturday."

Maggie shook her head. "Nope. I don't have that kind of cash flow, Billy. I'll have to wait till I get the insurance check. It was my old Eclipse, but the Bluebook value ought to be high enough I can manage to get him a pretty good one without a car payment through the roof."

"I'll handle his car, Maggie, don't worry about it."

"You don't have to—"

"Oh, I see. It's *our* home, yours, mine, and Jake's, but you still have to handle everything by yourself. I said I'd handle his car. He should've been mine, too, Maggie. I missed the first bike, the first glove, the first football, the first everything. Not just Jake's, the kids we should have had and didn't. I'm handling Jake's car."

Maggie glanced over him. His own firsts had mattered only to his mother, not to his father. Not ever. Something he'd sworn to her would never happen to a child of his.

"As long you're not planning to buy him a brand-new souped-up Mustang to try and make it all up at once."

Billy laughed. "Thought did cross my mind. But I won't go that far if you don't want me to. Don't worry about his car, Princess."

Maggie smiled. She'd always been his Princess. Not too many folks knew it was short for "Princess Bitch".

"You know, Jake wouldn't have been mine either, if I'd never gone to Georgia."

"Which is proof all things happen for a reason. Because he was *definitely* supposed to be yours."

Maggie sped down Highway 80. A few new houses set back off the road but it hadn't changed that much. They ran across the bridge over Turkey Creek proper. Toward—

"Princess, do you really live this close to Big John's house?"

"Hell, no. *Our* house is back the other side of town, part of the old Harris plantation. Way back in the woods. You'll love it."

"And we're near Big John's house because—"

Maggie turned sharply right onto a painstakingly maintained gravel road and sped straight down it. Directly into Big John territory.

"Maggie—"

She pulled up, threw the car into first gear and pulled the brake. "I wasn't going to tear out the oil pan, Billy. Nothing changes at Big John's. Not the mailbox, not the drive, not the house. No road on his property would dare tear up a car."

"That's not exactly what I—"

He broke off. No stopping an immutable force of nature. Maggie wanted to talk to Big John, and God help the man who tried to stop her. He threw open the car door and hurried after her. Her forceful strides ate up ground at an alarming rate. He caught her before she charged up the steps and through the massive front door, always left unlocked. The Kincaid house got a lot of traffic, and nobody in his right mind would try to burglarize Big John's home.

"Hey, Charlene!" Maggie waved at Big John's current housekeeper and kept walking.

"Miss Maggie? Miss Maggie, what you doing, you can't just—"

"Sure I can, Charlene. Just watch me."

She flung a door open and walked straight up to Big John's desk. He stared at her and then looked past her to Billy, standing in the doorway. His eyes widened.

Maggie slapped her hand down in front of him, leaving the laminated clippings lying on the desk.

"You daughter-fuckin' son-of-a-bitch."

Big John leaned back in his chair and laced his hands behind his head.

"Well. Looks like the white trash blew back in town. And at least this time, girl, you're right down on his level. You been practicin', Maggie? You look like hell."

Billy moved forward. Maggie laughed.

"Oh, don't even try that mind-game shit with me, like I give a damn what you think. Yeah, I've been workin' like a dog all day and probably look like one. But you know what? I clean up real good. 'Cause this kind of dirt, it washes off. Your kind of filth never will."

She turned on her heel and started back out.

"And you, boy? Content to let a girl do your talkin', are you?"

Billy smiled.

"Oh, I have no problem at all with a *woman* like Maggie talkin' for me, no, sir. But you and I, we'll talk later. Unfinished business." Billy walked up to the desk and scooped up the old clippings. "Had these a long time, think I'll hold on to 'em. Put 'em in Maggie's scrapbook next to my obituary."

He started after Maggie and then turned back. "Almost forgot. Just wanted to remind you—there's no statute of limitation on murder."

Maggie threw one last volley on her way into the main foyer.

"I'm sure you won't be upset to hear you're not invited to the wedding. Seein' as how you threw the bride away a long time ago."

Charlene stood in the hall, mouth hanging wide open.

"Have a good evenin', Charlene!" Maggie threw the front door open and bounded down the steps.

"Feel better or you still drivin'?"

"Better. But I'm still drivin'." Maggie cranked up. This time she did let him close the door before she pulled off.

"Daughter-fuckin'-son-of-a-bitch?" Billy raised his eyebrow.

"Yeah, I just made that up. Pretty good, huh? Figuratively speaking, of course. Literally, it's one of the few things I can't accuse him of."

She stopped the car out of sight of the house and turned to look at him.

"So. Let me guess. You would be the new Chief Investigator for the County now, wouldn't you?"

"That's been beating on the tom-toms, huh?"

"Oh, yeah. How they kept a name out of it, I don't know. Good thing, though, I'd ever caught the name. I'd have probably been lying in wait with a shotgun."

"You hate guns."

"I'da made an exception. I did wonder how the hell the county ever landed anybody with that kind of credentials. According to scuttlebutt, you've been everything from ex-Ranger to ex-Green Beret."

"Oh, no, nothing that dramatic. Military police. Hit it early, about all I've ever done. I'm a cop, Maggie. Even as a soldier. It's what I was born to be."

She looked him over. "That really doesn't surprise me much, now that I think about it."

"And you figured that out so damn fast because?"

She laughed, pushed in the clutch and turned onto Highway 80. "Are you *kiddin'*? That absolute chill politeness. *Sir*. The level tone. I just about expected to hear *make my day*. But no statute of limitation on murder? What was that about?"

"Princess, I'm not in that coffin, but somebody is. Somebody so close to my build and coloring it fooled you. With his face blown off. At the least, that's mutilation of a corpse. No chance it was a wax dummy?"

"No chance. I stood there and held your hand a long time."

"God, Maggie! You're goin' to really kill me yet before the day's over!"

"It was, as they say, one of those defining moments in life." She stared straight at the road, her expression as hard as any that ever crossed Big John's face. Billy reached over and covered her right hand with his own. "I didn't have another one for seven years. Then I got the call Jake's parents had been killed in an interstate pileup. Sara'd asked me when they got pregnant if they could name me guardian in their wills. I said sure, but nothing's goin' to happen to you, don't be silly. Yeah, right. So I tore up I-75 to Atlanta, got there about one o'clock in the morning. I stood in front of his crib, knew I shouldn't wake him up, but I couldn't help it. I reached down and picked him up and put him on my shoulder. By all rights, he should have been screamin', getting picked up like that from a sound sleep. I'd visited a few times since he'd been born, not often enough for him to know me. He pulled his head back off my shoulder and looked at me. And giggled. And I started to live again. Funny, I hadn't realized until right that minute I'd ever stopped."

Billy squeezed her hand.

"Nothing rocked my world again till today. When you walked through the door." She shook her head and shifted her hand to squeeze his. "We were one month and one week from driving out of this town together and never lookin' back, Billy."

"Yeah, I always thought that was kind of ironic, Big John setting me up so I had to join the army. Since that's exactly what I was going to do, anyway."

They'd had it all planned. A Vegas wedding, even. Maggie would take classes at whatever community college they were stationed near, get a little part-time job for a few luxuries. They'd been young but realistic.

"Shouldn't have waited for graduation."

"The most rational thing we ever decided to do, wait for graduation. Funny, huh? Caused us more trouble than any of the impulses."

"What's the 'unfinished business' you've got with Big John? 'Cause I don't think you meant just us, did you? You came back to take him down."

"Never told you, but back that spring, I got an offer. One of those offers you probably shouldn't refuse. Well, you should, but you need to be real careful about how you do it. Drug-runnin' ain't the safest of all professions, but refusin' to do it can shorten your life, too, depends on who you're refusin'."

"From who? And what's that got to do with Big John? And why the hell didn't you ever tell me?"

"Never wanted any of that shit to even touch you. Especially since—Maggie, you don't think all the Kincaid money's from legitimate businesses, do you?"

"*What?* You think Big John's a *drug-runner?*"

"You're surprised?"

"Nothing he does would surprise me. It's just—the family's always had money, Billy. Farming, mining, banking, I don't even know what all else, never stuck around long enough as an adult to figure it out. Why would he get involved in something so *blatantly* dirty? I got no illusions, hell, he'd commit murder if it suited him—and if he thought he could set it up to get away with it. I got no problem believing that at all. But the drug trade? That'd be so— he'd consider it *common.* Beneath him."

"There's no way farming and mining produce the kind of money organized crime does, Princess. And I don't think he's just *involved* in drug dealing and I don't think it's just for money, that wouldn't be good enough. I think he's one of the masterminds, considers it sort of like three-dimensional chess, a challenge he enjoys. Maggie, he put a *body* in that coffin. He knew you'd look, wanted you to, that's why it wasn't sealed. Had to be real so you'd believe. The average citizen can't just come up with a spare body. Not even Big John.

"And that spring, well, I sort of stumbled on some stuff goin' on 'round town that was stuff you really didn't want to stumble into. Right after that's when the offer came. Like, okay, we've hinted enough, let's see if you're willing to play. And when I wasn't—think about it, Maggie. He at least *tolerated* me that winter. Probably because of that bad boy reputation. Bet he thought it might come in handy. In the long run, handy enough to put up with a white trash son-in-law. That'd give him a family lieutenant, expendable, in the front lines. So he made sure I started getting sniffs of—stuff—around town. And when I'd sniffed enough, they moved in to recruit. But I didn't bite. And got framed for armed robbery a week later."

"*Mafia* stuff?"

"Believe me, Maggie. There's nowhere in the world there isn't a mafia or its equivalent. And now, since I was dead, I think I know the missing pieces of the puzzle on Jonesy, too."

"Like?"

"First, I think something went wrong somewhere in Big John's master scheme, like the wrong deputies on duty at the right time. For me, that is. Because I think I *was* supposed to be the body in that coffin. Just a lot sooner. Killed trying to escape. When that didn't happen—everybody knew I lived more at T-bone's than at home. Who else would I try to contact? So I'd be willing to bet Jonesy'd knew if I ever came back home, there'd be another body. In an unmarked grave. Plus one for his son, too. I bet they were *real* convincing when they talked to him. Made it crystal clear. And just think how easy they coulda made that happen if I'd come back when I was still a green kid."

"Oh. My. God."

"Feels right, now that you think about it, huh?"

"Absolutely. Now hang on. We're almost home. And this driveway ain't Big John's."

They were past the four-way and Maggie slowed. She turned right over the railroad tracks and then immediately left. She took the rutted gravel drive slow. The Mustang bounced and Billy cringed.

"Damn, Maggie! Don't you think we need to see about gettin' a little work done on this road?"

"Oh, hell no! Keeps the riff-raff out. I see folks all day long, don't want 'em driving down just 'cause they take a notion. I know exactly where to drive, and so does Jake and all his friends, and anybody else I want down here in the first place. Close your eyes."

"What?"

"Close your eyes. Humor me."

He did.

"Okay. Open."

"Maggie, oh my God!"

They stopped at the top of the last slope down to a little hollow in the midst of tall hardwoods. The house blended into the trees, taking advantage of the natural terrain. A mountain cabin both contemporary and rustic, constructed with natural wood and big sheets of glass. Not large, not pretentious. Country comfortable. *Exactly* the house they'd planned to have. One day.

"Thought you'd recognize it. Welcome home, Billy."

Chapter Eleven

Jake bounded out of Aunt Lulu's house. His first call was T-bone. He waited for the whoops and hollers to die down.

"So, you happy about this or not? I couldn't really tell, reaction I got."

"Boy, you work too hard at being a smartass."

"I don't work hard at all, it's natural talent."

"Yeah, well, you just don't know, Jake. You don't know what they were like back then, got no idea what it did to Maggie. Couldn't, of course. Probably shouldn't, either. Kids just ain't ready for some things."

"Well, wanted you ready. Billy said tell you he needs a best man. I get to give the bride away. They think they're just gonna walk in the courthouse and get married, I know. But that ain't happenin'. I got calls to make and people to see, a courthouse wedding's fine with me, but they're gonna have an audience. And a—whatcha call wedding stuff? Reception. Yeah, they're gonna have as much of the whole deal as I can manage. So I got to get with Junie Bug."

"Hold on! Just wait a minute! You call Junie Bug, she gon' call Janet Weldon, and Janet's gonna pull out all that fancy stuff like meatballs and wedding cookies and fruit platters and those lil' ol' chicken things takes a dozen of 'em to make a real drumstick, and God knows what all else! And set up in one of the church halls or something. Maggie and Billy, they don't want none of that frou-frou stuff!"

"Frou-frou? Damn, T-bone, didn't know you spoke French."

"Boy. Quit it. Now, here's what we're doin'. You call Junie Bug and tell her to get with Janet Weldon 'bout a wedding cake. And that's it. All we want from there. Tell Junie Bug to get over to the café tomorrow and fix up a big batch of them baked beans she makes. Potato salad, maybe coleslaw, too. *Big* batches. Just tell her we're having a barbecue, she can take it from there."

"We are?"

"We damn sure are. I just had some meat butchered last month, got plenty for this, gonna call Danny Gordon, get him to get out that big barbecue grill he made, him and me got to get started, gonna take us all night. Now what I really need is for you to stop 'em from getting married 'til late afternoon, so we can have a nighttime field dance."

"T-bone. One, I'm gonna be lucky if I can stop 'em from gettin' married by noon. Two, I'd have to talk to 'em to figure out what they're actually plannin'. Three, I ain't about to call 'em right now. Or anytime the rest of this evenin' or night. Probably ain't even goin' home for the next few nights, either. I'm thoughtful that way. So scratch the night-time dance idea. Afternoon barbecue, early supper thing we can handle."

"Well, hell, coward. I'll call 'em then!"

"T-bone. They're the loves of each other's lives, torn apart like Romeo and Juliet. They haven't seen each other in years. They thought they were *lost* to each other for all eternity and all that shit. You think they're just sittin' on one of the porch swings having tea and cookies right now?"

"Oh. Well. Yeah."

"'Bout damn time it clicked, I was gettin' worried 'bout you. Why's night-time so important?"

"Told you. Field dance, numb-nuts! Y'all don't do line dancin' out in the fields anymore? 'Course you do! And so did we, you turkey! You think y'all invented 'em?"

Jake grinned. T-bone surprised the heck out of him sometimes. And on this, he was right. Mom and Billy wouldn't want any of that frou-frou stuff. They'd much prefer a barbecue and it didn't have to be night to have a field dance, after all. The afternoon would work just as well. Turkey Creek kept a pasture and a lake in perfect condition for exactly such social events.

"Okay, I'm on it! Later, dude!"

He pulled up in the parking lot in front of Clean Class and dialed Junie Bug before he got out. Initial explanations took a while, seein' as how Junie Bug was two classes below Billy's Senior Class and knew every Maggie Kincaid-Billy Brayton story ever told.

"That boy on a football field, Jake, that was magic! Ain't been none to touch him since! And him and your mama in that red Mustang! Just like one of them glamour couples you see on TV! They both looked so good they looked artificial!"

"Neither one of 'em looks bad now, either. Now, about tomorrow." Jake proceeded to outline the basic plan.

That part of the conversation took a while. Junie Bug wanted 'the real deal.'

"That's what I thought at first, but no, think about it. T-bone's right. So whatcha think we can do with the time we've got?"

"I think you leave the food to me. The flowers, now—"

"For a barbecue?"

"No, son, for your mama! And the *wedding*! I'll call Joyce, you go on 'bout lettin' everybody know."

"Miss Joyce? Why?"

"Jake! Your mama's best friend, President of the Garden Club? *Your* best friend's mama, 'member her? Leave it to us, you just run on along and get the word out."

"Thank God. I was beginning to think my ear was gonna fall off just between you and T-bone."

"Don't get smart with me, boy! Now, you get movin'!"

"Yessum."

Chapter Twelve

Maggie gave Billy a tour of the house and settled him on the sun-porch off her bedroom while she showered. There wasn't any awkwardness, just unspoken agreement to savor these few hours, to re-adjust to each other's presence, to absorb as much as possible of the other's last twenty-five years.

Billy whistled when she emerged.

"Yep, you clean up real good."

She laughed. "Even with comfort clothes and no makeup? Glad to hear it. Not that much make-up was left, anyway. Just *lots* more character lines." She settled on the porch swing beside him and slipped comfortably under his arm. She leaned back and sighed.

"You've never needed makeup. I like your hair shorter. Other than that, you really haven't changed."

Maggie's hair at eighteen had cascaded half-way down her back, a dark brunette with natural highlights of varying shades of brown and an occasional touch of reddish-gold. The color was the same, but now it swung slightly below her shoulders.

"Men always say women don't need make-up until we don't wear any. Then they ask us if we're sick. You've changed a lot. And then again, you haven't."

Billy raised his eyebrows.

"Face is the same, just a little older. Few character lines yourself. But you've certainly filled out."

"I'm fat?"

"Smartass. No, filled out. Your shoulders are to die for."

Billy grinned. "Twenties and thirties have a way of doin' that to guys. Jake'll do it, too, I can tell. Trick is to keep it going in the forties."

"Hmmm. I think a considerable amount of time on a considerable amount of gym equipment had something to do with it, too."

"And Jake's definitely got that," Billy said. The main back porch was filled with weight benches, stationary bicycle, abs cruncher, Bowflex.

"Which I tend to think the two of you'll be using together. A lot."

"Working out's a lot easier with the right partner. Wrong partner's hell, but Jake—that's one impressive kid, Maggie."

"Very. I have no false modesty at all when it comes to my son. Like the porch? Not too feminine, I hope? This is my one indulgent luxury. The deer come out at dusk to feed in the yard."

The porch opened off Maggie's bedroom through French doors and faced the side of a sloping, wooded hill. The main back porch was Jake's. This was a woman's private retreat. Rattan furnishings, colorful throw pillows, painted glass wind chimes, green plants, old-fashioned wooden swing full of cushions.

"It's perfect. Absolutely perfect. Feels just like you." They watched the quality of light change while twilight settled in. Pools of shadow rippled.

They talked through twilight, on into full dark. They told each other everything they could think of to tell, attempting to catch up years in just a few hours. They laughed and talked and touched and enjoyed the feel of each other. Maggie leaned back against Billy on the swing while he rubbed her shoulders.

They let the dark come down around them, and the rest of Turkey Creek talked, too. Word of the biggest news to hit this town in nobody could remember when hummed over the telephone wires and skipped like a stone over lake water from cell tower to cell tower.

* * *

"...and he's not really dead, can you believe it? And I swear, I don't know how that big a mix-up could happen. I remember they actually ran an obituary, and had a funeral and everything! And Maggie was just..."

"Mix-up my left foot! Now, Helen, you know dang well that was Big John, all the way! Didn't want that boy near Maggie!

Though Maggie's real forgiving you ask me, I mean, he never came back..."

"You didn't hear that part? Somebody'd—and I guess we all know who that was—sent that boy Maggie's wedding announcement! Now, why on earth would he have come back?"

"Well, still..."

"Oh hush, Agnes! And they're gettin' married tomorrow, isn't that just the most romantic thing you ever heard tell of..."

"I got enough layers frozen for a good cake, don't worry about that, but I'm gettin' some other stuff together for a pretty table, I don't care what Jake and T-bone want, this is Maggie's wedding, for heaven's sake..."

"...tea olive! The tea olives are blooming, and I'll use that for accent! I'm puttin' together a bouquet with every color camellia I got, those dark, glossy leaves make a beautiful green, don't you think? Thank God they're out early this year! I'm bettin' she'll wear cream, but I wish I knew for sure, Maggie's as like as not to show up in blue jeans..."

* * *

While the town hummed, Maggie and Billy talked.

"...and so I used the money I had in trust from my mother's family to finish college, got a campus job, didn't take any more from Big John after that first semester, wouldn't have taken that if I hadn't been afraid it'd tip him off not to. And then I used what was left on the house, I figured why not, 'cause I put all the insurance money from Jake's parents up in trust for college and just left it there, thought that'd be one less thing to worry about. So I don't really have a very big mortgage left."

"*We* don't have a very big mortgage left. And considering the years it's been just yours, let's just consider what's left something you don't need to worry about, okay?"

"But—"

"No arguments."

"This might take some gettin' used to."

"…kind of surprised you put him in Rockland Academy, actually. You really fell in love with the high school and the high school kids our senior year."

"Yeah, I did, and if it was still the same, that's where Jake'd be. But Billy, it's just not the same anymore, the *town's* not the same anymore, there're so many factions and divisions. The Academy's not that great academically, but I know it's safe and all the boys still keep their hunting guns in the backs of their trucks and nobody thinks a thing about it…"

"…and I didn't really think I'd like Alaska at all, didn't think the Southern blood could take the cold, but the Northern Lights, my God! Every time I saw 'em, I imagined you standing there watching, too, framed in fur, that look of wonder you always got on your face over thunderstorms and rainbows and sunrises. Wasn't really that fond of Hawaii, believe it or not, so humid it almost felt like home, and it just felt so little, kept missin' the roads stretching out for miles in front of me like in the plains.…"

"…but you have to swear to me you'll let me die first this time. Buried you once, I don't think I could do it again. But I'm not sure that wasn't easier, actually. At least it was final. Easier than just waiting, day to day, finally realizing I wasn't coming."

"I don't know. I think about standing in front of your coffin and seeing you with no face—God, Maggie, that woulda' killed me, I'd have lost my mind! And your voice, when you told me that—felt like I was getting stabbed in the heart just listenin' to you. And then to hear you talk about holdin' my hand—no, I don't know if I could have done that. How often did you wake up screamin'? For how long?"

"First few years were real bad. I didn't actually scream, you know, not at the time—"

"Wouldn't give him the satisfaction."

"Hell, no. But I made up for it afterwards. That's how I got so close to Sara. Jake's mother. Sort of have to tell your roommate why you wake up screaming a couple of times a week…"

"…and I'm really glad he's not playing football this season."

"He's not playing football? His senior year? That boy was born to play football, you can tell by lookin' at him."

"Broke his leg sliding into third last game of the season last year, so he was out of commission for a lot of the summer practices. And then I think he kind of liked not sweating himself to death. Besides, he might've been scared to. I kinda had a bad reaction at one of the games last fall. Volunteer coach slapped his hand down on top of Jake's helmet so hard while they were huddlin', I saw his shoulders buckle. And it takes a *lot* for Jake's shoulders to buckle. Almost went over the fence, might have been a little more vocal than I realized at the time."

"You don't say."

"Yeah, real shocker, I know. But I don't think I've ever been that mad at anybody but Big John before. Well, except you this afternoon for never coming back."

* * *

The news spread like wildfire, through every social circle of every age group in town. Jake's circle was buzzing. The girls swooned over the sheer romanticism of the thing.

"Miss Maggie's gettin' married tomorrow, did y'all hear! And after thinkin' he was dead all those years!"

"Won't be the same up at the store, I'll bet. She ain't gonna have time for all of us now."

"Not Miss Maggie, you'll see. And he has to be super himself if she's stayed in love with him all this time."

The boys, however, quickly honed into a more important point, at least insofar as the masculine mentality was concerned.

"Did you hear? My daddy told me it was him!"

"Who him?"

"Him! You know the story, the dude who stayed from midnight clear through to daylight out at Clayton Chapel! My daddy told me it was Billy Brayton. And that he was the biggest bad-ass ever came out of this town!"

"Damn! Jake gets all the luck! Miss Maggie for a mom and now he gets that dude for a step-dad?"

"All night out there, man! I stayed maybe ten minutes and ain't ashamed to admit it! You?"

"'Bout that. All night? Jeez..."

***

The town kept talking, and so did the subjects of their conversations.

"…it was my Sergeant in the first Gulf War. Saved my life a couple of times, for sure. He's the reason I ended up in the Military Police…"

"Did you ever come close? To getting married?"

"Not really. Wasn't a monk, don't get me wrong, but nobody ever felt like forever. Never felt like us. Like it would be—settling, I guess. How 'bout you? Ever come close?"

"No. Good description, settling. I mean, I even already had a child—without morning sickness or stretch marks. Besides, didn't know any men I'd trust to do right by Jake except for T-bone, and my sacrificial maternal instincts just ain't *that* strong!"

Positions on the porch swing shifted periodically through the hours. Billy lay stretched out across the swing with his back against the cushions of the right arm rest, Maggie in his lap with her legs on top of his, leaning back against his chest. They'd finally about talked themselves out. Maggie stretched, her muscles finally loose and relaxed, a state seldom achieved.

"You finally windin' down, are you?"

"Limp as last year's corn stalk. Don't get shoulder rubs very often. As in never, actually. What time is it, anyway?" She glanced at the clock she'd hung on the side porch wall. "Oh, hell, I didn't know it was this late! And we haven't eaten anything either, are you hungry?"

"Starvin'."

Maggie bounced up. "Well, why didn't you say something? I brought plates down from the café earlier, I usually do—"

Billy pulled her back and lowered his head.

"Not for food."

And while Maggie and Billy were otherwise sweetly engaged and the hour grew later, the quality of the phone conversations running along the wires changed. New participants entered the wires and cell tower interstates.

* * *

"There some reason I never caught the name of that new investigator y'all just hired?"

"I didn't know the name. Sheriff kept it close to the vest. Is it important?"

"You might say so. And you might say you've just fucked up big time. And you might say you're goin' be real sorry 'bout that."

"Hey, hold it! Wasn't my decision even if I did know, I don't have final say on—"

"You got enough say. And you didn't use it. And now I'm gonna have to fix it. So you just get the word on out. I'll handle it. You keep the little play cops out of my boys' way."

* * *

"Boss Man's on the warpath. He got a history with that Brayton fellow, the new investigator?"

"Oh hell yeah."

"And you didn't tell me that?"

"Well, I might have, you'd ever bothered to tell me the name. But I don't see what it mattered. We ain't got enough pull to have stopped him from getting hired, that's the sheriff's call."

"Not the way the Boss Man sees it. And he's pissed as hell I didn't ever tell him the name."

"You never told him it was Billy Brayton?"

"I didn't know the name to tell him, I tell you! And how the fuck was I 'sposed to know it'd matter if I did? I'm not one of you local yahoo rednecks!"

"Well, shit. Bet he is put out on that. Well, don't worry too much. He's probably just pissed 'cause he didn't have time to figure out how he wanted to get rid of him 'fore he got here. Probably glad of the second chance."

"Second chance?"

"Yeah, Brayton's one of the Boss Man's few failures. But he won't be this time."

* * *

Later still, while most of the town slept, yet another contingent made an appearance on the wires.

"We might have trouble with the new County Investigator. He's got a personal vendetta, won't be just a job for him."

"I don't think we need to worry about it. He knows how to handle himself. And lots of people I know take Big John personally. I'm talkin' to one, matter o' fact."

"We've worked too long and risked too much for anybody to fuck it up now, we'll have to be real careful."

"He might even be useful, you know. Ever think of it that way?"

"And he might fuck it up and get himself killed while he's doing it."

"Not a chance. By all the signs, he's got nine lives."

"Yeah, well, you'll forgive me if I worry about it anyway."

* * *

Billy stretched and stirred and pulled Maggie closer. She smiled and shifted.

The town finally slept. And so did they.

Chapter Thirteen

The ringing phone, coming from some muffled location, roused Maggie from the deepest sleep she'd had in years. Cellphone. Jake's ringtone. What time was it, anyway?

She rose on her elbow and looked over Billy at the clock.

"*Shit!*" She punched Billy's shoulder.

"What?" He sat upright, fully alert.

"It's already ten o'clock! I don't believe this. I haven't slept this late in *years!*" She threw the covers back, reached for her discarded T-shirt and looked around for her cell. "Shit!" she exclaimed again. Still in her pocketbook. "Quit grinning!" She glared at Billy. "Okay, I haven't had a night like this since I was eighteen, either! That satisfy your male ego?"

"It's a start."

"Jake? Hey, buddy, where are you?"

"Still at Ben's. You said don't go to school, but I don't know anything about any other plans or times or anything."

"Honestly, I don't quite know yet—you're not going to believe this, but—"

"I woke you up? I actually woke *you* up?"

"Yeah, yesterday between thinking you'd killed yourself in a car crash and Billy walkin' through the door—too much excitement for this one-horse town. Wore me out."

"I hope to hell that's not all that wore you out."

"*Jake!*" He got that in both ears at the same time from both Joyce Clayton and Maggie. "Sorry, but you *got* to stop leaving yourself wide open on that, Mom. So, got a time frame, estimate, something?"

Muffled noises sounded in the background. "And Miss Joyce is kind of excited, she's pulling the phone away from me right now, actually—"

"Maggie Mae, *please* tell me you're not gonna wear blue jeans."

"No, I'm not, and you know I hate it when you call me Maggie Mae."

"Watch it, girl, or I'll tell the Judge to use your real name during the ceremony."

"You wouldn't dare."

"Watch me. Is Billy just as big a hunk as he ever was?"

"Hunkier."

"Some damn. Now listen, girl, I know how private you are, but Ben and I aren't waitin' on an invitation, we're just comin'. You know that, don't you? Benjie would be out of town, you sure you want a husband? Never around when you need 'em anyway."

Maggie laughed. "Yes to both questions. But I don't know what to tell you yet, we overslept."

"Well, here's what you need to do. Just call Eddie Thompson and ask him when he can do the ceremony today. You can just go up a few minutes before and get the license. That won't take ten or fifteen minutes, you'll be all set. Call us back and let us know. Oh, and that long cream linen sheath you bought for Miss Luellen's big birthday party last year would be perfect!"

"Even my fashion-challenged brain knew that. Any more orders?"

"No, I figure if you overslept you're doing fine on your own. At least *my* ass isn't in a sling over it, I was always *petrified* you were going to slip up and oversleep one of those mornings. And who would everybody have come after when you weren't at school? Me, that's who!"

"And that's why you were and are and always will be my dearest friend in all the world."

"Well, don't let's get sappy over it, okay?"

Maggie laughed. "Okay, okay, let me get moving."

She clicked the phone shut looked over at Billy.

"Set-up. For sure."

"What?"

"Set-up. She even told me what to wear. I don't think we're havin' a private wedding. Might not even be particularly small."

"Do you mind?"

"I don't care if the whole damn world watches. Now, let me get the Probate Court number so Eddie Thompson can tell me when the whole thing's already set up for."

"Chunk? He's the Probate Judge?"

"Yeah, well, after all, the town bad-ass is a cop. Life moves in mysterious ways."

"Past mysterious if Chunk's a lawyer."

"Don't be silly, this is Rockland County. Probate Judge is just an elected citizen."

* * *

Over at the Clayton residence, Jake swatted Ben.

"Will you *quit* trying to put flowers behind my ears!"

"But you look so *sweet*!"

"Ben, you do that one more time, I'm gonna flatten you!"

"Boys! Just get those big ferns in the back of the Tahoe, please." Joyce Clayton, intent on lining the biggest courtroom of the Rockland County Courthouse with every green plant in Rockland County turned to find two teenagers looking at her.

"What?"

"Why would *your* ass have been in a sling if Mom didn't show up at school 'cause she overslept?"

"We're best friends. Best friends cover for each other. Y'all think we don't have any idea how often both of you are spending the night here, as far as Maggie knows, and at Maggie's as far as I know?"

"Mom!"

"So where was Mom when she was supposed to be at your house?"

"Take a *wild* guess, Jake. 'Bout time y'all realized you've never come up with anything your parents didn't do first."

"Some damn."

Joyce exited the kitchen, fern in hand, heading for her SUV.

"Know what I heard from Blake Elbert this morning?" Ben asked Jake. "His dad told him."

"What?"

"Billy's *that* guy!"

"What guy?"

"Guy that stayed at Clayton Chapel from midnight to dawn!"

"No shit?"

"Shit, man. Nerves of steel or what?"

"Well, I could've told y'all that," Joyce said, coming back in the kitchen. "If you wanted to know who it was, why didn't you just ask?"

"You sound like it's nothing!"

Joyce shrugged. "Well, that's just something you'd expect from Billy."

* * *

"Maggie, this is just unbelievable! Who'da thunk of such, I swear? Is Lightnin' handy, can I holler at him?"

"Sure." Maggie passed the phone to Billy. "Chunk wants to talk to you."

"Hey, Chunk."

"Damn, man, hasn't no one called me that in years!"

"Yeah, I don't hear Lightnin' much anymore, either."

"Funny how things like that go, nobody uses my nickname, nobody hardly remembers T-bone's real name. Now, let's see, I got a couple of hearings set for this morning, they won't take long. How 'bout one o'clock? Y'all come up around twelve-thirty, plenty of time to get the paperwork done, we'll have the ceremony right after, that suit y'all?"

"We'll be there."

Billy looked at Maggie. "Set-up is for one o'clock. Got the distinct feeling we're not supposed to show up 'til twelve-thirty—or later, seems that gives us plenty of time to get the paperwork done. So I figure we need to just hang around here and keep out of everybody's way."

"Well, good. Guess I don't need to rush around after all. So, let's see—"

"Princess, I'm starvin'."

"You're kiddin', right?"

"No, I mean I'm *really* starvin'. Can we have breakfast, you think? First, that is."

Maggie laughed. "Yeah, I think I can manage. I do own a restaurant, you know."

"But can you cook? 'Cause I can do a pretty passable breakfast."

"I'm a better cook than Junie Bug, actually, but for God's sakes, don't tell her I said that."

* * *

They lingered at the table over coffee, a rare event for Maggie, who almost never sat for longer than a few minutes at a time.

"Have you got a suit with you, by any chance? Since it seems this might be a little more formal than I'd thought?"

"Yeah, a couple. I need to get the clothes I brought out of the car, I guess."

"The closet in the guest room's pretty empty, that'll do for right now. I've always taken the whole closet in my room, but I'll shift the out of season stuff to the guest room so you'll have a side."

"I can walk to the guest room, Maggie, it's not that big a deal."

"Yes, it is. Never thought I'd see your clothes hangin' with mine. One of those little things I don't intend to miss. I'll rearrange later. What about the rest of your stuff?"

"I travel pretty light. Got some stuff in storage, but not a lot. I really thought I'd just get a room at the hotel off Ninety-Six for a few days while I looked around for something. Never thought the something would be this." Billy looked around at the bright kitchen and the view of the woods. "I've got navy and tan with me, but not black. That all right with you?"

Maggie shuddered. "I buried you in a black suit. I don't *ever* want to see you in a black suit. If you own one, burn it. Even navy's too close, wear tan."

Chapter Fourteen

Billy pulled up to the courthouse at 12:40 p.m. No parking space available.

"Good Lord!" Maggie pointed to the café. "Park over in the café parking lot. They've got most of the town here! I wonder if they're goin' to jump out and yell 'Surprise!'"

"You have to act surprised anyway. Somebody pulled double over-time last night to pull this together."

"Oh, I will. Feel underdressed for this crowd."

"You're beautiful."

"Well, it's a wonder I'm even halfway pulled together! When we settle into something resemblin' normal next week, you've *got* to stay out of my morning shower. You almost made me late for my own wedding!"

"Don't count on it, Princess."

"Oh, hell! I never called anybody back! You think they even noticed?"

"Nope."

Thelma Davis, long time guardian of the town's licenses and death certificates, came around the counter bestowing hugs.

"There you are! Heard you were coming, got everything all ready for you! I swear, Billy Brayton, I coulda just *cried* last night when I heard! Well, I did cry, matter of fact. All this time, all of us thinking you were dead, son, *why* didn't you come back home? Well, I heard that part, too, but I swear, what goes aroun' comes aroun' and one day, it'll come back to haunt your daddy, Maggie, what he threw away, what he did to y'all. And look at you now, Billy, always tryin' so hard to prove you weren't your daddy, you never seemed to realize how much of your Mama's in you, sweetest woman ever drew breath, she'd be so proud of you!"

Billy, long absent from the ebb and flow and tides of small-town life, felt himself being swept back in. He was absurdly touched at the reference to his mother.

"Thank you, Miss Thelma. I'm glad you think so."

"Here, here. Y'all waited long enough for this, I already filled everything out, y'all just throw your drivers' licenses down so I can copy 'em for the documentation, and we'll be all ready!"

"Miss Thelma, how'd you—"

"Now, Maggie, you don't think I don't know everybody in town's birthdays and addresses and parents and mother's maiden names, now do you? Give me some credit, child!"

"Lightnin'!" Eddie Thompson walked in.

"Chunk!" Billy responded.

"You can say that again. Fits a lot better now than it did when we were young, sorry to say. But you—damn, you kept yourself in shape, now, didn't you?"

"I tried."

"Well, com'on, I figured we'd go over to one of the courtrooms—"

"Eddie. I'm not stupid, I know Joyce Clayton like a sister and I know my son even better. I'll act surprised, but what are we lookin' at exactly?"

"Why, Maggie, I don't know what—"

"There's more cars out there than for a two week trial term, Eddie."

He sighed in defeat. "Well, just hang on to your hats, okay? You comin', Miss Thelma?"

"Heaven's yes! Wouldn't miss it for the world!"

"Oh, I forgot! Y'all got anything special you wrote or—"

"I've waited a long time for this, Eddie. Traditional is perfect."

"But leave the 'obey' out," Billy interjected. " I don't want her to say hell no and walk out on me."

"Good thinkin', Lightnin'." He threw open the door to the main courtroom.

"Oh. My. God."

"Surprised after all, ain't you, Maggie?" the Judge asked.

There was standing room only in the biggest courtroom the courthouse had. In just one glance, Maggie saw Jake's entire Senior class of Rockland Academy, her entire Senior class of Rockland Academy, every football player who still lived in the area who'd played with Billy, a goodly portion of Billy's senior class, which was much bigger than hers, the girls of the Scales of Justice Café, and a huge number of the café and Clean Class regulars.

At second glance, she caught the rows of huge green ferns and pot plants lining the banisters and aisles, the ivy twined over the courtroom railings and shook her head at the speed and effort she knew it'd taken to transform the Courtroom into a wedding bower. Joyce rushed up, dressed in a short cream sheath that complimented Maggie's, and thrust the huge bouquet of vari-colored camellias into her hands.

"There! I knew it! I knew the camellias would be just perfect with that dress! Now, let's get in position, here. I'm Matron of Honor, I know you didn't think to ask, but that's okay honey, I forgive you, know it was a lot to handle at one time, and I'm ready anyway, coordinated and everything! Now where's T-bone?"

"Joyce, I really—"

Billy's former teammates and classmates surrounded him.

"Damn, Lightnin'! Sure is good to see you, nobody ever thought to see you again!"

"Yeah, but you had a real nice funeral!"

"Well, that's real comfortin', guys, glad to hear it." Billy grinned and shook hands with the mob. The boys from Jake's class rushed up.

"Mr. Billy, did you really stay at Clayton Chapel all night? Till morning?"

"Billy's fine, guys, and yes, I did."

"*Man!*"

The females surrounded Maggie and clamored for attention.

"Bridesmaids! She has to pick bridesmaids, and that should be—"

"'Scuse us, little girls, that's us!" Junie Bug and Leola pushed through, armed for battle.

Maggie shook her head. In usual unflappable Maggie style, she solved the problem.

"Okay! Attention! Line up behind me. Curve around the corner there, down the wall side!"

"Who?"

"All of you. Who else?"

"Maggie, that's just not gonna work! That's too many! We're out of balance with the men! And where the heck is T-bone?" Joyce turned and looked toward the back.

"Right here!" T-bone rushed in, clean-shaven and immaculately dressed in a light brown suit, his hair impeccably combed.

"Holy shit!" Jake whispered in her ear. "I've never seen him like that! Man, that'll take some getting used to!"

"Well, get down here! Now, we've got too many bridesmaids here, this won't—"

"Sure it will, Joyce." Billy knew how to defuse tense and volatile situations. He figured cutting any bridesmaids would make for a pretty volatile situation. "Okay, football team! Guys, Senior class, Rockland High! Guys, Jake's class! Over behind T-bone, com'on, let's go! Might not be exact, but it's close enough."

"Okay! Are we ready, people?" Eddie Thompson tried to restore some order.

"Now would be good, Chunk. Before the ladies start rioting."

"Then let's do this! Dearly beloved, we are gathered here…"

The crowd gathered in close.

"…and by the power vested in me, I now pronounce you husband and wife. You may kiss the bride!"

The room exploded into applause and whistles. Chunk shouted over the roar, "Ladies and Gentlemen—Billy and Maggie Brayton!"

Chapter Fifteen

Maggie and Billy finally separated and the crowd surged forward. Jake's arms circled his mother from behind, claiming first hug.

"Love you, Mom."

"Love you, too, baby," Maggie managed, squeezing one of the arms circling her waist.

"Mom? You cryin'?"

"Maybe."

And then the crowd was on them, with laughter and hugs and tears.

Joyce wiped her eyes and tried to hug them both at the same time. "I swear, Maggie Mae, y'all are making me ruin my make-up. I'll have raccoon eyes."

"Well, you're not the only one. And *don't* call me Maggie Mae."

T-bone shouted for attention. "Okay, people! Field by the lake! Barbecue! Let the guests of honor out first, don't want 'em caught in traffic, make 'em late for their own party. More room to hug out there anyway!" He maneuvered Billy and Maggie in front of him and out of the room.

"C'mon, let's go. Ain't got but a few minutes to clear out before the crowd hits."

"Barbecue?" Maggie asked. "For this crowd? Y'all pulled all that together since last night?"

"Nobody ever gives me enough credit, I swear. Unloved, unappreciated, that's me."

Maggie kissed his cheek.

"You're not either. Not unloved, not unappreciated."

"Don't go giving all our secrets away to your new husband, girl, you ain't been married ten minutes yet."

With a wave of his hand, he jumped into the driver's seat of the pick-up he was currently driving and tore out of the parking lot in front of them.

"You okay?" Billy pulled out after him.

"Never been this good in my life. Why?"

"You do sort of have raccoon eyes."

"Oh, hell, I was afraid of that!" Maggie flipped the visor down for the mirror and reached for her purse.

"Don't worry about it, men wore mascara, I'd have 'em, too. But don't tell anybody."

"It'll be our deep, dark secret. One of 'em, anyway."

"And do you, who told me years ago you wanted to get married in Vegas 'cause you didn't want to fool with all that wedding crap, realize you had forty or fifty bridesmaids and groomsmen?"

Maggie laughed. "I did, didn't I? Well, they were attendants of the sweetest kind. Completely unplanned. Oh my God! Would you *look* at *that*!" They pulled into the field by the lake, pretty much the town's common for crowd events.

Danny Gordon's big homemade barbecue grill, called into service for almost every local church and school fundraiser, stood to the side, steam still rising. Two tables draped in white tablecloths stood over to the right. One was loaded with big bowls of barbecue side dishes and picnic paper-ware, the other full of trays loaded with fruits and cheeses and cookies. A huge white wedding cake held the place of honor in the center of the table. Big vases of camellias and tea olive peeped between the bowls and platters. Janet Weldon waved and Danny Gordon stepped out from the grill.

"Maggie! Billy! We're sorry we missed the wedding, but somebody better have a video waiting for me! Somebody had to stay, make sure the food didn't get hijacked by the local wildlife."

"Janet, I don't know *how* y'all did all this! The courtroom, the flowers, the ferns, all *this*! Since last night! A real wedding cake?"

"Now, Maggie, don't be expecting me to tell you all my professional secrets."

"And *you*!" Maggie turned to T-bone. "I thought your eyes were bloodshot 'cause you'd gotten the boys together for a bachelor party without Billy! You and Danny were up all night, smoke goin' all in your eyes, weren't you?"

"Well, hell, biggest thing to hit this town in none of us remember when, whatcha expect?"

"Now, listen, this is too much! Janet, this is a *huge* catering job, and I know that meat came from your stock, T-bone! You *have* to let us pay you back for—"

"Maggie. Don't ruin it, girl."

"Don't, Maggie," Billy said. He circled her waist with his arm and pulling her closer. "Don't even. This is the town's wedding present."

"Damn straight, don't even. And looka' here, just in time, the line's coming!"

Jake headed the line in Maggie's car, Aunt Lulu in the front seat. Her chocolate face split into a blinding white smile, all teeth still her own.

"Com'on, Billy, let's go help her out of the car. I'd like to get to her for a minute before the crowd moves in."

Aunt Lulu beamed and stretched her arms out.

"Never thought to see it! I'm so happy, honey, so happy!" She released Maggie and turned to Billy. "You weren't near good enough for her back then, boy, but I always figured you would be one day. Jake tells me you are, don't you be disappointin' me, you hear?"

"I won't."

The crowd parked and headed toward them and the food tables. Coats and ties lined the backs of the folding chairs, ladies' jackets scattered among them. The crowd mixed and mingled.

"Got a big case of hero worship goin' on, you know," Maggie said in his ear. Jake's class couldn't keep their eyes off Billy, the legend who'd stayed all night at Clayton Chapel. And still held the running back record for most total yardage at Rockland High besides.

"Most of 'em practically live between our house and Joyce's house, by the way. Probably should have told you that up front, but I didn't want to scare you off."

"Take a lot more than that to scare me off. Lookin' forward to it."

"Yeah, well, say that when they decide they're having a scavenger hunt in the back woods at midnight and we have to worry about one of 'em breakin' a leg or steppin' on a snake."

A dark-haired man in a gray suit tapped Maggie's shoulder.

"Hey, Maggie. Congratulations. Haven't met your husband, but I've spoken with him a few times."

"Sheriff Raines," Billy said. He caught the voice immediately. Good law men had an ear for voices, a memory for faces.

"Yes sir. Not being a native local, I'd never heard the story, at least not in enough detail to connect your name with any of the town history. Must say, it's quite a story. Fairy tale ending."

"Yes sir."

The two men measured each other.

"If you want to change your start date for a few days later, that'd be all right with me, all things considered."

"Thank you, sir, but I said I'd be there Monday morning. I'll be there."

The Sheriff nodded. "Maggie, what about you? You back to business Monday, too?"

"Of course. Have to feed my boys."

"And they 'preciate it. Your wife really looks after my deputies, gon' make 'em all fat yet with those free desserts."

"They could get their heads blown off every time they walk up to a car, Clint. Least I can do. Besides, I guess I'm a little more connected to the force now than I ever thought I'd be."

"Yeah, seems like. Well, Monday then."

"Monday."

Billy looked after him as he walked away.

"Hmmm," Maggie lowered her voice and moved close to his ear. "So whatcha think?"

"Whatcha mean?" Billy matched her low tones.

"I mean, what do you think of him? Considering I'm pretty sure your credentials beat his by a country mile and back. Which I'm also sure he knows. So since he hired you anyway, he's either very good himself or very stupid."

"Too soon to tell. What's local scuttlebutt? He clean?"

"As far as I know. Or at least clean enough for it not to be common knowledge if he isn't. Which is quite a change, all things considered. But I'm sure you intend to find out."

"I sure as hell do." Billy looked down at her face. "Hey, not so serious, please, this is a party. Who's that, by the way?" He pointed to a lady several groups over, blonde by way of the bottle. "Looks familiar, but I can't—"

Maggie laughed. "Shame on you, Billy Brayton. I'd think you'd remember somebody you got *that* up close and personal with!"

"Excuse you?"

"That's Angie Malone. Davis. James. Rowe. That might be all her last names, all I can remember right now, anyway."

"Shit."

"Be nice to her, 'spect you gon' see her a good bit. She's my waitress."

"You're kiddin', right?"

"'Course not. What better employee can you have than somebody already knows you can kick her ass?"

"Mmmm. Got a point there, I guess."

"Oh, look! Here come some of your new boys."

Two cars and an SUV pulled into the field, all painted in gray and gold and blazing the logos of the Rockland County Sheriff's Department.

"I'm sure T-bone sent out the word for the deputies to stop by and eat when they get a chance. We try to look after 'em. Hard, dangerous job. Which I said even before I knew it was yours. And T-bone's the official wrecker service for the County, even if he didn't like 'em, which he mostly does, he'd have to play politics."

"Have to find out which ones he mostly doesn't."

"I'm sure that won't take you long on your own. And I'd be pretty sure they'll be the same ones you don't."

"'Spect so. All of 'em headed for you."

"What can I say? I butter their bread. Literally. Hey, boys! Glad y'all could stop."

All three of the uniformed deputies hugged Maggie and introduced themselves to Billy. "Lieutenant" and "sir" figured heavily in the conversation.

"Y'all want to loosen up a little bit before you break?" Billy asked.

"Sorry, sir. We're looking forward to working with you."

"'Preciate that. See y'all Monday. Better go get up to the tables before everything's gone. Maggie, who's that waving for you over near the lake?" He steered her away from the deputies.

"Like you don't know that's Joyce?"

"The guys are nervous, I'm an unknown. Let 'em enjoy their food. Taylor's one of the one's T-bone doesn't like, isn't he?"

"Damn, you *are* good! How'd you get that so quick?"

"Ass-kisser. They usually cover their own ass pretty good, don't much care about anybody else's. Other two are just young. Are they all?"

"Most of 'em, yeah. Sheriff fired a lot of 'em pretty quick. After he made 'em clean up the jail, which I hear was pretty filthy. Sorry, I don't know that for a fact from personal observation. Either the firin' or the filthy."

"Both, I'd be pretty sure. Well, that bodes well for him, I think. Is Taylor his hire, or do you know?"

"Yep, you really were born to be a cop. Even on your wedding day, that brain's just turning, isn't it?"

Billy laughed. "Sorry. Forget it."

"I don't mind."

"Too close to the crowd for this conversation, anyway."

Joyce waved them down and pointed to some chairs.

"Maggie Mae, don't you dare sit on that grass in that dress! Never get the grass stains out! And I don't believe you've been walking around barefoot!"

Maggie'd shed her shoes long since. "Well, if anybody'd thought to tell me about the barbecue, I could've thrown some sandals in the car. I wore my best heels to get married in, I'm not about to ruin 'em in this pasture."

"But ruining your feet, that's okay."

"It's not like there are ever *cows* in here, Joyce, it's not a big deal." Maggie glanced down at her hand and smiled.

Joyce caught her glance. "I always loved those rings. And it's really good to see 'em together, finally. That engagement ring looked so lonely by itself. Always amazed me you picked out something so—well, so Maggie, you know. Most men can't do that, 'specially young as you were."

Maggie laughed. "Yeah, and one of the first things he wanted to do was buy new ones. 'Cause bigger's better."

"Well, that's a man for you, for sure. Looks like we're winding down. I better see about getting those plants back to everybody."

"Don't worry 'bout it, Joyce." Eddie a/k/a Chunk waved his hand casually. "Tell 'em to come get 'em tomorrow between ten and twelve. I'll go over and stick around, let 'em in."

"You will? Eddie, you're wonderful."

"Spread the word. Next year's election year."

"And you sure don't want to have to actually get a real job again, I know."

The crowd was breaking up.

"Why don't you two go ahead and take off?" T-bone suggested.

"With this mess to clean up?"

"Girl, if you even *think* about throwing a paper plate away, I'll personally throw you in that lake!" Joyce exclaimed.

"No, you wouldn't, it'd ruin my dress. Where's Jake? I need to—oh, never mind. There they are!" She waved Jake and Ben over.

"And where've you been hiding? Avoidin' your mother?"

"Well, she's been in hot demand today." Jake leaned down and kissed her cheek. "Y'all 'bout to cut out? Okay, I'll see you Monday afternoon after school, how's that?"

"Excuse you? You're never planning to come home again? We'll see you tomorrow after you get up, how's that?"

"Now, Maggie Mae, c'mon! You just got married. Let Jake and Ben have a weekend out. Or if you've just got to have a teenage boy runnin' around the house, I'll send you Ben and keep Jake, that work for you?"

"Joyce, you've been trying to swap kids since they could walk. No deal. I'll take Ben too, but you can't have Jake. In fact, send Ben over with Jake tomorrow if you want. It's all right."

"Mom, com'on, y'all should have a few days—"

"Well, all right, but you'll have to take what you get if you don't come with us. Can't be complainin' you don't like it if you don't come lookin'." Billy said.

"Sir?"

"Thought we'd see about replacing your car tomorrow."

"Tomorrow?"

"Yeah."

"But there hasn't been time to get with the insurance company or anything. Don't we need to do that first?"

"It'll be fine, buddy, don't worry about it."

"Mom?"

Maggie threw up her hands. "Oh, I was way overruled on that one. No, we're goin' car shopping tomorrow."

"Well, you know what?" T-bone said. "Before y'all go into Macon, stop by my place, why don't you? Might save you a trip."

"I thought you'd sold off all the cars you were fixin' up right now, T-bone, starting a new crop?" T-bone's family lived and breathed cars. The junkyard provided a ready source of treasures just waiting to be reconditioned.

"Well, yeah. But if Jake don't want the one I'm thinking about, I'll be real surprised."

Chapter Sixteen

Several members of the Rockland County Sheriff's Department sat in the back of the Huddle House off 96 and I-16. They preferred the Justice Café, but it wasn't open on Saturdays anyway, even if the owner hadn't just gotten married.

"Don't know 'bout y'all, but *I* ain't takin' no shit off that new hotshot. Don't know why we had to go out of county, anyway, should have just moved one of us into that job." Sgt. Davis Taylor of the elite K-9 Crime Prevention Squad, known to the county as the CPS Unit, was in rare form.

Cpl. Shane Attenborough snorted. He partnered with Taylor, not by choice.

"What? You don't think one of us should'a had a shot at that job?"

"Sure we should. After all, all our résumés list armed combat, hostage negotiations, forensics, K-9 handler, SWAT, stand-offs, shoot-outs, and all that other stuff I don't even remember, it was so damn long."

"Damn straight they do! Ain't that what I just said?"

"Taylor. You really don't get it, do you? The difference in what we've only had courses on, and what he's actually done?"

"Whatcha mean? We've all had courses in all that! And you sayin' we ain't K-9 handlers?"

Shane bit his tongue. Taylor was an asshole who shouldn't be trusted with such a valuable resource as a trained drug dog. Shane didn't say it—not a good thing for a corporal to tell the sergeant—but he came close.

"Our armed combat's been taking a gun away from a drunk redneck. None of us have ever been in front-line military like he was in the first Gulf War. We don't work forensics at all. The only hostage deal we've ever had was when George Haynie threatened to shoot his wife and she cold-cocked him before we ever got there."

"Well, I'm glad to know you don't think we're worth a shit!"

"I ain't saying anything couldn't happen to any of us at any time. And I ain't saying we won't do the best we can with what we have when it happens. What I am saying is we've had courses and simulations on most of that shit, and he's been doing the real deal. Guess who I want to go in behind, something like that happens?"

"Well, shit! I didn't know I had a fuckin' pansy for a partner!"

"Let up, Taylor." J'Nita Stevens was one of the two female officers on active patrol duty and the first female on the force. She'd been hired because a female officer was *de rigueur* when searching a female suspect. "You lettin' your mouth run without having your brain in gear. Like always. Looks like we got company." She nodded toward the window. Alec Wimberly got out of his F-250 pickup.

"Alec!" Taylor pounced as soon as Alec walked through the door. "Get over here! I need some backup, eatin' with a bunch of fuckin' idiots!"

"One of them idiots could have your back tomorrow, Taylor. I'd be more cautious how I insulted 'em." Alec walked over to the table, mostly because of the others.

"Shit! I'm the one'll be bailing them out. Like always. Too bad you were off duty yesterday. You missed meetin' the new boy."

"No, I met him. Caught Jake's accident Thursday, new Lieutenant was the one coming by when it happened, he stopped to pull him out of the car."

"Yeah, damn kid. Wouldn't have wrecked if he knew how to drive. Prob'ly goin' ninety around those curves."

"No, he wasn't. Would have been dead if he had been. And if he *didn't* know how to drive."

"Call that drivin'? Kid thinks he's something special just 'cause he's Maggie's son. Though why he thinks that gives him any pull in this town, I don't know."

"*Miss* Maggie's special to lots of folks 'round town." Alec emphasized the "Miss" in front of Maggie's name. Any Southern child raised right referred to people older than themselves as 'Miss' or 'Mr.' and their first name. Taylor'd been raised right, but it hadn't taken real well. "And Jake's a good kid, you got no reason to be bad-mouthin' him like that."

"Kid always short changes me when he's working the cash register at the restaurant."

"That's 'cause you always try and tell him you got the vegetable plate when you've been sittin' right in front of him chomping down on fried chicken and complainin' to Junie Bug one piece wasn't cooked right and the other wasn't big enough so she'll let you have two more pieces. You're a real piece of work, Taylor."

Alec worked patrol and didn't have to contend with Taylor on a regular daily basis. Thank God. Taylor was trouble.

"Well, anyway, I was just tellin' the guys here—I ain't takin' no shit off that cocky bastard."

"And that's why he was callin' him 'sir' and 'Lieutenant' every other word at the barbecue yesterday." Voncile Chapman was as big, solid, and usually as silent as a tree trunk, but when he did speak, his voice rumbled.

"Figures," said Alec.

"Hey! That's just politics. We all got to talk the talk. Don't mean we got to walk the walk."

"You couldn't walk the walk if you had to, Taylor." Alec turned and headed to the counter to place his order before he got so sick of Taylor he walked out without any food. He'd have kept driving when he saw Taylor's Tahoe in the parking lot if there'd been any decent food anywhere else handy to drive to, but Anna Grace had been pretty damn clear no odors remotely associated with bacon and eggs were coming out of her kitchen in the foreseeable future. She was having a hell of a time with morning sickness. She'd been equally clear he'd better come back with the largest chocolate milkshake the Huddle House made, or not come back at all.

"Hey, Alec! I wasn't through talkin' to you!"

"Well, that's tough, Taylor. I'm off-duty and I'm through talking to you."

"But what'd you think of him? The new boy?"

"I think the new *boy's* gonna see right through you, Taylor. Probably already has if you stopped at the barbecue and opened your mouth for more than hello and goodbye. I think he's gonna eat you for breakfast, Taylor. And that it's about damn time somebody did. That's what I think."

Alec marched on up to the window to place his order. Taylor stared after him.

"Now, what damn burr got up his ass?"

* * *

While Taylor talked the talk like he could walk the walk, Billy, Maggie, and Jake headed up the driveway to check out T-bone's must-see special vehicle. Billy cleared the gate and headed up 80 to the four-way.

"You *sure* we can't get that driveway worked on?"

"You drove it just fine, even first time up yesterday! What's your problem?"

"I grew up on those types of roads, yeah, but damn, Maggie! You just like having an obstacle course? One wrong move, you'd break an axle or tear out an oil pan. And a good rainstorm's gonna shift the path some every time anyway, you know that!"

"Wuss. By the way, Taylor's not his hire."

"Huh?"

"Yesterday. You asked me if Taylor was Clint Raines's hire. No, he's not. He's Davis Brown's grandson. Need I say more?"

"I see." Billy nodded. "Just what I need. Sheriff couldn't fire him when he was weeding out and still can't, not till he really, really screws up. Probably sleeps with that badge and gun, too. Especially the gun."

"He's a royal ass," Jake said from the back seat. And in his mind, he's really royal, too."

"Ever hassle any of y'all, Jake?" Billy asked.

"No, not exactly. But it's just—like if he's the one who pulls working the games and stuff at school—it's always how much better the teams were when he was on 'em, how much tougher he was than any of us. You know."

Billy nodded. "Know the type, for sure."

"This is the first time this year I'm kinda sorry I'm not playing."

"Really? Why?"

"I'd have liked for you to see me on the field."

"I'd have liked that, too, son."

Billy turned down the road leading the junkyard. T-bone waved to them from the front of the main garages.

"Okay! Glad y'all said something yesterday, I've been saving this for Jake's graduation present and I woulda been *pissed* if you'd *bought* a damn car! Things movin' so damn fast since Jake wrecked, I just ain't got around to it yet!"

"His graduation *present?*" Maggie's eyebrows lifted. "I'm not taking a *car* for his graduation present, T-bone, have you *lost* your *mind?*"

"You'll take this one. Betcha. Follow me." T-bone passed the closed garages where he kept his private stock of automobiles on the way to reconstruction. He stopped in front of a smaller outbuilding hiding between the bigger ones."

"I've never noticed this building before," Jake said.

"Didn't intend for you to." T-bone opened the padlock. "Okay, stand back while I get the doors."

T-bone pulled the doors open.

Dead silence. T-bone stood, savoring the looks of wonder. Finally Billy walked closer and stroked the satin finish of the right fender.

"I don't believe—this isn't really—"

"Believe it, buddy. 'Cause it sure as hell is."

"How did you—why did you—"

"Really, it was Daddy. That first night. The night they dropped the frame on you. Had it towed out here after they took you in. Said you'd put too damn much work in that car, wasn't nobody else gettin' their hands on it. Said we'd keep it safe for you till things worked out. Daddy and Mama loved you, Billy, don't know if you ever knew that, you never seemed to think anybody did. Daddy knew it was a frame from minute one. Actually went out there, that same night, tried to talk some sense into Jim Ellis. Didn't work, of course."

Maggie and Billy exchanged quick glances. Bad move on Jonesy's part. Of course they'd have to shut him up.

T-bone didn't notice. "And then, of course, when you came back—or when we thought you came back—you sure as hell weren't gonna be driving. So Daddy said Maggie should have it. And Mama, she threw a fit, said Maggie would crack like a piece of crystal if she even saw that car on the road, let alone tried to drive it. So Daddy said, well, way 'Sixty-five and 'Sixty-six Mustangs were going, that car was gonna be worth something someday. So why didn't we just finish restoring it, keep it in shape, see what happened. So we did. Thought at the time Maggie'd be ready for it one day. Then Jake came along. And Daddy was right, it being a 'Sixty-six Mustang, I figured it wasn't gonna do nothing but increase in value, 'specially if it was kept up right. And that's when I decided it'd be a real nice thing for Maggie—hell, for me, too—watching Jake drive off to college in that car, like he was taking part of both of you with him, even though he'd never had the chance to know Billy."

Maggie's fingers lingered on the satin red finish, the custom paint job complete with racing stripes and the silhouettes of the wild racing mustang on the doors, the paint job Billy'd sacrificed to buy her rings.

"Jack, have I told you often enough over the years how much I love you?"

"Now, girl, I told you yesterday not to tell your new husband all our secrets. Jake, you still haven't said anything, buddy. Whatcha think?"

"That's Billy's Mustang? For real?"

"Sure as hell—"

"No," Billy interrupted. "No, it's not. My Mustang was nothing compared to this. You finished everything. Dual exhaust. Hurst shifter. Modern sound system. Custom paint, leather upholstery. I'm scared to look at the engine. What you've done to this car, Jack—this is priceless."

"Oh, hell, Billy! Wouldn'ta been nothing but rust for years now if you hadn't pulled it out of the junkyard. 'Sides, it's been a real nice hobby. So, Jake! Am I right? This the car you want?"

"T-bone, that's—that's Billy's car, and he's back. Give it to him!"

"Whoa! Nobody's *giving* this car to anybody! Jack, this car is worth—"

"It's worth the look on y'all's faces when you saw it. Better than I thought it'd be, 'cause for damn sure I never thought you'd see it again."

"Won't take it if you don't let me pay you for it and don't give me any shit about it bein' my car anyway. 'Cause without you, it *still* would have been nothing but rust for years. And don't try and bullshit me, I know a little about classic cars, too!"

T-bone hedged. "Jake still hasn't said he wants it, what about it, Jake?"

"You've got to be *kiddin*! Who *wouldn't* want it! But it's Billy's, it's not—"

"No, son," Billy said. "It *was* mine. And my time with it's done. It's yours. But not as a graduation present, and we're not takin' it without paying for it, so you'd best be doing some fast talking to your Uncle T-bone there."

"T-bone, please! You can't dangle this in front of me and take it away! Let him pay you for it! Don't do this to me!"

"Well, *hell*! Okay, you can give me a couple of hundred for parts!"

"You have *got* to be shittin' me!"

"Okay, okay, a couple of thousand, how's that?"

"You're crazy as hell. I cruised around some of the auction sites on the web before I bought the new Mustang. Just curious, finally decided the past was past, let it go. But there was a 'Sixty-six Mustang on one of 'em, great restoration job but probably not as good as this. Listed for twenty-seven thousand, no reserve. Get a car like this at an auction, some of the pony car collectors start bidding, it could go sky high. You know it, and I know it."

"*Damn it*, Billy, no way in hell I'm taking anything near that, it was *your* freakin' car! Five thousand. Highest I'll go."

"Twenty-five."

"Seven."

"Twenty-three."

"Nine."

"Twenty."

"Twelve."

"Eighteen. Lowest I'll go. And that's still robbery."

"Fifteen. Highest I'll go. I mean it, now. This discussion's over."

Jake went down on bended knee, hands laced in supplication.

"Com'on Billy, give! He's serious, I can tell, he's not going any higher. I'll adopt you, I'll change my name, I'll be the son you never had—"

Billy laughed, reached out and shook Jake's shoulder.

"Whatcha talking about? You already *are* the son I never had!"

"So—negotiations over? Y'all satisfied with each other?"

"Well, I don't think either of us is satisfied, but I can live with it if T-bone can."

"I guess," T-bone grumbled.

"Man, I've never seen anything like that in my life! Talk about reverse horse-trading!"

"Yeah, I guess it was kinda funny. So, you sure you want it? You don't have to take it just because it was mine."

"Billy. It's a *fully restored* nineteen sixty-six Mustang. Red. Hello, earth to Billy Brayton? Does this baby have keys, please?" Jake held his palm out, wiggling his fingers.

T-bone dropped the key tab into his outstretched hand.

"It ain't got a remote now, buddy."

"Who cares? Is it okay with you guys if I go show off a little? I'll be home before dark."

"Sure it's okay, and you haven't had to be home before dark since the first couple of weeks you were driving."

"Oh, I want to be! I don't want to take it down the driveway the first time in the dark! I just have to go show Ben. And everybody else, of course!"

"Of course. Be careful."

"Oh, man! Like you need to say that! I'm parking a mile away from every other car in every parking lot." Jake got in. His eyes closed in sheer bliss when the engine growled to life.

"Now, watch the gears, Jake! It's restored like the original—these babies were three-speeds, real long gears, got it?"

"Got it!" Jake pushed in the clutch and worked his way through the gears to get their feel before engaging first. "See you guys! Oh, and just so all of you know—this is the greatest thing that's ever happened to me. Except the three of you!"

They watched him drive off, taking a part of all three of them with him.

"Billy?"

"Hmm?"

"Call Shelton Brothers Monday. Get the driveway fixed."

Chapter Seventeen

With Jake off making his rounds in his new-old classic, Maggie and Billy drove to Mt. Olive. Billy wanted to say hello to his mother.

"I probably need to tell you this before we get there. Your father's buried out there now, too."

"Beside my *mother*? And who the hell bothered to bury the bastard?"

"I did. Billy, somebody had to."

"Should have let the county handle it, Maggie. I would have. Is he right by my mother?" He pulled the brake.

"That'd be kind of hard, since she only has two sides and your grandmother's on one and you're on the other," Maggie said. "And that's a lie, you wouldn't have let the county bury him. You'd have done it for your mother. You didn't ask when he died or of what."

"Don't care when." Billy opened his door. "I can guess of what. And you're right, of course, I'd of buried the bastard. Didn't mean to shout at you. Sorry."

"That's okay. First place you ever shouted at me was in this cemetery."

"Yeah, still sorry about that, too."

"Don't be. That memory's one of my prized possessions."

Billy laughed and held out his hand. She took it and they walked over to his family's markers.

"Well, good. Beneath her feet. That's fittin'."

"I thought you'd have liked it. But that's not why I did it. Your mother—Billy, don't you think she'd have wanted him close? And that was about the closest left."

He sighed. "Yeah, hell, I guess she would have. And look at that. Not many men can say they've stood at their own grave." He gazed down at the black marble marker bearing his name. The vase built into the base of the stone was filled with a big arrangement of fall leaves in the boldest of fall colors, accented with fat brown cattails. The base of his mother and grandmother's graves held fall arrangements, too, more feminine in style. His father's grave was clean but flowerless.

"Nice headstone. You made Big John pay through the nose on that, didn't you? Before you got to college and told him to go to hell."

"Jake must have told you. Sometimes it amazes me he knows so much about all of that. I've never actually talked about any of it myself."

Billy squeezed her hand. "Thank you. For keeping up Mama and Grandma. I'm glad you didn't feel compelled to keep flowers on his, though."

"Are you kiddin'? I actually tried to once or twice and I swear to God I heard you yellin' at me, asking what the hell I thought I was doing. Though I suppose I'm predisposed to hearing you yell at me here."

"Christ, Maggie. I should have come back. Just once. To check and make sure you were all right, that you were happy. You'd never have even known I'd been here, if you had been."

"Kiddin' yourself on that one, son. You couldn't possibly appear in Turkey Creek without somebody knowing."

"Trust me, darlin'. If I hadn't wanted anybody to know I was here, they wouldn't have."

"That good, are you?"

"Yeah, I am. But I didn't, and now every time I turn around, something else is twisting the knife—what you've been doing all these years. All by yourself. Keeping my graves for me. Running the businesses. Looking out for T-bone. Building our house. Raisin'—that's funny, you know. I was about to say, raisin' my child. When I saw him for the first time two days ago, got no claim to him at all. But Jake—there's so much of you in him, Maggie. Almost from the first minute I met him—after he decided he didn't have to kill me, that is—I felt like I'd known him all his life. Like I'd watched him grow up. That any child we'd had would have been just like him."

Maggie rested her head on his shoulder. "He's my life's work. Except I've always seen you in him, used you as the measuring tape. Every crisis, every milestone. How would Billy handle this? What would he think I should do? Well, I guess that goes for everything, not just Jake. But as far as raisin' him—that was easy. I just wanted him to believe in himself, not because he had to, to survive, like you had to, just because he was so special. Like you. Except I wanted him to know it. You never did. And that's funny, too, because he doesn't. Think he's anything special, I mean. Which I guess is part of what actually *makes* both of you special."

"You know that body's got to be exhumed, don't you?"

"Yeah. Think y'all can find out who it is? After all this time?"

"Time's not the problem. Depends on how many records he left behind, whether he was ever reported as missing, whether he was a good guy or a bad guy, whether he was ever on anybody's radar. And why."

"Got any theories on that?"

"Maybe. We'll see. Com'on, you ready to go?"

"If you are." They started walking back. "You know, after I got Jake—I actually started going to my mother's grave. I keep flowers on hers, too."

"Really? What made the difference?"

"Jake. It's just—after I got him, I started thinking. That I could never just *choose* to leave him alone in the world. Especially not as a small child, not knowing he'd be raised by a man like John Kincaid. And that led to—well, she's a part of me, too. And it's nice to think that part's enough like me—or I'm enough like her—that she wouldn't either."

"I see. So you think maybe—it wasn't suicide?"

"I hope. I hope she didn't die by choice."

"Princess, by definition, suicide is by choice. If it wasn't suicide, there's only one other explanation."

"Yeah. Pretty twisted, hoping your mother was murdered, huh?"

"Not when you only have the two alternatives. Interesting thought. You caught that bit about Jonesy back at T-bone's, too, I know."

"He went to Jim Ellis that night. Shouldn't have done that. Put him on their radar, let 'em know he might be a threat."

"Big-time. Jonesy was an independent cuss. He'd never have believed they could make him do something he didn't want to, never have believed he'd give in. Because he'd never believe they could make a threat big enough to make him give in. I hate that, Maggie. I hate that so bad for him. It would have been—well, hard to describe exactly what it would have been."

"Emasculating is the word you're looking for. Yeah, I get that."

"And a threat big enough to make him live with it for the rest of his life—"

"Would have to involve a few more graves. Probably of the unmarked variety. Because he had to look me in the face almost every day. For years, Billy. Knowing you were alive. I don't know how he did it."

"He told me you were happy, you know. The last time I called and got him, before the home number was changed to unlisted. I usually hung up when he answered but that time—it was a couple of months after the wedding announcement and I tried to talk to him, make sure you were okay. He told me you were happy. Said if I'd ever thought about anybody else in my life except myself, to do it now and leave all of you alone."

"Funny, what age does to a person. Ten years ago, I'd have been in such a rage to hear that. And now—"

"Now, I just hate thinkin' what that must have done to him. 'Cause I know—I mean, *I know*—he was just trying to keep Jack safe. And me. Maybe even you."

"Yeah."

Chapter Eighteen

Jake and Ben cruised the Dublin side of Highway 80 on their way to Deanna Durham's. Deanna's was holding a romantic comedy movie marathon with the Rockland Academy Senior girls. Jake drove a responsible 60 miles per hour. Which was driving Ben crazy.

"Jake, com'on! It's an *eight* cylinder! Let it go!"

"Ben, shut up! I am *not* going to hotrod this car! Not today, not ever! Get over it!"

"Yeah, but *sixty* miles an hour—"

"You know damn well you never know when the guys are goin' to be patrolling out here, not to mention the actual state patrol, and I am *not* going to go home havin' to tell Mom and Billy I got a damn speeding ticket the first day I have this car."

"Most of the guys like you, they'd never give you a ticket unless you were really, really flyin'."

"Well, maybe, but it's not right to put 'em in the position where they ought to and don't. 'Specially now. I mean, Billy's on the force and all."

"Bet *Billy* never drove this thing sixty miles an hour."

"When Billy had it, it was a junk car he'd pulled out of the graveyard he was fixin' up with his own money. It wasn't a fully-restored classic like it is now worth I don't know how much at a classic car auction. And they just handed it over to me. So *can* it already!" Jake threw a glance up at the rearview mirror and swore loudly. "*Shit!* I don't fuckin' *believe* this! Ben, did you have to talk about it, I swear you jinxed me!"

"What?" A wailing siren gave the standard 'pull it over' signal behind them. "Oh, hell. It's one of the CPS guys, not regular patrol. Who is it?"

"Who the hell you think? Nobody but Taylor'd stop anybody doing sixty."

* * *

Taylor almost salivated as the Mustang pulled over on the shoulder. Stranger in town, had to be, he'd never seen that Mustang. Fresh meat in strange territory. Nothing better for a certain type of deputy, the kind who gave law enforcement a bad name. Taylor's door slammed. The Mustang's driver's window was coming down.

"Keep your hands where I can see 'em!"

"Taylor, it's me. Keep my hands where you can see 'em? For *real?*"

"Damn, boy! Thought you were trying to run there. Goin' kinda fast, weren't you? And where in the *hell* did you get this?" He pointed at the car.

"I was doing sixty, Taylor. All the time. I don't see how you think I was trying to run."

"Speed limit's fifty-five, boy. And you didn't tell me where you got this."

"Shit, Taylor! You don't think he stole it, do you?" Ben asked in exasperation.

Well, this was going from bad to worse. Ben was a Clayton, one of the oldest families in the county, not to mention an Attenborough on his mother's side. Both his grandfathers were every bit the social and financial equal of Taylor's. Small town society was a funny thing. Taylor couldn't harass Ben and get away with it and Taylor knew it. Worse, so did Ben. But Jake Rubin? Oh, just hell.

Technically and legally, Jake's grandfather was Big John Kincaid. Under ordinary circumstances in normal families, Jake would be Crown Prince of the county. Big John and Jake had never even spoken to each other, though, so that didn't give him much protection. On the other hand, Maggie pulled a lot of weight in town in her own right. All in all, this wasn't going at all the way Taylor'd planned.

He glared at Ben. "Watch it, boy. Nobody pulled your string."

Jake took over before Ben's mouth caused unnecessary problems. "I got it today. T-bone's been working on it a long time. It was my dad's."

Shit! Taylor'd forgotten about that. Maggie Kincaid was now Maggie Brayton and Billy Brayton was his superior officer. Bad to worse.

"Well, you got no business running along at that speed. Trying to set a record for most wrecks in two days?"

"Taylor, I was doing *sixty*. Everybody does sixty."

"Except you," Ben threw out. "You're always running at least ninety."

"*I'm law enforcement, boy!* You watch your mouth!"

"You run ninety if you're just cruisin' in your own car!" Ben shot back.

"Ben. Shut up. So, Taylor, if you're giving me a ticket for this, let's get it over with."

"Naw. I see how a car like this could get away from you, Jake. But you watch it. 'Cause from now on, I'll be watching *you*."

Taylor turned on his heel and headed back to the Tahoe.

* * *

"*Fuck, fuck, fuck!*" Jake sat until Taylor pulled the Tahoe back on the road and shot past them.

"Look at that asshole! Got up to ninety in ten seconds flat! On Highway 80 and all these curves! What the hell you doin', Jake?"

"I'm going home." He turned into a side road and threw the car in reverse. "Don't feel much like celebrating right now."

"Jake! C'mon! The girls are waitin' on us! You're not in trouble for this, you know that! Miss Maggie and Billy won't believe Taylor over you! You're golden boy, all the grownups always believe you! Hell, even *my* folks wouldn't believe *Taylor* over me! Believe anybody else, probably, but not Taylor!"

"That's not it. He's gonna go back and make it sound like he was doing me a big favor, only cut me some slack 'cause of Billy. And didn't you hear him? He's gonna be ridin' my tail from now on, and he's gonna try to cause trouble for Billy somehow, I know he is. Billy don't need that crap, he just got here!"

"*Billy* ain't gonna worry one damn bit about that asshole! And man, did you just pop Taylor with Billy or *what?* Proud of you, son, didn't know you had it in you!"

"Huh?"

"Slicker'n goose shit, the way you popped that to him. You know. When you told him it was your dad's car. Did you *see* the way his expression changed?"

"I said that?"

"You don't *know* you said that?"

"No."

"You mean you didn't do it on *purpose?*"

"*Hell* no! Mom'd crawl my ass she thought I was trying to use family connections to get out of something!"

"You didn't do anything to get out of! Well, even if you didn't do it on purpose, it still worked. So if you didn't do it on purpose, why'd you do it? He's one tough dude, but you just met him."

"No, I don't think I did," Jake said slowly.

"Huh?"

"It's like—it's not like your parents got divorced or something happened to your dad and Miss Joyce got re-married. Mom's never been married. I've never had a dad. Well, I know I did, but not one I remember. Billy's like—ever since I was old enough to start piecing the story together, it's like he's always been there. In the shadows. The dad I would have had, if things had been different. Which is stupid, 'cause if they'd gotten married when they were supposed to, Mom wouldn't ever have met my mother at college and she wouldn't be my mom. But anyhow, I guess I've just always thought of him as the missing part of the family. Shadow Dad. I think I've always thought of him as Dad, even before I met him. Even when he was dead."

Ben looked at Jake thoughtfully and shook his head. "I have *definitely* been hangin' out with you too much, man. I actually *understood* that!"

"And I want to go on home and tell 'em about this."

"Jake, c'mon! An hour or two! Shake it off, man! Don't let that asshole ruin this for you. This is the only time in your *life* you'll ever be able to show everybody a new car over forty years old."

Jake looked over at his life-long best friend. "You mean it's the only time in *your* life you'll be showing off a new car over forty years old."

"Well, yeah, that, too."

Jake laughed. He backed and headed toward Deanna's house.

"Okay. But I don't want to stay too long."

* * *

"Home already?" Maggie, cubing cheese on a cutting board, looked up when Jake came through the kitchen door. I know you said before dark but this is like three *hours* before dark!"

"Yeah. I wasn't feelin' all that social. Hmmm. Nachos?"

"Thought if you were really goin' to be home early, this'd be a good football night supper. Wanna tell me about it?"

Jake smiled slightly and shook his head. "Not with a knife in your hand. And how'd you know there's something to tell?"

"I'm your mother. All mothers can do that. Something happen to the car?"

"No, the car's fine. Where's Billy?"

Heavy steel clanged. The sound of the weighted bar hitting the rack. Somebody was making use of Jake's equipment on the back porch.

"Oh."

"Said it had been a few days and he was feelin' kinda tight." Billy came in with a wet towel around his neck. Moisture sheened on his arms and legs.

Maggie handed Billy a bottle of cold water and Jake a glass of tea.

"Home already? Didn't expect you this early. Want to go for a run, show me your route?"

"Yeah. Yeah, I would, that really sounds good. But first—I want to tell y'all up front. Taylor pulled me over on Highway 80. Sort of put a kink in the afternoon."

"Taylor did what? Com'ere, sit down." Maggie pulled a barstool from under the counter bar. "How fast were you goin', buddy?"

"Sixty, Mom. *Sixty* miles an hour. Swear to God."

"You don't have to swear, buddy. You've never given me a reason not to believe you. Well, except a few things here and there you wouldn't be normal if you didn't do."

"I'm a good kid, I got no secrets from you, Mom."

"Oh, good! Then I *was* supposed to see the Trojans in your underwear drawer, I wondered about that."

"*Mom!*" Jake turned purple. He slid off the barstool and ducked his head underneath the counter.

"Maggie, stop! You're killin' him, you got no idea what you just did to that boy!" Billy tried not to laugh, which only made him choke.

"Billy, help!"

"Don't know if there's much recovery from that one, son. I'da died, Mama'd ever said that to me! Probably for real, 'cause she'da probably killed me! Which is why I kept 'em in a toolbox in the shed, if you want any suggestions there."

"Got your mind off Taylor, though, didn't I?" asked Maggie. "Now com'on out!"

Jake and his red cheeks sat back on the barstool. Billy came around and pulled out the stool on the other side of him.

"So, did he actually give you a ticket for five miles over the speed limit?" he asked.

"No, but I got the idea it might have been better if he had. It was like, *big favor you just got, kid, and I'm watching you from now on.*"

"I don't have a problem with you getting pulled over for actually doing something, you know that," Maggie said. "Well, I do, but it'd be with you, not the guy that pulled you over. But to do it for nothing—"

"I want to know why he was on Highway 80. He's CPS, he's supposed to be on the interstate."

"How you know that? You haven't even been in the office yet!"

"Sheriff sent me the organizational charts. And the rosters, personnel sketches. Photos. I know who everybody is and where they're supposed to be. Didn't really need introductions yesterday, just didn't want to make anybody nervous."

"You could recognize *all* of 'em? Anybody on the force?"

"Yeah."

"And there's how many?"

"Four CPS units, those are the K-9 drug interdiction units, they're supposed to concentrate on the interstate, where the drugs run. Eight patrol, they're supposed to concentrate on the state and county roads. Eight detention officers, they stay in the jail, obviously. They've got a captain and lieutenant. Another captain runs the patrol unit, the major runs CPS. That would be Miss Luellen's son, I'm assuming, can't be that many Lamar Simpsons around. Eight dispatchers. Three office staff. One other investigator, the Sheriff, the Chief—he's pretty much internal affairs—and now me. That's thirty-nine total."

"And you'll recognize all of 'em when you walk in?"

"Yeah."

Maggie and Jake looked at each other.

"What? It's what I do. What'd Taylor say, Jake? 'Cause the type radar we've got is just ordinary radar. You can't prove the radar read unless it's at least fifteen miles over the limit. Five's not worth bothering with."

"I think he pulled me over mainly because of the Mustang. I mean, a classic car running 80? Seemed surprised when he saw who was in it. And then he did a big song and dance about how fast I was goin' and how he thought I was trying to run. And I *wasn't*, I pulled over as soon as he flashed me."

Jake's cellphone went off. A shrill, annoying series of beeps. Ben's ring tone.

"Crap! Can he ever give it a rest! He knows I just got home!"

"Might as well get it over with, Jake. You know he'll be ringing mine if you don't answer."

"He will?" Billy asked.

"Impatience, thy name is Clayton. He can't get Jake, he'll call me to see why not. Joyce calls Jake if I don't answer mine. Don't give 'em your cell number. They'll add you right on in."

Jake swiped across his phone face.

"Ben, let up! I just got home!"

"You're not in trouble, are you? 'Cause you know I got your back!"

"Oh, yeah, you're a *great* character witness, Ben! Like you wouldn't back me up no matter what!"

"Jake. You mind puttin' Ben on speaker for a minute?"

Jake raised his eyebrow, but he put Ben on speaker. "Ben. I need to know how Taylor acted. I'm guessin' like a really big asshole, but I don't think Jake's gonna tell me how big 'cause he don't wanna sound like he's whinin'."

"Jake was only doing *sixty*, Billy! Swear to God!"

"Don't got any doubt about that at all, Ben. It's how *Taylor* was acting I want to know about. 'Cause if he pulled y'all over for no reason and acted like an ass, he'll do it to anybody. And if that's so, I want to know about it. We serve and protect, we don't harass."

"Oh, man, jeez! You feel like he's throwing off slime when he talks to you, you know? He didn't know it was us when he started up, actually hollered for us to keep our hands where he could see 'em, like a bad cop show! And when he did know it was us, he just kept on harping, where'd you get it, where you'd get it, like we'd *stolen* it or something! Well, that and how fast Jake was goin' and he *wasn't*—it's just he'd started something and he was damned if he was gonna back down, you know?"

"Oh, yeah."

"But you'da been proud of Jake, Billy, you and Miss Maggie both! He punched Taylor's lights big-time! When Taylor kept asking where he got the car, Jake told him it was his dad's! You should have seen Taylor's face when he registered who that was!"

"Thanks, Ben. Might not be a bad idea for the two of you to stick together next couple of weeks when you're out."

"Oh, we pretty much do that anyway. See y'all later!"

Maggie and Billy looked at Jake.

"It wasn't what y'all are thinking," Jake said. "I didn't tell him it was my dad's car to try and get away with something or anything. I didn't even *know* I'd said it till Ben told me. He thought I did it just to remind Taylor you outranked him. But I didn't. It's just—ever since I was old enough to hear the stories, I always knew you were supposed to be here. So you were always *here*, you know, just *not* here. Shadow Dad. And now you're here for real. Not a shadow anymore. Just Dad. Like you were always supposed to be."

Billy reached over and put his hand on Jake's shoulder. "I'm honored."

Maggie smiled. "My cup runneth over."

Chapter Nineteen

Over the weekend, the cell towers and phone lines of Turkey Creek buzzed. They usually did, even in such small rural strongholds as Turkey Creek.

"There's been a new development. We've put some support out in the field, little back-up for you."

"Back-up? For us? *Now*? What the hell good is that going to do us? The time it'll take to get anybody up to speed ain't even worth it!"

"You don't have to get anybody up to speed. You won't even know who it is. Nobody will know who the two of you are either. That's the beauty of it. Working an entirely different angle, going places the two of you can't go. We don't even want you to talk to the new operative by phone. No chance of recognizing a voice."

Another voice took over. The two receiving this unwelcome news weren't together for this conference call, but they'd been partners in red-neck espionage long enough to know when the other was about to blow. And they didn't need to be looking at each other to know it, either.

"We aren't exactly novices, just in case you've forgotten to check our personnel files and résumés lately. We're not giving another operative away, and it's damned insulting that you think that's even a remote possibility. And in case you didn't know it, we've got enough problems with new guys here in town already. Sheriff's Department has a new investigator with a personal vendetta we're going to have to side-step and now you come in here and tell us you've got somebody else in play and we can't even *talk* to him? How the hell are we supposed to coordinate with *that*?"

"Already heard about the new guy in the Sheriff's Department. You aren't going to tell me the two of you can't handle some little hick cop that passes for an investigator, are you?

And don't worry. You don't need to coordinate. You won't overlap. If you do, we'll know. We'll handle it."

"Oh, so you'll tell us what we need to know when we need to know it, huh? Well, you'll forgive me if I'm not exactly overwhelmed with the sufficiency of that response!"

"See what you did?" the original speaker took back the conversation. "Now Poison Ivy's using all them big words!"

"Kiss my butt, Cyanide!"

"Will you two can it and stop calling each other those ridiculous names?"

"Just our way of injecting some humor. God knows we always need some after a conference call with you. And we weren't the geniuses that blessed this operation with a code name like Country Justice, either, so I'd be more careful about insulting *our* code name choices! What angle is the new guy working you don't think we can handle?"

"Something the two of you can't do."

"Well, not to imply that home operations hasn't thought this through, but just suppose there's a reason we actually *do* need to communicate with each other? Like maybe we'd all like not to *shoot* each other by accident?"

"We've thought of that. New operative has your emails. You've all got phones, don't you? With a few extra apps the teenagers would kill for. Or didn't you notice that's what you're talking on right now?"

"And what's the new operative's email?"

"I guess you'll know when you get an email, won't you?"

"You are *shittin'* us!"

"Not at all. Operation Country Justice has now merged with Operation Country Time." The speaker shifted to a fake Southern accent any native Southerner would tell him was just *nasty*. "Y'all have fun now, you hear?" The line went dead. The long-time partners were alone again.

"Asshole!"

"Calm down. We can handle any new boy they've put on the playing field."

"Be nice to know who. Be nice to know *where*."

"We'll figure it out. Ours is not to reason why, just to *git her done*!"

"Oh, God! Will you cut the redneck comedy act? This is *me*! You've got a Master's in Criminal Justice, for God's sakes!"

"Yeah, one day I'm gonna go on tour myself. We'll make a fortune and retire."

* * *

Big John Kincaid sat behind his mahogany desk and barked orders into his phone.

"Where the hell are we going to find *that*?"

"That's your problem. Just set it up."

"How soon?"

"Yesterday."

"This is going to *seriously* piss off the whole town."

"Just do it."

Big John turned back to Davis Taylor. Damn, that boy was stupid. A useful tool, but stupid.

"You back off for a while."

"Back off? *Back off*? You tellin' me you want us to leave Brayton alone?"

"You didn't pull over Brayton. I hope to God you're not really that stupid. You pulled over the boy."

"Well, I didn't know it was him at the time. And you're not gonna tell me you're gettin' sentimental about that smartass kid, are you?"

Big John looked at Taylor. The look was enough.

"Sorry, sir."

"Keep it up, boy. I'll hand you your ass on a platter. Right now, goin' after the kid is the same as goin' after Brayton. Don't do it. I'll do it. When I'm ready. You understand me?"

"Yes sir."

"You sure now? Don't want any confusion."

"Yes sir."

"Then how 'bout you get your ass out of my study? And don't be comin' in here while you're on duty. On I-16. Ten miles east of here. Not here. Not on Highway 80, where you got no business being. Or don't you remember that?"

"Yes sir. Sorry, sir."

Taylor left. Big John shook his head at his back. Taylor hated Jake. Big John, master psychologist without a degree, understood exactly why. Jake was everything Taylor'd always pretended to be growing up, but never had been. Leader of the Pack. Now why the hell couldn't Maggie have been sensible and given him a grandson like that who actually had Kincaid blood flowing in his veins? Damn, what he could have done with a kid like that. Intelligence and personality. If he'd known how the boy'd turn out, he might have overlooked the mongrel blood. Oh, well. No use cryin' over spilt milk. It might have come to nothing in the end anyway. After all, Maggie hadn't worked out exactly the way he'd planned, either.

Neither had Brayton. Taylor'd detested Brayton on sight, for the same reason he detested Jake. Brayton'd always been a Leader of the Pack. Not for the first time, Big John wished he'd been sensible all those years ago. What a front-line lieutenant he'd have been. And probably a good breeder, too. Cross those genes with Maggie's, damn. Talk about an heir. Maybe he should have waited. Big John shrugged. More split milk he wasn't going to cry over.

* * *

"We need *what*? Now, where the hell are we gonna get that?"

"Try one of the Florida labs. Check the internet. I don't care where you find 'em, just find 'em. Get 'em here."

"Whose damn bullshit idea is this, anyway? What are we gonna *do* with 'em?"

"The Bossman's, that's who. So do you *care* what we're gonna do with 'em?"

"Nope. Not a bit."

* * *

"Country Justice's been advised of your presence, Country Time. And they're not very happy about it."

"Don't blame 'em. I'm not real happy about it, either. Those no contact orders—c'mon, what's up with that? And don't give me that shit about not wanting us to recognize each other's voices, either. We're actors. First and foremost. It's what keeps us alive. No good field agent's gonna give anybody else away. And I hope to hell it's safe to assume they're pretty good."

"They're better than that. Which is what makes them so damn hard to handle. Just like you. You can contact them if you really need to. Just don't talk to them. And I'd really appreciate it if you followed orders just this one time. A personal favor to me, maybe?"

"I don't even like you. Why would I do you any personal favors?"

"Because you're a damn good field agent?"

"I'm a damn good field agent because I don't follow stupid orders. Stupid orders could get me killed and that's not gonna happen. Not to me, not to the other agents I'm not supposed to talk to."

"Which means you're emailing 'em as soon as we hang up?"

"Hell yeah."

"And if as a group you decide you're talking—"

"Then we'll talk."

"Will you try not to for at least a month or two? We're so damn close."

"Maybe. But I guarantee you we'll know who each other is before the takedown. I'm not taking the chance of shooting one of the good guys. Pretty sure they're not gonna chance shooting me, either."

The line went dead. The man known as "Lifeline" shook his head. Damn thankless job. Damn good agents, all. Trying to keep all of them alive was going to kill him yet.

* * *

The agents of Operation Country Justice clicked open the new email showing on their special issue Agency phones at the same time.

"Hey, Country Justice. Country Time here. Don't hold it against me, I didn't make the name up."

The emails flew back and forth. "Hey? You a southern boy?"

"Good with local dialects, that's all. We were in the Bronx, you'd think I was Joe from Thorty-thord Street. Don't wanta step on any toes. Would appreciate the same consideration."

"Contacting us against orders?"

"Yeah."

"So we're agreed not take any chances on shooting each other later?"

"Hell yeah."

"Our kind of guy."

"So we're solid?"

"Proud to meet ya, Country Time. Later."

"Backatcha, Country Justice. Later."

Chapter Twenty

The Rockland County Law Enforcement Center, the LEC for short, occupied a small building adjacent to the courthouse. When Billy Lee Brayton'd made the acquaintance of a jail cell in 1985, the Sheriff's Department and the jail facilities were on the third floor of the courthouse. Billy walked into the new LEC for the first time on Monday morning as Lt. Billy Brayton, the newest member of the Rockland County Sheriff's Department.

Billy hoped Sheriff Bo Franklin was watching from wherever he now resided in the hereafter. And had indigestion.

"Mornin', ladies! I believe y'all might be expecting me?"

"Billy!" Warrant Officer Betty Jean Lewis came around her desk for a big hug. "Lord, Lord, I never thought I'd see this day! Com'on, give me another hug for your mama! If you don't have the look of Kathleen! Those dark eyes and dark hair! She'd be so proud of you, son!"

Miss Betty Jean'd been the closest thing to a best friend his mother had in the years before her early death. His mother's fierce pride and embarrassment had pushed everyone away except Miss Betty Jean. She'd pushed back.

Miss Betty Jean continued. "I slipped away for the wedding but I couldn't get to the barbecue. It's *so* good to see you and Maggie finally happy! I'm just so proud for you!"

"Thank you, Miss Betty Jean. I know you always tried to keep Mama close but I was too young and dumb to ever thank you for it. I want you to know I always knew, and I always appreciated it. Still do."

"Lord, son!" Miss Betty Jean's eyes were suspiciously bright. "Wasn't nothing. I loved your mama. Com'on, sheriff's waiting for you."

Billy followed. He nodded to the others in the office as they passed, connecting names and faces from his memory banks. Monticia Williams was the Dispatcher on duty. Aurelia Andrews, the Sheriff's secretary. Hmmm. Odd. That she hadn't taken over the introductions.

"Ladies, nice to meet you. Lookin' forward to working with all of you."

* * *

"Well, good mornin'! Have a seat. We'll get all the preliminaries outta the way." The sheriff waved Billy into the chair across from his desk. "So. You and Maggie back up with business as usual this morning, huh? Saw the café was up and running. Hope you took advantage. Nobody can fry eggs like Junie Bug."

"Maggie can."

"Yeah, well, I'm not in tight enough with the owner for her to cook my breakfast. You know, I spent most of the weekend wondering if I'd made a big mistake with you."

Billy raised an eyebrow.

"See, I kinda fudged there at the barbecue. Yeah, I knew from the git-go who you were, knew about the frame-up, why you joined the army. Knew you were supposed to be dead."

"Really? You let me walk back into this town knowing Maggie thought I was dead?"

"Well, see, I figured you were comin' back for a personal reason but I didn't think it was Maggie. Figured that was a teenage flash in the pan. Thought your reason went by the name of John Kincaid. Why else would you? Man with your résumé, you coulda gone anywhere. Atlanta, hell, New York or LA if you wanted to. So why here? Kincaid's the only reason I could think of. You wanta take him down. So do I. *Really* bad. But he's run this county for damn long he's pretty much immune. Sure, I've put a crimp in his style. But the locals, he knows way too many skeletons in too many closets for anybody to be pullin' out any of his. And Charlie Jenkins—that's my other investigator—he's a good ol' boy and he's got a great nose for marijuana fields in the middle of other fields—but Big John? Naw, way outta Charlie's league. Figured somebody like you, you'd be my best shot. That's why nobody knew your name but me before you got here. I mean *nobody*. Wanted the shock value when Big John knew you were back."

"Then you pretty much lost it the first hour. First thing Maggie did when she got coherent enough was march straight into his study and call him a daughter-fuckin' son-of-a-bitch."

"Damn, I'da paid money to see that. She went to the house? Scuttlebutt has it she ain't crossed his door since all that happened."

"And scuttlebutt would be right. So let me get this straight. You knew Maggie thought I was dead, and you knew I wasn't. And you still let me walk right back into town with no notice, to hell with what that might do to Maggie?"

"That I screwed up on. And I'm sorry. Like I said, I thought y'all were just a teenage flash in the pan, long over. I mean, surely to God you'd have been back long before otherwise. Didn't have a clue about the fake engagement-marriage thing on Maggie's end. Nobody did. So I didn't know y'all were the real deal till I saw you together. And there's more to it than that fake engagement thing anyway, has to be. Anybody seein' you together with half a brain can see no newspaper announcement would keep a man like you away from a woman like her, I don't give a damn how young y'all were. So there's another story there. What is it?"

"None of your damn business."

The Sheriff sighed. "Yeah, figured you'd say that. But anyhow, when I realized exactly what Big John'd done to the two of you, that's when I started wondering if I'd opened a whole can of worms shouldn't be opened. Because what he did to you and Maggie—hell, you don't want revenge. You want blood and guts. I would, anybody cost me twenty-five years with a woman like Maggie Kincaid."

"Brayton."

"'Scuse me?"

"Maggie Brayton. I'm a little sensitive 'bout that. Took me a lot longer than I planned on to change the name."

"Yeah. My point exactly. I wanna take him down. And I intended for you to do that for me, 'cause I *knew* you wanted to take him down. But I don't need no vigilante justice won't hold up in court, and now I'm wonderin' if you can build a watertight case with no loopholes. You know, like entrapment. Or, say, beatin' the hell out of him while he's resisting arrest."

"He's in his seventies. Wouldn't be a lot of satisfaction in that." Billy leaned forward and tapped his open personnel file with his finger. "You don't think all this means I'm capable of working a proper case, tell me now and let me trot on in to Macon. Like you said, I could go to New York, I don't think Macon'll turn up its nose. But if you're lookin' to get rid of me entirely, ain't gonna happen. That's about as far away as you're gonna get me."

"And you'll still be watchin'."

"Damn straight."

"Well. Okay, let's get you sworn in, get your truck. Force uses four wheel drive F-150's for the investigators."

"Not the same one, I hope."

"Same one?"

"You don't think I know you need a new investigator because the old one was found in his vehicle with his head blown off on a dirt road out near Clayton Chapel?"

"I could always hope you hadn't done any digging."

"And it would say what for me if I hadn't?"

"Not a lot."

"No, it wouldn't."

"So, you got any ideas on your plan of action yet?"

"First thing, I think, is to visit the DA. For an exhumation order. Like to know whose grave my wife's been changin' flowers on all these years. That's a real teenage flash in the pan for you there, huh?"

"She has?"

"She has."

"I didn't know. What happens when an outsider thinks he knows all the inside stories. Won't happen again. And I'm sorry for messin' up so bad on that. Anything else?"

"Are you insider enough to know the stories about Clayton Chapel?"

"That it's supposed to be haunted? Yeah, I know that."

"Do you know the teenagers use it as a rite of passage? The night they get their driver's license. They have to go out and see how long they can stay out there alone. If they want to hold their heads up with their friends ever again, anyway."

"Yeah. Haven't really worried 'bout that. None of 'em stay past five minutes."

"You don't really worry about that but one of your men got his head blown off two miles away?"

"Think I should worry?"

"Maybe."

"Think I dropped the ball there, huh?"

"Maybe."

"Okay. Anything else?"

"I might be asking for another exhumation order but I don't know for sure yet."

"Another one? On who?"

"I'll tell you that if I decide I need one."

"Would I be the one wearing the Sheriff's badge here, or would you?"

"Oh, you would. Here. But they wouldn't even put you on the force in New York or LA. And if they did, you'd get yourself killed. Pretty damn quick, I think. I wouldn't. You want me for the express purpose of taking Big John down. So let me do it."

Billy's southern accent disappeared. His words were precise, clipped, military.

"And should I worry about my job come next election?"

"They couldn't pay me enough to do your job. You can have it and all the county politics and paperwork and administrative crap that goes with it. And speaking of county politics, you do know Davis Taylor is a loaded gun?"

The Sheriff sighed. "Yeah. Haven't figured out how to get him out of here yet, though."

"Maybe I can help with that, too."

"You ain't been here long enough for him to piss you off that bad."

"Yes, I have. He pulled my son over on Highway 80 Saturday for doing sixty and did a big bad 'Got my eye on you' number on him while he did it."

"Well, technically, sixty is over the speed limit."

"Get real."

"Son, huh? Now, that happened kinda fast, didn't it?"

"He's Maggie's son, that makes him mine. Like he was always supposed to be. I just didn't know it."

Billy waited for the Sheriff to mention that Taylor had no business on Highway 80 in the first place but he didn't. Billy found the omission very interesting.

"Well, com'on. Let's get you saddled up."

The Sheriff walked over to the door. Billy followed, making a slight detour over to Dispatch. He didn't bother to confirm his memory banks with her name plate.

"Mornin', Monticia. Could you do me a favor and pull the log for Saturday afternoon? See what you got for any calls on the Dublin side of Highway 80 between say, three and four?"

"Sure, Lieutenant." She scanned the computer screen. "Nothing. Was there supposed to be?"

"No, I really wasn't expecting anything. Thanks."

Chapter Twenty-One

Maggie resumed her usual routine while Billy immersed himself in a small-town Sheriff's Department. She pulled into the parking lot of Clean Class to open the store side of her combination laundry and ladies' store business at 2:30 p.m. A group of older ladies always met for a coffee klatch at 3:00 p.m. in the store side. A few years before, Maggie'd introduced them to espressos and lattes, thereby extending their regular bedtime by several hours. A few husbands appreciated that. A few could have done without it.

She hummed, moving around the store, switching on lights and setting up the espresso and regular coffee pots. She looked up from the side sink at the sound of Joyce's voice.

"Hey, Maggie Mae! Only woman I know'd be working today, couldn't y'all have taken a couple more days off, for Heaven's sake?"

"Oh, hey! I didn't hear you, need a new battery in the door chimes. Damn thing never gives me any warning it's about to go out. Glad you came by. Hand me the espresso beans."

"I've yet to walk through that door without you puttin' me to work. Gonna stop comin'."

Maggie laughed. "Yeah, handing me a canister is gonna put you in bed for a week, I know."

"Anyway, this is not a social call, this is serious business."

"Do tell. What serious business would it be?"

"We're gonna pull out some of your catalogs before the little ol' ladies get here and order you some serious lingerie."

"Say what?"

"Maggie. You just got married. You need some new sexy, transparent stuff. Don't need to be in T-shirts with a hunk like Billy in your bed!"

"This may shock you, but with a hunk like Billy in my bed, I'm not in a T-shirt. Or anything, actually. Not for very long."

"It's the principle of the thing, girl! Keeps the mystery going. Hides the imperfections till he's panting so hard he won't notice 'em!"

"Joyce, he doesn't *care* about any imperfections. Don't think he sees 'em. And what imperfections would you be referring to, anyway? I don't think I'm too bad for forty-three!"

"No, damn it, you're not. 'Course you've never had a baby, don't have to worry about stretch marks—"

She came to a dead stop at the look on Maggie's face. "Oh God, Maggie, I'm sorry! I forgot."

"Don't worry about it, it's okay."

"No, it's not okay, and you've never gotten over it. Did you—did you tell Billy?"

"No, I did *not*, and I don't ever intend to! Why would I at this late date?"

"Maybe because it was his baby, too?"

"He didn't even know about it. I didn't know till he'd already been railroaded. No, I'm not tellin' him, not goin' there. He's already got enough reasons to hate Big John without knowin' he caused me to miscarry, too."

"Now, you don't know that! First babies miscarry real often, you might have lost it anyway."

"Well, you'll forgive me if I think standing there holding his dead father's hand had something to do with it! Because *I* was dead inside, Joyce. *Nothing* could have kept living inside me! The last bit of Billy, just bleedin' out of me that night!" Maggie gave a shaky laugh. "Sorry. Overdramatic much?"

"And you always call it 'he.'"

"Had to be, Jake's his replacement. If he'd of been a girl, Jake would be, too!"

Joyce shook her head. "Damn, girl, you got some convoluted reasoning on that. You—" Joyce broke off at the look on Maggie's face.

"Well, hey! I have *got* to get a new battery in that door chime!"

Joyce turned. Billy stood inside the door.

"Anything else, Maggie? Anything else you didn't tell me? 'Cause I'd really appreciate it if you'd go ahead and do it now, while I'm still bleedin'."

"Billy, I'm sorry. I didn't see any reason to tell you about the baby after all this time."

"The baby's an abstract, Maggie. It's *you*, damn it! Knowing you stood there, holding a dead man's hand, losing a baby nobody even knew you were carrying! *Burying* me the next day! Alone! All by yourself! It's *you*!"

"And that would be my cue to leave," Joyce said softly. They didn't notice.

"I'm sorry," Maggie repeated.

"*Damn it,* woman, will you *stop* saying that? Like you think it was something you did on purpose?" He stalked down the aisle of the store toward her and pulled her close. "Christ, Maggie, what did I say Saturday in the cemetery? Every time I turn around, I find another hell you were going through and I didn't even bother to come back one damn time to check! Did anybody but Joyce even know you were pregnant?"

Maggie rested her head in the hollow of his shoulder, her arms around his waist. "No. And she didn't know I'd miscarried until a couple of weeks later. After word got out you were dead, Joyce's mother called Big John and begged him to let me come to them or at least let Joyce come to me, but he wouldn't. So it was a while till I could tell her what happened."

"Were you *completely* by yourself?"

"Aunt Lulu. She held me all that night, on one of the sofas in the living room. I cried and cried, and she thought I was crying so much I was making myself sick, and that was part of it, I know, but it was mostly the baby. I don't think I've ever been that gut-wrenchingly sick before or since."

"You sure she didn't know why you were really so sick?"

"I'm sure. Nobody but Joyce. And I know she's a scatterbrain, but she really wouldn't have slipped up. Not on that. She never has. She never even told Benjie. I asked her once and believe me, she can't lie worth a damn. I'da known."

Billy led Maggie to the loveseat in the coffee area of the store and pulled her into his lap. "So. Is there anything else? *Anything* else that's gonna jump up and stab me in the heart when I find out about it?"

"Not that I can think of."

"You're goin' to really kill me yet, Maggie. I swear you are. And while I know you'd of loved Jake just as much no matter what—"

"Yes, I would have. But that's the reason, don't you see? The reason he's so much like you. So much like me. He's our replacement child."

"Maggie, he's like you because you raised him. And he's like me because you and I are very much alike."

"That's some of it. But not all. And okay, I know it's stupid, but you know the big debate on the abortion issue? That life begins at conception. And that if it does, then so does the soul. So miscarried babies—their little souls go somewhere. Don't they?"

"Back to God, don't you think?"

"But they never actually lived, so maybe He gives them a second chance."

"Only you, Maggie. Only you could come up with that."

"Yeah, I know. But it just always made me feel so good to think so. And very logical, too, now isn't it?"

"You never stop surprisin' me."

"And that's a bad thing?"

"Of course it's not. You okay? I just stopped to say hey. I need to get back out."

"I've been okay with it for a long time, Billy. I just—I didn't want you to have any more reasons to hate him than you already have gettin' in your way."

"Yeah, well. Seems another one turns up at every corner, huh?"

"Yeah."

He grabbed a quick kiss. He was almost out the door when she called after him.

"Hey! Did Jake happen to mention what position he played when he played?"

"No. What?"

"Running back."

"And of course you never accidently on purpose sort of pushed him in that direction?"

"Never gave the first push."

"It doesn't matter, Maggie. He was yours the first time you picked him up. So now, he's mine, too."

"Yeah. Good stuff, huh?"

"Yeah. Good stuff. See you tonight, Princess. Love."

"Love."

His phone vibrated as he got back in the truck. Not the phone clipped to his belt, now programmed with all necessary numbers connected with the Rockland County Sheriff's Department. The phone with the extra Apps a teenager would kill for. The phone in his side pocket no one in Turkey Creek had ever or would ever see.

He hit the screen impatiently.

"What?"

"Well?"

"I'm in. And I'm not in a talkative mood right now."

He cleared the screen and pulled out of the parking lot of the Clean Class.

Chapter Twenty-Two

Billy sat in darkness in his official vehicle, out of sight among the trees, out by Clayton Chapel. Danger zone. Thinking was easier in close proximity to a danger zone, not that Clayton Chapel was a danger zone at the moment. He wasn't there in his capacity as county investigator, the retired MP the County'd been lucky to get. Billy Brayton hadn't been regular army in a very long time. He was a specialist. The Agency's take-down specialist.

Not for him the years of patience exercised by the agents of the Country Justice team, the years of dangerous milking. Profitable years. Years in which Rockland County served as a clearing house. Drugs made their way to the Florida coast and up the Florida interstates, most often veering onto Georgia Interstate 16, frequently stopping off in Rockland County to parcel out a portion of the merchandise for distribution in the central Georgia area prior to their transport up I-16 to I-75 to Atlanta and routes up the eastern seaboard.

The Country Justice team walked a high-wire balancing act, rapidly using up all its nine lives. Over the years, they'd brought down four Florida operations and five Atlanta operations, and that was a good enough score for any team. The Agency thought it was time for them to shut down. Country Justice didn't agree with the head honchos real often. But they did this time. It was time to shut down. Billy was there to ensure they got out alive.

Collin O'Brien, now. The county investigator who'd gotten his head blown off two miles from here. What the hell had he been thinking? Careless. He'd known full well Clayton Chapel was the clearing house. The perfect clearing house, its already sensational history augmented with bells and whistles special effects. Lord knows, though, the place didn't need any special effects. Billy knew that first hand. After all, he held the record for the longest stay at Clayton Chapel.

Over the years, memories of that night, like memories of Maggie, peeked and teased and surfaced and retreated. For certain sure, though, that night insured he'd never become a pothead. An encounter like that on the night of the first—and only—damn time he'd ever been stoned out of his mind—talk about a drug-prevention program.

Before his mind slid off into memories triggered by the nearby cemetery, his phone vibrated. His "public" phone, not the special edition private one. He glanced down. Jake.

"Yo, buddy."

"Can you talk?"

"Sure."

"Good. I thought you might like to know where your wife is right now."

"Which would be where? She's not at home?" Billy glanced at the clock on the dashboard. Ten-thirty p.m. Surely even Maggie'd called it a day.

"She got wind the health inspector's gonna be at the restaurant tomorrow. So she's in the kitchen freakin' killin' herself! I saw the light when I closed down Clean Class and headed home. And I tried to stay and help but she knows I've got a calculus test tomorrow so she wouldn't let me!"

"What the hell's she doing?"

"You don't want to know. Includes but is not limited to moving every piece of equipment in there and mopping underneath. Taking the kitchen fans apart and cleaning the blades. Wiping down all the shelving with bleach—"

"Okay, I get the idea. Shit." Maggie did way too much, way too often. She'd been fine Monday night, showed a bit of strain by Tuesday night, a good bit more than that by Wednesday night. He didn't intend to let that continue, but she'd been on her own a long time and he couldn't barge in and change things overnight. But was she trying to put herself in a coma?

"You don't know what all she does during the week yet 'cause she shut everything down for a few days when you got here! But it's way too much and by the weekends, she's always so tired I don't know how she's moving! And she's got no business—"

"I'll handle it, Jake. On my way now." Billy was, in fact, already on Highway 96 heading back into Turkey Creek.

"And she's gonna kill me for calling you."

"Got your back, buddy. She won't know you called."

"Yeah, she will. But I don't care. Wish the damn place'd burn down. Clean Class isn't so bad, but that restaurant—"

"I know. Better than you think. I watched my mother work herself to death there. Didn't know that, did you?"

"No, I never caught that."

"So don't worry. You're not gonna watch yours do the same thing."

* * *

He pulled into the back of the restaurant in seven minutes flat. She didn't even have the damn door closed all the way, let alone locked. He stalked to the screen and yanked it open.

"What in the *hell* do you think you're doing?"

Maggie straightened up, mop still in her hand.

"Are you blind or stupid? I'm mopping the floors!"

"No, you're tryin' to kill yourself is what you're tryin' to do! Now put that damn mop down! You're going home!"

Maggie threw the mop forward.

"Who the hell you think you are and why the hell you think you can issue orders? This is *my* business, damn it, and I'll take care of it any way I damn well please!"

"Not if it means killin' yourself, you're not! Step up to that mirror over there by the sink and look at yourself, Maggie! And what in the *hell* have you done to your hands?! You're using bleach without gloves! Maggie, they're almost *bleedin'*, don't you know what they're gonna feel like tomorrow?"

"I'm not in a beauty contest at the moment! I'm taking care of the business that helps me take care of my son!"

"I watched my mother kill herself in here for pennies, Maggie! And now you want Jake and me to stand back and watch you do the same thing? Like hell! I fuckin' *hate* this damn place, Maggie! Jake wishes it would burn down! Did you even *know* that?"

"Jake called you, didn't he?"

"I saw the light on my way home."
"Bullshit."
"C'mon, let's go. I mean it now."
"Or what?"
"Or I'll throw you over my shoulder and carry you out. Don't believe me, you try me." She stared him down. He knew that look. "Don't you even think about it, woman, you don't have a prayer's chance in hell of takin' me down! I ain't Angie Malone!"

She stalked to the table and grabbed her keys and pocketbook. The screen door banged. Her car door slammed so loud he figured better check it in the morning. She took the driveway fast enough to tear the engine out if the Sheldon Brothers hadn't finished grading it. She flung the car door open and stalked up to the kitchen porch. She marched through the great room, ignoring Jake, and paused when she hit the hall.

"We'll be talkin' later, little boy."

The bedroom door slammed. Billy and Jake looked at each other.

"Wow," Jake said softly.
"Yeah." Billy sank into the couch.
"So. What now, you think?"
"Well, I think I'm goin' sit here 'bout half an hour, watch a little ESPN, and unwind some. And then I'm goin' check and see if the bedroom door's locked. And if it is, I guess I'll find out how good the mattress is in the guest room."
"Oh, c'mon! You tellin' me you don't know how to jimmy a lock?" Jake grinned.
"I know how, all right. Just ain't that stupid."
"It's really great, you know. Havin' somebody around can pull rank on her. I can't. Obviously."
"Well, I don't think one of us has any rank over the other, but I'm big enough to throw her over my shoulder and carry her out and she knew I was about to do it. You are, too, of course, but in your case, I wouldn't recommend it."
"I hate that damn place."
"I do too, son. She's breaking her back to break even, isn't she?"

"Oh, hell, yeah. You know that song and dance she gave you about the driveway keeping unwanted company out?"

"Yeah."

"That's a crock. We didn't have the money."

"I figured that might have something to do with it. Think we got a chance at convincing her to sell it?"

"To who? Turkey Creek ain't got a lot of entrepreneurs, you know."

"What a vocabulary. I'm impressed. I was thinking Junie Bug. She's the cook. If she owned it, that cuts the salary and payroll taxes right there. Much less expense of operation, right from the start. Does Maggie own the building?"

"No, she leases the building, it's just a month to month thing. She bought all the kitchen equipment and stuff but everything else goes with the building. But I don't think Junie Bug could get a bank loan. And I actually mentioned that to Mom once 'cause the main reason she won't throw in the towel is Junie and Leola would lose their jobs. She said she didn't think Junie Bug could handle the business end and that she'd end up doing all the accounting stuff anyway."

"Your mother has *got* to stop trying to take care of the whole world. I'll front Junie Bug. Don't really give a damn if it gets paid back as long as Maggie's not killing herself."

Jake gave Billy an appraising glance.

"Okay. The car. The driveway. Loan to Junie Bug. What the hell you been doing all these years?"

"I've been in a profession with low living expenses and no one else to spend the excess on. By Kincaid standards, I'm a pauper, but by mine, I'm pretty well off." Well, that was true, and applied to both the army and the Agency.

"Then by Mom's standards for the last twenty-five years, you're filthy rich. But you're not going to stay that way at this rate. Fifteen thou for the car, I know that driveway was at least two or three, now you're talking twelve or fifteen."

"Jake, borrowing from me to pay Maggie keeps the money in the same spot for all practical purposes. And would make Junie Bug feel like she'd actually paid Maggie for it. Doesn't matter though, everything I have belongs to all of us. Nobody ever said families were cheap. But trust me on this. They *are* priceless. And on that Kodak moment, I think I'll see if the door's locked."

"Kodak moment?"

"Damn. Gettin' old. Welcome to the digital age. You ready for that calculus test? 'Cause if you're not, go get ready."

Jake sighed. "Waited eighteen years to have a dad and I get one with a memory like a steel trap."

* * *

The door wasn't locked after all. Maggie was in bed, but from the rhythm of her breathing, she wasn't asleep. Billy smelled the clean scent of body wash and lingering steam from the bathroom. Well, a shower would feel good. And give Maggie another ten minutes or so to cool down.

She still wasn't asleep when he came out.

"You speakin' yet?"

"No. I don't want to talk to you. But I spent too many years sleeping without you to ever want to do it again. So get in the bed, stay on your side, and shut the hell up."

"Okay." He threw the covers back. "I can live with that."

Chapter Twenty-Three

Something wasn't right. Billy knew it as soon as he surfaced from sleep. He was alone, that was it. Maggie was already out of bed. Out of the bedroom, even. The day started early around here. By 6:00 a.m. Junie Bug was up at the restaurant starting the grits, bacon, sausage, and homemade biscuits that were the staples of the café breakfast. Maggie usually left the house between 6:30 and 6:45. He glanced over at the clock. Five fifty.

He'd made her leave the bucket of mop water in the middle of the floor. Health inspector. Right. She'd probably thought of some other fine-tuning, too.

He got up and pulled on his jeans and T-shirt. The coffee pot, timed to start at 6:00, still hadn't gone off yet and he hit the start button to get it going. Yep, her car was already gone. His phone went off in the bedroom. Damn, Maggie's ringtone. So she was talking again. He hurried down the hall, not wanting to push his luck by letting it go to voicemail.

"You speakin' to me, Princess?"

It wasn't Maggie.

"Billy!" Junie Bug's voice, edging toward hysteria. "Get up here! Now!"

"What's wrong?" No answer, only background voices as Junie passed off the phone to Leola. "Here, take this. Maggie! Miss Maggie! Miss Maggie, honey, don't go in there!"

Billy ran down the hall for his keys and shoes. He paused by Jake's door. If Maggie was hurt, Jake would never forgive him for not waking him up.

He pushed the door open. "Jake. Something's wrong at the restaurant. I don't know what. If you're comin' with me, you got two seconds for jeans and shoes while I grab my keys."

He didn't linger to watch, but he heard the mattress shift and Jake's feet hitting the floor. He came out his door right behind Billy as Billy ran back down the hall.

They cleared the driveway and pulled up to the restaurant in under three minutes. Junie Bug and Leola stood on the front porch wringing their hands.

"Where's Maggie?"

"She won't come out, Billy! We tried to stop her from going in but she wouldn't listen, and she won't come out!"

Billy pushed the front door open on a restaurant owner's nightmare vision of hell. Maggie stood frozen in the middle of the dining area. Clouds of roaches swarmed in colonies over the tables, up the walls, over the floor. They streamed in lines over the steam heated serving bar, shifted in and out of the compartments cut to hold the big pans of fresh-cooked food. The blackish-brown waves of clicking, hissing darkness moved over the floor like the tide. Billy was no expert, but any fool could see the invaders weren't all the same variety, mute testimony this infestation wasn't an act of nature, but a man-made disaster.

Billy rushed to Maggie. Carapaces crushed under his shoes, echoed by Jake's feet as he followed.

Maggie's head jerked up.

"I'm done. I'm through. I guess this makes both of you happy."

"Maggie, don't. We just want you to slow down."

"Slow down? *Slow down?*" She laughed. "I'm *shut* down! Can you guess what the kitchen looks like?"

"Mom, please, let's get you out of here, okay?"

"Oh, I'm out of here! There's two, three thousand dollars' worth of food in that kitchen I'll have to throw away. They're in the *freezers*. The *refrigerators*. The *stove*. The *grill*. The *deep fryers*. I'm done."

"Honey, this was vandalism, it's a crime scene. Your insurance—"

"*I don't have insurance!* I don't own the building, the owner insures the building! The price of renter's insurance on the equipment was so high it wasn't worth it! Even if I could have afforded it!"

"Just come out, Maggie. We'll figure out how to handle it."

"*I'll handle it! Like I always have! I don't need you!*"

"I hope you don't really mean that, Maggie. 'Cause I sure as hell need you."

That got through. The frozen mask covering her face crumpled as she shook her head.

"I'm so tired, Billy. I'm so damn tired."

"I know you are, Princess. So let us help. I'm here now. Jake's not a little boy. You don't have to handle everything by yourself anymore."

He pulled her close and wrapped his arms around her. And then Maggie did something she hadn't done in a long, long time. She burst into soul-wrenching, shoulder-shaking tears.

Billy ran his hand up and down her back. "Let it out, Princess, let it out. But finish somewhere else, okay?" He bent down, picked her up and carried her out the door, the sobs now muffled against his shoulder.

* * *

By 9:00 a.m., the cell towers and phone lines buzzed with the news of disaster at the Scales of Justice Café.

"Janet, did you ever? I've always been scared of restaurants, Lord knows what really goes on in the back and—"

"Agnes Peters, if I hear one word around town that Maggie was running a filthy restaurant, I'll come after you myself! You know full well that place was spotless! This was deliberate and it don't take much to guess who did it!"

* * *

"Joyce, you'd know. Tell me the truth. Are they just saying this was deliberate or was the restaurant really that bad? Has it always been dirty?"

"What the hell are you talking about?"

"You didn't hear? The café was just crawling with roaches this morning when they went to open up! Just swarming. They're sayin' somebody broke in and dumped 'em but c'mon! That's just a little too far-fetched if you ask me, I mean, who on earth would even think about such?"

"Don't you even go there! This has Big John written all over it! And she didn't call me? I'm goin' to crawl her ass for this!"

"But was it really dirty back there?"

"Hell no, it was not, and I'd better not hear one word around this town saying that it was! Now, I've got to get to Maggie so go find somebody else to gossip with! But be nice! Or I won't be!"

* * *

"Now was that really necessary?"

"I liked it."

"Well, you've completely destroyed the social network of Turkey Creek. Where's the Dead Dick Society goin' to congregate now?"

"The who society?"

"That's what the girls call all your ol' fart wannabees. You know, the ones think they're the movers and shakers in town. Like Davis Brown."

"Fits, got to admit. Hell, they can get their wives' fat asses out of bed to make their breakfast. Or pay a cook. I do."

"Much as they'd like to think so, not all of the Dead Dicks have your resources, you know."

"You're not telling me you're goin' to miss that damn greasy spoon, are you?"

"Hell to the no."

"Didn't think so."

* * *

"Just heard about the restaurant. You have any idea that was comin'?"

"Not the slightest. Did you?"

"No. I'd have told you if I had. Well. Guess that shows where we sit on the totem pole."

"You know Big John. Absolutely nobody's going to know everything. Except him. But we know lots he don't know we know."

"God, I hope so. Only edge we got."

"I am so ready for this to be over."

"Yeah, me too."

* * *

Shane Attenborough wasn't having a good morning. Nobody having breakfast with Davis Taylor was having a good morning. He glanced around the Huddle House for rescue and spotted Alec Wimberly walking in for a coffee re-fill.

"Alec! Back here!" Shane called, shamelessly sharing the joy.

"Guys. Mornin'." Alec stood by their table but didn't sit down. "Got to get back out."

"Yeah, all of us need to get back out. Gonna be pulling extra duty today 'cause of all the guys they got up at the damn café. Flat disgustin' sometimes, all the strings get pulled in this town."

"What the hell you talkin' about, Taylor? Billy's up there and the Sheriff's up there. And they pulled Jenkins in to double document the evidence 'cause it's Billy's wife's café, for God's sake! Nobody's off patrol. How you think that's causing any back-up anywhere?"

"Makes you sick, don't it, many times as we ate up there. Kitchen's probably always been crawling with the damn things. Wonder we ain't all dead from some disease!"

Shane snorted. "Many times as you walked back there to make sure Junie Bug was cooking you three eggs and not trying to sneak you two—mostly so you could grab an extra piece of bacon off the grill—seems like you'da seen something, there'd been anything there to see. Or somebody would have. We all stick our heads in the kitchen all the time."

"Hell, bugs don't come out in the day time!"

"Not unless four or five million of 'em get dumped overnight, Taylor! Think about it!"

"Shit, she's always getting' special treatment. Put a crimp in that damn kid's style last week, though. Tearing down Eighty in that 'Sixty-six Mustang. Kid ain't got no damn business with a car like that."

"I got to get back on the road," said Alec. "Taylor, you're too stupid to understand this, and I know I'm wasting my breath. But if you think you can hassle Jake just to aggravate Billy, you picked the wrong target. All you're doin' is paintin' a bulls-eye on your heart. I got to get back out. Shane, my sympathies, buddy."

Taylor scratched his head as Alec walked out.

"Now, what the hell did he mean by that?"

Chapter Twenty-Four

Aunt Lulu moved about her kitchen, stopping occasionally to stir the big pot of homemade soup simmering on the back of the stove. Making soup for Aunt Lulu was at least a two day endeavor she embarked on one week every mid-summer when the southern fields were at their best. She didn't let being in her seventies stop her from putting up enough to last all winter and through to the next soup-making. It wasn't easy and got harder every year, but it was worth it. She could put out a good homemade meal for any visitor just by pulling a few pints of soup out of the freezer and mixing up a batch of cornbread.

Her youngest son Lamar should be driving up any minute. They had a standing Friday lunch date. Lamar'd done good for himself, no question about it. Major Lamar Simpson. Direct Supervisor of the elite K-9 SWAT CPS team.

Lulu wished she didn't have a niggling suspicion there were other reasons for Lamar's success beside his brains and hard work. It wasn't anything she could put her finger on, exactly. Lamar'd been a difficult child, an unwanted child. Born when her then youngest was already eight, she hadn't wanted another baby. It felt like she'd been a mother since she was sixteen. Oh, wait! She *had* been a mother since she was sixteen. And she'd handled most of the raisin' herself. She'd thought she'd picked a good man, but she sure wasn't the first woman who'd been wrong.

Lulu'd resented every minute she carried Lamar, raged against every labor pang, fought every contraction of delivery. And she'd loved him beyond life the minute he was placed in her arms. She'd always been afraid the love had come too late, that the resentment she'd harbored for the child and his father through those long nine months had taken seed, nurtured by her unhappiness. Maybe it had rooted deep down in her child's soul, taking his childish joy even in the womb.

Lamar worried her, always had, always would. So did Maggie. She hadn't wanted another child, and here came Lamar. She sure as hell hadn't wanted yet another, and here came Maggie. Maggie wasn't physically her child, of course, but she was her child where it mattered. In her heart.

It hurt Aunt Lulu to think of Maggie and the backbreaking hours of work that had gone into keeping the café going. She did a lot more physical work up there than she needed to or should have. But did Maggie listen when she tried to tell her? *"Can't ask anybody to do anything I'm not willing to do myself, Aunt Lulu,"* she'd say, and there seemed no way to get through to that girl that being *willing* to do anything you had to didn't mean actually *doing* it yourself when you were paying other folks to do it.

She gave the corn sticks a final check. Perfect. And just in time. There was the slam of Lamar's car door.

"Hey, Mama!" He bent and kissed the top of her head while she pulled the hot cast iron pan from the oven.

"Hey, baby!" Lord, what a good-looking man, with his father's height and presence. She prayed every night that was all he had of his father. She wasn't sure. "Good to see you, you hungry?"

"Ain't I always? That your soup I smell?"

"Sure is."

"Don't get no better'n this." He washed his hands at the sink and settled in at the table with a large bowl of soup and the plate of hot buttered corn sticks.

They passed pleasantries and tidbits of family, town, and church news across the table while they ate.

"What about the café?" Lulu asked. "Things settlin' down?"

Lamar shrugged. "I guess. No reason for me to be up there, not my case."

"Now, son, you and Maggie practically grew up together! You don't think you coulda checked on her?"

"Mama, you've always done enough checking on her for the both of us."

"Raised her, just like I did you!"

An indefinable something flashed in his eyes. "And gave a lot more attention to raisin' her than you did me, at that. Didn't you?"

Aunt Lulu sat back in her chair. "Maggie was a girl, son. A little girl without her mama. Girls more complicated to raise than boys. Don't mean no insult, they just are."

"Yeah, well, I know lots of little girls—and boys—trade a lot for a daddy with Big John's money."

Aunt Lulu snorted. "Money don't mean nothing, son. Man's a demon in human form."

"He's not so bad. Always done right by me. Helped me out when nobody else would, that's for damn sure."

Aunt Lulu closed her eyes. Yes, Big John'd gotten Lamar hired in the first place. That scared the hell out of her. Because why would Big John care if Lamar Simpson was a member of the Sheriff's Department unless it gave him another deputy in his pocket? Though why Lamar mattered to him, she didn't know. Wasn't like he didn't already have enough badges in his pocket back then. She liked to think he'd lost a few, these days.

Lamar pushed his chair back. "Well, I got to get goin'. Thanks for lunch, Mama. Just as good as always. Can't nobody touch that soup and cornbread, never will."

Aunt Lulu pushed back her chair and walked to the door with him.

"Son, don't ever think John Kincaid does anything for anybody out of the goodness of his heart. Ain't got one. I was in that man's house over twenty years. You got no idea who he really is."

Lamar's eyes flashed. "Mama, I know *exactly* who that man really is."

Jagged fear shot through Aunt Lulu's chest, sharp as a heart attack.

"Now, what does that mean?"

"Whatever you want it to, Mama. See you later. Don't you work too hard now, you hear?" He kissed her cheek and walked out. Aunt Lulu looked out the doorway after him, watching a good bit of her life's work walk away, praying she'd done a good job. She wasn't at all sure it'd been good enough.

Chapter Twenty-Five

Harve Preston, owner of the café's building, stood outside with Billy.

"Lord, Lord, I just don't know how Maggie's gonna be able to handle this, Billy. I mean, this is gonna cost a fortune—"

"*Maggie's* not gonna be handling this by herself, Harve. This is your building. It was vandalized. So I suggest you call your insurance agent."

"Wait a damn minute! I'm not runnin' the restaurant—"

"Harve. It's *your* building. You want to leave it the way it is, that's your call. But it's just goin' to sit if you do. 'Cause I happen to know Maggie doesn't have a lease with you, she's month-to-month. She can cut her losses pretty easy. You leave it like this a few days, you'll have to tear it down. Pretty damn quick. That helps your wallet a lot, doesn't it?"

"But I don't own any of the equipment—"

"You still own all the furniture in the dining room. You own the walls themselves, Harve. Now, you get an adjuster out here, I've already called the pest control company, they're on the way. They do their thing, we'll find out how soon we can get a professional disaster company out here to start clean-up and get everything sterilized. I'll handle any pro-rated bill for equipment clean-up. The food's a total loss, and I'll handle that. But you are not just gonna sit there and expect Maggie to pay for everything when that's what insurance is for. Are we clear on all this? Because if that restaurant's not operating, you're not getting any rent till it is."

"Now, Billy, that's just not right! I got a bank note—"

"Who the hell you think you talkin' to, Harve? Some idiot who just blew into town? You don't have a bank note on that building. If you do, it's the longest-running mortgage in history. It's a shell of a building, lousy insulation, backyard construction.

The heating and cooling just flies out the cracks. Didn't cost ten or twelve thousand to build, not worth $30,000.00 now. You want any money out of it while it's down, you better include a loss of use claim when you file that insurance. And you'd better go ahead and get 'em the hell on out here. Longer it sits, longer it's goin' take to get it back up and runnin'. So, one more time. Are we clear on this?"

Harve sighed and scratched his head.

"Yeah, hell. I just hope Maggie can pull her part—"

"I said I'd handle it, Harve. Don't you even mention money to Maggie. You got me?"

Harv sighed again. "Yeah, hell, I got it." He pulled out his cellphone and began running down his contacts for his insurance agent.

The sheriff emerged from the depths of the roach hotel and Billy walked over.

"Well, I think that's about all she wrote, for right now, don't you?"

Billy wiped his forehead with the back of his hand. "Yeah, for all the good any of this'll do. All we really needed was a picture of the three pairs of latex gloves on top of the kitchen table."

"Hell, even if they hadn't left a sign announcin' they wore gloves, the fingerprints are useless. You know that. Everybody in town's got prints in this place. Even in the kitchen. Folks step back there all the time."

"Maggie was on a cleaning marathon last night, though. Bleach and industrial cleaner all over the place."

"And that mighta helped if we didn't know they were wearing gloves."

"Maybe. I doubt it."

"Me, too. Well, let's go home, get cleaned up. You need to check on your wife. Don't hurry back, you think she needs you to stick around a while."

"Thanks."

* * *

Not knowing what to expect when he got home, Billy yelled out from the yard. "Maggie! Nobody else here, are they?"

She appeared on the kitchen porch. "No, why?"

"Just makin' sure." He started stripping in the yard. No way these clothes were coming in the house, and there were lots of advantages to living in the middle of the woods.

She reached out to touch his arm as he walked by.

"Hey. I'm really sorry. I don't know where the hell that came from. In the café. Because I've never stopped needing you. And you've always been there. Even when you were dead. I wasn't kidding when I said I've always asked myself *'What would Billy do? What would Billy say?'*"

"And did you always listen?"

She grinned. "Maybe not. But I always took it into consideration."

"Then let me get cleaned up and I'll tell you what Billy says. And you can take it under consideration."

"Want some company?"

"Always. But I need a few minutes to scrub down about five or six times. Nasty in there."

"Bastard."

"You're calling me names already? I haven't even started tellin' you what I think."

"Big John. He knew you'd be the one have to work that scene."

"Yeah. Two for the price of one, huh?"

He'd only scrubbed down three or four times when she slipped into the shower, but he figured it was good enough. Billy broached the idea of selling out as they recuperated, twined together in their bed.

"Probably gonna shock you, but I think you're right. No point in me re-opening when he could do it again anytime he wanted to. But I hate you laying out so much money when I don't know if you'll ever get it back. Junie Bug—"

"Will surprise you. She'll do just fine. And now you can concentrate on feedin' the three of us. 'Cause if last weekend was a sample, you're right. You are a better cook than Junie Bug. That southern-fried grease'll kill you."

"Billy Brayton! That's treason!"

"Oh, it's the best-tastin' food in the world. Nobody ever said it was healthy."

Chapter Twenty-Six

Friday night football, the heartbeat of America. Billy and Maggie sat in the stands by the field at Rockland Academy. For some reason, Jake'd seemed unusually intent on making sure they'd be at the game.

Maggie'd had a week of relative leisure and Billy marveled at the difference. She'd been near total exhaustion when he'd come home, but he'd had no frame of reference when he first arrived and hadn't realized just how chronically exhausted she'd been. Tonight, though, she was rested, happy, beautiful. She called out blithely to all the spectators in the rickety wooden stands.

New country music classics played over the loudspeaker, courtesy of this year's sports announcer, the self-proclaimed "Voice of Rockland Academy," Patrick Lewis, one of Miss Betty Jean's younger grandsons.

Billy looked around for Jake but didn't see him. The players lined up to run through the night's banner. *Who Let the Dogs Out* blared from the speakers. The team broke through just as Joyce and Benjie Clayton settled in beside them.

Maggie clutched Billy's arm. "Oh my God!"

"What?"

"Number Twenty-One! On the field! It's Jake! No wonder he insisted we come to the game tonight! He went back to the team!"

"But twenty-one's—"

"Your number. I know. And no, I didn't have a damn thing to do with it! Not then, not now!"

"You swear?"

"On your mother's grave! I don't think I can get much stronger than that!"

"Damn."

"Well, I mighta had something to do with it." The familiar voice drawled behind them.

"Should have known," Billy said, without turning around. "T-bone, why'd you want to go do something like that?"

"Watching Jake run's always reminded me of you. Even when he was as young as six or seven." T-bone settled down beside them and sipped his coke. "So when he got football size and asked me what number I thought he ought to ask for, I told him. Simple as that."

"You could have told me!" Maggie said. "I always thought that was just plain damn spooky."

"You never asked, babe. Always thought you kinda liked thinkin' it was one of those meant to be things."

"I did, actually. Kinda sorry you told me."

"Ah, c'mon girl! You got flesh and blood back, don't need a fantasy anymore."

Billy looked at the best friend he'd ever had in his life and wondered, not for the first time, if Maggie had any idea Jack Jones was in love with her and had been for as long as Billy had been himself.

"You could have told us about this, too," Maggie scolded.

"Not on your life. He wanted to surprise you. Wants Billy to see him play."

"Joyce, you knew! Ben couldn't possibly have kept it a secret!"

"No, believe it or not, he never said a word. I'm as surprised as you are."

Billy watched the players go through their warm-ups. They looked lean and in shape, smaller in statute than the players most public schools fielded, but small private schools didn't have nearly the player pool to pull from. So that's why Jake was so conditioned. There were exactly eleven players on this team. Total. They played offense *and* defense. They never came off the field. Billy looked across the field at the opposition. At least 30 players stood on the sidelines. Damn.

"We call it Ironman Football," Maggie said, reading his face. "Yeah, they're tough. Don't win much, they're okay the first half but so tired by the second half the defense is gone and they can't get any momentum going on offense. Most of the coaches on the other teams we play always tell us after the game if we had eleven or twelve more just like 'em, we'd take State. For them, it's not winning. It's just taking the field and playing a whole game, week after week. Pretty much knowing they're goin' to get their asses kicked."

The microphone whined briefly from the Press Box. Patrick Lewis started introducing the team. "Sorry 'bout that, folks! Wouldn't be a game without that first whine, now would it?" The crowd laughed. One thing a small private school didn't have was a top of the line public address system.

"Well, here we are again! This is Patrick Lewis, your voice of Rockland Academy, and here's our line-up for tonight! First things first—let's give a rousing welcome to our returning running back, Number Twenty-One, who took a few games off at the first of the season! We don't hold it against you, buddy, breakin' a leg'd make anybody take some time off!"

Jake waved from the field.

"Now, got to tell you—there's another change in the roster. 'Cause there's been a change in Jake's house. And on behalf of all the seniors, let me say thanks to Jake's new dad, Billy Brayton, for coming back from the dead, 'cause he makes hangin' at Jake's house even more fun than it used to be! No offense, Miss Maggie, your pizza and nachos rock, but you can't talk football strategy worth a darn! And that's the change in the roster, 'cause Jake's in the process of changing his last name to match the rest of his house! So here's our running back, Number Twenty-One, Jake Brayton!"

Jake raised his arm high in the victory sign, his smile visible even in the stands. Billy shook his head slightly and cleared his throat.

"Did—did you know about this?"

"Not a clue. So, ah, whatcha think about it?"

"Don't think I could begin to tell you. Jack, you knew?"

"Sure. But Jake's my bud. We always got each other's back."

Patrick finished introducing the players.

"Well, com'on, guys!" Maggie got up and started toward the fence.

"Oh, hell." T-bone groaned. "Com'on, son, Maggie don't sit if Jake's on the field. She walks the damn fence with the action. The whole damn game."

"Joyce, you coming?" Maggie demanded.

"Do I ever?"

"No."

"Exactly. That's what bleachers are for."

* * *

At half time, Billy worked his way through the crowd, into the gym, and down to the locker rooms under the bleachers. The team was wearing out, but there were things they could do offensively to counter that. Coach Daniels taught social studies. He'd never played even first string. Billy would bet the bank on that. And besides, he wanted to talk to Jake.

The masculine smells of sweat, testosterone, and wet towels hit him as he walked in, a smell an athlete never forgot. Jake sat on a bench by the wall, his helmet off, his hair plastered to his head, his head hanging low while his hands braced themselves on his knee as he breathed deeply.

"Hey, buddy!"

Jake raised his head. "Hey, Dad." He smiled slightly, but it wasn't convincing. He was just too damn tired.

"Full of surprises tonight, aren't you?"

Jake's eyes clouded. "You don't mind, do you? I didn't think you would."

"I'm so proud it's got to be a sin. Did you really want to, or did you just think it'd make your mother and me happy?"

"Always been two names in the house. Mom never changed my birth name when she did the formal adoption. Understood why, she hated being a Kincaid. And I always felt like she thought changing my name was takin' something that wasn't hers to take, that she'd be trying to replace part of me somehow. But you don't replace something you don't even remember. And now—you're here and there's still two names in the house. You know? Sort of makes me odd man out."

"So, you just want to change the name? Don't know much about adoption law but—"

"I could change the name by myself. Couldn't do an adoption without y'all. Didn't ask, but I sort of figured it'd cost more than I had in my bank account."

"You and your mother, I swear. I've got that much in my bank account, Jake."

"Yeah, but this was my present to you. And Mom. And me."

"So an official adoption can be mine. To all of us. What would you think about that?"

Jake smiled. "And you want to do that?"

"Damn straight. If you do. No pressure."

"I do."

"Coach plannin' on talkin' anytime tonight?" Billy gestured over to the far wall, where the Coach appeared to be hypnotized by his clipboard.

"Oh, yeah, in a few minutes he'll tell us to hang in there, we're doin' a good job, yadda yadda, you know. He's kind of used to losing. So are we."

"Y'all win just by finishin' a game. That's brutal, Jake. I never played both sides."

"Somehow I think you've done a lot of things a lot more brutal than that."

"Well, yeah, but not when I was sixteen or seventeen or eighteen. Not till basic anyway. Please tell me you don't want to join the army?"

"No thanks."

"That's a relief. Think the guys'd mind if I talked to 'em?"

"You kiddin'? You're a legend."

Billy shook his head. "That damn church is gonna haunt me till I really do die."

"Well, that too. But we all know you still got the county record for the most runnin' yards."

"I do?"

"You didn't know?"

"I didn't know I had it in the first place."

Billy walked to the center of the room.

"Guys! Huddle up, okay?" The boys raised their heads and moved in. "Hard to see when you're actually on the field, so I thought I'd mention this to y'all. The quarterback throws a little off. Got sort of a right sheer on the ball. Doesn't get much air under it, either, and the defensive line's weaker on that side, too. Keep your eyes open, you think you got a chance at one of his passes, take it. You don't get an interception, you might knock it down. Worst that can happen is you don't touch it. And when he sets to throw—he holds the ball down low to his side and behind his back for a few seconds before he starts raisin' his arm. And one more thing. Ben and Parker, y'all control the field. You're the two biggest linemen out there, and wherever y'all are, Winston Academy don't go. Y'all are natural decoys to get 'em in the position you *do* want 'em in. Understand?"

Varying voices chorused.

"Cool!"

"Sweet!"

"Maybe we can get some sacks off that, you think?"

"Well, I'm sure Coach Daniels was goin' to tell y'all the same thing. Hope I didn't butt in too much." Billy held out his hand as he passed by Dan Daniels and the men shook hands. "Sorry, excitement of the game, I guess."

"Oh, anytime! Yeah, I was gonna mention all that, but sometimes it's better when it comes from somebody besides me, you know how it is, they listen closer."

"Absolutely. See y'all back on the field."

"Well, finished spreadin' pearls of wisdom?" Maggie asked, as he rejoined her. She'd settled down on the bleachers next to Joyce, but he knew that wasn't going to last when the team came back on the field.

"We'll see."

"Quarterback's got a right spin on the ball," T-bone said. "Holds it low when he's settin' up, too."

"Yeah, that didn't escape my notice."

From the first, the tone of the second half was different. Winston Academy moved no more.

"Oh my God! Did you *see* that?" Joyce's voice came simultaneously with Patrick Lewis's excited shout. "And that, ladies and gentlemen, is a *sack* of the *quarterback* by Number Fifty-Eight, Ben Clayton!"

"Hot damn!" T-bone slapped Billy on the shoulder. "You musta done some talkin'!"

"They must'a listened."

On the next play, at the fifty-yard line, the ball left the quarterback's hands and started its spiral down to the waiting receiver. A Rockland Academy uniform leapt up into the golden haze cast by the field's lights and captured the ball.

"It's Jake!" Maggie jumped up and down and tugged on Billy's arm. "It's Jake!"

Patrick Lewis screamed over the microphone.

"*Go, Jake! Go! Jake Brayton, Number Twenty-One! He's going, he's going, he's gone!*"

Billy leaned forward, muscles straining almost as hard as they had when he'd been the one running down the field. Jake stood in the end zone and held the ball high over his head in triumph.

"*Yes, yes, yes!*"

Billy and T-bone pounded each other's shoulders. Maggie and Joyce and Benjie jumped up and down in a circle of three. The crowd went wild.

The game settled into a grim holding pattern. Both teams tried series of short drives going nowhere, right up until the last minute and a half of the fourth quarter. Winston had possession on their thirty. Their quarterback got off a decent pass to the running back. He fumbled. Opposing uniforms dived for the ball that skidded around on the ground It escaped the grasping hands of both sides and came to rest covered in a mound of sweating and straining bodies.

The referee blew his whistle.

"Winston ball!" He signaled toward their goal.

Oh man!" shouted the Voice of Rockland Academy. "Somebody call the sheriff, we done got *robbed*!"

Winston's quarterback set up for another pass. The ball spiraled through the air with that peculiar right twist. Again, a Rockland Academy uniform leapt high into the gold and grabbed the ball in mid-air. He turned and ran.

"*He's done it again, folks! Go, Jake! Goin', goin', goin'—gone like a freight train!*"

"Oh, my God! He is, he is gone, he's—"

"*Greeeeezed Liiightniiiiin'!*" T-bone shouted.

The crowd roared. Patrick Lewis screamed from the Press Box.

"You 'da man, Jake, *you da man*! Jake Brayton, Number Twenty-One, Rockland Academy *M–V–P!*"

Final score, Rockland Academy 21 – Winston Academy 14. Maggie pushed Billy forward. "Don't be polite, get up front. You need to be the first person he sees coming off the field."

"You comin'?"

"No. This is your night. Yours and Jake's. He did this for you."

* * *

Davis Taylor watched from the sidelines. It was his night to work the games, a perk the deputies didn't mind collecting at all—extra pay for watching the county kids play ball. As a rule, Taylor didn't mind himself. This game he could have done without. Damn kid'd be so full of himself now nobody'd be able to stand him. And using Brayton's name now, too. Fuck. Just fuck.

Well, appearances were everything. Might as well act like he gave a damn. He walked up to the team, moving in a group toward the gym, with Billy in their midst. The boys didn't want to let him out of the crowd.

"Well, guys, good enough job. Pulled that one out of your asses, didn't you?"

Billy looked at him.

"Taylor."

"Sir?"

"Shut up."

Chapter Twenty-Seven

During the next few weeks, Billy stitched himself back into the fabric of life in Turkey Creek as seamlessly as though he'd never been ripped out of it. He was Maggie's husband, Jake's dad, a damn good lawman. A good man to have as a friend, a bad man to cross. Life was perfect except for two things—Davis Taylor and the identity of Country Justice.

Taylor was everybody's problem. Nobody on the force liked him, trusted him, or felt safe when he had their back. That didn't bother Taylor a bit. He didn't even realize it. But Country Justice? Oh, hell, their real identity was driving him crazy. The blazing intelligence behind the redneck hick act cracked him up.

One afternoon he and Lamar Simpson grabbed a cup of coffee out of the department break room at the same time.

"How's it goin', Lamar?"

"Usual." The taciturn answer didn't surprise Billy much. Lamar didn't like him. Didn't like Maggie, either. Never had. Billy understood that. Must have been hard, growing up watching your mother tend a rich man's child.

"Well, that's good. Thought you might be havin' a rough day, short-staffed and all."

"Meaning?"

"Bobby Wainwright's on vacation and Taylor called in sick. Again. Does that a lot, I've noticed."

"Yeah? Well, how 'bout you worry about your case load and let me worry about my squad."

He turned and walked away. Billy looked after him thoughtfully. Nobody'd ever had any hard evidence he was dirty. But there was no way any commanding officer with any experience didn't know Taylor was a bad cop, even if they couldn't get rid of him. Billy settled in behind his desk in his cubbyhole and picked up a file. He was deep into a small-time bust down around Tolbert Road when he heard Alec Wimberly's voice.

"Hey, Jake! Looking for your dad?"

"Yeah."

"My office, guys," he called out. "What's up, son?"

Jake stuck his head in the door.

"Just stopped in to tell you I won't be home tonight, so the guys won't be over." The football practices that counted were now held with Billy in the big cleared bottom at the slope of a gentle hill in their yard. "You and Mom could probably use some down time from us anyway."

"Okay. Anything special? Hot date in the middle of the week? Alec, don't just stand there holdin' your coffee, come in and sit down a minute."

Jake and Alec both walked in and settled in visitor's chairs.

"Austin Peters got his driver's license today."

That time-honored rite of passage for Rockland County teens, the solitary stay out at Clayton Chapel, always occurred the night any teen acquired his driver's license.

"Oh. So y'all are keeping him company till midnight, are you?"

"Yeah, we're gonna hang at Ben's house till it's time to head for the Chapel."

Billy hesitated. He didn't want the kids hanging at Clayton Chapel, but nothing he said was going to stop them. Before he could say anything, Alec shifted restlessly in his chair.

"Jake, I really wish y'all wouldn't do that."

"Why not? You did it, didn't you?" Jake asked.

"Yeah. Yeah, I did. For a whole two minutes, maybe. But that place, night checks, you know—it's got a real bad feel, Jake. Worse than it used to be. Or maybe I'm just older. But I wish y'all wouldn't go. Any of you. Ever."

"Ever see anything?" Jake grinned.

"Probably not."

"Probably? Either you did or you didn't, Alec."

"Mind plays tricks on you in places like that, Jake."

"What about you, son?" Billy asked. "How was your midnight out there?"

Jake shrugged. "Never had one."

"What?"

"Never had one. Mom asked me not to. She didn't *tell* me not to, it wasn't like an order, it was—she said she knew no matter what she said, I'd do it anyway, and she knew it was a point of honor for us and all that but she'd take it as a personal favor to her if I didn't go. I mean—well, hell, Mom doesn't ask for much. I'da felt like a jerk if I'd gone anyway. And if I'd gone and she'd asked me and I told the truth, she'd have been disappointed and if I'd lied, she'd of known it, she always does, and then she'd be really disappointed. But she never asked."

"Take much ribbin' for that?" Billy asked.

"No, not really. Kind of surprised me, I figured everybody'd give me hell about it, and I'd just have to take it. But when I said Mom'd asked me not to, nobody said anything else. Then again, all of us'd pretty much do anything Mom—or Miss Joyce—asked us to. They're—different. Grown-ups, but not exactly."

Billy seized the chance.

"Would I qualify in that category, by any chance?"

"For me? Hell yeah, sure. Surprised you'd even ask."

"For the guys."

"Well, yeah. Hadn't thought about it, but—sure, yeah, you would."

"Then can you get Austin on the phone for me?"

"You don't want him to go, either. Are you guys really serious?"

"As a heart attack."

Jake pulled out his phone and rang Austin, passing the phone to Billy.

"Hey, Jake!"

"No, sorry, it's Billy. Listen, guy, I asked Jake to get you on the phone 'cause I hear tonight's your big night. Don't want to steal anybody's thunder but here's the thing. I'd take it as a personal favor if y'all didn't go out to the Chapel tonight. Or any night, actually." Well, it worked for Maggie.

"You're kiddin' me, right?"

"Nope. Know y'all gonna do what you're gonna do, but I'd really rather you didn't."

"You're the last person on earth I ever figured would say that, you stayed out there all night!"

"Make you a deal. You don't go—none of you guys go, not on anybody's driver's license night—and we'll have a Halloween bonfire down in the bottom next week and I'll tell y'all all about my night at Clayton Chapel. Whatda' you say?"

Long pause. None of the kids ever *really* wanted to go to the Chapel anyway. This was an honorable out. With an almost irresistible bribe.

"Well—you'll tell the guys it's 'cause you asked me not to and not 'cause I'm chicken?"

"Got your back."

"And you'll really tell us about it?"

"Promise."

"Well, okay then!"

Billy handed the phone back to Jake.

"Give," Jake demanded.

"Halloween bonfire."

"Not after that build-up. Give. Right here, right now."

Alec joined in.

"Give. Right here, right now. I'll be on duty Halloween night, can't make the bonfire."

Billy sighed.

"Close the door, son," he ordered. "This involves some conduct unbecomin' a police officer."

Jake complied, and Billy leaned his chair back.

"Well, it was like this…"

* * *

Sixteen-year-old Billy Brayton drove his ramshackle pick-up behind Clayton Chapel and parked between the Chapel proper and the Fellowship Hall. He didn't quite hate the thing yet. Nobody really hated their first ride, not when they first got it. The new driver's license was burning a hole in his wallet, not that he hadn't already been driving for some time now. Most of the kids in a county with nothing but back roads drove long before their sixteenth birthday.

He reached over to the passenger side and grabbed the brown paper bag containing his supplies for the night. His mother'd been dead for almost two months and Billy was still raging at the entire world. He'd remain in that state for the next two years, when meeting Maggie would begin to mitigate the situation. He'd never have done it if his mother'd still been alive. He'd raided his father's marijuana stash. That hadn't been hard. His ol' man was lying on the sofa in the dilapidated rental house, a beatific expression on his face moving in and out of view in the haze of pot smoke surrounding him. Hell, there was enough second-hand smoke to get high.

Billy knew what being drunk felt like, as most of the county kids did by the time they were sixteen. He didn't much like it. He didn't like it at all, in fact. He had so little control over the circumstances of his life in general he couldn't see why anybody'd want to sacrifice what little control they did have in an alcoholic stupor. He'd never tried pot, though. He didn't figure he'd like it much, either, but what the hell? One time couldn't hurt. Wasn't like he was planning to go any higher up the drug chain, pot was his outer limit. He might be poor as dirt, and he might be the county bad-ass, but he wasn't *stupid*. And this night, this place—again, why the hell not? Probably put him in such a daze he wouldn't notice Jack the Ripper stalking around the headstones.

Maybe he'd even beat the current record, believed to be three hours. Nobody really knew, because it was lost in the shrouds of time. And though nobody was really sure and it had never been confirmed or denied, rumor had it the record belonged to Big John Kincaid. Be kinda neat to beat the King of the County at something.

He strolled among the headstones of the side cemetery, carrying his stash to a stone bench situated in the midst of the markers. He sat down. Hard as hell, but at least it had a backrest. Opening the bag, he rolled his first joint and lit up. Huh. He wondered what all the fuss was about. He really didn't feel much different. So he rolled a second and lit that up. Must be more tired than he thought, he was getting drowsy as hell. So thinking, while marveling at the quality of the moonlight, shimmering with far greater intensity than he'd ever seen, he slept.

Then he woke up. Or at least, he thought he did, but he must not have, because a lady sat on the bench beside him. A beautiful lady, with long straight hair that yet had a hint of wave, dark as lake water, shining with highlights gleaming gold with a hint of red under the moon glow.

"I hope you don't make that a habit," she said, gesturing to the bag on the bench beside him. "Life's too short to waste in a stupor."

"No, I don't. First time. Last time. Just for tonight."

"Good. On the other hand, it kept you here long enough to visit. Nobody ever stays long enough to visit. Gets quite lonely, you know."

"It must. Uh, excuse me, but—where'd you come from?"

The lady waved her hand in the general direction of the side cemetery.

"Oh, you know. Here and there. Now and then."

"But where'd you come from right here and now? And why?"

"My, you are bright, aren't you? The kids all come, they never stay. But if they had, they wouldn't stay long after I said hello, you think?"

"Don't guess so."

"But you're still here."

"I'm stoned out of my mind. For sure."

"Why?"

"Because you can't really be here. I can't really be seein' you. Can I?"

"Actually, I think you might be seein' me even if you weren't stoned out of your mind. Which, by the way, you're not. Not right now, you've slept it off already. So for heaven's sakes, don't try it again. Or anything else. You've obviously got a very high tolerance, it'd take a lot to have any effect if you ever got hooked on anything. No, the after-affects helped a little, but you, my boy—no, I shouldn't call you that. You left boyhood behind a long time ago, didn't you? You, young man, are a sensitive."

"I'm a *what*?"

"You're a sensitive. I don't just mean you've got a sensitive soul, though you do. I mean you're sensitive to the world beyond."

Billy snorted. He'd been called many things, especially by his ol' man, but sensitive had never been one of 'em.

"You can laugh," the lady said. "Doesn't mean it isn't so."

"Then why just you? This is a cemetery. Ought to be seein' more folks from the world beyond. Shouldn't I?"

The lady sighed. "This is an old cemetery, you know. Mostly everybody's moved on. Oh, there's been a few over the years have lingered a while, but right now, I'm all by myself. But that's okay. I've pretty much always been all by myself, even when I was with somebody else. Sometimes, especially when I've been with somebody else. You know?"

Yes, he certainly did know.

"So why haven't you? Moved on?"

In the space of a heartbeat, the visage before him shifted and changed. The lovely face transformed into a wreck of blood and bone, brain matter oozed from the shattered skull. He wanted to scream like a girl and run like hell, but stayed frozen in place, his eyes reflecting his inner horror.

In the space of another heartbeat, the visage shifted again, returning to its former state of beauty.

"Oh, dear! I'm so sorry about that! You took me by surprise, can't imagine why, of course you'd ask, bright boy that you are. Takes a lot of energy to maintain, it's much easier to stay in the state you crossed over in."

Billy, still in shock, remained speechless.

"Are you all right? I didn't mean to scare you, I'm really sorry."

"Who—how—what did that to you?"

"Oh, you got it right the first time. It was definitely a who. My husband."

"Your husband killed you?"

"Yes."

"On purpose?"

"Now, don't make me rethink my opinion of you, young man. Of course, on purpose. You're so surprised a husband could kill a wife? That's classic, isn't it?"

"No. I mean, no, I'm not surprised. My father killed my mother, after all."

"I thought you'd lost someone recently, makes you even more open than I'd guess you usually are. Literally or figuratively?"

"Huh?"

"Don't play dumb, it doesn't become you. Did your father kill your mother literally or figuratively?"

"Figuratively. But he killed her, just the same, wouldn't be any more his fault if he *had* used a shotgun. Uh, if you don't mind my askin', was it?"

"A shotgun? No, handgun. Magnum, I think."

"Pretty close range, huh?"

Short laugh. "*Very* close range."

"And that's why you haven't—what'd you call it? Moved on? He got away with it?"

Shorter laugh. "He gets away with *anything*. *Everything.* Always has, probably always will. It'd be nice to think my stickin' around could change that, but it probably won't. No, I wouldn't stay just for that, satisfying as it would be. It's my little girl. Not so little anymore, probably your age. She hates me. She thinks I left her on purpose, but I'd never have done that. I tried so hard to stay, even with—well, you saw. Pretty impossible to stay with my head in that mess, wouldn't you say?"

"Oh, yeah."

Deep sigh. "I see her every now and then. Oh, she doesn't come to *visit*, not with me, but she comes occasionally when all the kids do. That thing y'all have with your midnight vigils, you know. Well, of course you do, that's why you're here. I'd really like for her to know how much I love her and how much I hated to leave her before I move on over. Mostly I don't think that's very likely, but hope springs eternal. I think she could be a sensitive, too, just like you are, except she's too tight, too guarded. She's never had enough love not to be. You did. You hate the world right now and you hate your father and probably always will, but you were loved. Your mother loved you to the moon and back, I can feel it, and that, young man, is going to be your salvation."

"Do I know your daughter?"

"No, I don't think you do, unless you just know her in passing. I'd sense her around you if you knew her well, I think. But I hope you meet her. You and she—I think you'd be very good together. Very strong, both of you." The lovely lady looked up. "Oh, my! Dawn's about to break, I've kept you long enough. It's not impossible to maintain in daylight, but it's a lot harder, I might shift back to the horror show. And you need to go get some real sleep. In a bed. It was very nice to meet you, young man."

"Billy. Billy Brayton."

She was beginning to shimmer, almost but not quite transparent.

"Very nice to meet you, Billy."

"Wait! Who are you? Who's your daughter? You never told me!"

* * *

Billy came out of his midnight trip back to Clayton Chapel's cemetery abruptly, grabbing every shred of thespian talent he had, the talent that kept every good field agent alive.

"Dad! Don't just quit! What was her name?"

"I don't know. She shimmered on out. And then her voice came back. 'Sorry, young Billy, some secrets stay in the grave.' So I don't know."

"For real?"

"For real."

"Not just the name, I mean the whole thing."

"Swear." Well, everything up to the name, anyway, and close only counted in horseshoes and hand grenades.

"Damn! The guys'll freak *out* on that!"

"Good. Maybe that'll keep all y'all away from there."

"You making it up just for that?"

"No, I told you. I swear. So, you guys still gonna hang at Ben's tonight? I'm probably goin' to be late, have to go do an interview this afternoon. Probably goin' to have to go back out tonight, too."

"Yeah, we'll go pick on Miss Joyce tonight, share the wealth. Probably thinks we abandoned her. She's kind of sensitive, you know."

Billy laughed. "But she hides it so well."

"Don't she though?"

Billy closed the door after they left. He settled back in his chair and deliberately threw himself back into the state of almost total recall he'd attained as he relayed the story. He could even feel the dew of the early dawn, see the faint traces of pale color beginning to mingle with the darkness of the horizon.

* * *

"Very nice to meet you, Billy."

"Wait! Who are you? Who's your daughter? You never told me!"

She solidified again for a moment. "Oh. Sorry, that was silly of me. I'm Magdalene. My daughter's Magdalene, too. I always liked my name, thought it was rather distinctive. But she hates it, just like she hates me, won't let anybody use it. She uses—"

"She uses Maggie," Billy whispered. "How the *hell* could I have forgotten that? Never connected that?"

Well, easily enough, after all. Because he really didn't believe that night ever actually happened while simultaneously believing, oh, hell yes, it had. So he didn't think about it much. From the first, he'd *tried* not to think about it. It was confusing as hell and that was reason enough not to think about it, especially given the two whole years between that event and the time he met Maggie. Two years was a century to a small child and at least a decade for a teenager.

And his Lady Magdalene—his mind deliberately turned the designation into the title of honor born in the Middle Ages, because she was a Lady, for sure—dear God, the resemblance was uncanny. He'd known Maggie only as a teenager just entering young maturity, and he'd come back to find her a fully mature woman. He'd never seen the progression from then until now. But he was certain down to the depths of his soul that she'd looked just like his Lady Magdalene when she'd been in her twenties, early thirties. He was certain if Lady Magdalene hadn't taken early residence in Clayton Chapel's Cemetery, she'd have looked just like Maggie at the age of forty-three.

So. Where did he go from here? Walking into the DA's office and asking for an arrest warrant because Big John's wife's ghost said he'd murdered her wasn't going to work. Definitely. But she'd sure as hell given him somewhere to start. He needed the file on her suicide, which might be dicey, considering it had been in what?

1967? Long before the miracles called computers. He especially wanted the low-down on the gun allegedly employed in the alleged suicide.

But first things first. He needed to confirm that Magdalene Kincaid was actually buried at Clayton Chapel. Considering the exhumed occupant of his own grave currently resided at the Georgia Bureau of Investigations headquarters in Atlanta awaiting identity and everybody in town knew it, it wouldn't be very bright to go asking about another grave, especially that one.

He didn't want to ask Maggie. But he could ask somebody else. Somebody who knew how many sets of clean underwear were folded neatly in each bedroom of the Kincaid house at any given time. He closed the file on his desk and headed out the door.

Chapter Twenty-Eight

He pulled the F-150 into Aunt Lulu's driveway. She rocked slowly on the front porch in the pool of sunlight slanting over her rocking chair, a coffee cup in her hand.

"Well, well!" she called in greeting. "Didn't you time it just right! Just ran out of coffee!" She held the empty cup out to him. "How 'bout you save these ol' legs a walk? Get me a refill when you grab you a cup, maybe throw a few of those brownies coolin' on top of the stove on a little plate for us?"

He bent for a hug and took the offered cup.

"How do you *do* that? Always have something fresh-baked whenever anybody pulls up?"

"Shoot, son! Make some little treat every afternoon, somebody mostly stops in sometime or other 'fore the day's done!"

"Then how do you keep that girlish figure?" Billy's voice floated back down the hall as he headed for the kitchen.

"Some folks gain weight in their ol' age, some lose it. This the smallest I ever been in my life, no matter how much I eat."

Billy came back, balancing cups and brownies on the small tray Aunt Lulu kept on her counter.

"So." Aunt Lulu reached for her cup. "Whatcha come to ask me 'bout?"

"You know I like checkin' on you every now and then."

"Middle of the week, four o'clock? You checkin' on me, you stop in on the way home. And I 'ppreciate how often you do. But this, no, this ain't no social call."

"Okay, caught me." Billy settled back in a vacant rocking chair and picked up one of the still warm brownies. "Maggie learned how to cook from you, didn't she?"

"Mostly. Girl's good, ain't she?"

"Very. Tell me about Maggie's mother."

"Miss Magdalene? Why on earth, son? What you wanna know?"

"Do you think she killed herself?"

Aunt Lulu's face closed down. A repository of secrets, Billy was sure, and she was, for the most part, good at maintaining a poker face, but she wasn't good at masking reactions to the unexpected.

"I believe I'll take that expression as a no." Billy sipped his hot coffee.

"Son, it's not that simple. Nothing's ever really black and white. 'Cept skin color, of course, and even then, folks come in varyin' shades of both, though no Georgia redneck ever gon' say so."

"What was she like? Much like Maggie? Or I guess that oughtta be, is Maggie much like her?"

* * *

Aunt Lulu tried to pull herself out of confusion. Damn, it was hell getting old. Harder to keep your mind straight on what you should and shouldn't say. And Billy Brayton—it wasn't just that he was a trained lawman and had been for years, it was more than that. One thing Aunt Lulu knew was people. And Billy had the knack, with no clue that he did, or that it was something most folks either didn't have or never used. He could see—or sense—the underlying currents always moving in even the most seemingly placid folks. Hard man to lie to. Or to misdirect.

And you know what? She was seventy-five years old. She was tired. She wasn't ready to just start talking and spill forth everything she'd learned about Big John over the years—Lamar was still her child, after all, and she wasn't at all sure what *he* knew about Big John—but she was tired of watching her every word.

She looked Billy straight in the eye.

"No, son, she wouldn't have killed herself. Wouldn't have left Maggie. Not with John Kincaid. And yes, Maggie's a lot like her. And no, she's not. Magdalene was a lit'le girl in the fifties, girls still raised to think they gon' grow up and get married and have babies and live happ'ly ever after. And John, he tried to raise Maggie like that, too, 'cept of course, he intended her to grow up and marry who he wanted and have both of 'em do whatever he say. Up to jumping off a cliff, did he tell 'em to. But times done changed. And they'd long changed by the time Maggie hit twelve, thirteen. So he didn't have a lot of luck with that. 'Sides, Maggie's got a lot of John Kincaid in her, too. Too much to take orders from anybody. Tol' Jake that once and he looked at me like I'd done grown two heads, but you know what I'm sayin', don't you? 'Cause if you don't, you don't know her half as well as you think you do."

Billy rocked in rhythm with Aunt Lulu.

"That absolute confidence there's nothing she can't handle. And usually does. She just isn't arrogant about it. That uncanny knack of lookin' straight through to your soul. But she looks for the good things, doesn't use the bad things to take advantage of folks. Except when she's really pissed, and then that tongue cuts like a knife. But that doesn't happen often. And that damn brain that computes things so fast, you got to run to keep up with it."

Aunt Lulu nodded in satisfaction.

"Glad you didn't disappoint me, son."

"So what do you think happened? Did Big John kill her? Did he ever love her at all? Did she ever love him?"

"She thought he did, once. She thought she did, once. Notice you didn't ask me why I never said nothing to nobody iff'n I think John killed her."

"I'm a realist, Aunt Lulu. Turkey Creek, nineteen sixty-seven? King of the County and his black housekeeper-maid? You'da been crazy. But do you absolutely know he did?"

Aunt Lulu made a fist and thumped her chest over her heart.

"Here I do. Did I see it? Naw. One thing John ain't never been is stupid. Nor careless. No matter how arrogant he is."

"Happen in the house?"

"Naw. Found her body in the woods, out near a hunting cabin John kept about five, six miles off the road on some of the farmland he owns. She liked that cabin, went out there right often, said it was her thinking place."

* * *

Shit. It would be. Billy bet he knew exactly where that cabin was, too. Though it'd been abandoned and stripped for years—probably for sixteen, to be precise, if Maggie had been two at the time of her mother's death—by the time he'd made its acquaintance.

He'd upset Aunt Lulu, he knew. And she knew a lot more about a lot more than she wanted to talk about. He wouldn't push any further. Not right now, anyway. He just needed one more thing.

"Where's she buried, Aunt Lulu? Maggie doesn't talk about her."

"Why, Clayton Chapel, of course. She was a Clayton."

* * *

The witching hour of midnight approached. Billy walked toward the stone bench that still stood in the side cemetery of Clayton Chapel. He'd been home, but one of the advantages of his job was the ever-present possibility of keeping odd hours for reasons he really wasn't supposed to talk about. Maggie never asked questions when he needed to go back out. He'd tell her about this later, because he'd have to tell the same story at the bonfire that he'd told Jake. And there was no way Maggie wouldn't jump all over it with both boots, even without the name. There was just too damn much coincidence.

Good thing he'd thought to grab a jacket. Chilly tonight. He settled down and prepared to wait. He waited. And waited. Flipping out his phone, he saw he'd been waiting for two hours. Maybe now since Maggie'd started visiting her grave, Lady Magdalene'd finally moved on. Or maybe the whole thing had been just an hallucination triggered by the pot. Damn lot of coincidences if it had been. Or maybe he was just nuts. Definitely the most likely theory. Well, in that case, he had nothing to lose.

"Miss Magdalene?" he called softly. "You still here? Remember me? Please don't make me smoke pot this time, I'm a *cop* now, I'd hate to have to explain it if I get busted!"

Nothing. Hell, it was late. Maggie was lying in a warm, queen-sized bed with an empty side just waiting for him. He stood.

He heard her laugh before he saw her.

"My, how impatient! Do sit and visit awhile, Billy Brayton! I certainly don't want to be responsible for a *cop* getting busted!" She was sitting on the bench, and reached down to pat it in invitation. Then she stiffened. "Well, well. You've done a lot more than meet my daughter, haven't you? I feel her all over you."

"Married her. Long story."

"Must have been fairly recent. You've been gone a long time. I've never felt anyone on her, except Jake. She comes to see me now. Several times a year. She's softened a good bit, motherhood'll do that to you. Beautiful boy. Shouldn't use beautiful and boy together, but he is. Hers, and not hers. And strangely enough, now that you're here again, that's what I've never been able to pinpoint about him. Yours. And not yours."

"Like I said, long story."

"But do you love her?"

"To the moon and back," he said.

She laughed. "You stole that line from me."

"Yes, ma'am, I did."

"Must have been quite the whirlwind romance."

"It was. But it started a long time ago. Two years after I met you. When we were eighteen."

Billy figured fair was fair. She'd waited a long time to hear about her daughter. So he talked. And talked. And told her everything.

"Your turn," he said, when he finished.

"My turn?"

"I'm a cop now, remember? So how 'bout you help me take Big John Kincaid down?"

Chapter Twenty-Nine

Billy slipped under the covers beside Maggie at 5:30 in the morning. She roused, sighed, and threw her arm over his chest.

"Wha' time is it?" she asked.

"Shhh. Go back to sleep."

He didn't expect to sleep very long. His mind was churning. The problem was, it wasn't churning profitably. A couple of hours was all he needed and he'd be up to speed again. Besides, sometimes he solved whatever sticky problem he was working on while sleeping. Right now, he needed to figure out how to get his hands on an ancient file in what had been ruled an open-and-shut suicide. And he had to do it without anybody knowing about it or figuring out why he wanted it if they did find out.

He slept. And woke to Maggie's dismayed wail.

"Oh, good Lord! Billy! We overslept! It's *nine o'clock!*"

"Don't worry about it." He reached up and pulled her back down. "Already told 'em to expect me when they see me this morning. And you don't have anywhere you have to be this early anymore, remember?"

"What time did you get in last night, anyway?"

"Early mornin', actually. Five-thirty or thereabouts."

"Damn."

She settled back and then bolted upright again.

"Jake! Oh, I forgot. Never mind."

"What?"

"I was afraid he'd overslept right along with us but he stayed at Ben's last night. Damn it."

"Damn it?"

"It was Austin's birthday. I hate them all goin' out to the church. But I know they did."

"No they didn't."

"And you know this because?"

"I asked them not to. And then threw in a bribe. Said I'd tell 'em about my night at the Chapel at a Halloween bonfire down in the bottom if they didn't go."

"And you know they didn't go anyway because?"

"Oh ye of little faith. Because I was out there from midnight on myself."

She settled back again.

"Keepin' that world record of yours that important to you, is it?"

"Yeah, it's how I define myself."

"Well, I'm glad you have something. God knows you've accomplished nothing else in life to be proud of. So why were you out there? I don't like 'em goin', but sittin' out there all night yourself to make sure they didn't—that's a little extreme, don't you think?"

Billy ran a series of possible segues into the actual explanation through his head. As he'd hoped, the solution to his sticky problem of how to get his hands on the old Kincaid suicide file without arousing suspicions had been right there waiting on him when he woke up.

"You won't think so when you hear all this. And by the way, I need you to develop a sudden interest in the details of your mother's suicide. Burning questions that have to be answered for your continued peace of mind. Which will allow me to pull the file without anybody thinking I have any interest in re-activating any investigation."

"Again I ask. Because?"

"Remember when you told me you didn't think—or hoped—your mother didn't kill herself?"

"Yeah?"

"She didn't."

Maggie sighed. "This is getting old, Billy. And yet *again* I ask, you know this because?"

"She told me."

* * *

The road had deteriorated over the last twenty-five years. It didn't need a four-wheel drive back then, not all the time, anyway, though he'd always swapped vehicles with T-bone and taken one anyway. Nobody would know or care if he'd gotten stuck out there for a week, but he sure as hell wasn't about to risk it with Maggie. It definitely needed the department's F-150's four-wheel drive now. He glanced over at Maggie, trying to read her face. He hadn't wanted to come out here yet, but like Maggie's march up to Big John's desk on the day of his return, some things you just couldn't stop. She needed to see the place again, feel it, absorb it. He understood.

"I really should have gotten the file before we came out here."

"Why? It says what Big John wanted it to say, not what we know happened."

"Oh, by the way—thanks for not trying to have me committed."

Short laugh. "It just confirmed what I knew about you from the minute you asked me to visit your mother with you."

"And that was?"

"Well, I didn't know you *were* a sensitive, but I knew you had a sensitive soul."

"Hell of a thing for the local bad boy to have. Do you remember this place at all?"

"*Excuse you?*"

"I don't mean us, I mean, do you remember your mother ever bringing you out here to play? She said you loved it."

"Billy, I was *two* when she died. I don't even have any memories *from* two, let alone before."

"You might not know you do, but maybe that's why you remembered it was here at all."

"I remembered it because I was Maggie Kincaid and it was the only place in the county I could think of where nobody was likely to see us. And it had to happen *here*."

"Not actually in the cabin, Princess, it happened in the woods."

"Because he brought her here after he caught her and took me away from her. But she wouldn't tell you why she'd decided to take me and run?"

Billy shook his head. "Your mother had—has—a very strong code of honor. Almost as though it's from another time. And I guess what with the way everything's changed it pretty much is. As soon as I remembered enough—I've never *tried* to remember that night, let alone ever let myself go into total recall on it—I started calling her 'Lady Magdalene.' She's got that type of poise, that type of manner. She only said he'd hurt someone she cared for very much which was neither here nor there as to the facts of her murder, and that part of the story wasn't hers alone, not her secret to share. That bothers me. Like I ought to be able to figure it out if I just thought about it the right way. The obvious person is you—but I never took Big John for a pervert or pedophile, just a megalomaniac. And since you have no memories of anything—" The inflection in his voice turned the words into a question.

Maggie shook her head. "No. I don't. And not because anything's repressed, either. I don't ever remember him touching me at all, actually. No hugs, no goodnight kisses."

"Jesus, Maggie, that's—" Billy broke off. He remembered no signs of affection from his own father, but his mother'd made up for it. Maggie'd had no one except Aunt Lulu.

"Yeah, ain't it, though?"

The woods had thickened so much they almost ran into the cabin itself without realizing it. The walls sagged under their heavy burden of thick, twining vines, the front door hung half open from one hinge. There'd been some glass left in some of the windows in their day, but not now. Gaping holes yawned in a roof almost bare of shingles.

Maggie opened the truck door. "Somewhat the worse for wear, I see."

"Hold it!" Billy grabbed for the box of latex gloves on the seat. "Put these on, remember? Don't want our prints in here until I can manufacture a reason for us—or me—to be here. And then it'll be with somebody else, too, so there's no question of us—or me—planting anything. If she's right, and if he stashed the actual gun in the safe he had in the cabin. She apologized but said she might be a bit fuzzy on that, navigating while being dead was a new experience. At least I know now where you got that dry sense of humor."

"Okay, okay!" Maggie grabbed the gloves. "But our prints'll be all over the inside anyway."

"No, they won't. Fingerprints are nothing but oil. They don't weather well, don't last. Extreme heat or extreme cold destroys 'em in a matter of weeks, let alone years. You ready for memory lane?" He held his hand out to her and they slipped through the waiting door.

The musty smell of rot and mildew hit them in the face.

Maggie tugged his hand.

"Still there." She pointed to a back corner where the rotting shreds of their double-sleeping bag still remained. God, it'd been cold in here in December and January and February, not that they'd noticed the cold for long, and by April and May, they'd been sleeping on top of the bag instead of inside it.

Echoes whirled in the air, just out of earshot.

* * *

"Maggie, we shouldn't be here. I wanted so much more for you than a damn sleeping bag on the floor—"

"Shhh. This is what we've got. And it's perfect."

"Maggie—"

"What if I told you you weren't the first?"

"I don't give a damn if I'm the first, I just want to be the last."

Startled gasp of surprise and pain. Absolute stillness.

"Liar."

"I never said you *weren't* the first, I just asked what if."

"Because?"

"Thought you were about to go all noble on me."

"Don't know me as well as I thought you did, throwing out words like noble."

"Oh, yes. I do."

Feather kisses on his throat, pressure pushing upward against him from the slender body beneath. Cessation of all coherent thought.

December, and a small cedar stood in the corner by the sleeping bag, now fortified with extra blankets, decorated with berries and scattered with sweetgum balls, two small boxes beneath it.

Maggie's delighted laugh.

"I don't *believe* you! What made you think of it?"

"Oh, I don't know. Haven't had a tree at home in a couple of years, just seemed like the thing to do. Makeshift home, makeshift tree. For now."

"Yes, but I don't want to open any presents when I don't have one of yours here, you should have told me."

"Well, maybe one of 'em's mine. Depends on if you like it."

Quizzical glance as she settled on the bag beside the tree.

"Here," he said, settling beside her and picking up the box, wrapped in silver foil. "This one."

She knew, he could tell. It was obvious in the almost reverent way she peeled the foil away.

"*Ohh!*" Soft breath of delighted awe.

"It's little, but later on—"

"Don't you dare! It's beautiful. And I will wear it till I die! Don't ever think about trying to replace it!" Flinging arms encircling his neck. "And the band, too! I can't wait to put that on! The other box is yours?"

"Yeah, matches your band. Figured you'd probably better take 'em and keep 'em together until—well, until—"

"Graduation. I don't want to stick around that long but it'll complicate things so damn much if we don't already have our diplomas when we drive out of this town. June's not that far away, I guess we can survive that long."

* * *

"Well, we did."

"Did what?"

"Survive. Didn't think *you* did, for a long time. But good things come to those who wait. And wait. And wait."

"Old times' sake," he said. Long kiss. Long sigh.

"You okay?"

"Yes. Though it seems—sacrilegious, almost—to be looking for evidence of murder here."

"Lady Magdalene said the safe was under the floorboards near the fireplace," Billy said, "but I don't want to move around too much. Too much dirt and dust, don't want to leave a line of clear footprints. And I sure as hell don't want to pull up any floorboards, it'd be too obvious the flooring's been pulled up, never be able to explain that. So let's go." He tugged her hand and they backed carefully out the door.

The F-150 pulled out and left another series of echoes replaying in the trees that had taken over the cabin's yard.

* * *

"John, don't do this! Maggie needs—"

"Sorry about this, Magdalene but Maggie doesn't need a mother just waiting to take her away from me. Shouldn't have tried that, Magdalene. You know, I might have actually let you go, you been a real disappointment from the start. Elsewise wouldn't be needin' any side dishes, now would I? But this—" Kincaid shook his head thoughtfully. "Now, I'm not about to wait around while you try to run with her again. Or haul me into court with your stories of how I'm an unfit father."

"You aren't fit to touch her! Or me, or anybody else!"

"That child's mine! First time I looked in her eyes—she's me made over, Magdalene, she has nothing of you, never will." Cold feel of gun metal close to her skull. Hard click as the hammer engaged. "Not even memories."

Chapter Thirty

Billy spent Saturday morning catching up on the bane of a law enforcement officer's existence. Paperwork. He returned home with a four-footed guest, one of the county's elite K-9's.

"Oh! Which one is it?" Jake rubbed the big head and then pulled back. "Oh, shit! Am I supposed to touch him?"

"Sure. This is Riley. Shane Attenborough's dog. His wife's mother had an accident in Savannah. Shane needed to go, so I said Riley could stay with us. Been a while since I've handled a dog, thought it'd be fun. Where's your mother?"

"Great! I've missed a dog. Oh, Mom went to Macon with Miss Joyce."

"I've wondered why we didn't have a dog, hoped I wasn't screwing up bringing Riley home, but Maggie always loved animals. So why don't we have one?"

"We did. She was a Dobie. Well, mostly a Dobie, anyway, it was real obvious, she was a stray T-bone found up around Tolbert Road when I was four. I remember I wanted to name her Princess—well, hell, I was four—but Mom said everybody's dog was named Princess so we named her Belle. And now I know why she didn't want me to name her Princess. Which, by the way, really doesn't suit y'all. Too sweet, somehow, why *do* you call Mom that?"

Billy laughed. "Short for Princess Bitch. That sweet enough for you?"

"You're kiddin'."

"No, one of the first things I ever said to her was 'Excuse me, Princess Bitch.' So Maggie didn't want to get attached again when Belle died, huh?"

"God, Mom loved that dog, I caught her crying for weeks later. Been almost a year now."

"Well, maybe Riley'll help us get past her on that. Been thinking 'bout getting my own dog and training it myself, what'd you think about that? Never liked gettin' close to a department dog, they can swap around on you without notice."

"You could train one yourself?"

"Mostly. Need some fine-tuning probably but not much."

"I've heard the guys giving commands. You can do that?"

"Yeah. They're mostly trained in German or Dutch. Sometimes French or Czech. Riley here speaks German. Good thing, I never had one that used French or Czech."

"That's so they won't listen to anybody but their handler?"

"No, that's what folks think but the language is whatever they're initially trained in and it's easier for an officer to learn a few foreign words than to retrain a dog. A lot of 'em are trained in Europe. You could train one in Martian, if you knew it. We get one, I'll use English, how's that?"

"Awesome!"

Billy bent to take Riley's leash off. "Here, go give him a run."

"C'mon, Riley! Catch me!" Jake tore off like a six-year-old. Riley barked madly beside him, anxious for the chance to play. Then he stopped dead still, heading for Jake's car. He circled the Mustang a few times and sat down by the driver's door.

"Riley! C'mon boy!" Riley remained firmly in place, staring intently between Jake's car door and Billy.

"Son of a bitch," Billy said softly, walking over.

"Dad? What's he doing?"

Billy opened the door. "Riley, *such rauschgift*," he ordered, and Riley climbed in the backseat and sat, lowering his head and insistently trying to poke his nose under the driver's seat. "*Lass es!*" Billy ordered, and Riley desisted. Billy backed away. "Riley, *hier!*" Riley jumped out of the car and trotted over. "*So ist brav,*" Billy reached into the truck and retrieved he rubber cone that rewarded the dogs for good performance. Riley accepted the toy with a universal doggy smile.

"Dad?"

Billy reached under the seat. He held up a plastic bag of whitish pink crystalline lumps.

"Crack," he said. "Automatic felony. Probably close to six ounces. Say thirty-five to seventy-five hundred dollars' worth."

Jake's face went stark white.

"Dad, that's not mine! I swear to God, I don't know where the hell that came from, but *it's not mine!*"

"Jake, calm down! I never thought it was, and even if I had any doubts, which I didn't, nobody knowing crack's in their car's goin' be playing right beside it with a drug dog. Besides, you got that much money handy, you can start payin' rent."

"But there's *no way* that should be there! I don't know *how*, I don't know *why*—"

"I do."

"But—"

"Who was working the game last night, Jake?"

"I don't—Taylor. Wasn't he?"

"Oh, yeah. Wondered about that, Taylor doesn't like working very much, thought it was a little soon for him to have another game."

"But *why*? How?"

"How's easy enough. None of y'all lock your cars in that parking lot, do you?"

"Well, no. I mean, why would we?"

The Rockland Academy kids were family. There was only one class for each grade level in the school, and none of them had twenty students. Some of them had a lot fewer than that. Most of the kids had been together in that one class since Pre-K. They were virtually brothers and sisters, a closed unit. Among the older kids, it didn't matter whether they were freshmen, sophomores, juniors, or seniors. The distinctions of grade so firmly drawn at public schools and bigger private schools didn't exist for them. They co-mingled in one big group. Naturally, some kids were more popular and well-liked than others, but they didn't steal from one another. Everyone had each other's back.

"And Taylor knows y'all don't lock your cars. And even if you did, anybody could get into a sixties car with a wire coat-hanger. No problem for him to open your door and stash that."

"But *why*? I never did anything to him!"

"It's not what you did, son. It's who you are. You're Maggie Kincaid Brayton's son, key name now being Brayton, and for a bonus, now you're my son, too. You announced that at the first football game. Taylor feels threatened by people he can't control. By you, by me, by your mother. Because we're something he's not, and he knows that but he doesn't know why."

Jake sat down on one of the iron benches under a group of water oaks in the side yard.

"But to come up with something like this? Just because? On his own?"

"Oh hell no. Not on his own. How much sweat did you see your mother pour into that restaurant, how important was it to her? But what's the most important thing in her life? You are."

"And you."

"And me. But you're different, you're her *child*."

"Big John?"

"Of course. Been expectin' something actually, didn't know what or when, but I've been on the lookout. Family's the weakest link. Always."

"I just—it feels so—no way I can tell you how it feels!"

Billy walked over and sat beside him. "Riley, *hier*!" Riley trotted up and sat at their feet, hassling happily.

"Let's see. It feels like it doesn't matter whether you did or didn't, 'cause nobody's goin' to believe you no matter what you say. And that you must have done something for this to happen, so somehow or other it's your fault anyway. And mostly, you just feel dirty."

Jake raised his head and half-way smiled. "Okay. So you do know. I forgot."

"Try sittin' in a jail cell for two weeks with an armed robbery charge hangin' over your head when you never so much as thought about lifting a candy bar from the grocery store when you were a kid. This is one country boy grew up scared to death of his mama's wrath and not ashamed to admit it."

"Sorry I never got to meet her."

"Me, too. She'd have loved you. And Maggie. To the moon and back."

"Good one. I like that."

"Yeah, so do I. Just remembered hearin' it again a few days ago."

"Dad? What now?"

Billy gazed thoughtfully toward the woods.

"I need to see a man about some crack. I think. If I'm right about where this came from. Got to run back to the evidence locker first to be sure."

"You're goin' to *Taylor*?"

"Oh hell no, not about to give him any warning. But he and Lexie had a pretty big bust on Sixteen three days ago, crack, packaged just like this, rank amateur style. Not professional, not exact in weight. Four bags. Except I'd be willing to bet there were really five bags. The four checked in were in this type of baggy, one side green, one side yellow, so it turns blue to show the seal's tight. See? And it's pinkish, too, color differs from batch to batch, depends on who's processing it. Double-bagged, just like the ones he turned in. I'm bettin' a chemical analysis'd show it was all cut from the same batch. Which seems a little stupid for Big John, though it's what I'd expect from Taylor, so maybe he didn't have specific instructions on that. The sheriff and I need to have a little talk."

"Dad, he's not goin' to believe me—"

"Yes, son, he is. Trust me. This is his chance to get rid of Taylor, he's goin' grab it with both hands." Billy stood. "Now while I'm gone, pull the car close enough to the side porch for an outlet and vacuum it out. Everywhere. Carpet, mats, under the mats, seats, get the attachment and go under the seats, trunk. Wipe down everything you can wipe with Armor-All. Everything."

"So the dogs can't smell it?"

"Hell no, nothing's goin' to stop the dogs from smelling it. For *a while*. But I don't want any trace dust or powder lingering, which it probably isn't, bagged like that, but just in case. Now, try and lighten up a little, shake it off. You got a big scene comin' up."

"Scene?"

"No point in plantin' it if he wasn't goin' pull you over to pin it on you. We'll talk about it when I get back. You want Riley to stay?"

"If it's okay."

"Sure. 'Come' is *hier*. That'd be about all you'd need."

* * *

Billy punched his secret phone as he roared up the driveway.

"My, my, what an honor! You don't usually bother to check-in—"

"When?"

"Excuse me?"

"This is goin' on way too long. And I know damn well you have more than enough. I want this over, I want that son-of-a-bitch shut down!"

"Patience has never been your virtue, Country Time. But what's the immediate rush?"

"He planted crack in my son's car."

"Your *son*? Why, Country Time, your personnel file says you aren't even married, let alone expecting, and you have a son *driving* already? Fast work, congratulations."

"Bite me. I know damn well you know all about it. Country Justice would've told you, even if you weren't monitoring the locals yourself."

"Wouldn't have heard about it from you, though. Oh no, marrying Kincaid's daughter, that couldn't *possibly* be anything important—"

"Kiss my ass. He's targeting my *son*. I was lucky as hell I caught this."

"Jake Rubin—oh, excuse me. Jake *Brayton* now, I understand. He's got guardian angels, Country Time. He was born under a lucky star. Nothing's going to happen to him. We're moving, chill out."

"What guardian angels?"

"Well, you for one."

Billy swore as the line went dead. He headed back to the office. He needed confirmation before he brought the sheriff into it. It was just too far-fetched for a kid like Jake to emerge full-blown on the drug scene carrying that much crack. A few eight balls or a few ounces of weed would have been a lot more believable. Big John would've thought of that, but this overkill fit Taylor's hick mentality perfectly. Bigger had to be better. If he'd altered orders on his own, Big John was going to make him very sorry. Almost as sorry as Billy was going to make him.

"My, Lieutenant! Back so soon?" The Sheriff's secretary, Aurelia Andrews. Shit. Billy avoided her like the plague. Most of the guys did.

"Forgot something I wanted to check the first time I was up." Billy didn't pause or turn to look. It wasn't a good idea to encourage a man eater.

"Really? I wouldn't think you're a man who forgets much."

"We all have our days."

Billy pulled out his key ring. In this instance, rank didn't have the advantage. Job description did. Only the investigators went in and out of the evidence locker. Yep, just what he'd thought. The bag in Jake's car had to be from the same bust. He locked up behind himself and left. Next stop, the Sheriff's house.

Chapter Thirty-One

They stood in the sheriff's driveway. This wasn't a conversation for other ears.

"That stupid son-of-a-bitch! You sure it's the same crack?"

"Oh yeah. And I'm sure a chemical analysis would confirm it. But that's not the problem right now. Tonight is. Taylor's on duty. Which screams 'warning' all by itself, 'cause he volunteered to swap with Bobby Wainwright today so Bobby could go to his niece's birthday party. When's Taylor ever given a damn 'bout anybody else's family functions?"

"How the hell you know all this about everybody's schedule? *I* don't know all this about everybody's schedules!"

Billy shrugged. "I notice things. The guys talk to me."

"Yeah? You be talkin' to me, you didn't have an explanation for where that crack came from?"

Billy shrugged again. "I'd like to think you'd be a little leery of the idea that a kid like Jake just all at once came up with that much crack."

"Yeah, overkill, all right. But would you be talkin' to me?"

"Doesn't matter if he did it or not. You know that. Folks just remember the bust. Positions reversed, you be talking to me?"

"I honest to God don't know. Then again, I never got framed for anything. That'd probably tip the scales a little. So. Whatcha think the big plan is?"

"It's the weekend, Taylor swapped for tonight. Kids'll have some plans, but I didn't ask before I left. I'll call you back."

"You do that. I want in on this."

"Don't want to ruin your Saturday night."

"Thoughtful of you, but I'd kinda like to be sure I don't have to arrest you for murder, you're kind of handy to have around. I mean, a few bruises, that's nothing, but a dead body I couldn't ignore."

"Only a few bruises?"

"We'll see how big Taylor's mouth is, how's that?"

***

Billy called T-bone as he headed down 96.

"I need to swap my car tonight. For something nobody'll notice. Whatcha got for me?"

"You ain't tom-cattin', are you? Heard the sheriff's secretary's got the hots for you."

"Get real. She's got the hots for anything male. And where'd you hear that, anyway?"

"Maggie-pie, o'course. She thinks it's funny as hell."

"She would. She's not the one fendin' off a barracuda. So whatcha got for me?"

"I can fix you up, com'on over. Uh, just out of curiosity, you ain't fixin' to do something gonna get your ass blown off, are you?"

"Tell you about it when I get there. I'm on my way already."

Billy returned home satisfied. The car was freshly washed and Jake was still vacuuming, Riley beside him.

"Son! I didn't say suck the carpet up, you can stop now!" Billy came up behind him.

"Oh!" Jake started. "Sorry, didn't hear you."

"How many times have you done this?"

"I don't know, lost count. I did stop for a while, to wash the car, but then I thought one more vacuum couldn't hurt. It was something to do. What the *hell* is that? Where's your Mustang?"

"Horse-traded with your Uncle T-bone."

"You got rooked." The old Chevy truck had originally been purple. You could tell if you looked inside the bed. Now it was some color between black and gray, a flat neutral shade that resembled gun-metal. On a gun that hadn't been oiled or maintained worth a damn. The tatters in the upholstery stuck out like a bad haircut.

"Oh, I don't know. Reminds me of the old truck I drove while I was fixin' up your Mustang."

"That's carryin' nostalgia a little too far."

"Yeah, I hated that truck. But this one runs like a son-of-a-bitch. It'll work real good for tonight, who'd even look at it twice? Just somebody's old huntin' truck. So what're y'all plannin' for tonight?"

"You think it's tonight?"

"Oh, yeah, Taylor even swapped shifts with somebody to be sure he's workin'. And if that don't scream by itself, I don't know what does."

"Field dance. Tyler Stewart's house."

"That's off Cold Creek, right?"

"Yeah."

"Okay. Here's what's happenin'. And nobody's ever gonna know it except you, me, the Sheriff, and Taylor. Understand?"

"Taylor. That means the whole town."

"Hell, no it don't. Not this time."

"What about Mom and T-bone?"

Billy sighed. "Well, that kinda goes without sayin'. I can't not tell your mother, don't have that right. And I'm not jokin' when I call Jack your uncle T-bone, he loves you, loves your mom, he's family. I'll owe him the rest of my life for the way he's looked out for y'all the time I wasn't here. And besides that, he's all over the place, all the time, and I can use another pair of eyes on the lookout for you. So T-bone's gon' be staying here, 'cause Maggie definitely can't go. Now, she might not give any fight about that, and then again, she might. I'm honestly not sure how she'll react. But Jack's about the only person I trust to keep her here. And knowing he's got to keep her here's 'bout the only thing I can think of that'll keep him out of it. So I figure it's a trade-off. Beats handcuffing 'em, anyway."

"And you think Mom's not gonna run all over T-bone?"

"Not this time she won't, not over this. It's a guy thing."

Chapter Thirty-Two

Billy pulled out onto Highway 80 in the beat-up Chevy truck. The sheriff sat in the passenger seat beside him. He hung back to let Jake get a half mile or so in front. Maggie hadn't argued, but she was wearing a hole in the floor. Riley followed her every step. That had been some instant bonding. Even with Maggie's seeming acquiescence, Jack kept an eagle eye on her.

Billy's phone sat open on speaker on the truck's tattered front seat. Jake's phone sat open on speaker in the '66 Mustang. The headlights of the borrowed truck, out of sync with each other, skewered a bit sideways as they cut into the total darkness of the late October evening.

"Dad?"

"Right behind you, son. We're here, don't worry."

"That rat-trap you're in's not gonna break down on you, is it?"

"What's the matter, you don't trust your Uncle T-bone? Just get through town. You might not see us after you get on open road, but we'll be there. Look for the crazy-ass headlights."

Small laugh. "Yeah, I noticed that. Just don't run off the road, please, are they good enough for that?"

"Oh, yeah."

They ran through town, picking up speed as they passed the 45 miles an hour zone and hit open Highway 80, running through alternate pools of shadow and darker shadow. About three-quarters of the way to Jake's right turn onto Cold Creek Road, a big, dark SUV with the fluorescent decals and distinctive roof accessories of an enforcement vehicle pulled out of a dirt farm road and turned behind Jake. It gained speed silently. No swirling blue lights, no siren.

"Dad?"

"I see him, son. Just stay steady. Pull over as soon as he flashes you, now."

"Hate soundin' like a wuss, but damn, I'm nervous."

"Good. Stay that way."

Billy braked suddenly. He and the sheriff swore as a van pulled out of a driveway in front of them, speeding up gradually to a cautious 40 miles an hour.

"Shit!"

"Dad?"

"Car pulled out in front of us. We're coming, where's Taylor?"

"He's—oh, hell, there's the flashers."

"Don't argue, whatever he says. We'll be there in a few seconds."

Billy started to pull around the van but it was a blind curve and he had to pull back behind.

"Won't help Jake if we're dead, Billy."

"I know." He saw a chance to pass and ignored the double yellow lines. He pulled out and bulleted past the van, gaining more speed once he pulled back on the right side of the road.

"Well, there's some righteous citizens right there probably moanin' no cops ever around when you need 'em," Raines drawled.

"Out of the car!" Taylor's voice came over Jake's phone. A car door slammed. Something in Taylor's voice crawled every nerve in Billy's body. It wasn't the disciplined voice of law enforcement, firm and calm even when loud. It was excited, tense, keyed, maybe even a little high. The voice of a man savoring something he'd been anticipating for a long time.

It wasn't Billy's imagination, either. Beside him, the sheriff ordered, "Floor it."

"Taylor! Christ, Taylor, what the *hell*—" Jake's voice. Scared to death. No mistaking that.

A body thumped against a car. There they were, on a wide shoulder fronting a pasture. Billy saw Jake in the headlight. His back was pushed against the side of the car. Taylor waved a gun in his face.

"Motherfucker!" The sheriff reached for the door handle. Billy slammed to a stop beside the Tahoe, half on and half off the road.

"You get your asses away from here before I run you in for interference with a law officer!" Taylor didn't even look around.

Billy reached him first, even with the Sheriff's head start. He grabbed Taylor's wrist and hand and bent downward. The gun aimed at the ground. For just a moment. Then Billy's hand pushed and angled, and the gun poked straight into Taylor's crotch.

"Drop it, Taylor! Drop it or I'll make you blow your own balls off!"

"Breakin' my wrist! You're breakin' my wrist!" The gun fell to the ground. Billy pulled Taylor's arm up behind his back, shoved hard, and slammed him into the side of the car. He held him in position with his own body, grabbed the back of Taylor's neck and head-slammed him into the car roof. Blood spurted, black in the darkness of the night.

Billy leaned close to Taylor's ear.

"Next time you come within a hundred yards of Jake or Maggie, they'll find another deputy on a dirt road with his head blown off, *do you understand me*?"

"Billy!" The sheriff came up behind. "Let go. My turn."

Billy slammed Taylor's head down again and backed off. Taylor slumped against the car. Then he pulled himself up and turned.

"Sheriff! Thank God! He tried to *kill* me, I'm pressin' charges!"

"Damn, Billy, I sure hope you didn't put a dent in that car. Car like that, that'd be a shame."

"Sheriff! Didn't you *hear* me, didn't you *see* that?"

"You know what I heard, Taylor? Know what I saw? I saw you pull out of a side road and follow a car without probable cause. Which you pulled over without a siren—and I know that because—"

Raines leaned over, opened Jake's door, and reached across for the phone.

"I know that because I didn't hear one. And drivin' up, I saw you holding a kid against a car door waving a gun in his face. Not just any kid, either—Rockland Academy's star athlete and valedictorian. Without probable cause. 'Cause I heard every word you said and every word you didn't. Just like I heard Jake. Now that's what I saw and heard."

"The gun was on safety! And he's got crack in that car! I know he does!"

"And you know that how?"

"Got a tip."

"Love to know who that snitch is. Now, what exactly were you lookin' for? This, maybe?" The sheriff held up the plastic baggie. "This one, the one any fool could see came from that bust you had last week on 16? The one you didn't turn in?"

"That's—that's—see, it was there! That crack was in that car! I told you!"

"Taylor, you didn't turn in evidence. You planted it on an innocent kid. You pulled him over with no probable cause, without proper protocol. You *pulled your gun on a kid!* And you just turned in your resignation, effective immediately. Or I'll have the other four bags analyzed right along with this one and you know damn well that'll show they were cut from the same batch. And believe me, those two little rednecks you busted'll get offered a *really* good deal if they'll testify they had five bags instead of four when you busted 'em."

"You can't do that to me!"

"Watch me."

"I'm pressin' charges against Brayton, didn't you hear me?"

"Go ahead. He's been with me all evenin'."

"You—you—this ain't regulation, I got rights, you can't do this. *Do you know who I am?*"

Clint Raines grabbed Taylor around the throat, and pushed him back against the car again.

"I know you're a dirty cop, Taylor, a disgrace should never have been wearin' a badge and you're finally, thank God, out of my department. I know I don't give a flyin' *shit* about followin' regulations or any of your *rights*. Dirty cops don't have any, not as far as I'm concerned."

Raines broke off, reached down, and grabbed Taylor's flashlight from his utility belt. He clicked it on and angled it for a view at Taylor's face.

"And just look at that! You're high, Taylor, your eyes are screamin' it. On duty, handlin' a gun. And how fuckin' long has *that* been going on? Give me your keys, the Tahoe's goin' back with me. And you give me your ankle gun right now, right along with that department phone." The sheriff reached up and jerked the radio mic from Taylor's shoulder. "And just look here, radio's flat turned off. Out of contact while on duty. Wonder why'd you do something like that, Taylor? Billy, you got that Glock he dropped?"

"But—but—you can't just *leave* me out here!"

"Sure I can. You get back in the Tahoe, you'll bleed all over it. Head wounds bleed a lot. Now, Jake, come over here and chat with me a bit. Let's give your dad a few minutes with Taylor. You know, Taylor, Jake's *dad*—the man who just watched you wave a gun in his son's face, probably wonderin' what would'a happened here with nobody to see it if he hadn't taken Riley home with him this afternoon."

"Sheriff! Sheriff, don't let him near me, he's gonna *kill* me, you know that!"

Billy twisted Taylor's arm behind his back, so fast Taylor never saw it coming. Billy hissed in his ear.

"Don't come near him. Don't come near Maggie. Ever. I'm career army, Taylor. Trained by the best. Nobody'd prove a thing."

He let go and walked over to Jake. He reached over and tousled Jake's hair.

"You okay? Holdin' out on me, huh, you never told me you were goin' to be the valedictorian."

"Not a lot of competition there, Dad."

"So, you okay?"

Shaky breath. "Yeah. Yeah, I'm all right. But I just want to go home right now."

"You feel like drivin'?"

"Yeah, I'm—" Jake broke off. "That's a lie. No, I don't. I really don't feel like drivin'. Keys are in the car. You drive home. But what about T-bone's clunker?"

"I'll pull it over on the shoulder, we'll come back for it."

Billy glanced back. Taylor sat slumped on the ground holding a bloody handkerchief to his forehead.

"Maybe Taylor'll still be here when we do. Without the sheriff. That'd be nice. Me, Taylor, your Uncle T-bone."

Taylor's head jerked up. He stood and started walking down the shoulder of Highway 80.

Chapter Thirty-Three

It might not have been the biggest fit ever thrown in Big John's study, but it ranked in the top five. Maybe even in the top three. Davis Brown sat erect in one of the armchairs while Big John threw his fit. His eyes flashed but he didn't interrupt. He knew better. Davis Taylor slouched miserably in another chair. He held an ice bag to his forehead.

Big John stopped for breath and Davis Brown jumped in.

"You hold it, there, John! Just *look* at my grandson! Don't you see what that son-of-a-bitch did to him? You just gon' let that go? Let somebody do that to one of ours?"

Big John stalked over to the speaker's chair.

"You shut that whinin' stupid mouth of yours! He ain't one of *mine!* He's lucky I haven't killed him myself! Of all the *stupid, fucked up, moronic* things to do—"

He whirled in mid-tirade and swooped down on Taylor.

"What the *fuck* were you *thinkin'*, you stupid son-of-a-bitch?"

"It was your idea! You said—"

"*My idea!* Except you didn't wait on me to tell you *my idea*, give you what I wanted planted! You had to go out on your own, use some *shit* you got from a *bust!* You're supposed to be a goddamn lawman, remember? We all know you're not, but goddammit, you're supposed to *fuckin' act like it*! Now both of you get your asses out of here and let me see what I can salvage out of this!"

Davis Brown stood up.

"John, you got no right talkin' to me like—"

"*Get out!*" The shrillness factor hit a ten on that one.

"Com'on, son, we better head to Dublin, you probably need stitches for those gashes."

"Good! Hope to hell they do it without Novocain!" John shouted out the door after them. The rich, drawling voice came from a chair in the shadows, soothing as warm velvet.

"Feel better now?"

"Stupid, stupid, son-of-a-bitch! And why aren't you yellin'? Especially as much trouble as you had keepin' the idiot on CPS, I know it wasn't easy. Ever since that fucker Raines got elected—never had anybody cause me this much trouble. 'Cept Brayton, of course, but that's gettin' handled. And I'm about sick of it, tired of waltzin' around."

"Ever think it might be time to pull back a little?"

"Pull back? I don't pull back."

"Times change, power shifts. The days of the One Man Show might be over, that ever cross your mind?"

"Only one other person got enough guts to say something like that to me, you know that?"

"Yeah, I know. Part of the reason we're valuable. Makes you be a little bit honest, anyway."

John walked behind his desk and sat. He slumped a bit in fact, something he wouldn't have done in front of any other human on earth. Well, except one. His tirade had exhausted him. The years were catching up. He'd built an empire and every now and then, he felt it shift a little, minute slippages like mini-quakes before the fault line gave way. Occasionally, not often, he even admitted it to himself. He was seventy-five, with high blood pressure and borderline diabetes, though he seldom admitted that to himself either. But he couldn't deny the shaky shortness of breath that overcame him when he allowed himself to give free rein to the rages that were now beyond his ability to control.

And all for what, for whom? Well, partially for the man with the velvet voice coming from the shadows. In the end, blood called to blood. This blood was from the wrong side of the blanket, but that seemed to matter less and less. He'd never thought he'd consider the boy anything but a useful tool, but he must be getting soft in his old age. And wondered yet again how it was that nobody'd ever tumbled onto his paternity. It was in the cheek bones, in the height, in the sheer force of personality that preceded him into a room. Just as it had always preceded John himself. Yeah, who'd have thought. A son to be proud of. He'd never have believed he'da said that.

Once again, he came close to regretting the speed he'd removed eighteen-year-old Billy Brayton from the equation. Billy'd rejected one recruitment offer but they might could've won him over. Which brought him back to Jake Rubin—no, officially Jake Brayton now, wasn't that a hoot, after all the trouble he'd gone taken to make sure that name died when Billy supposedly did—and what an asset he'd have been. New blood, next generation. Well, shit. All right, so he'd made some mistakes over the years. Didn't mean he had to admit to 'em.

"It's just as well," the rich voice spoke again. "Taylor's started using. Hasn't been going on long, not even long enough for me to be sure. Till tonight. You noticed, didn't you?"

"He is? Guess I was too damn mad to notice anything much. Got to get a handle on my temper, I guess."

"Been getting worse, that's for sure."

"You don't have to agree with me."

Deep laugh. It matched the soothing voice.

"That'd be a first. Well, let me get movin'. See what's shakin'. I don't know what kind of story the sheriff's goin' to put out. Or even if he will. Might just let Taylor dig himself deeper, see what bullshit he comes up with. I'm bettin' he'll have gotten jumped by four or five suspects he pulled over and can't keep workin' with guys don't provide proper backup when a deputy's ass is on the line. Yeah, that sounds about right."

"That's pretty good. Probably exactly what he'll put out."

"I have my moments."

The tall man moved into the light and headed to the door.

"Son?" Now, where the hell had that come from?

"Yeah?"

Well, shit. Guess it wouldn't be the end of the world to admit it. "Proud of you, boy."

"Damn! Better watch it, I'll start callin' you Daddy in public."

"Ain't that proud."

"Now, why doesn't that surprise me? See ya later, Pops."

"And don't call me Pops!"

* * *

Billy glanced over at Jake on the ride home. He'd been lucky, *they'd* been lucky this time. Time to reinforce the armor. Jake wouldn't be happy a bit, but he'd survive. No help for it. He cleared his throat.

"Jake."

"Sir?"

Billy smiled. That southern raisin'. Couldn't beat it. You responded to a question from a lady with "ma'am," to a question from a man with "sir." No Southerner ever shook it.

"Son, here's the thing. Like I told you this afternoon—family's the weak link. You're the weak link. It'd be better if you weren't alone with anybody else. Like for the rest of the year, until you take off for college. Except Ben, of course. And even at that, y'all don't need to be out by yourselves. You need to stay with a crowd."

"Why?"

"Because anytime you're alone with somebody, it's their word against yours. About anything."

"Dad, I grew up with those kids!"

"Whose parents were mostly born and raised in Rockland County and who might have connections with Big John we don't know about. And I swear I'm not trying to ruin your social life, but you really, really, don't need to be alone with any of the girls. Any of 'em. Of all accusations, rape and sexual assault by their very nature mean it's one person's word against another."

"You're kiddin', right? We're all like—"

"Yeah, well, I spent every Saturday for four years workin' for Jim Ellis at the Chevron, too, but it was his name listed as the witness on those armed robbery charges. Would you ever have believed tonight could happen, Jake?"

"No."

"But it did. So, can you humor me? Until we get through this year and you get off to whatever school you're goin' to?"

"Yeah." Long sigh. "Yeah, if you think it's better."

"I do. I wouldn't ask for anything like this from you if I didn't. I know it seriously sucks. I know it's your senior year. And I'm really sorry about that."

"It's okay. Like you said, it's not that much longer."

"So, any progress on decidin' where you're goin'? What you think your major might be?"

Jake hadn't declared firm future intentions as yet, or as firm as any eighteen-year-old ever had. Too smart, Billy figured. Too many options for that brain and personality.

"Maybe," Jake said.

"Really? Don't keep me in suspense."

"Well, tonight—yeah, I was scared, and yeah, it was—*dirty*—gettin' set up like that. And I won't lie, I didn't know it was possible to be that scared, watchin' that gun wave around in my face. But you know what? It was—well, it was still a rush, know what I mean? And watchin' you, I mean, you knew exactly what to do. Sort of like watching an old *Dirty Harry* movie. Only I was in it, not just watchin'. And you were *tough*, the real thing, not movie tough. But so controlled, somehow. So I think when we get home I'm headin' to my room to get on my laptop and re-check some stuff. Like which school's got the best criminal justice program."

"Say what?"

Jake laughed. "Well, you came to the party late, Dad. Never got to pass out those cigars. But you're here now, man. So congratulations, I'm a clone."

"Four years is a long time. You might change your mind."

"Maybe. But I wouldn't bet on it if I were you."

Chapter Thirty-Four

The two men leaned back against the hoods of their cars, parked out of sight behind the overgrown hedges hiding abandoned church yard of Mt. Olive Baptist Church. They were engaged in that ancient past-time of men—waiting on a woman.

There, finally. Gravel crunched under incoming tires. A trim figure bounced out and hopped up to sit on the fender of her own car.

"Okay, folks, this special-called meeting of the new generation of the Kincaid Cartel is now in session." She moved too far back and her rear hit the hood. She jumped back down. "Damn, that engine's hot!"

The men laughed.

"Think you'd remember that by now, you do it every damn time." Rich, velvet drawl.

"I have short-term memory loss."

"Like a barracuda."

"I don't think barracudas are noted for their memories."

"Just their teeth."

"Don't feel the same," said a third voice.

"What doesn't?"

"Meeting in broad daylight. In the *mornings*. Meetings like this need *night time*, you know? The dark. Thunder. Lightning."

The woman laughed. "Sorry. Not as easy for me to slip out at one a.m. as it used to be."

"A sacrifice you gladly make for the cause."

"It has its moments." The woman grinned.

"Okay, com'on, com'on. I got to get back. Big John's really losing it, you know. Threw a temper tantrum Saturday night after the Taylor fiasco 'bout worse than any I've seen. Thought for a few minutes there he'd finish the job for Brayton."

"Couldn't happen to a nicer guy," the woman drawled.

"Taylor or Big John?"

"Works for both the bastards, as far as I'm concerned."

"Doesn't bother you a bit, watching Big John deteriorate, does it?" asked the velvet voice.

The woman shrugged. "Hey. We're all in it for the money. That's it. None of us ever made any claim otherwise, we're just like him, you know. Only reason he trusts us even as much as he does, only thing he understands."

"So you got the next one set?"

"Oh, sure. For a hell of a lot more than he has any idea it's worth. Man really should keep up with the rise in street prices, you know."

"Like I said, he's really losing it."

"Not fast enough."

* * *

The sheriff grinned. Aurelia Andrews had Billy cornered in the hall outside his half-open door. She'd fixated on Billy in the months he'd been with the Department. Her reputation as a femme fatale was at stake.

Billy finally made good his escape and knocked.

"Hey, got a minute?"

"Sure."

Billy carefully closed the door. He wiped his forehead as he sat down.

Clint Raines leaned forward at his desk and sotto-whispered. "You still alive there? Got all your parts?"

Billy leaned forward and did the same. "What the *hell* is it with that woman?"

"You, right now. Don't worry, somebody'll come along snag her attention in a few weeks or so, she'll leave you alone."

"I thought she and Ricky O'Donnell were an item anyway. Didn't they move in together last month?"

"Yeah, but variety's the spice of life to those two. Rumor has it they're into the swappin' scene. You might not be the only family member on the hit list. And she likes breakin' in the young ones, too, been surprised she ain't tried to latch on to Jake, much as he's in and out of here now. Don't know how she's ignorin' that build."

"Coulda gone all day without knowing that, thanks. No other qualified secretaries in town?"

"Oh hell, son! I been married twenty-five years. Got to get some vicarious entertainment somewhere. So what's up?"

"I need to get my hands on something without everybody in Turkey Creek knowin' about it."

"Well, if you can do that, you're a better man than me. Whatcha need?"

"An old file."

"How old?"

"Pretty damn old. Forty plus years old."

"Good luck with that. We ain't even got most of the files from Roy Lee's time, let along any from ol' Bo's."

"You're shittin' me!"

"You been in the big leagues too long, Billy. You don't think Bo Franklin or Roy Lee Rollins goin' leave any files laying around might come back to haunt 'em, do you? Particularly any that old, pre-computer . Even if they *had* wanted to keep 'em, their organizational skills weren't what you'd call top-notch, they pretty much had no system whatsoever. We'd never find what you're lookin' for, even if it still existed. And I'm pretty sure it don't."

Billy made a disgusted sound in his throat.

"You're right. Must have been havin' an Alzheimer's moment, that was stupid."

"So what'd you want?"

"Personal. Maggie's been mad at her mother her whole life. You know she killed herself when Maggie was two, don't you? That one of the local stories you know?"

"Know that's the story."

"She's had her mother on her mind a lot lately, thought it'd be a help for her to see the file. Don't know what I was thinking."

"Bullshit. I don't know all of what you're thinking, either, but I'm damned insulted. Wouldn't have thought you'd think *I* was that stupid. So whatcha got? Anything concrete?"

"You could pretend to believe me."

"I could grow wings and fly home, too, but I ain't expectin' it to happen. You got anything concrete?"

"Not yet." Billy wasn't about to admit he had the whole story—or most of it—straight from the purported suicide's mouth. "Maggie's never been satisfied with the suicide thing, thinks no mother would leave a two-year-old baby with a man like John Kincaid. And Aunt Lulu—that's—"

"Lamar's mama. Yeah, I know who Miss Luellen is, what she did for a livin' most of her life. Now that's a deep-runnin' river, could you get her to break the dam. Considers Maggie another child, too. She tell you anything?"

"She doesn't believe Magdalene Kincaid killed herself. But she doesn't have anything we can use. Or doesn't know she does. Or hasn't told me yet. Take your pick, probably a combination of all of the above."

"But you're workin' on it. Miss Luellen like you?"

"Well, she'll never really believe any man's good enough for Maggie, but she's decided I'm probably close as any man'll ever come."

"Well, see what you can do there. She probably knows a lot she doesn't realize she knows. And I'm sure she knows a lot she *does* know she knows, she just don't wanta talk about it."

"I'm a patient man."

A fresh burst of new voices sounded in the outer office. The Sheriff motioned toward his door.

"Now that's what you call fortuitous, Alec Wimberly coming in. Been meaning to talk to you 'bout Alec. Whatcha think about runnin' CPS by him, see if he might want to do some canine training?"

"I think you got to quit gettin' in my head. Yeah, Alec's the best potential cop you got, no contest. But don't you think you might ought to talk to Lamar first? He is head of CPS, you know."

"Oh, I know."

"But you don't much like it?"

"Do you?"

"Jury's still out on that. He's Aunt Lulu's son, got to be a good soul in there somewhere."

"For a lawman, you're sure naïve."

"Well, that's a new one, don't think anybody's called me that since I was eighteen. Maybe ever."

"Go call him in, why don't you?"

* * *

"Sit down, Alec. Billy and I got something we want to run by you."

"Sir?" Alec sat.

"Whatcha hear 'bout last Saturday night?"

Alec grinned. "In connection with what? Or should I say who?"

"And what's the who puttin' out as to the reason his Tahoe's sitting in the parking lot and why he's sporting five stitches in his forehead?"

"Well, he was in the fight of his life, bunch of drunk rednecks he pulled over Highway 80 drivin' like maniacs. And would you believe, they jumped him? Fought like a wildcat now, but one man can just do so much. 'Specially when he's callin' in for help and nobody comes, I mean, puttin' your life on the line's one thing, but damn, who could work for a department when you can't depend on your backup?"

"That's pretty good," Billy admitted.

"Yeah, classic Taylor. Y'all goin' to tell me the whole story?"

"Maybe later."

"So which one of you put the splits in his head?"

"That would be me."

"I'da paid money to watch that."

"Well, speakin' of money, how'd you like to make a little bit more?" Raines asked. "Not *much* more, mind you, but still. We've got an offer for you, Alec. What about moving to CPS? You interested?"

"Am I *interested?* Are you *serious?*"

"Well, now, before you get too excited, remember. Means six weeks of K-9 training down in Savannah, only coming home on the weekends. How's your wife goin' to feel about that? Present circumstances being what they are and all."

Alec's face assumed the expression of a little boy who'd been offered the candy shop and then reminded it was subject to his mother's approval.

"I've wanted K-9 for a long time, something not everybody can put on their résumé, and Anna Grace knows it. And we've still got three months or more to go till the baby's due, and she's real near her mama and daddy, so even though I'd hate to leave her, I wouldn't feel like she didn't have anybody around."

"You shouldn't feel like that anyway, Alec," Billy said. "We look after our own, you know that."

"Yeah, but it's not the same. I want to say yes, right now, but I have to talk to Anna Grace. And I really think she'll say yes, but I don't want to commit till she does. And I don't think she'll have to think about it very long, but I just don't know. Can I have a day or two?"

"Sure. Y'all take all the time you need."

Chapter Thirty-Five

Billy left the office in a disgruntled mood. The sheriff was right. He'd been in the big leagues too long. No way a file that old in a department that small could be pulled out of the stacks just like *that*, not to mention it would only contain what Big John wanted it to contain in the first place. But the Sheriff was right about something else, too. Aunt Lulu was the key. And as a fringe benefit, it was lunchtime.

* * *

"Well, timed it just right, didn't you, boy? You still country enough to eat salmon croquettes?" Aunt Lulu ushered him in the door. Salmon croquettes was a Southern specialty. Not only was the canned salmon delicious when mixed with the proper portions of cornmeal, flour, and egg and fried in small patties, it was also cheap. "With a side of greens and black-eyed peas?"

"You got to ask? Don't believe you still cook like that for just one person, though."

"Eatin' right's one of the things keeps you goin'. 'Sides, I still like cookin'. And Lord knows, you gettin' to be a real regular. What you want to pump me about this time?"

Billy wrinkled his nose. "I hate bein' obvious."

"Gotta get some benefit outta getting old. You still on that Miss Magdalene thing, ain't you?"

Billy sat down in front of the full plate Aunt Lulu placed on the table.

"If we could prove Big John killed his wife, well, that's one of the few things might get a Rockland County jury stirred up enough to take him down."

"Might be one of not a few things Big John'd love to kill you over, too, you know."

"Been quite a few things in my life folks'd love to kill me over. Sort of goes with the job description. Were you already workin' for him when they got married?"

"Oh, yeah. Had been for 'bout two years or so. Didn't have much choice 'bout it. Had three young'uns to take care of with a daddy not much good for nothing 'cept drinkin' and shootin' craps. Got hisself shot over one of them crap games. And then Lamar come along, too. Didn't even have the decency to keep hisself alive till he was born."

"Big John bein' who and what he is, it occurred to me if Magdalene tried to leave him, that'd be guaranteed to send him over the edge. Especially if she tried to take Maggie. Not because he loved them, because he owned them. They were his. What you think 'bout that idea?"

Aunt Lulu, in the process of raising her tea glass to her lips, set it back down carefully. She shrugged.

"Good a guess as any, I reckon."

"Were you and Magdalene real close?"

"Son, she was the lady of the house and I was the maid. How close you think we were?"

"I think you were two women pretty much at the mercy of a man they both detested, a man who could have—and I'm pretty sure did—make their lives miserable. Misery loves company. Wasn't she a good bit younger than he was?"

"Yeah, 'bout ten years. Her folks tried to talk her out of it, but young girls bein' what they are—" Aunt Lulu shrugged again.

"And him bein' such a charmer when he wanted to be. And even then, one of the most powerful men in the county. Made her feel like a Princess in a fairy tale, I bet."

Aunt Lulu's head came up at that.

"You gettin' scary here, son. Men ain't supposed to understand women that well."

"And then she married him. And found out there were all sorts of secret doors and windows in the castle she wasn't supposed to open. And havin' opened 'em, found out she didn't like what was behind 'em very much. And then one day, she opened one she just couldn't tolerate and so she tried to run—"

"Billy. Women talk like that. Men don't. Not about fairy tales and castles and secret doors and windows. You almos' sound like—"

"What do I sound like?"

"Not what. Who. You sound almost like you repeatin' what—" Aunt Lulu broke off. "Well, if I didn't know better, I'd think she'd been talking to you herself. Magdalene."

Billy took he last bite of the salmon on his plate and sipped his tea before speaking again.

"Aunt Lulu, did you know I hold the record for the longest stay at Clayton Chapel? Didn't know that myself till I came back home, but all the kids sure as hell did. Don't take any credit for it, I was asleep most of it. Stoned out of my head, in fact, only time I ever smoked weed. And even when I thought I'd woken up, I figured I must not have. Because when I woke up, I had a conversation with—"

"Magdalene Kincaid," Aunt Lulu whispered.

"Though I never made the connection till I told Jake the whole story, tryin' to keep the kids away from there. Not 'cause of all the ghost stories, actually, 'cause of the investigator found dead near there. When I did remember, just takin' a chance it might happen again—"

"You went back. And she was still there."

"You're sure takin' this seriously. Most folks'd either be laughing their heads off or trying to have me committed."

"Son, try and remember who you talkin' to. You ain't gon' see no movie like *The Amityville Horror* got black folks livin' in no horror house with no ghosts and demons. That's cause we be gettin' our asses out of there. Believe it was Richard Pryor I heard doin' a comedy routine 'bout that, years ago. One of the funniest men ever lived, one of the funniest routines ever done. But he was sho' 'nuff right. We got too much sense for that."

"Well, she wasn't—isn't—scary at all. Except when she does what she calls 'loses control' and looks like she did when she—crossed over, I believe that's what she called it. Instead of what she looked like when she was alive. Which is beautiful. Maggie looks very much like her, doesn't she?"

"Spittin' image. So if you been talkin' to Magdalene, why you need to talk to me?"

"Because she told me about it. And then again, she didn't. I know she took Maggie and ran, and I know he caught her. And I know he gave Maggie to ol' Bo—and I don't even want to think about how scared a two-year-old must have been, jerked away from her mama and handed over to that bastard, or how much she must have screamed—and I know he took her back to the old hunting cabin and killed her. But I don't know why she ran in the first place, she said he'd hurt someone she cared for very much but it wasn't her secret to tell. Thought that meant Maggie at first, but that doesn't wash, a two-year-old wouldn't remember anything anyway, so you couldn't count that as a secret—"

Billy broke off. The changing expressions on Aunt Lulu's face told their own story.

"You," he said. "Of course. Nothing you could do, no one to tell, no place to run. 'Cause you had kids to take care of with no help from their daddy—and believe me, no one understands that better than me, that's my mama for sure—and no one else in the county would hire you if he put out the word not to. She walked in on it, didn't she?"

* * *

In Aunt Lulu's mind, she went back to that room, bent over a chair. Big John moved behind her, grunting like the pig he was. She'd carefully schooled herself to wear a stoic, expressionless face during such times. It helped, at least a little bit. It sent her into a secret room in her brain where this wasn't really happening. Turn of a door knob, crack of a door. Startled gasp. Her only consolation—no woman looking at her face could never mistake the situation for anything other than what it was. Magdalene certainly hadn't.

"How many years did it go on?"

"From the time I started workin' for him. Until Miss Magdalene was found dead. Never laid a finger on me after that."

"Of course. Lamar's his son, isn't he?"

"Yes," she whispered.

"John knows that?"

"He knows. My husband—I had a little back house behind the main house, me and the kids, part of my pay. That house was the main reason I went to work for him in the first place, better'n anything I could get on my own. Wasn't 'bout to live off welfare and social services, even though all that was around already by then. My husband'd moved out on us right before John hired me, in with a new party girl not bothered with having to take care of young'uns."

"Does Lamar know?"

"I don't know. I've tried his whole life to make sure he didn't, but I just don't know."

"So what do you remember? About that night?"

Aunt Lulu closed her eyes again. "Lord, son, spent over forty years trying to forget. She knew, you see—knew it wasn't anything I wanted to do, knew it was what I had to do for my family to survive."

* * *

Echoes of shouts flew across her brain, spilling from her mouth. She'd never thought she'd tell this story. She'd never thought anyone would believe it, let alone care. She knew Billy believed. And cared.

"How dare you! You sick son-of-a-bitch! To use someone like that! To control someone like that! When you know she's got no choice!"

"Christ, woman, man's got to do something, cold bitch like you in his bed."

"You can call it anything you want, John, it's rape!"

Big John casually zipped his pants and brushed past Magdalene.

"Good God, woman, it's nothing important, get over it, both of you. I got to go meet somebody, be home by supper."

Magdalene looked at Lulu as the door slammed.

"Go to the back house and stay there. I'm getting Maggie's bag and going to my parents. But don't worry. I'll be back. And I'll get all of us out of here."

* * *

"And then what?"

"And I went to the back house and stayed there. But she never came back. Sheriff's car pulled into the yard 'bout an hour later. Ol' Bo. And Maggie, screamin' like she'd never stop. I ran to get her, Ol' Bo told me 'Git that brat in the house and shut her up.'"

Aunt Lulu raised her tea glass to her lips. Her hands shook. "I figure his meetin' didn't take long as he thought. Or else he got to thinkin' real hard and turned around. Must have passed her. And she never came home. John didn't neither that night. Not till the next day. After they'd found her body. Story he put out was he'd spent all night lookin' for her."

"I'm so sorry, Aunt Lulu. Not just for Magdalene, for you. For all he did to you, for how you must have felt, knowing in your soul what happened and no one to tell who'd believe you."

Aunt Lulu shrugged. "Life, boy. Life'll get you every time. Couldn't give up. 'Cause now I had *four* young'uns I had to feed, and another one with nobody but me to take care of her. Nobody that gave a damn about her, anyway. Magdalene's parents made some noise 'bout trying to get Maggie away from him, but they weren't no match for him. Not even with the Clayton name. Old family, you know. Most of their money and power done gone. So now you know. Whatcha think you gon' do 'bout it?"

"Damned if I know. Involving you like it does, sort of puts a crimp in my style. Because I would never do anything to cause you any more pain over this than you've already been through. Thought I could get the old file and go from there, but that was really stupid, sheriff says all the old files are gone."

"No, they ain't."

"Excuse me?"

"The one on Magdalene ain't gone, son. Sittin' right there in his study, has been for years. So's the one on you, showed up right after we buried you."

"Battle trophies," Billy said. "To the victor go the spoils."

"Yeah, somethin' like that."

"His study. Shit. So I'm still royally screwed."

"Right often, I'd hope, as many years as you and Maggie been apart."

Billy laughed and felt a faint tinge of red creeping up his cheeks.

"I don't believe you can joke about it, considerin' all the hell men have put you through in your life, Aunt Lulu."

"My husband wasn't always a no-good drunk, son. Would'na ever married him if he had been. I got memories of some good years, some good lovin'."

"Well, I'm glad. You sure got enough bad ones."

"I do, and that's a fact. But I ain't the only woman in the world been in that boat. And I'm still alive to tell about it."

Chapter Thirty-Six

Billy knocked on the door of Nate Bennett's old farm house outside of Barnesville. He'd gotten some names from the state K-9 Training Center in Savannah and made some calls. Plans had changed. Billy didn't have time to train a puppy himself. Taylor'd joined the Macon PD, so he wasn't riding Rockland County roads throwing his official weight around, but he still lived in Rockland County.

Billy wanted a trained dog in the house as soon as possible. Cross-trained, in fact, would be pretty damn good if he could find one. Narcotics and guard-attack. Such a dog wouldn't be cheap but hey, it was only money. Billy wanted a dog sitting in Jake's front car seat. Yesterday. Jake couldn't take a dog to school with him, but he could take one everywhere else, that'd help ease up a little on the restrictions Billy'd felt compelled to impose on Jake's social life for safety reasons. If Jake didn't change his mind about majoring in criminal justice—and Billy was sure hoping to hell he did—then for all practical purposes, by the time he graduated from high school in the spring, he'd already be a trained dog handler. Trained in a few other things, too. Like the Glock Billy'd already bought to go under the Christmas tree. Jake's first serious gun. A hand gun. It wouldn't be as good as a first bike or a first football, but it'd have to do. A big, jovial good ol' boy opened the door, a handsome German Shepard close by his side. Jovial until you got a look at the eyes. Lifelong law enforcement. Those eyes didn't miss a thing.

"Yo, buddy! You Brayton?"

"Yes sir."

"Told you on the phone now, I don't sell my dogs to just anybody. You say you're actual law enforcement yourself? And a trained handler?"

"Sure am."

"Then you know what you're talking about here, you know a dog like you're looking for ain't cheap."

"Damn sure ain't."

"Ain't sellin' one of my dogs to a nervous parent only wants him to check out the kids' bedrooms. I like my dogs a lot better'n I like most folks. They got to be part of the families they go to."

"I'd train a puppy myself if I didn't have a pissed off psycho ex-deputy goin' after my kid to get to me. Already tried to frame him once. And no, I'm not a stupid parent believes everything his kid tells him."

Nate smiled. Man was good. For sure, that woulda been the next thing he asked.

"And I reckon that's why he's an ex-deputy now, huh?"

"Ex in our county, anyway. Sheriff wasn't real happy. Scuttlebutt has it Macon PD hired him."

"Dog like you want's a lotta dog for a kid to handle." Nate Bennett gave Billy the once-over, coming back to his eyes. "Kid anything like his dad?"

Billy grinned. "He's a clone."

"That a good thing?"

"Not all the time, no. Means he's gonna be a tough son-of-a-bitch to tangle with full-grown, though."

Nate Bennett laughed and stroked his K-9 companion's big, beautiful head. "Sarge, check this guy over. See whatcha think of him."

The dog moved forward and gave Billy a smell-over. Billy held out his hand.

"Hey there. And aren't you a good-lookin' guy?"

"Take him out in the yard. Get acquainted. He's trained in English."

"This dog? He's not yours? I mean your personal dog?"

"All the dogs are mine. Until they belong to somebody else."

The dog trainer stood on the porch, watching the man and the dog. Good voice, firm, calm. Man could put a dog through his paces, for sure. And then play with him. Nate liked that. Dogs weren't machines, you didn't put 'em up when the work day was done and forget about 'em till the next shift like you did your gun.

And Sarge liked Brayton, too. Maybe more than liked him, already.

They were playing tag now. Sarge knew he was playing and not working. He leaped and twirled like a puppy. Brayton laughed, sliding down on the ground beside the dog, grabbing him around the upper body and tussling with him like two kids playing touch football. Oh yeah. The trainer's instincts were intact. Brayton was the one for Sarge. He'd been almost sure just from the phone inquiry. This clinched it, sure 'nuff.

Billy and Sarge walked back up the steps. Sarge's tongue hung out of the side of his mouth. He was a happy boy.

"So. You think you got a dog?"

"I know I got a dog. Got my checkbook with me, and the check'll be good but I came on a weekday on purpose so I could run back into Barnesville and get a certified check if you'd rather. Wouldn't take offense, that's a lot of money."

"How much money you think it'd be, son?"

"A cross-trained dog? Guard-attack and narc? That's a twenty thousand dollar dog, think I'm an idiot don't know the business? And this one's worth every penny."

The trainer grinned. "Oh, you know the business. You didn't, you wouldn't be gettin' this dog. But keep your pennies. He's yours."

Billy started. "Excuse me?"

"He's yours. This dog's not for sale."

"I don't—"

"This dog ain't mine. Belongs to the widow of a retired K-9 officer who died of a heart attack two months ago. He trained Sarge himself, I helped a little. She's in bad health, can't exercise him or play with him, 'bout to have to go into assisted living. Wants Sarge in a family that'll love him. Appreciate him. She says you don't sell family, you just do what's best for 'em. So he's yours."

"The widow of a retired law enforcement officer ain't rich. She's gonna need that money, 'specially if she's 'bout to go into assisted living. Surely you can make her take something?"

"Talked till I was blue in the face, son. But she ain't takin' money for that dog. Said it'd be like selling a child."

"I'm—hell, I don't know what I am."

"One lucky son-of-a-bitch. But that's okay, 'cause that makes Sarge one lucky dog. He wasn't goin' to just anybody, son. I'da kept him myself the right owner hadn't come along. His name's Sergeant Murphy, by the way. Call name Sarge, of course. And yeah, that's the family name. The widow's Miss Mary Ann Murphy. I'll get you her address when she gets settled in her new place, it'd be a nice thing were you to let her know how Sarge's doin' now and again. She loves that dog."

"Get me that address as soon as you get it. Though she might be sorry if you do. 'Cause she just got adopted right along with Sarge. You don't know my wife. Miss Mary Ann just got her an extended family. Hope she likes us."

* * *

Miss Mary Ann liked the Braytons just fine. They took Sarge up to visit her twice during the holiday season between Thanksgiving and Christmas. Maggie brought her down to their house to spend a Saturday after the house was decorated for the holidays so Miss Mary Ann could see Sarge in his new home.

Billy'd never had a Christmas like this one. As a child, Christmas meant Billy and his mom. As an adult, until this year, the holidays were mostly just another day. This year was magic.

Even the Kincaid Cartel and the Agency stayed quiet. Until the first week in January.

Chapter Thirty-Seven

"Well, kids, I missed y'all."

"That s'posed to be a southern accent? Damn glad you ain't in the field, son, you'da got your ass shot off years ago." The Country Justice duo hated fake Southern accents.

"Now that's just rude. Though that's why I never I worked the Deep South even when I was in the field. So you guys ready to get some action going? Gotta love Small Town, USA. Only place in the world where crime takes a holiday. Sort of. So, end of the month?"

"Good Lord willin' and the creek don't rise. "

"Don't know what I'll do for fun and entertainment without you two. Com'on, reconsider. You both got another operation or two in you, I know you do."

"When hell freezes over."

"So, talked to Country Time lately?"

"You know damn well we haven't 'talked' to Country Time at all. Orders, remember?"

"Don't be so literal. And I don't recall orders ever having much influence on you. Or on Country Time."

"How long you been coordinating that boy, anyway?"

"Don't ask. Too long. Bigger headache than you are. Try and stay out of trouble now, y'all hear?"

Lifeline clicked out of the three-way conversation, leaving the agents of Country Justice on the line together.

"God, I can't wait."

"Me, neither. How shocked you think we should act when we meet Country Time?"

"You finally admittin' it, huh?"

"Admit what?"

"You've never said a word, but you got to know who he is."

"You think he's got a clue about us?"

"Doubt it. We've got the edge there, been here too long. Just too damn much coincidence, Billy Brayton walkin' back into town, that kind of background, just strollin' right on in to the Sheriff's Department."

"Yeah. I know."

* * *

"Miss me?" Lifeline asked, checking in on his other charge.

"Like the plague."

"Now, that's just rude. You and Country Justice, I swear, your lives' mission's to make me feel unwanted and unloved."

"You are. The only thing I want from you is a date."

"End of the month. Final details pending. Understand it's one of the biggest the Kincaid Cartel's ever run in."

"Don't keep me in suspense."

"Figure of a thousand kilos been tossed out."

"Then I hope to hell Country Justice's as good as you say they are."

"Woulda been dead a lot of kilos ago if they weren't."

* * *

An Arctic blast and a stalled high pressure system turned the first two weeks of January bitterly cold. Temperatures in Middle Georgia rivaled the Great Lakes temperatures. One thing about a truck, the heater made the cab feel like the tropics in about ten seconds flat. Sarge rode shotgun with Billy. Sarge and Jake were inseparable other than when Jake was in school. When Jake was in school, Sarge rode with Billy. He let Billy know the truck was too damn hot. His tongue hung out over his lower lip as he panted.

"Okay, okay, I get the message!" Billy reached over to turn the heat down and lowered Sarge's window a bit. "Don't drool on the seat, somebody'll complain and you'll get grounded. Or they'll tell us I'll have to put a kennel in the back. Know you don't want to ride around in the back of a truck in the cold and rain, now do you?"

Sarge woofed softly. His expression told Billy clearly the dog knew that was a load of shit.

"Tell you what, we're real near T-bone's. You want to stretch your legs and get a bowl of water you can slurp?"

Short bark of assent.

"And with that enthusiastic response, I s'pose you got to take a leak, too?"

Confirming short bark.

"Damn, boy, you're worse than a toddler. Always something."

Billy turned off Highway 96 and headed down T-bone's road. He spotted T-bone over on the side of one of the mechanic's sheds by a truck he didn't recognize. No surprise there, T-bone was always in a different truck. T-bone slammed the truck door as Sarge bounded out of Billy's truck and raced to Jack.

"Well, hey, guys! Didn't expect to see you!" T-bone started forward. He stopped. "What the hell?"

Sarge came to a full stop and sat abruptly in front of Jack. "What's the matter with you, Sarge?"

Billy stared at T-bone. There was no way, no way in hell, just no way. Except it appeared there was.

"Sarge! Find!"

Sarge stood and moved to the truck. He barked once and sat down by the door.

Billy went cold, a total body coldness that had nothing to do with the current frigid temperature. He walked to the truck in rapid strides and jerked the door open. An open satchel full of banded hundred dollar bills sat on the floorboard.

"You want to explain this?"

"Don't know why I'd have to. Don't appear to me you stopped me with any probable cause to search, you just showed up on my property and yanked that door open without a by-your-leave now, didn't you, Mr. Investigator? And as far as you know, I just sold a big load of scrap metal and got cash for it. So call the IRS."

"Bull fuckin' shit. That's drug money, residue's all over it. Sarge smelled it on you and he smelled it in the truck. Why in the hell did you get into this? How *long* have you been into this?"

T-bone shrugged. "Man's gotta make a livin'. This is Turkey Creek, Billy, where you break your back to break even."

"Don't give me that bullshit, your business came from your dad, it's old and established and it makes money. There's no reason in hell for you to have gotten into this. And just how long have you been doin' this shit and takin' it around my wife and son?"

"Hey! You weren't here for Maggie, not *ever!* I was! And don't you go givin' yourself airs about your precious fatherhood, either! Where the hell were *you* when he was little and we were in the emergency room with him at midnight with an ear infection and a hundred and four temperature? Where the hell were *you* when we were in the waitin' room or the exam room takin' turns walkin' him to keep him quiet, feelin' that little body throwin' off enough heat to bake the meat off your shoulder? What do you know about that? You don't know *shit* about bein' a father! 'Cause that was *me*, buddy-ro, not *you!* Doin' all the shit work of a husband and father with damn few of the fringe benefits! *Me!*"

"Well, it *would* have been me if your son-of-a-bitchin' father'd bothered to tell anybody I was ringin' the phone off the goddamn hook tryin' to get to you or Maggie! Until he changed the home number to an unlisted! After he told me for the hundredth time nobody wanted me back to cause any more trouble, especially Maggie! It *would* have been me!"

"That's a goddamn lie! He'd *never*—"

"Well, he *did!* And how the hell'd you keep Maggie from findin' out all this time, she goes over your books, I don't understand how you kept her from—"

Jack's face went blank.

"No," Billy whispered. "*No!*"

Billy walked back to his truck. Sarge whined and bounded in front of Billy. He jumped into the seat as soon as the door opened, distressed by the violent emotion whirling around the men.

Jack watched Billy drive away.

"Shit," he said. "Just shit."

Gail Roughton

Chapter Thirty-Eight

It was Charlene's day off at the Kincaid house. A slim figure lounged in one of study's leather chair, its hanging over the arm, very much at home.

"So I guess you're full of yourself these days," John said.

"It's only the biggest deal we've ever done. Wasn't easy to set up, you know. I would say the Feds are gettin' smarter, but they're not. The cartels are gettin' harder to deal with, been stung too often."

"But you managed."

"That dumb, helpless, female Southern charm gets 'em every time. I'm a *woman*. Of course they think they're smarter than I am."

John snorted. "Well, glad to see women's lib didn't ruin your brain."

"Hell to the no, you got an advantage, use it."

"Knew you were just like me the first time I ever looked in your eyes."

"You'll forgive me if I don't consider that the highest compliment I've ever received."

"And after all I've done for you."

"You haven't done a damn thing for me, old man. No love lost on either side, never pretended there was."

"No, but I knew the money'd win out in the end. Knew that righteous poverty'd get old pretty damn quick."

"I've *earned* that money, old man."

"Yeah, got to say you have. But I've done a few things for you, bonuses you don't know about."

"Such as?"

"Well, got you out of that damn restaurant where you were breakin' your back, didn't I?"

"Like I don't know about that?"

"Hell, you think you were hurtin' for money when you finally broke down and came to your senses? S'pose you'd had a whinin' brat clingin' to your leg since you were eighteen instead of the one you took in? At least you were already in your twenties."

"What the hell you talkin' about?"

"Think I didn't know you were pregnant, girl? Think I'm that stupid? Expected it from the first, you takin' up with that white trash."

"Okay. So you knew about it. So what?"

"Good God, you don't leave things like that to chance. And in this county, you don't have to. Don't you know root doctors still around, girl? All kind of things they can do with their brews and potions."

"You slipped me some poison you got from a *root doctor*?"

"Worked, didn't it?"

"You could have *killed* me!"

"I didn't figure it was much of a risk."

"Well, I'm so glad it didn't cause you any concern. Though I suppose yeah, that was a big favor. Been aggravatin' enough raisin' the one I got stuck with."

"Like you said from the start, damn good cover, though. And he has turned out to be a bright kid. You sure you don't want—"

"Hell, no, I don't want him in the business. Why the hell would I want it split into any more shares than it already is? I want him to trot on off to college next year. And not come home very damn often, either. Most kids don't, after all. Anyway, the cover worked too well. Don't think he's got this in him, takes a special gene for this kind of work. Like you keep reminding me, no Kincaid blood there. Besides, I want to start enjoying some of that money stashed away. New life. Away from this God-forsaken place. My own tropical island, maybe. Yeah, that sounds about right. Free at last, God, free at last!"

"Did you forget you married Brayton the minute he showed back up in town?"

"Figured that'd make you ecstatic, me knowin' what he was doing every minute." Maggie Kincaid Brayton shrugged. "And besides, you don't intend for him to be around much longer, now do you? 'Cause I *am* gettin' a little tired of always havin' a live-in nursemaid thinks I can't pee by myself. Gettin' real old."

"Nope, I sure as hell don't. Anybody stupid enough to pass up the kind of offer I sent out to him—shit, what the two of you coulda had by now. Anybody that dumb by rights ain't got enough sense to keep breathing. But you sure as hell enjoyed that scene, didn't you, waltzing into my study the afternoon he came back. Now was that really necessary?"

"I liked it. Funny, I seem to recall askin' you the same thing the morning I walked into the roach hotel. Enjoyed it about as much as you enjoyed the thought of me walkin' into that horror movie you engineered."

"Yeah, we're two of a kind all right. Three, actually, your brother's just as bad as we are."

"Long as he keeps his ass where it's s'posed to be. 'Cause I sure as hell ain't walkin' around town claimin' *that* relationship." Maggie pulled her legs back over the arm of the chair and stood. "I better get goin'."

"Too early in the afternoon for your husband to be lookin' for you, ain't it?"

"Actually, I told Joyce I'd go shopping with her. I'm just a regular little Suzy Homemaker these days."

"Well, we all have to make our sacrifices."

"Don't we, though?"

Maggie walked out of the study and left through the kitchen. She always came into the property on a back driveway that wound through several miles of woods and left her car up in the trees. She drove halfway back to the highway and stopped.

Her hands shook. She leaned her head forward and rested it on top of the wheel. A low moan spiraled upward into a high, keening wail. When the echo died, she raised her head from its bowed position, straightened her shoulders, and drove on.

* * *

Billy was in shut-down mode and he knew it. It was an old and familiar survival technique he'd mastered long ago. It had kept him sane during the days he'd waited for Maggie to appear at his current base. Later, it had kept him sane and alive during the first Gulf War. It'd been a long time since it had taken him over so completely.

He drove home on remote control. His mind registered necessary things, the curve of the road, the speed of the truck, the sight of a stop sign. It registered nothing else, not even Sarge's soft, worried whines.

He navigated the long driveway mindlessly, parked, and shut off the engine. He went to the bedroom and stripped, exchanging the dress pants and sports jacket for nylon gym shorts and an old gray T-shirt with cut-off sleeves. He double-knotted the strings of his Nikes and headed to the back porch. Sarge dogged his every step with soft, questioning whines Billy didn't even hear.

He moved to the weight bench. The bar currently carried Jake's body weight of 200 pounds. Instead of adding the twenty pounds needed for his own body weight, he added forty, lay down on the bench, and started doing reps. When he'd done three sets of ten reps each, he got up and added another twenty pounds to each side of the bar and repeated the process. Then he added another twenty to each side of the bar and did another set, feeling nothing but the strain of pumping muscles, the slickness of sweat running down his arms. His mind registered no thought other than the silent commands of up and down running from his brain to his arms.

"Dad? Hey, Dad, aren't you home early?"

Jake's voice penetrated the black vacuum of his brain. He had no idea how many times he'd added more weight to the bars or how much weight it now carried. But all at once he was aware it was too much. His muscles quivered. No way he'd lift that bar back up again by himself.

"Out here!" He heard the strain in his voice.

"Dad?" Jake rushed to the weight bench. "Jesus Christ, Dad! What the *hell* do you think you're doing?! There's close to four hundred pounds on this thing! And you're sweatin' like you been liftin' an hour!"

Jake grabbed from the top and Billy pushed upward. The bar safely clanged into position in its resting slots. Jake reached an arm down and Billy grabbed it, pulling himself back up.

"Now, what the hell was all that about?"

"Stupid, huh?"

"Stupid, *duh*. You'd be reaming my ass I tried a stunt like that!"

"Yeah, I know, sorry. I was—thinking." Well, the mindless state was his pre-requisite for intense thinking.

"Couldn't prove it by me. Where you goin' now?"

Billy wiped his face and arms down and headed out the back screen.

"I need to run a while."

"*After that*? It's thirty-two *degrees* out there and dropping fast! You're over-heated and sweatin' like a pig! And you want to go *run*? Wait a minute, I'll come with you!"

"No. Sorry, buddy, but I've got something goin' on I need to think about, this is how I think. I need to run alone a little while, okay?"

"Well, I don't guess there's much I can do about it, is there? What direction you goin' in and how long do I give you before I figure you've collapsed and I need to come pick your ass up?"

Billy grinned in spite of himself. No, he shouldn't go running right now and Jake knew it as well as he did. But he had to. That's when the actual thinking started.

"Trail around the perimeter. You can come look if I'm not back in an hour, okay?"

"How 'bout half an hour?"

"I'll go slow, son, I'm not that hard-headed."

"Only if you take Sarge."

"He can stay with you."

"I *said*, take Sarge!"

Jeeezzz. "Okay, okay! Com'on, boy, let's go!"

Sarge bounded out in front of him. Billy headed for one of the winding trails threaded throughout the fifty acre tract.

"You got an hour!" Jake shouted after him. "And I'm setting the alarm on my phone for it, you hear?"

"I hear!"

Chapter Thirty-Nine

Jack punched the "End" button on his phone viciously for about the twentieth time. He cussed.

"Fuck, fuck, fuck! Com'on, Maggie-pie, turn your damn phone on!"

* * *

Maggie and Joyce strolled the grocery aisles of Dublin's Super Wal-Mart. Maggie stopped at the meat counter.

"I swear, Maggie Mae, you're the only person I know thinks the meat counter's the high spot of a shopping trip! Last time I take you anywhere, you didn't even give me time to go through all the after Christmas sales racks at Belks!"

"Don't think you're in much danger of goin' around naked. I think you can manage on what's already in that closet of yours." Maggie inspected the sirloin tip roasts. "Oh, good, nice big one. Leftovers have a short lifespan at my house."

"Benjie says my roasts are dry as sawdust. And you spend way too much energy on cookin'. I swear, you worry more about the state of their stomachs than—"

"Any other person I know," Maggie finished for her. "Yeah, but I missed a lot of years worryin' about the state of Billy's stomach. I like fixin' his favorites. What you do is, you rub it down good with garlic salt and wrap it up real tight in aluminum foil and slow roast it for five or six hours. You should try it, Benjie'd like it."

"Benjie'd faint dead away. And then he'd be expectin' what I cooked to taste good and then he'd actually expect me to cook. Now I ask you, why the hell would I want to start something like that?"

"'Cause you love him?"

"Com'on, girl, most of the time I don't even *like* him!"

"Liar."
"I don't like him *that* good."

* * *

Jack kept calling. Maggie's phone kept going to voicemail. "Shit, damn, hell! *Call* me! Don't go home until you do!"

* * *

Taylor sulked in his grandfather's living room on his day off. The Macon Police Department hired him within hours of submitting his application, but he sure didn't like the job. The city streets were very different from the country roads of Rockdale County. The neighborhoods of his new patrol routes scared him shitless. Most of all, he didn't like actually working. Especially in a department where his grandfather's name and local connections meant exactly squat. It was a new experience for him. He wasn't enjoying it at all.

"Boy, you nervous as a dog smellin' a bitch in heat. What's the matter with you?"

"Nothing. Just tired of waitin' is all. Thought Big John woulda taken Brayton out by now."

"John does things in his own time, son. Ain't you ever heard—now what's that phrase? 'Revenge is a dish best eaten cold.' John's past master at that."

"Yeah, well, he's waited too long this time."

Davis Brown looked up.

"Boy, you ain't gone and done something stupid, have you?"

"Why do you *do* that? Always think what I do's stupid?"

"'Cause it usually is, son. I love you, but you don't think things through. You ain't gone and put another move on Jake Brayton, have you?"

"No. No, I didn't put a move on Jake Brayton."

"You done something to somebody. I can read you like a book. Out with it. What the *hell* have you done now?"

"Maybe Brayton's 'bout to find out he ain't Superman."

Country Justice

Chapter Forty

Billy ran up the steepest hill of the rolling trail circling the boundary lines of the property. He'd promised Jake he wouldn't run full out after the weight-lifting marathon but he did anyway. He couldn't outrun his new knowledge.

He'd lost Maggie. He'd never had her. And he'd lose Jake, too. Jake sure as hell wouldn't want anything to do with him after he took Maggie and Jack down with the Kincaid Cartel. And they were in the Cartel. There'd been a hundred thousand dollars plus of drug money in that truck, easy. No way anybody handling that kind of money wasn't part of the Kincaid Cartel, not in Rockland County. A few homegrown homeboys making recreational sales was one thing, but that much money? Hell, no, that had Kincaid written all over it. No way any rival dealer with that kind of money resources would be tolerated.

Billy couldn't pinpoint when his instant liking for Jake had shifted and deepened. He supposed it didn't matter. Something about watching an almost mirror image of yourself every day—not in looks, so much, though they were very similar, but in personality—seeing all the things that were good in you and, insofar as Billy could tell, almost none of the bad—God, he loved that kid. He didn't think he'd have loved the long-ago child that never was any more than he did Jake. That was the worst of it, the thing that would burn with the hottest fury when he'd finished sorting all this out. That the last five months had been full of home and family, something he'd never thought to have, and now wished he hadn't. You don't miss what you never had. But he'd had it—or at least he'd thought he did. Losing it? He'd be an amputee.

And even if he could figure out a way to take Maggie and Jack out of the take-down, what then? Who and what would he be if he did? How in the hell could he keep living with a woman who was moonlighting in the drug trade on that kind of scale, who was that good a liar? Who was using him for nothing but cover anyway.

Because the rumor mill had it that Big John's second in command was a woman. He'd known that before setting foot in Rockland County again. Aurelia Andrews, he'd figured. Barracudas of that caliber gravitated to power as naturally as the tides followed the moon. Jesus, he was in the wrong business.

How the hell could he have been so stupid? And how the hell could someone change so much? Maggie, his Maggie, who loved thunderstorms and rainbows and sunrises and cried over Disney movies? And stood by an open coffin holding a faceless dead man's hand? Because that was true, he knew that from Aunt Lulu. What the hell had happened to her?

"*Folks don't change much. Not in their center.*" He could hear Jake's voice as clearly as he'd heard it in his car, heading into Turkey Creek his first afternoon back. *But they do, son, they do. They just mask the changes.*

Or did they? While he'd sulked and licked his wounds on his changing army bases, believing himself forgotten, Maggie'd finished college on her own, worn his ring, tended his graves, built their house, and raised a child just waiting to become his. Because it was good cover? Or because it was the truth? The center?

"*Folks don't change much. Not in their center.*" The words echoed again. His thoughts moved to his old buddy T-bone. He'd always been happy-go-lucky. If he didn't have bad luck, he'd have no luck at all. But he'd always had a heart of gold. He'd never refused anyone a favor, especially Billy, not then, not since he'd come back. But when God said brains, T-bone thought he said trains, and he'd missed his. Or had he?

"*Don't appear to me you stopped me with any probable cause to search, you just showed up on my property and yanked that door open without a by-your-leave now, didn't you, Mr. Investigator?*" Smart enough to know that, anyway. He was right, no way to make a charge stick under those circumstances. But of course, everybody in the drug trade was a jailhouse lawyer.

"*You don't know shit about bein' a father! 'Cause that was me, buddy-ro, not you! Doin' all the shit work of a husband and father with damn few of the fringe benefits! Me!*"

Straight for the jugular with the precision of a scalpel wielded by a fine surgeon, a study in psychology.

Sherlock Holmes had one basic tenet. When you eliminate the impossible, whatever remains, no matter how improbable, is the truth. He hadn't believed his gut twenty-five years ago when it told him Maggie wouldn't forget him. Not believing, he'd never come home. He'd lost twenty-five years. There was one alternative explanation to all this. Just one. It felt right in his gut. And if he didn't believe his gut this time—or if his gut was wrong—he'd lose her forever.

He stopped running and looked around to see where his was. Closer to keep going than to turn around. He started up the last big hill on the way home. Sarge's expression lost a little of the worried frown he'd carried since the drama at the junkyard. He even grinned as little as he held his pace back, staying even with Billy.

* * *

"Where the *hell* have you been? And why the hell has your phone been off all afternoon?"

"Well, damn, I didn't think it was a matter of national security! Spent the afternoon with Daddy Dearest, so I turned the phones off. It was an—unsettling visit. Forgot to turn 'em back on."

"Well, you ain't the only one got unsettled, sugar, let me tell you."

* * *

Billy came in through the side porch and headed for the bedroom. Jake sat on the floor in the great room with his back propped against the sofa, notebook and book in his lap, ESPN on the television. Sarge bounced over and lay down beside him.

"Hey. Sorry if I was snappy."

"No problem. You cut it pretty close, you only had another five minutes on the clock before I was headin' out after you. It's almost six o'clock in case you hadn't noticed. Only a few minutes till full dark."

"Sorry. You heard from your mother?"

"Said something this morning 'bout goin' to Dublin with Miss Joyce."

"Oh. I've got to go back out for a while. You keep Sarge here, I don't know how late I'll be."

"Okay."

Behind the closed door of the bedroom, Billy sent a message out to Country Justice via email.

"Meet me. Mt. Olive Cemetery. 6:30 tonight."

He stood waiting, pretty certain a reply would be forthcoming in the next minute or two. He was right.

"Meet? Our orders changed?"

"Fuck orders. 6:30. Tonight."

"Why there?"

"I fucking said so."

Billy cleared the screen, stuck the phone out of sight in a drawer, and headed for the shower.

He parked the Mustang at 6:29. No vehicles he could see, but he was pretty sure Country Justice was here. They'd be holding the high ground. He threw his door open and shouted out into the darkness.

"Maggie Brayton, you get your ass out here! And bring Jack's with you!"

Chapter Forty-One

"Well, and aren't we pissed?" Maggie's voice floated out of the darkness. Her silhouette, spotlighted by the full moon, emerged from behind the overgrown bushes forming a protective fence around the graves. "And you shouldn't have shouted like that. Suppose it hadn't been us?"

"Had to be. No other alternative."

"So glad you figured it out, I'd have hated like hell to divorce you but I think the mutual trust thing is sort of absent if your husband thinks you're a drug dealer."

"Maggie, are you fuckin' *crazy*, woman, what in the *hell* would have happened to Jake if you'd gotten yourself killed?"

"Joyce, of course. I mean, odds were if I was dead, Jack was, too, so that wouldn't have worked. A Will's one of the first things I did after I got him. I didn't have Jake when all this started, and by the time I did, it was too late. I was in it."

Billy shouted into the darkness again. "Jack, I'm not seeing your ass out here yet!"

T-bone emerged from the shadows. As he walked, the slumping shoulders disappeared, adding at least two inches of height and two more of shoulder width. The incipient beer belly disappeared. The tightened torso radiated muscled strength instead of soft flab. The raised chin changed the whole profile. Without the cap, the close-cut hair and shadowed beard shouted toughness. This was a dangerous man to cross.

Billy stood immobile for a few seconds, looking back and forth between his wife and his best friend. Twenty years they'd done this. This one operation. Eleven major take-downs and one more to go. Still standing. He bent low in a formal bow.

"I'm in awe. Of both of you. Was even before I got here, just on your record. You're legends. And I bow at your feet."

"As well you should in the presence of greatness," Maggie said. "Especially when it comes to Jack. I mostly just play myself, I only have to act when I'm dealing with Daddy Dearest and the cartels. Jack's on stage all day, every day. He's got a Master's degree in criminal justice, by the way."

"Yeah, I did my thesis on how to convince your best friend you're a drug-dealing scumbag."

"I'm sorry."

"Don't be, pretty big compliment."

"Yeah, it is. But that's not what I'm sorry about."

Jack shook his head. "Don't. Explains a lot. Knew there had to be something, some other reason than a newspaper clippin' you never came back. And Daddy—if it's any comfort, it turned Daddy into an old man real fast. Saw it happenin', never knew why. Guess I know why now, must have eaten him alive. Maggie told me the whole thing while we were waitin' on you. Well, actually, while we were waitin' on you to put it together."

"Damn good thing you did, too." Maggie said."Believin' I'd forgotten you when we were eighteen, after what Jonsie told you, even needin' a couple of hours this afternoon to think it through, considering the business we're all in, that's one thing. But not believin' in me after livin' with me for the past five months—if you hadn't figured it out—"

"I know," said Billy. "I know."

"And then you picked Mt. Olive. So I knew you knew. When I asked you why I half-way expected you to send back, 'Maggie, don't even go there, woman.' But I guess it's a good thing you did get out of the car shoutin', 'cause if you hadn't, I'm not sure I'd have believed you when we walked out and you claimed you knew it was us all the time. After all, lying's the stock in trade for all of us."

"That thought occurred to me, yeah. Hence the shout. I'm assumin' you knew who I was a long time back. When'd you figure it out?"

Maggie laughed. "Oh, hell, almost from the first. As Jack kept tellin' me, we had the home team advantage. You just appearin' out of the blue, somebody with your background, waltzing right into the Sheriff's Department at the same time Lifeline tells us there's a new player on the field—well, hell." Maggie shrugged. "Just too damn much coincidence there."

"Why'd you get into this? How? Either of you? Both of you?"

"You. Of course."

"For Maggie, yeah. She did it for you. For me, sure for you, but it was more for Maggie. Somebody had to have her back. You didn't see her, standing there by the coffin, holdin' your hand. Knew she had to have a cool head with her, couldn't let her get into something like this with no backup she could trust. And I'm glad—as much as I hate Daddy havin' any part in it—I'm glad you had a reason to think you shouldn't come back. 'Cause I'll tell you, buddy-ro, I was havin' a real hard time with that, the why in the hell you'd never come back."

"You didn't act like it even crossed your mind to wonder."

"I *act* for a livin', Billy."

"And would have won many Oscars by now if you were doin' it on the screen, too. Never seen anybody to touch you."

"And I'm sorry, too," Jack said.

"Shouldn't be. Every word was true."

"Yeah, it was. But it wasn't your fault. And in spite of everything, I'm glad to know it."

"So," Maggie said. "Everybody ready to kiss and make up now?"

Billy and Jack gave her identical looks. Maggie laughed.

"Okay, allow me." She rose up on her toes and kissed Billy lightly on the lips, then repeated the process with Jack.

"Won't know how to operate now, knowing who everybody is," Billy said.

"Wellllll—" Maggie drawled out and scrunched her nose.

"What don't I know now?"

"Did you by any chance know this is an interagency operation? With maybe one of their agents bein' in the mix with us?"

"What other agency?"

"GBI."

"No, Lifeline left that out."

"Lifeline's left a lot out. And I'm goin' have a talk with that boy about that very thing in the very near future. Tripped him up last night, he admitted he's been coordinating you for years. And the Agency knew, Billy, they *knew* why I got in the business in the first place. They *knew* I thought you were dead and they knew exactly where you were almost the whole time."

"Let's both talk to Lifeline about that. In person. Not on the phone."

"Think we can find him?"

"Hell, we're secret agent men."

Maggie laughed. "Yeah, well, back to the GBI thing—"

"Okay, rub salt in my wounds, go ahead. Who the hell else is workin' this operation I don't I know about? The Sheriff?"

"Not exactly." The velvet voice preceded the figure emerging from the shadows. "And I'm damn glad you changed your tone so fast. That shout when you first got here, thought for a minute you were mad enough to get physical and I'da laid your ass out into the next county, you'da laid a hand on Maggie."

Billy shook his head. He'd have sworn this man detested him and hated Maggie Kincaid. He'd have sworn this man was a dirty cop.

"I'm in the middle of a cluster-fuck and I'm the one gettin' fucked. That's never happened to me before."

"A little humility's good for the soul," Maggie said.

"And you do *not* seriously think I was goin' to manhandle Maggie."

"Oh hell no, but I got three sisters and three daughters. I love givin' that speech, given it for all of 'em except Maggie. Figured this might be the only chance I ever had."

"Now that he might not know about, Lamar."

"Yeah, I did. Didn't know if you knew."

"Well, shit. We just be stumblin' all over each other, ain't we? How'd you know?"

"Aunt Lulu. I think she might be—"

"Pretty worried about me. Yeah, I know. My own mother believes I'm a dirty cop, T-bone, don't know why it bothers you Billy thought you were a drug-dealin' scumbag."

"Yeah, but you got that Kincaid gene thrown in for her to worry about. And both of you are just like him," T-bone said.

"*Excuse you?*"

"Totally ruthless. Just like he is. Don't even bother denying it. Only difference is, the two of you got to have a righteous cause before the ruthless kicks in. Nothing as tangible as money'll do it."

"So now what?"

"Now we're goin' to run in the biggest deal in Rockland County history, we're goin' to take him down, and we're goin' to fry his ass. For the murder of Magdalene Kincaid. Just like we always planned to." Maggie's face hardened. "Billy, that was always our strategy. We always knew. And Lamar, Billy figured that out very early in the game. That Big John killed my mother."

"But I don't know how much luck we're goin' to have with that," said Billy. "Thought I could get my hands on the case file, till the Sheriff told me all the old files were mostly destroyed. Except Aunt Lulu says it's in his study.

"Yeah, some extra evidence wouldn't hurt," Lamar said. "But it's a file that's been out of the chain of evidence for years. Still, it's good side dressin', if we can get it in."

"So if y'all always planned on the murder charge, how you plan on makin' it stick? Aunt Lulu didn't actually see anything."

"Damn, man, you know more about what my mother knows and don't know than I do. That sucks. We're not much worried about physical evidence. We got an eye witness."

Billy started. "Maggie, you weren't there. And if you were, you couldn't possibly remember anything. And even if, God forbid, you did, no jury would believe the memories of a two-year-old child."

"Well, no," Lamar's drawled. "But a smart five-year-old—now that, I'm thinkin' they'd believe."

"You?"

"Me."

Chapter Forty-Two

The smart five-year-old under discussion was playing with his cars in the kitchen the day Big John came in, grabbed his mother's hand, and walked toward the study. He'd watched this scene many times before. He knew what he was supposed to do. Get out of the house and go back to the little white cottage in the back yard. He didn't know exactly what happened after Big John grabbed his mother's hand, but he knew it was best to leave her alone the rest of the day.

His big brother and his two sisters were at school. Nobody was home in the back house. Miss Magdalene had loaded the baby up in her little car and driven toward town. Come to think of it, she was never home when Big John grabbed his mother's hand. He hoped she came back soon. He loved Miss Magdalene. She'd sit on the floor and play with the baby for hours. She always called him over and included him in the rolling balls and building blocks. Little Maggie was kinda boring, but for a girl and a baby, she was sorta cute and he did love to hear her laugh. Her giggle cracked him up. And when she tired and crawled into her mother's lap, Miss Magdalene would sit on one of the big couches, lay Maggie down with her head on her lap, and pat the seat on the other side of her for Lamar to climb up. And she'd read. Even when Maggie fell asleep, she'd keep reading to Lamar. Lamar had already sorted the black squiggles into letters and was beginning to sort the letters into actual words.

Right now, though, what to do to entertain himself? He glanced around the yard and spotted John's truck. The pickup bed was covered over with a tarp. Very interesting. What was under it? He climbed up and over to see.

Well, shucks. Nothing much, just some old crates and barrels. Still, they had possibilities. He thought about his favorite television shows. That one, now, that'd make a good fort. If he got in, he could probably hold off a horde of bad guys, like the Lone Ranger and Tonto. Or that barrel—it looked sort of like the tunnel Zorro used to enter his secret cave. And that one, that was a good castle, like the White Knight's castle in the last fairy tale Miss Magdalene read him.

He was thus busily engaged in make-believe when he heard the car. Miss Magdalene, back already?

"Stay right here, baby doll," he heard her say. Well, that was kind of dumb, wasn't it? Maggie was strapped in her car seat, after all. Wasn't going anywhere without help. "I can't believe I forgot your bag, I'll be right back."

Oh. Well, no point even getting out if she was just running in and coming right back to drive off. He continued to guard his fortresses, glancing toward the car every few minutes from under the tarp, keeping an eye on the baby. She seemed happy from the sound of the babbles coming from the front seat.

Lamar resumed his play. He was guarding the White Knight's back when the front door slammed. He peeped out from under the tarp and dropped the covering material back down. Big John was heading toward the truck.

Well, nothing to do now but hide and ride. He'd have to come home sometime. John had never been *mean* to him, mostly he just ignored him, but Lamar didn't think it'd be real smart to advertise his presence. And based on past behavior patterns after Big John took his mother's hand and walk her toward the study, she might not even notice he was gone until he was back. He settled back into one of the crates stuffed with rags. He'd been up a long time; it was getting on into the afternoon. He hated naps and his mother didn't insist on them anymore but the lull of the truck tires was hypnotic.

The abrupt braking of the truck woke him. Disoriented in his fantasy surroundings, it took him a few minutes to remember where he was. And why. But he was sure gonna be staying exactly where he was, because Big John was furious.

"Get your ass out of that car! Where the hell you think you're goin' with my daughter?"

He heard a short gasp of startled pain. From the sound, John had whipped someone's arm up and back behind their shoulders. It couldn't be anybody but Miss Magdalene. Then he heard a loud wail of fright. Maggie. He'd know her cry anywhere.

Even under the tarp, he knew from the rapidly revolving pattern of light that a Sheriff's patrol cruiser pulled up.

"Goddamn, you idiot!" John shouted. "Shut those damn lights down! Now get over to that car and get that baby out and take her home!"

"*No!*" Miss Magdalene's shout. Outrages. Scared to death. "Don't you touch her!"

"Will you *hurry the fuck up?*" John's voice again, raised over Maggie's cries. They escalated rapidly into the ear-splitting shrieks of a terrified toddler.

"John, you're scaring her to death! She doesn't *know* him!"

"Won't hurt her to scream a while."

"You son-of-a-bitch!"

"John, this kid's kickin' like a mule!"

"*Just get her back home!* Jesus Christ, do I have to do *everything* myself, you stupid bastard?"

Maggie's shrieks muffled. He heard the patrol cruiser's door slam. It drove off. Scuffling gravel, another cracking sound and a sudden yelp of pain. The driver's door of the truck opened and a body fell across the seat. Immediately, he heard the sounds of a door trying to open.

"Goddamn, woman, you'd ever shown that kind of fire where you're supposed to, none of this would have happened!" Lamar heard a dull thudding sound, like the one he'd heard when his big brother Dwayne got in a fight with Willie Johnson and Willie'd punched him in the jaw and knocked him out. And then he didn't hear Miss Magdalene anymore.

They drove a long time while he lay huddled in the rags lining his castle-crate. The truck turned off the highway and down a dirt road. It bounced and shook. Miss Magdalene moaned just before the truck stopped. John pulled her out of the truck. The sound of fabric sliding over the front seat grated on Lamar's ears like squeaky chalk on a chalk board. John didn't bother to close the door. Peeking out, Lamar saw them, clearly limned against the beginning dusk.

John dragged her into the clearing in front of the hunting cabin where Miss Magdalene took him and Maggie for summer afternoon picnics. He shoved her to the ground.

"John, don't do this! Maggie needs—"

"Sorry about this, Magdalene. But Maggie don't need a mother just waiting to swoop her away from me. Shouldn't have tried that, Magdalene. You know, I might have actually let you go. You've been something of a disappointment from the start. Otherwise, I wouldn't be needin' any side dishes, now would I? But this—" Kincaid shook his head thoughtfully. "Now, I'm not about to wait around while you try to run with her again or haul me into court with your stories of how I'm an unfit father."

"You aren't fit to *touch* her! Or me, or anybody else!"

"That child's mine! First time I looked in her eyes—she's goin' to be me made over, Magdalene, she has nothing of you, never will." Hard click as the hammer engaged. "Not even memories."

Lamar tried to close his eyes, but he couldn't. Blood spray rained with the sound of the exploding gun, the memory of shattering bone and bits of gray matter printed indelibly, forever, in his five-year-old brain.

* * *

"Holy. Shit." Billy breathed softly. They sat close to each other on different levels of the Church's old stone steps

"Sort of made a lastin' impression, yeah. I loved that woman."

"One of the greatest gifts anybody ever gave me." Maggie and Billy sat on the step below Lamar. She leaned her head over and rested it against her brother's knee. "Memories of my mother."

"We've held the advantage so far 'cause that motherfucker thinks we're just like him. That money and power are all we care about. Ego won't let him think anything else. We're his blood, his genes, even if I'm black. So it's never crossed his mind we're in for something else, that the money don't mean shit to us. He's never cared about another living soul in his life, wouldn't occur to him Maggie and me are in it for our mothers. 'Cause both our mothers—well, they were both mothers to us both. Then you got in the mix, too. Because Maggie's my sister, bastard's gonna ruin her life and not pay for it? Oh, *hell* no. One for all and all for one. And that bastard's goin' *down*."

Chapter Forty-Three

As the next generation of the Kincaid Cartel initiated its newest member into its elite ranks, Clint Raines shot the shit with an old friend who'd called to catch up, one of the head honchos at the state's K-9 training facility in Savannah.

"Good man you got there. That last one you sent us."

"Alec Wimberly," said the Sheriff. "Yeah, he's done real good since he's been back on the job."

"You got a good team overall, Clint. Real impressive when you consider what you started with."

"Yeah."

"'Course, I know there's still some rough spots you're workin' on. Must be glad of the extra help."

"Extra help?"

"Oh, com'on, buddy! You know the state's got men on that force. Been plantin' 'em here and there for years. Be stupid not to, that shit with Bo Franklin. Ol' Roy Lee Rollins wasn't that much better. Some Feds get thrown in now and again, too, I hear."

"Oh, sure. But it's been a while."

"Well, play dumb if you want to. Scuttlebutt has it they're 'bout ready to finish cleanin' up the county."

"Where'd you hear that?"

"Don't worry, won't get leaked anywhere it don't need to be heard. But when word gets out they've sent in their best clean-up man—well, shit. Don't take much to figure what's comin'."

"No, I guess it don't, at that."

The Sheriff swore as he hung up. Son-of-a-bitch! Plant in his department and he didn't even know it? Sure, there'd been plants before. But he'd known it. The county'd been dirty for years and of course the Feds and the GBI rode herd on it—or tried to—even after his election. And he'd always figured out who real quick, too. This time, though, he'd slipped up. And it was so damn obvious, too. Because why in the hell else would Billy Brayton come back to this hick town and this hick force? The personal vendetta thing only went so far. Of course it was Brayton.

The Sheriff felt like a fool. He didn't much care for the feeling. So much for professional courtesy in his own county. They coulda' *told* him. *Brayton* coulda told him. Gonna be damn sorry he hadn't, too. No way anybody was stealing thunder in *his* county.

* * *

"Left my car at T-bone's. So, how 'bout a ride, mister?" Maggie slipped her arm under Billy's as they walked away from the old Church. "Believe you're goin' my way."

"Believe I am."

"Then let's hit the road. I'm 'bout frozen, can you turn the heat up?"

"You know, we could have sat in the car with the heat on instead of freezin' our butts off on those cold stone steps."

"Oh no, secret meetings, they need the open night. Preferably with thunder and lightning. The law according to Jack Jones."

"Where are they? Should we wait?"

"No, go ahead. They parked further back, didn't want to spoil the effect by you seeing the cars, now did we?"

"Enjoyed yourself, didn't you?" He cranked up and pulled out.

"Oh, yeah. Billy, you know what Big John told me this afternoon? What he *bragged* about this afternoon?"

Her face darkened and lightened as they ran through the tunnels of dark overcast shadow thrown onto the road by the overhanging trees.

"What?"

"I always blamed him 'cause I lost the baby, you know that. But he really did kill him. He knew I was pregnant. Slipped me some back country poison he got from one of the local root doctors."

"Nice to know he didn't care if he killed you gettin' rid of the child."

"Hell no, he didn't care. Wouldn't care if I died tomorrow as long as it wasn't in the middle of a big buy. That'd be inconvenient. When I was younger, just startin' this, I almost chewed my tongue off a couple of times, but that—and I sat there and acted like yeah, that was a big favor, would have been God-awful to be saddled with a kid, the one I had was bad enough. That's how I keep him away from Jake, pretendin' he's never meant anything to me except a good cover story. John thinks I can't wait for him to grow up and leave home. I couln't *ever* give him the leverage of lettin' him think I loved Jake. My God, he'd of had me."

Billy shook his head. "I'm so outclassed by you and Jack, it ain't even funny. I don't know how I'm still *alive*, I'm so far out of your league."

Maggie laughed. "Ironic, huh? That if he'd just left me alone and let me have my baby, I would have majored in business and had a quiet little career while I raised my child. Wouldn't have spent my whole adult life workin' to take him down. Can't wait for him to know."

"Life's full of little ironies. Like Jack. So—why aren't the two of you a couple?"

"Excuse you?"

"At first, you know, I assumed both Country Justice agents were male. But after a few emails, it was pretty obvious they weren't. And I'd started to think they might even be married. Not that common in our business but not unheard of. There was just something in the banter—can't explain why, exactly, just got the impression they were a couple. Maggie Kincaid and T-bone—that's stretchin' the bounds of reason. Maggie Kincaid and Jack Jones—the real Jack Jones I just met—you're damn near perfect together."

"Key words. Damn near. When you've had perfect and you had it so young—" Maggie shrugged and continued. "Very perceptive of you, though, because we did give it a shot. For several years. I can see why you assumed Country Justice was a couple because in a lot of ways we are. But the other—well, like I said, we did try but it was a Catch-22 thing. Because of you. He's Jack Jones because of you. And me. Without you—and it follows that without you, there'd never have been a me—he'd have been T-bone. For real, not just his cover character. You made the bed seem crowded, somehow. So it never worked out real well for either one of us."

Billy bit his lip. "Well, I asked."

"Yeah, you did. We've been apart a long time, and without even talkin' about it, we both just did the don't ask, don't tell thing. But if you feel the need for details, now's the time. 'Cause the deceptions and omissions are over. They're done. Any questions you just gotta ask, details you gotta know, comments you want to make?"

"Just—I'm so damn glad the bed was crowded. Would that be safe?"

"Smart man."

* * *

"What the *hell* is wrong with that boy?" Big John Kincaid shouted into the phone. Davis Brown grimaced and pulled the phone from his ear.

"He's just tryin' to help, John," Davis attempted a soothing voice, but the attempt was wasted. There was no one on the other end of the line.

* * *

"Hell of a profession, hell of a life," Billy said. "I feel like—I hate it's been such a lonely life, Maggie. For you and Jack."

"It's been worse for him. Like I said, he's on stage damn near twenty-four/seven. He just *amazes* me sometimes. But he has his distractions." Even in the dim interior, Billy heard the grin in her voice. "Been married a couple of times, we both knew they wouldn't last. I mean, who but a female T-bone would marry T-bone, and God knows, there's plenty of 'em in the county. But he said a few years of convenient sex'd be worth it. And for a back-up, there's always Angie Malone. And Aurelia Andrews. Though that's kinda mixin' business and pleasure. You do know she's one of Big John's plants in the Sheriff's Office?"

"Yeah, I always figured—"

Maggie's phone—one of Maggie's phones, anyway—erupted into a shrill, standard ring.

"That's strange," she said. "Daddy Dearest. He almost *never* calls me, I call him." She hit the phone screen. "You bellowed?"

"Where the hell are you?"

"I'm at home, where you think I am?"

"Where's Brayton?"

"Out. Would I have answered if he was sittin' right next to me?"

"Good. Maybe it'll work out after all. Long as you're not in his car with him."

"Why shouldn't I be?"

"Taylor. Davis just called me and told me the idiot's messed with the brakes on Brayton's car, half-cut the line or some shit, I was in too big a hurry to get to you to catch it exactly—"

"Gotta go. Sombody's home." Maggie punched the screen. "Try the brakes. Taylor's half-cut the line. We don't have any, cut the engine and run off the road. We're just starting down that big hill before—"

"The curve from hell," Billy finished, his foot already on the brake pedal. It depressed all the way to the floorboard. "Shit." His brain ran rapidly through any alternative and couldn't find one. Not in a stick shift with a cut brake line. There was no way in hell to negotiate the waiting curve at the speed the car would have as it approached it.

"Off-road—is this pasture? I'm rememberin' right?"

"Yeah. Do it. Quick."

"Shit." Billy turned the wheel to the left and cut the ignition. The Mustang bounced as it cleared the roadside ditch and broke through the fencing. Billy fought the dead wheel, turning to the left to angle the car back toward the incline, rather than the decline, of the hilly terrain. The car gradually slowed and started rolling back down. Billy cut the dead wheel again, not without considerable effort, and wished like hell he hadn't spent so much energy that afternoon pumping iron. He brought the dead weight sideways. The car was still.

Maggie reached out and joined hands with Billy.

"Now *that* was some damn good drivin'!" she exclaimed.

Car doors slammed behind them. Pounding feet raced toward the car. T-bone jerked on Maggie's door, Lamar jerked on Billy's.

"Hey! We're okay, give me a second!" Billy hit the unlock button.

"What the *hell* was all that?" T-bone reached over Maggie and released the seat belt. "Stay still, girl, don't be movin' around till we make sure you're not broke!"

"I'm not broke," Maggie threw her legs out of the car.

"I *said*, stay still!" He bent down and ran his hands over her legs.

"You just want a chance to feel me up. Stop fussin'!"

"Any chance I get. Billy? You alive over there?"

"He's fine," Lamar finished duplicating the same procedure on Billy.

"Yes, he is. And he can talk, too. Y'all back off. And quit feelin' up my wife over there."

"Come make me. What the hell happened?"

"Daddy Dearest just saved our lives. Though mine was the only one he was worried about. 'Cause it'd be real inconvenient if I got killed right now with this big buy comin' up.

"Say what?"

"Called me 'cause he was afraid I'd get in Billy's car. Taylor messed with the brakes. Half-cut the brake line or something. Would that work?"

"Oh, hell yeah," Jack said. "Slow leak, extra pressure, line'll eventually break all the way through, no brakes, no warning."

Lamar whistled. "You're a hell of a driver, Billy, I'll give you that. I don't think the car's even hurt that bad."

"Couldn't have done a damn thing if he hadn't called right when he did, we'd never have made it all the way to the curve. And I'd never have held it if we had."

Lamar took over. "Okay, here's the deal. I'll call in and tell dispatch I was behind you when your brakes failed, so I'm takin' the scene. That way we'll have the accident report for the insurance company with nobody else pokin' around."

"Insurance company, hell! The Agency can pay for this."

"Good luck with that, my brother, they yell about batteries for a flashlight," Lamar said.

"Hey, I can't be here! I told Daddy Dearest I was home and Billy was out. And anyway, my car's at Jack's and I don't want to freak Jake out. Findin' out Billy lost his brakes is gonna freak him out enough."

"Good point, little sister. Jack, you take Maggie for her car and come back with the tow truck."

"We can get it tomorrow," Billy said. "All of us had enough excitement for one day. And for God's sakes, check Maggie's—"

"Hey! You think I'm really T-bone, buddy? And hell, you wouldn't even have to tell *him* to check her car!"

"Sorry. Wasn't thinkin'. Whose pasture am I in, anyway?"

"Ricky Russell's?" Lamar looked over to Maggie and Jack for confirmation.

"Yeah, I think so."

"Okay. Let's get things goin' and after I report in, I'll give him a call and tell him where the extra car in his pasture came from. I'll take Billy home, Jack, you go ahead and get Maggie out of here. Let's roll, boys and girls!"

* * *

Big John Kincaid looked at the phone for a few minutes. Enough was enough. Davis Brown was as close to a friend as anyone'd ever been to the Boss Man, but he was sick of this shit. And he might be old, but he still practiced one guiding rule. Never let the right hand know what the left hand was doing. Not even if the right hand was blood. He still had a few hidden aces Maggie and Lamar and the village idiot they used as their personal assistant didn't know about. He pulled the phone over and punched in the number.

"Yeah?"

"Time to earn your keep."

"I always earn my keep."

"Taylor's crossed the line. Take him out."

"What's he done?"

"You care?"

"No. Just curious."

"Stupid fuck coulda' killed one of my seconds. Take him out."

"'Bout damn time."

"Yesterday."

"I hear you."

The line went dead, and John leaned back, satisfied with the night's work.

Chapter Forty-Four

Alec Wimberly loaded Lexie into her kennel in the back of the Tahoe. He was on the 7:00 a.m. to 7:00 p.m. shift, and under ordinary circumstances that beat the hell out of the 7:00 p.m. to 7:00 a.m. shift. With a new baby in the house, he'd probably get more sleep pulling the night shift. The Sheriff pulled his unmarked Crown Vic in beside him.

"Alec! Glad I caught you. Hop in here a minute, will you?"

Alec hopped.

"Had a chat last night with one of the K-9 boys in Savannah. Said some good things about you."

"That's good to hear."

"Thinks we got a winner with you. So do I. That's why I got a special, sort of on-the-side job I'd 'preciate you taking on. If you can. How's sleep these days with that new baby boy?"

"He's doin' real good. Worth the lost sleep, for sure. And folks tell me this stage doesn't last forever, even if you don't believe it at the time."

"That's a fact. Well, here's the thing. I need you to start swinging off the interstate a couple of times on your shift. Circle 'round Big John's territory now and again."

"Something up?"

"Something's always up with him. Think you can do that for me?"

"Sure, no problem."

"Good man. Oh, and uh, by the way—you might keep your eye out for Billy Brayton while you're out there."

"Sir?"

"Welllll—few things come to my attention lately make me sort of want to know what Brayton's doing. Let's leave it at that." Brayton could drop beneath anybody's radar in about six seconds in any real town traffic and the Sheriff knew it. Turkey Creek and Rockland County was another story, though. All it had were clear views and open roads. Seeing a Tahoe in his rear view mirror off and on all day—and the Sheriff intended to have all four of the Tahoes on his tail by lunchtime—that'd drive Brayton crazy. Teach him to come into Clint Raines's territory without a by-your-leave and work an operation.

"Sir—you can't be serious!"

"Alec, it's a dirty world."

"There's no way—"

"Humor me on this, son. Or do I need to ask somebody else?"

The sheriff was off base. No way in hell Billy Brayton was dirty. But if he was bound and determined to put a semi-tail on Billy, it needed to be somebody who *knew* he wasn't dirty. Otherwise—well, otherwise, some shit could happen didn't need to be happening.

"No sir. I'll handle it."

"Knew you were the man to ask." One of 'em, anyway, but what the CPS guys didn't know wouldn't hurt 'em.

* * *

Jake stumbled to the kitchen, already dressed but bleary-eyed.

"Well, good mornin'! Thought you were goin' to oversleep and I'd have to come in and wake you up. You're not usually this glassy-eyed at seven."

"Had to finish a book report. Had to finish the book first."

"Not like you to wait till the last minute, buddy," Maggie said. "And you've always loved to read. You feel okay?"

"Mom. It was *Tess of the D'Ubervilles*."

"Well, that explains it. Told me that, I'd have bought you the Cliff Notes myself."

"I almost borrowed Ben's. Closest I've ever come." He looked over at Billy. "So—you solid this morning?"

"Excuse you?"

"I don't know what was goin' on with you yesterday, but you were freakin' me out. Did whatever it was have anything to do with your brakes last night?"

"Yeah, you could say that," Billy said. He sipped his coffee casually and mentally kicked himself in the ass for being so obvious. Then again, what was obvious to some folks was Chinese to others, and Jake was not one to miss the nuances of life. "Over now, buddy, I'm fine. Sorry I freaked you out."

"It's okay. Hope you don't make it a habit, though."

"Don't worry, I won't."

"You know, Dad and I are eating pancakes and sausage as we speak," Maggie said, as she watched Jake nuke a slice of leftover pizza.

"Gotta go, thanks, don't have time."

"This early?"

"Things to do, places to go. Later, dudes."

He was almost out the door when Billy called out. "Hey, Jake!"

"Yeah?"

"I love you, son."

"Love you too, Dad."

The door slammed. Maggie looked at Billy.

"Male bonding's a beautiful thing."

"Sarcasm?"

"Truth."

The Sheriff's Department ringtone blared from Billy's phone.

"Brayton."

"We got a situation," said Clint Raines. "Taylor's out off a back road with his face blown off."

"Where?"

"Out by Clayton Chapel."

"Same spot as O'Brien?"

"Sho' 'nuff."

"On my way."

* * *

Billy spotted the sheriff's unmarked Crown Vic and the twin of his own F-150 two miles down the dirt road that cut through the woods by Clayton Chapel. Investigator Charlie Jenkins was already on the scene. Not, in Billy's opinion, a particularly good thing. Charlie's specialty was finding pot fields. One of the Tahoes was there, too. Bobby Wainwright. And just so nobody'd get lonely, there was a patrol unit parked over on the side. Reggie Metts. Christ. Between them all, there wouldn't be a tread-mark or a shoeprint left.

"Nice of you to join us, Lieutenant." The Sheriff walked toward him.

"Maybe if you'd called me as soon as you called everybody else, I'd have already been here. Who found him?"

"Lucky there. Charlie was cutting through from Cold Creek to Ninety-Six. Likes to run the dirt roads, keep an eye out in case it looks like anybody's got something going on."

Bobby shouted from across the clearing. "Reggie! Don't *walk* over there, you've already puked by the car!"

Billy groaned. "How 'bout you get everybody pulled back from there and let me do my thing? Think you got enough feet trampin' through the scene? Anybody called for a medical examiner? 'Cause Stuart's not goin' to be a lot of help." Vince Stuart, like most of the coroners in rural counties, was the local mortician. A little more finesse would be needed on a murder scene.

"Charlie's an investigator, too, remember. He's been doing his thing, you don't need to worry."

"You think Charlie's got it, why'd you call me?"

"Just thought it was sort of—coincidental."

"With O'Brien?"

"With you."

"With me?"

"Well, I did hear you tell him he might get found on a back road with his head blown off. So where were you last night?"

"Excuse me?"

"Oh, you heard me. Where were you last night?"

"Check the department logs. Pull last night's accident reports. Lost my brakes. Lamar handled it. And then I was home."

"Simpson don't impress me that much. And home's pretty lame."

"Do you want me to look at this scene before it gets completely fucked to hell and back? Or do you want my badge? Which is it? Make your mind up right now and then live with it. "

"Well, hell, that's respect for rank."

"I thought we'd passed the pissing contest stage, Clint. I don't give a shit if you fire me or not and you know it. So whatever's stuck in your craw, either fire me it or get over it and get out of my way."

The sheriff shifted to the side. "Sorry. Little on edge."

"Okay, people!" Billy shouted. "Get away from the car and then everybody come show me where you've been! We're goin' be having a few in-house seminars on what to do and not do at a damn crime scene!"

Chapter Forty-Five

Jake sat on the lower bleachers in the midst of the Rockland Academy Testosterone Club in the far corner of the gym. It was a free period and the guys were holding important deliberations. To-wit: what to do for Tyler Stewart's upcoming eighteenth birthday. The senior males of Rockland Academy had their own Rite of Passage ceremony, separate and distinct from the gender neutral rite of passage conducted at Clayton Chapel marking a first-time driver's license.

This was different. This was a macho test just for the guys. Jake didn't know what the fuss was about. They'd talk big, and in the end, birthday boy camped out in the woods by himself. Thank God his birthday was in August. This January'd been colder than any he remembered. Then again, he'd about sweated to death on his own hot August night, fighting mosquitoes big as diving bombardiers and watching for snakes.

"Guys, good Lord! Will you hurry this up? Next weekend. Tent, sleeping bag, woods. Enough already!"

"I don't want just a camp-out," Tyler protested. "Everybody does that."

"Then why don't you go join the Marines? That tough enough for you?"

"It's the where, not the what! I want someplace different!"

"Okay, where?"

"Woods by Clayton Chapel."

"Say what?"

"Clayton Chapel."

"Dad doesn't want us—"

"Oh, c'mon, Jake! It's been months since anybody's been out there! And okay, yeah, probably the young kids and the girls don't need to be sitting out there at midnight alone. But this is one of us, not like *we're* sixteen or anything. Billy was out there all night.

Freaky bonfire story, but his ghost was pretty friendly. Maybe I'll get a chance to meet her."

"You're crazy. And Dad'll freak out."

"Why would he *find* out? *You're* not going to tell him, are you?"

Jake sighed. Somehow along the road between kindergarten and graduation, he didn't know when or where, he'd become everybody's big brother/guardian angel, the one who actually had some sense. He'd managed to keep several members of the tight-knit society from being, at best, grounded for life, and at worst, expelled.

Well, hell. No, he wasn't going to rat Tyler out. But he knew—he just knew—the ghost of Clayton Chapel wasn't the real reason Billy didn't want them out there. There was something else, something he couldn't put his finger on. And if he couldn't tell Billy, he supposed he'd have to truck on out there and check on the idiot a time or two himself during the night.

* * *

Alec cut across from the interstate over to Big John's territory. Keeping an eye on Kincaid territory was one thing. An obvious thing. It was the other thing that bothered him. He didn't like the sheriff's insinuations about Billy worth a damn.

From around a curve, he saw the glint of winter sunlight bouncing off car metal. All the land on either side of this road belonged to the Kincaid farm, had since the beginning of county history. Many dirt farm roads cut across it. From the position of that glint of sun on metal, a car was sitting at the top of one of those access roads, waiting to pull out. Alec slowed and pulled over to a dead stop, waiting until the glints of sun on metal told him that the car was on the road. He pulled on to the road again, maintaining a casual speed and caught up with the car.

 Holy shit. It wasn't. It couldn't be. Town legend centered around the feud between father and daughter. Miss Maggie hadn't set foot on her father's property or through his doors since the summer she'd buried Billy Brayton. Except for the day Billy came home, of course, when she'd marched into Big John's study and called him a daughter-fuckin' son of a bitch. The crown jewel of all the legends.

So what in the *hell* was she doing, pulling out of one of the Kincaid back roads? There was no way Billy was dirty. But *Miss Maggie*? If she actually did maintain a relationship with her father, why would she do it secretly? Which couldn't be that easy to keep secret now that she was married. And if Billy'd found out—was he *protecting* Miss Maggie? What the hell had the Sheriff stumbled onto?

He had to get off this road and pass Miss Maggie without making her suspicious. 'Course, she didn't know *he* knew she'd just pulled out, he'd hung back until he'd been certain the car was on the road. Law enforcement always went faster than the general traffic, even when it wasn't an emergency. He could just casually blow on by.

Feeling anything but casual, he hit the accelerator, pulled on around and passed.

* * * *

Maggie looked for the K-9 identification on the back. All the Tahoes looked alike and all the guys, being the same age and general build, looked pretty much alike behind the wheel. But every K-9 unit painted the dog's name underneath the tag.

"Lexie". Alec, then. *Shit, shit, shit*! She tried to be so careful when she left Big John's. She always used the back roads with bushy growth around the road, she never pulled out into plain view until certain no car was approaching from either direction. Where the hell had he come from? Had he seen her pull out? She hadn't seen him anywhere in sight when she'd turned onto the road, but he'd sure come into view mighty damn quick. Then again, all the guys drove pretty damn fast, including Billy. One of the perks of the job.

Oh, well. She gave a mental shrug. Nothing to do except shake it off. Billy'd need some extra TLC today, murder scenes had that effect on a man.

* * *

Billy walked into a kitchen full of the smells good enough to make a southern man weep. Maggie replaced the lid over a pot of some greens or other, and with that smell, he didn't much care if it was turnips, mustards, or collards. Mashed potatoes. Fried chicken. Fried okra. Staples of the Justice Café. Maggie didn't cook like this often at home, but if ever there was a night for it, this was it.

He kissed the back of her neck. "Smells like Southern Heaven, Princess. Maybe I should buy you a restaurant."

"Very funny. Had a feelin' comfort food'd be a big hit tonight. Was it rough?"

Billy shrugged. "Any death scene's rough. Wasn't nearly as rough as it would have been if it'd been anybody but Taylor. Clint Raines asked me where I was last night."

"Really?"

"Really. Couldn't have been any plainer if he'd flat out asked me if I did it."

"Did you?"

"*Excuse you?*"

Maggie laughed. "Sorry. Couldn't resist. I know you didn't have the energy to kill anybody last night."

"I was that impressive last night? Funny, I don't remember being impressive at all."

"You were that exhausted last night. Fell asleep in two seconds after you hit the bed. 'Course, pumping that much iron and running the property perimeter'll do that to you even without the rest of the night."

"You must have gotten back up last night. And Jake's got a big mouth."

"Couldn't sleep, you were snoring."

"Was not."

"Was too. And don't think I don't know you, Billy Brayton. Any threat to me or Jake, yeah, you could kill. You know it, I know it. I also know you came a lot closer the night Taylor waved a gun in Jake's face than you'd like for anybody to know. Clint Raines ain't that big a fool, he knows it, too. I can name three things you could have done just as easy as smashing his head into the car roof that would've left him dead. I could have done 'em. I'm pretty sure you know a lot more than three."

"Hell to live with somebody knows you that well."

"I'd have come a lot closer to killing Taylor than you did if I'd been there that night. And if you don't know it, you ought to. We've got something hard and dangerous in us most folks don't have, Billy. Everybody in this business does or they wouldn't survive very long. Sure as hell not as long as we have."

"So what you make of the Taylor thing?"

Maggie shrugged. "He crossed the last line Daddy Dearest intended him to cross with that brake thing. Figured that this morning when Raines called, but now I know so. I was out there this afternoon. Daddy Dearest picked up the phone last night soon as I hung up on him and put out the order. He didn't come right out and say it, but I know."

"You know to who?"

"No, 'fraid not. John Kincaid's cardinal rule. Never let the right hand know what the left hand's doing. He's got a few somebodies he always keeps off the radar. Always."

"Ideas?"

"If it was on the back road out by Clayton Chapel, how'd anybody find him so fast?"

"Story is Charlie Jenkins was just cutting through from Ninety-Six to Cold Creek."

"Possible."

"Or not."

"Or not. That night with Taylor—don't suppose the good Sheriff heard any threats?"

"Heard the exact threat. That if he ever came within a hundred feet of you or Jake again, there'd be another deputy found on a back road with his head blown off."

"Very interesting. His hearing the exact threat somebody made come true."

"Yeah, isn't it? What you think of Clint Raines, Princess? Really? Asked you once, but you were under cover at the time."

"Don't know. If he's dirty, he's real damn good at it. 'Course, Daddy Dearest protects his own. In the organization, Taylor was pretty much the same as he was in the department. A political favor for Davis Brown. Pretty useless and in fact, an actual liability. Surprised he lasted as long as he did. John always likes a big boy stashed in the wings. Although longevity would be good, too."

"So Clint Raines or Charlie Jenkins?"

"Or both. Or neither. Aurelia Andrews, remember? She could certainly have gotten Taylor on a back road with a good shake of booty. Might ought to call T-bone, tell him it was time to feel social. Is that where he was actually killed? Not moved, you don't think?"

"No, it was there."

"Well, she sure wouldn't want blood all over her sheets, now would she?"

"Charlie Jenkins is a good ol' boy, Princess. But he ain't that bright. 'Course, that's what I thought about my best friend until yesterday, too. Just like I knew in the depths of my soul my brother-in-law was dirty as a pig-sty." Billy sighed. "Life was much simpler then."

"Sounds like a country song."

A vibrating phone buzzed in Maggie's jean pocket. "My, my, that would be Lifeline. You wanta do the honors?"

She passed the phone over.

"And I thought my day was already bad," Billy said.

Faint hesitation. Lifeline was a trooper though. "My man! Hadn't heard from you in a few days, thought I'd check on you."

"Give it up. You didn't punch the wrong button. You called Maggie's phone."

"I'm screwed, huh?"

"You're screwed, *duh*."

"Maggie there?"

"Oh, yeah, you ain't that lucky."

"So—how screwed am I, guys?"

The voices came over Lifeline's phone together.

"We'll be *seein'* you."

Lifelife stared down at the dead phone. "I am *so* dead."

Country Justice

Chapter Forty-Six

Billy ran down Highway 80 the next afternoon. This was the third time today he'd passed one of the Tahoes, or had one of them pass him. Yesterday he'd seen one of the Tahoes twice. And not on the interstate where the Tahoes were supposed to patrol, barring special circumstances or special orders.

He hit Lamar's personal number, programmed in almost immediately after discovery of Lamar's actual identity. Or should that be, alter-ego? Too many phones, too many covers. And too damn many agents running around better at what they did than he was, which was a humbling experience for him. Especially considering he'd been sleeping with one of 'em for the last five months without a clue.

"Speak at me, my brother!" Just hearing Lamar's warm, rich drawl with the charm turned up high made a person smile. Until a few nights ago, frost coated his voice every time he'd spoken to Billy.

"You put out any special orders for CPS the last coupla' days?"

"No. Why?"

"They all seem to be crossing my path yesterday and today. And not on the interstate either."

"Where?"

"Sideroads and Eighty."

"What the hell they doin' there?"

"Hopin' you'd know, I damn sure don't."

"Well, *I* sure didn't tell 'em to be on no sideroads or Highway 80. And I don't think they'd decide to do it on their own."

"Can't think of but one other person with the authority to tell 'em to. Can you?"

"Nope, I can't for a fact. But why the hell would the sheriff do it?"

"He's been pretty strange yesterday and today, too."

"Murder in your county'll do that to a sheriff. I mean, nobody *liked* Taylor, but still—"

"Maggie's sure Daddy Dearest put the order out."

"I am too, but that don't help the good sheriff none. Wonder if he's gotten wind of something big comin' down, decided he wants his department to grab a little glory?"

"We got to get the boys back where they belong, can't have 'em showin' up unexpected. Gonna get one or all of us killed."

"Well, let's us have a little talk with one of 'em. I don't know 'bout you, but one of us gettin' killed'd really piss me off. Which one you want?"

"Alec. Good man, but still young enough he ain't gonna be able to keep a poker face. With either one of us, for sure not with both."

"Head over towards Chester Road, it dead-ends into dirt. I'm 'bout to call the boy to come meet me. You can come up behind him. Time for some double-teaming."

* * *

Alec turned down Chester Road, a narrow, barely paved side-road. Its original purpose was lost in distant memory. Damn, the major was far back, much further and he'd be hittin' dirt. And sure enough, there was dirt, and there was the major, his patrol car turned sideways. Please God, not another "special" assignment. This one was wrecking his nerves. He couldn't even fall asleep last night when he'd had the opportunity. Alec opened the door and cocked his head. Another car? Sure sounded like it, and sure enough—oh hell, it was an F-150. It was Billy.

The truck slowed and turned, blocking Alec's exit route. Not necessary, of course, but it added to the drama.

"Son, Billy tells me the Tahoes been all over the place yesterday and today, places they ain't s'posed to be. Apparently for a reason I don't know about. How 'bout you tell us why?"

Alec looked back and forth between them. He licked his lips.

"Major, could I maybe talk to Billy by himself for a minute?"

"Say *what*, boy?"

"I'm sorry, sir, it's not—it's—I don't know—"

Billy took pity. "Give us a minute, Lamar. Com'on, Alec." Billy led him back past the F-150, out of easy hearing range.

"Okay. Talk to me. Why the hell are all the Tahoes out in Kincaid territory? Or running up on me?"

Alec bit his bottom lip. "Because the sheriff told us to. Well, he told me to. I sort of figured he might have told the others, too, though. 'Specially since he wants—" Alec broke off. Billy wasn't dirty. But maybe his wife was. Maybe Billy knew that. Maybe he didn't.

"Since Lamar didn't, it pretty much had to be the sheriff. He 'specially wants what?"

"Wants us to keep an eye open around Big John's territory. And he wants—"

"I'm waitin'. Not too patiently."

"Wants us to keep an eye on you."

"On *me*?"

"I told him, Billy, I told him that was impossible, I know you're not dirty, I know it. But then yesterday—"

"You're pushin' my last button, son."

"Yesterday on the back roads—sun was glintin' up ahead, like off car metal, thought it was up at one of Big John's side roads. So I pulled off and waited for it to get on the road. Sheriff said he thought something might be about to go down with Big John. And when I got close enough, I saw it was—"

"It was who?"

"Miss Maggie. Comin' out the back way so nobody'd see her. And she don't have nothing to do with her daddy, or wants everybody to think she don't, so why else—and you—and she—and Billy, you can't! You can't throw your life and your career away to protect her, you just can't—"

"Lamar! Get up here!"

"Billy, don't get the major in this, don't put your ass out on the line for—"

Lamar came at a fast jog.

"Alec thinks Maggie's dirty, thinks I'm covering. Sheriff put 'em all out to tail me, and Alec saw Maggie coming out of one of the side-roads yesterday!"

Country Justice

"*Shit*! Boy, you tell the sheriff this yet? You tell *anybody* yet?"

"No sir. I wanted to talk to Billy, convince him not to do this, not to cover for her—"

"The sheriff's orders are countermanded, Officer. You did not *see* anything, you do not *know* anything, you do *not* talk to the sheriff. Are we clear on this?"

"Major, not tryin' to backtalk, sir, but he's the sheriff. You're not."

"Alec, you got a real shot in this profession 'cause you can think outside the box. You're thinking outside the box now, just in the wrong direction. But I trust you. Pretty much have to. Billy?"

"Yeah."

"And because we do, here's the deal. Neither of us carry any proof on us but trust me when I tell you this. Both of us can countermand the sheriff. We just did. What's more, *Maggie* could countermand the sheriff. And if you don't believe us, you can get us all killed, especially Maggie. And you don't want to be within a hundred miles of me or Billy if anything happens to her. Do you hear what I'm saying to you, boy?"

"*Miss Maggie?*"

"You have no idea who Maggie is, son, what she is. In fact, I think I'm about to make a call to put Sheriff Raines out of the picture till –"

"You can't. Suppose he's Big John's current secret left hand and suddenly disappears? You want a bigger tip-off?"

"The *sheriff?*" Alec whispered.

"Hell! Don't know what's wrong with me. You think he is, or you think he's just stupid?"

"Could be both. Too much of a chance to take, for sure."

"Well, just *hell!* Okay, let me round up the rest of the boys."

"You goin' to tell all *three* of 'em the truth? Like Alec said, he's the sheriff. You're not. Me neither."

"I can be pretty intimidatin', I get a mind to. I'm goin' try just tellin' 'em the sheriff's changed his mind before I blow cover any more than I already have, might buy us some time, anyway. Damn good thing we're so close. Twenty plus fuckin' years, that yahoo makes me break cover he's goin' be *real* sorry! *Son-of-a-bitch!*"

Lamar walked back to his patrol car, hissing curses with every breath.

Chapter Forty-Seven

Jake stood at his locker swapping out books. Tyler Stewart came up behind him.

"Hey! Guess what? My folks want to go to Savannah this weekend for my birthday, we're leaving after school Friday."

"And you're complainin'?"

"Wrecks my camp-out."

"Do it the next weekend, it's not that big a deal, Tyler."

"No, thought I'd do it tomorrow night instead."

"Whatever."

Jake shook his head as Tyler walked off. Hell. Tomorrow night was a Thursday night, and he had another infernal calculus test Friday. He'd have to grab his backpacking tent, set up out there himself where Tyler couldn't see him, 'cause he'd never get a chance to study running back and forth from home to the woods by Clayton Chapel. And it had been in the twenties every night for three weeks, with no sign of a warming trend. Thank God for Artic sleeping bags. This big brother status was getting *real* old.

* * *

Maggie slammed pots about in the kitchen as she emptied the dishwasher, venting frustration before she let the guys know about the change in the timetable. Florida had moved the deal up. Maybe he was antsy, maybe he'd gotten wind of something specific, or maybe he just wanted to yank her chain because she was a woman. Whichever, it meant a major overhaul in coordination, both the legal and illegal kind. Just *shit*!

* * *

The next generation of the Kincaid Cartel and their newest member leaned against their circled vehicles in the remnants of the parking lot of Mt. Olive Primitive Missionary Baptist Church at 9:00 p.m. that night. Maggie relayed the changes in scheduling.

"Damn! And you already got all that coordinated, little sister? With both sides?"

"I'm good, what can I say?"

"You 'de man."

"Am not!"

"Figure of speech, sis, don't get defensive just 'cause you got steel balls."

"Is that a compliment or an insult?"

"Both. Trust me."

* * *

Sheriff Raines sat back in his recliner, pipe in hand, in front of his fireplace. Brayton must have noticed by now that the Tahoes were tracking him. He hadn't bothered to ask any of the guys if they'd noticed anything out-of-kilter. Hell, he knew Brayton wasn't dirty. He just wanted to drive him crazy. But he'd check with them tomorrow. Because if any private—make that federal—or state—plans were shaking, he was damn sure going to know about them. Time to take his county back.

* * *

Tyler Stewart started setting up his pup tent in the woods adjoining Clayton Chapel's Cemetery at 5:00 o'clock Thursday afternoon. In January, it wasn't quite dark yet, but it wouldn't be long in coming. He'd parked out of sight further back on a maintenance road maintained by the church. He really liked Billy, all the boys did, but life just hadn't been the same since Billy'd manipulated them into abandoning Clayton Chapel as one of the rites of passage in the local teenagers' lives.

Tyler didn't know what all the fuss was about. There was nothing to it. The woods were just woods. They just happened to be by a cemetery. Though in the waning winter sunlight edging down toward dusk, everything was looking pretty damn spooky.

* * *

Lady Magdalene watched from the side. That child had no business being here. Tonight had that feel to it—tension was running through the air. Over the years she'd learned what that tension meant. Her dear husband had dirty business brewing. Leave it to John to make a church—and a very old one at that—the site of his unholy business dealings.

She moved in front of the boy and tried to catch his attention. He shuddered, but that was it. She'd never been able to make anyone but Billy actually see her.

And what was that noise? She turned her attention further back, to the dirt road that cut through the woods. The one where two men had gotten their heads blown off. Her finely tuned sensors picked up a well-known presence. It couldn't be. Why on *earth* would he be out here tonight?

She moved through the trees, visible to no one, and sure enough, there was her grandson, not by blood, exactly, but certainly by love, pulling out a hiking backpack and heading up into the woods closer to the cemetery. He was mumbling under his breath.

* * *

Jake was royally pissed. He was pissed at Tyler for insisting on this stupid ritual, especially on a school night, and he was pissed at himself for being here. If Tyler'd picked any spot but *here*, damn it, Jake wouldn't keep watch at all. But he had picked here, and it was the one spot in the county Billy'd ever tried to keep them away from. And when you got right down to it, who'd died and appointed *Jake* guardian angel? Nobody, that's who, and why he always felt like it was *his* responsibility to make sure his idiot friends didn't kill themselves, he just didn't know.

At least Mom and Dad weren't home, so he'd just left a note that he was spending the night out. Not a lie exactly, but he felt guilty about it anyway and that pissed him off, too. He slung his backpack on the ground and sat down against a tree trunk. Maybe Tyler'd spook out quick and he could get back home.

* * *

Lady Magdalene didn't want any of the local kids in the woods tonight. She especially didn't want her grandson out here. She'd never actually been alone with Jake before. Maybe if she just asserted a little more effort?

Jake's head cocked. Was he hearing her? No, he was—was he—actually *seeing* her?

His back moved higher and back against the tree. His eyes widened in shock. The Lady smiled. Well, what do you know? Another sensitive.

"Jake, sweetie, you don't need to be out here tonight, you know that, don't you?"

"Mom, I can explain!"

Chapter Forty-Eight

Silent figures in camouflage and camo paint slipped soundlessly through the woods, closing in on the Fellowship Hall of the old church. The leader, Billy Brayton by name, raised his hand in classic battle sign and dropped to the ground. He positioned himself in classic stance, body against the earth, arms, head raised slightly, tactical assault rifle on his back. A handgun was in his hand. He hoped to hell the assault rifles could stay on everyone's back. His wife, his best friend, and his wife's brother were in the line of fire.

* * *

The Sheriff leaned back in his chair. He propped his feet on his desk and laced his fingers behind his head. He hadn't gotten around to checking in with the CPS guys to see how much of a burr they'd been able to stick up Billy's ass the last couple of days, but Alec Wimberly was just coming in.

"Alec! Haven't had a chance to talk to you. Sit down. How's that special assignment goin'?"

Alec sat. Lamar's words replayed in his brain. *"The sheriff's orders are countermanded, Officer. You did not see anything, you do not know anything, you do not talk to the sheriff... Neither of us carry any proof on us but trust me when I tell you this. Both of us can countermand the sheriff...if you don't believe us, you can get us all killed, especially Maggie..."*

"Well?" The Sheriff raised an eyebrow.

"Well, nothin' much's been goin' on, Sheriff. I've swung by Kincaid territory off and on, haven't seen anything."

"Didn't really expect you to, but we could always get lucky. What's Billy been doin'?"

"Haven't run across Billy at all, Sheriff. Big county, you know."

"Yeah. Yeah, it is. Well, you get on home, rock that new baby awhile. Don't stay rockin' size long."

"Yes sir." Alec stood up. "Have a good night, sir."

"You too."

Raines leaned back again. Well, hell. Hadn't given Billy much of a headache, at least not from Alec. But there was Shane Attenborough coming in before he signed out.

He called out his greeting again.

"So, that special assignment we talked about. How's it shakin'?"

"Sir?" Shane looked puzzled.

"Your memory failin', son? Swing around Kincaid territory, keep an eye out for Billy? That ring any bells?"

"Well, yes sir. But the major told us you'd changed your mind about that, said we were supposed to stay out on the interstate."

"He did? And when in the hell did he tell you that?" Raines dropped his feet off the desk and leaned forward in his chair.

"Yesterday, Sheriff. Yesterday afternoon."

"*Son-of-a-bitch!*"

* * *

"And what are *you* doing out here, anyway?" Jake's first defensive shock wore off. The best defense was an offense and his mother didn't have any more business out here than he did. He didn't have a very clear view of the figure speaking to him. Dusk was settling in quickly and the woods were pretty thick right here. The voice was unmistakable. The figure moved closer. Jake did a double-take. Yeah, it was Mom. Sort of.

To Jake, as to every child, his mother was neither young nor old. She was just Mom. Every now and then when he stepped outside the role of child, he knew his mother was a beautiful woman whom no one would place at her real age. But right now, the way she looked must be due to the bad light, because she looked like he remembered her looking when he was little. When he was five or so, on up until he hit the teens. Like she'd looked in her early thirties, maybe.

He stood for a closer look. "Mom?"

"No, honey. I'm not your mom. I'm your grandmother."

He stepped back quickly.

"No. No, you're not—you're—Dad's seen you."

"Yes, he has. A couple of times, actually."

"That can't be right. He said he didn't know who you were. And you're—he had to— there's no way he wouldn't know who you are!"

Magdalene smiled. "I'm sure he had his reasons if he didn't tell you. Impressive man, your dad, even when he was sixteen. But please, Jake. You need to turn around and leave. Get your friend and take him with you. Please."

Chapter Forty-Nine

The Sheriff was not a happy man. If Lamar'd pulled Shane off, he'd pulled everybody off. Which meant Alec had lied like a dog. Two questions. *Why* would Lamar Simpson pull the CPS boys off any assignment the Sheriff made? And more importantly, *how* would he know about such assignment in the first place? Okay, three questions. Why had Alec lied about it?

The Sheriff punched in Alec's number.

"Sir?"

"Boy, you get your ass back in this office. Now."

* * *

Alec closed his eyes and winced. He wondered if he could support a family on a sales clerk salary. From the sheriff's tone, his days in law enforcement were limited.

* * *

The Sheriff sat in deep thought. Must have been pretty important to somebody that nobody tailed Brayton, though how the hell Simpson was in the mix, he didn't know. He'd suspected for some time Simpson might have some minor league role in the Kincaid Organization, the level of those suspicions rising and falling. Billy was Fed or State of some sort, though, for sure. Brayton could have broken cover and instructed Simpson to get the CPS boys off his back, but why? Billy didn't trust Simpson. At least, that was the impression he'd always given. And why the hell would he pull a *major* into an operation instead of him? Unless he didn't trust his own Sheriff. Which went back to the question of why he'd trust Simpson. The Sheriff sat bolt upright.

No way. There was *no way* Lamar Simpson had worked in his department right under his nose all those years without *somebody* having some inkling Simpson was Fed or State. Was there? Clint Raines didn't like the feelings these questions triggered. The feeling that maybe he'd been in the wrong business all these years.

* * *

"You sure do look like Mom." Jake shook his head. "Or I guess that ought to be, Mom sure looks like you. Dad's seen you. Now I have. Has Mom?"

"No, sweetie, I don't think she ever will. I think it's an inherited ability you got from from your father."

"Can't be. You *do* know I'm adopted?"

"Well, yes, you are. And then again, you're not. Exactly. I have a small request. Tell your mother she was right. Sometimes little souls who were meant to be do get a second chance from Heaven. And tell her she should tell you about it."

"I don't know what—"

"You don't have to right now. What you have to do is get out of here."

A blast of organ music peeled forth from the buildings.

"What the—"

"Jake, get your friend and get out of here!"

An engine roared through the woods.

"I don't think I got to worry about gettin' Tyler, Grandma." Jake stood, his head cocked to the organ music. "And that's about the fakest haunted church anybody could come up with. Sounds like a B-grade horror movie. That happen often?"

"I have to have a *bright* grandson! Yes, pretty often, it keeps folks away when they're not wanted. So will you *please*—"

"Jake? You talkin' to yourself, buddy? And what the hell you doin' out here, your dad's goin' to bust a gut."

* * *

Way to get busted, Alec. One of the other guys must have told the sheriff the major'd pulled them off special assignment. And it hadn't been Alec. But whatever Billy and the major were doing, it was *soon*. And now that he thought about it, as to where—Alec flashed back to his memorable night check at Clayton Chapel. Clayton Chapel threw off vibrations of eeriness. He'd known that his whole life. But those sensations were much more akin to Billy's story of his marijuana-laced ritual stay in the cemetery than to the horror show special effects that had almost made him wreck the patrol cruiser last September.

When he thought about it now, five months later, that's *exactly* what those back-lit silhouettes, the music spilling from the organ pipes, reminded him of. Special effects from a horror movie.

Good Lord! The Kincaid Organization used Clayton Chapel and its Fellowship Hall as the drop-off point, the special effects added to keep unwanted visitors—particularly any teenagers—away. Tonight? Maybe not. But maybe. If one of the other guys tailed Billy out there—or picked up on Miss Maggie coming out from a Kincaid side road and tailed *her* there—and if they told the sheriff about it—Billy and the major and Miss Maggie would be in deep shit and not have a clue.

Sales clerk, hell. After tonight, he'd be damn lucky to stock shelves in a grocery store. Because no way was the Sheriff going to interfere in this. He couldn't let him. Alec turned right onto Highway 96, heading to the interstate and Clayton Chapel.

* * *

The Sheriff walked outside, ready to nail Alec's hide to the wall the minute he pulled into the LEC parking lot. Otherwise, he'd never have seen the Tahoe turn right onto 96 at the four-way stop sign.

What the *hell*? The boy was running straight down 96? He wasn't coming back to the LEC? Was this his department or *what*? Did anybody in his freakin' *department* remember he was the freakin' *Sheriff*, for God's sakes?

Well, he'd just see about that. He cranked his Crown Vic and squealed out of the LEC parking lot after Alec.

* * *

"No! Jake, go! Don't trust him!" Jake's eyes widened. In her agitation, Magdalene lost control and slipped into her death head mode. She fought to reform her features, but Jake seemed to be taking her appearance in stride.

"Hey, Mr. Charlie, what's shakin'? Whatcha doin' out here?" Jake picked up his backpack and slung it over his shoulder.

"I could ask you the same thing, buddy. You well past sixteen, what's up with the backpack?"

"Oh, you know the guys. Manhood campout deal when we turn eighteen. Tyler got a wild hair to do it here, thought I'd keep an eye out on him, but I guess that's a pretty moot point right now, way he just peeled rubber out of here. So I guess I'll just head back home, too."

In the sudden transition between day and night that occurred in winter, full darkness blanketed the woods. Moonlight glinted off the gun in Charlie Jenkins' hand.

"No, buddy, I really don't think you will."

Chapter Fifty

"Let's take a little walk, son." Jenkins motioned toward the church with the Glock.

"Mr. Charlie, I don't know what's goin' on, but if I stumbled into the middle of a department operation, I'm sorry, be just as glad to stumble back out." Jake didn't figure the department blasted out vintage horror organ music in the middle of an operation, but it made for conversation, anyway. For the second time in three months somebody'd pulled a *gun* on him, for God's sakes. And even though Mr. Charlie didn't wave it wildly in his face, Jake figured it'd kill him just as dead.

"Well, that's not my call, Jake. Don't be stupid, son. Start walking."

Jake walked. His grandmother had disappeared. She had a plan. All he had to do was stay ready.

* * *

Lady Magdalene swirled through the woods. The atmosphere pulsated with electricity. It always did before her husband's business deals. Tonight was different though. More intense. More people were here. She navigated through the trees. Who was here? More to the point, could she *use* any of them?

She completed roughly a half-circle around the church and stopped. She smiled. Thank God. That young, rough, mad-at-the-world sensitive. He was here. Her son-in-law. Jake's father. In more ways than one.

* * *

Alec swore under his breath. Something was shaking at Clayton Chapel. Approaching the turn, he felt it, man, oh, yes, he did, and much further away from the source than usual. Alec wasn't strong enough to actually *see* Lady Magdalene or any of the entities who hung around temporarily before moving on, but he was tuned-in enough to feel them, just like he felt the undercurrents in the air that swirled around living humans. All humans gave off hints and signals of emotion and action and the best law enforcement officers could read them. Most of them never even realized they were doing it. It was simply part of them, like their eye color.

Clint Raines' Crown Vic appeared behind him. Damn, the sheriff'd probably been in the parking lot and seen him make the turn. As pissed as he'd sounded on the phone, he'd put on the blue lights and sirens any minute now. Unless he wanted to see where Alec was going. And in that case, if Alec kept going, maybe the sheriff would just keep going, too.

Alec passed the turnoff to the church and ran past it another mile or so, heading to one of the dirt roads that ran back into private property. He pulled in, braked abruptly, and cut the wheel of the Tahoe to turn and block the road. The Crown Vic's brakes squealed. Alec braced for an impact that didn't come. He grabbed his chance. He only had a few seconds. He jumped out of the Tahoe, handcuffs in hand.

He was halfway to the Crown Vic when the driver's door flew open. The Sheriff jumped out of the car.

"*Boy!* What the *hell* do you think you're *doin'?*"

Alec threw out his foot. The Sheriff couldn't stop his momentum and landed flat on his face. Alec grabbed both the sheriff's hands and handcuffed them behind his back.

"*What the hell?*"

"Sorry, sir." Alec whipped the sheriff's shoulder radio unit off his shoulder and pulled the connection loose. He grabbed the cellphone off Raines' belt, just for good measure, even though there was no way the sheriff was going to reach it. He sat down on the small of the sheriff's back.

Raines's bellows turned into incoherent roars. Alec understood them with no problem. They didn't bode well for Alec's continued career in law enforcement.

"Sorry, sir. But you ain't trackin' Billy or the major tonight. You'll get 'em killed, maybe some other folks, too. You're not talkin' to anybody, you're not goin' anywhere."

"You fuckin' *fool*! How long you think you can keep me here?"

"Long as I have to. Real sorry 'bout this, sir, you want me to help you up and put you in the backseat of the Tahoe, or you just want us to stay here on the ground? "

The roars changed to total incoherence. Raine's face went puce. Alec decided he'd better just hush. This situation wasn't getting any better till it got a hell of a lot worse.

* * *

Lady Magdalene spoke directly into Billy's ear.

"Billy!"

His head jerked, his eyes widened.

"Don't move! And don't talk to me, just listen! Jake's here and he's in trouble. A man—I don't know his name, but he's been here before. Jake called him Mr. Charlie. He's got a gun on Jake and he's taking him to the back house."

Billy belly-crawled to the supine figure on his other side and whispered in the man's ear. Then Billy was up, crouched, and moving through the trees toward the Chapel's back house.

* * *

Charlie Jenkins nudged Jake through a side door of the back house with the barrel of the gun.

"Sorry, folks, unexpected visitor."

"What the *hell*—"

Jake saw a group of people in the middle of the room surrounding large crates of stacked—*money*? Was that it? Yeah, it was, and a hell of a lot of it. His mother turned and stared at him. She was standing by a man Jake recognized but had never talked to. Big John Kincaid. T-bone was there, and the CPS commander,

Lamar Simpson. Along with four tough-looking street thugs with Florida tans.

His mother looked at him like she'd look at a roach. She'd never looked at him like that in his life.

"Damn! You haven't been *enough* trouble all your life, you've got to show up now?"

"Mom?"

"Well, hell," Big John said. "Your call, Maggie, whatcha wanna do about him?"

"Keep him out of the way for now. So, Charlie, had an idea you might be one of Daddy Dearest's secrets. You're pretty good. We get through, I guess we can leave the body as a warning to keep away from Clayton Chapel. Probably work better than those special effects from the carnival show you been using."

Jake's world reeled. "Who the hell are you and what have you done with my mother?" .

"Good God, kid, use that brain that's supposed to be so damn good. We'da starved a long time ago, I wasn't moonlighting at something!"

* * *

Billy peered in through a side window, so focused on Jake he didn't hear the footsteps behind him.

"Well, hey, good-lookin'! Fancy meetin' you here!" Aurelia Andrews laughed and pulled the pistol out of his hand. "Why don't I just take some of this extra weight off your back?" She slipping the assault rifle off his shoulder. "Now, where's that extra firepower I just know you're packing?"

She ran her hands down over his hips and legs and pulled out his ankle gun. "I'd have enjoyed that a lot more in other circumstances. Why've you been so stubborn? Let's go in and say hello, why don't we?"

Billy allowed himself one mental kick in the ass, but he didn't waste time on any more. He could disarm her in two seconds flat, but if she took him inside, he could concentrate on getting Jake out of the line of fire. Country Justice already had enough going on in there. Better just get inside and follow their lead. God knows they were better at this than he was, and didn't this just prove it. He moved forward with no protest.

"Hey, guys! Good grief, Jake too? Regular family reunion in here, ain't it?"

"Dad!"

"Just hang loose, buddy, gonna be okay."

"*Oh for God's sakes!*" Maggie rolled her eyes. "Will you just fuckin' *stay* dead this time?"

* * *

Jake wasn't sure where the gun came from. It was just there, in the hands of the woman he'd thought was his mother. It wasn't silenced. The discharge was very loud. It seemed to him Billy fell in slow motion. It took him a very long time to hit the floor. And then, in the miraculous way time slows down and speeds up, everything exploded around him. He flung himself down and over Billy's body.

He felt orphaned. He'd never call her mom again and in this moment, she was deader to him than Billy, the dad he'd waited eighteen years for. Shattering glass sprayed from the windows . For the first time, he noticed Billy was in camouflage. Oh God, this had been a stake-out. Billy'd been waiting, not by himself. And if Jake hadn't been here, Billy'd never have come in blind. Because of course that's where his grandmother had gone when she disappeared. She'd gone to find Billy.

In seconds the room was full of camouflaged figures holding assault rifles on the four toughs with the Florida tans. Jake risked a sweeping glance around the room and saw T-bone twisting Miss Aurelia's arm up behind her back. Major Simpson duplicated the move on Charlie Jenkins. Then he heard Maggie's voice, colder than ice crystals. She dug the barrel of her Glock into Big John's temple.

"Give me an excuse. Please. Move just half an inch."

One of the camouflaged figures moved up to her. "We've got it, Agent Kincaid."

"Brayton," Maggie corrected.

"Ma'am?"

"Agent *Brayton*. Don't you *ever* call me Kincaid. Especially not when I've got a gun in my hands."

Maggie hurried over to Jake. She knelt by Billy.

"*Don't. Touch. Him.*"

"Honey, I'm so sorry! I wish you'd never seen that." She patted Billy's cheeks. "Billy! C'mon, shake it off! You're scarin' your son!"

"What the *hell* are you doing?" Jake swatted her hands away.

"Jake, give it up! Do you *see* any blood? I had to hit him in the body armor before Daddy Dearest told Jenkins to blow his head off. Ol' Charlie favors head shots! You I could stall on, Big John's always had a soft spot for you, kept trying to talk me into bringin' you into the family business but Billy's always been a burr up his butt—"

Billy moaned.

"Billy? C'mon, that's it, say something!"

"*Shit. Damn. Hell.* That *hurts.*"

Jake stared at the two people he'd thought he knew better than anybody else in the world.

"He's really all right?"

"He don't feel real good right now, hurts like hell getting hit in body armor, but he's fine, honey, really." Maggie shifted, put her arms underneath Billy and helped him to a sitting position. "You okay? Just bruised, or you got a cracked rib?"

Billy whistled through his teeth. "Cracked rib, I think."

"Sorry."

"That's okay, Princess. I'm alive. You didn't have to warn me to stay dead, though, I coulda figured it out. If I'd been more than half-conscious, that is. Thanks for fallin' on me, buddy, best thing you could have done, got you down out of the way. Though I'd planned on pulling you underneath me instead of the other way around. You kind of left your ass hanging in the wind there."

Jake stared at Maggie. "*Agent* Kincaid?"

"No, Agent Brayton, don't you *listen*?"

"*Agent?*"

"Honey, one more time—we'da starved a long time ago, I wasn't moonlightin' at something. That much was sure true."

"And T-bone and the major?"

"Don't think you've ever been formally introduced. Hey, guys!" Maggie waved. "C'mon over here! Jake, this is my partner. And, of course, your uncle by love. Special Agent Jackson Jones."

Jake stared as T-bone headed toward him. One man started toward him. During the process, the slumping shoulders and incipient beer belly disappeared. The chin raised, the profile changed. Another man entirely stood in front of him.

Jake shook his head. "T-bone? For *real*?"

Jack smiled. "For real. Look a little different, huh?"

"Oh. My. God. I can't believe it. I just—I—I'm sort of embarrassed, I think. I mean, I always thought—"

"That's okay, buddy. You thought I hung the moon when you were little, but time you got eleven or twelve, you knew I was just a good ol' boy didn't have the sense of a twelve-year-old myself. Just your good buddy you had to look out for. 'Cause he sure didn't have the sense to do it himself. You believed the act, just like you were s'posed to. Biggest compliment you could ever give me."

"And you've never met this gentleman, either, not for real." Maggie motioned Lamar over and reached up for his hand. "Special Agent Lamar Simpson, Georgia Bureau of Investigation. Your uncle by blood. This is my brother, Lamar. Though he objects as loud as I do to being called Kincaid."

Lamar smiled and held out his hand. "Sorry you've never known I've always been here for you, Jake. But you've had an extra pair of eyes watchin' out for you your whole life, you'd best believe it."

Jake shook his uncle's hand. "Holy. Hell."

"So, quite a night you've had, buddy. Now make my day and tell me you've changed your mind about your major."

"Oh *hell* to the no! Everybody in the *family's* in it! Unless they're the bad guys, that is." He watched as his grandfather was led away.

"Really?" One of the camo'd figures broke away from the crowd and joined them. "You mean *another* one's coming up? Good things come to those who wait!"

"Lifeline," said Maggie. "Now that voice I'd know anywhere. Brave man, showing up here. Thought you didn't do field work anymore. You look good in camo, though."

"Figured it might be my last chance to try and talk the two of you into one more operation. Couldn't just sit up there in Virginia, now could I? And you just passed up a *great* opportunity there. Billy could've stayed dead, we'd set new identities in another state—"

"Not if hell froze over. And what do you mean the two of us? The three of us. This is Jack's last hurrah, too."

"Well, Maggie-pie, I been doin' a lot of thinkin' 'bout that. I'm really tired of bein' T-bone. And I'm really tired of loadin' up busted cars, too. Thought I'd reincarnate myself. Out on the Gulf maybe. Think I'll try runnin' a bar. Told 'em I wanna be Bo Franklin. What y'all think of the name? Though it won't be the same without you, darlin'."

"Give me a few years to get out there," Jake said. "We'll keep it in the family."

Maggie and Billy groaned. Lamar frowned and pulled his phone out of his pocket. He read the text message and laughed out loud.

"Okay, boys and girls, I got to go rescue the sheriff."

"What?"

"Alec. Sheriff figured out I called off the boys, tried to tail Alec to find us. So Alec's got ol' Clint handcuffed on the ground and cussin' a blue streak out off one of Scott Reardon's farm roads!"

Chapter Fifty-One

The County Commissioners called a special meeting the day after the take-down. They sent special invitations to Lamar Simpson and Billy Brayton. Billy would much rather have stayed home and nursed his taped cracked rib.

"Gentlemen, we've asked you both here because we have an emergency in the Sheriff's Department. Sheriff Raines has resigned."

"Say what?"

"Resigned. Says in his resignation letter his errors in judgment came close to endangering a joint Federal-State Undercover Operation and worse, endangering the lives of several agents."

"Well," Lamar drawled, "can't argue with that."

"And so we've called this meeting to ask if either of you would consider taking the interim position until the next election."

"Sure. Major Simpson will." Billy got up and headed to the door.

"Oh hell no, he won't! You sit your rear-end back down! You think I'm throwin' away a GBI pension for the *sheriff's* job? You crazy, my brother."

"That leaves you, Lieutenant. What about it?"

"No way. No how. No."

"Billy, we need you. The county needs you. And you're retirin' from all that undercover stuff, right? You know you're the best man for it, think of the county folks. We can't just throw somebody in there don't know the Department. Or the county."

Lamar laughed. "At least not anybody who'd work for that salary."

"Lamar, you hush now. Billy, c'mon, whatcha' say?"

"Shit. Just shit. But only till I can get one of the young guys trained right."

"We can live with that."

Country Justice

Chapter Fifty-Two

Monday's menu at the Scales of Justice Café: Fried pork chops, beef tips with gravy, black-eyed peas, okra-n-tomatoes, white rice, cream corn, string beans, squash, turnips, peach cobbler. Monday's menu was always the same. So was Tuesday's menu, and Wednesday's menu. A good thing in the midst of all the chaos. During this trial week, the town needed something to depend on. Turkey Creek'd been knocked right out of its orbit this past year since Billy's return.

The folks in the serving line waited to pick their one meat and three vegetables. Lawyers and law clerks and paralegals and witnesses and potential jurors mingled in the crowd. That didn't even count the folks who'd just come to gape. The girls of the Scales of Justice Café were ready to pull their hair out.

So far, there hadn't been much to gape at. Jury selection was a tedious process, barely even begun. Leola blew by Junie Bug on her way back to the kitchen to throw more chicken in the deep fryer. It was a double-duty day for them all. No way the waitress could keep up with the tea re-fills by herself. They were all frazzled.

The pressure of the crowd wasn't the problem, though. The fragments of conversation were driving them crazy.

"Complete waste of time and county money. Ain't never gonna get no jury picked. And no jury's gonna convict Big John Kincaid. Not in this county. Not in this lifetime..."

"It's a damn shame, what Maggie's done. Man's little girl turning on her daddy like that..."

"I just don't know what they're thinking with that jury pool. How many folks don't know Big John? I mean, they either work for him or he's screwed 'em over..."

"Blood's blood, just ain't right, you don't do that to your daddy..."

"They need to just hurry up and get on with it. 'Bout damn time the high and mighty found out they ain't God, can't just run all over folks doing whatever they want. Ain't nobody s'pposed to be above the law..."

"I heard something 'bout 'em trying to move the trial somewhere else. Now, what'd they call that? Change of something. Venue? Jurisdiction?"

The Dead Dick Table was the worst. Junie Bug and Leola had called that crew the Dead Dicks for years, the name being derived from the ages of the occupants. The Dead Dicks ran most of the businesses and between them, controlled most of the county money. And they were grumpy as hell when they didn't get the attention they believed their due. Like now.

Junie Bug gritted her teeth and wielded her serving spoons. What she wouldn't give to walk by that table pouring hot gravy over their heads. And if they didn't keep their mouths off Maggie, sooner or later she might just do that.

* * *

Tuesday's Menu at the Scales of Justice Café: Fried chicken, roast beef with gravy, butter beans, cream potatoes, yams, fried okra, collard greens, whole corn, cook's choice of dessert. Just like every other Tuesday, even though this second day of the trial wasn't like any other Tuesday Turkey Creek had ever seen. The only constant was the menu, and the café itself.

Like Monday, the lunch crowd overflowed the doors of the café, more impatient today than yesterday. It looked like the action might start this afternoon. It hadn't been easy, but the jury'd finally been picked and opening arguments given, more in spite of the attorneys than because of them. Lots of highly-paid, high octane legal education sat at the defense table, walking the finest line the judge allowed, trying to set up the defense while questioning prospective jurors during *voir dire*.

Arguments in the café came dangerously close to blows. Everybody had an opinion and nobody was shy about sharing it.

"Set-up! Nothing but a set-up! You're telling me they know how somebody died all those years ago? Bullshit!"

"Yes, they can tell! You never watch 'Cold Case'? Or 'CSI'?"

"The woman died from a gunshot to the head! Okay, they know that. They knew it then. But there's no way they can tell she didn't pull the trigger!"

"Well, you might have a point there! 'Cause if I was married to Big John, I'da sure been tempted to pull the damn trigger!"

"There you go! Just like everybody else. After all that man did for this County, the money he brought in—"

"That kind of money we don't need. Never did."

Over at the Dead Dick Table, Davis Brown, second in power in the county, held his own court, more feudal than legal. Dissention brewed at the Dead Dick Table.

"Don't know what the big deal is after all this time. So a drug-runner got his face shot off. Who cares besides his mama?"

"Well now, Davis, you got to admit. Came in mighty handy there for John."

"So he used it to get that white trash out of his little girl's head once and for all! Just took advantage of circumstances, that's all. C'mon, we're all fathers. What wouldn't you do for your kids?"

"Don't know as I'd blow somebody's face off just to fill a coffin. And it didn't work all that well, either, now did it? She married him the day after he showed back up in town."

"Now, ol' Bo just happened to have that little run-in! Can't blame him for wanting to get outta all the paperwork. The good guys ain't got a chance these days, damn lawyers and judges got 'em all tied up. Tell him, Roy!"

Roy Lee Rollins had served four terms as Sheriff between Bo Franklin and Clint Raines. Rollins hadn't been the overt enforcer for Big John Bo Franklin'd been, but everybody'd known there were certain times no Rockland County law enforcement officer would be found in certain parts of the county.

"That's a fact, I can't deny it. But just burying that body as somebody else—got to say that's a real inventive way of gettin' out of paperwork. Don't know as the thought would have ever crossed my mind."

Davis glared. "Oh no, you *never* thought about blurring any lines, did you, Roy Lee?"

"Well, I mighta blurred 'em a bit on occasion. But I never *erased* any, and ain't nobody can ever prove I did."

"Oh, and you think they can prove ol' Bo did?"

"Shit, I *know* they can. So do you."

* * *

Wednesday's menu at the Scales of Justice Café: Meat loaf, spaghetti, cream potatoes, whole corn, cabbage, English peas, fried okra, Texas toast or cornbread, cook's choice of dessert.

On Wednesday, the first of the state's forensic experts took the stand. His testimony concluded prior to the lunch break. And it had the lunch crowd buzzing.

"Now, Mr. Atkins, you've examined the contents of the official investigation file. And that file contains a gun that has always been labeled as the gun with which Magdalene Kincaid killed herself, isn't that correct?"

"Yes, it is."

"And that gun is a .22 caliber revolver, is it not?"

"Yes, it is."

"And that gun was, in fact, Mrs. Kincaid's gun?"

"Yes, it was."

"And .22's and .25's are frequently carried by ladies and referred to as ladies' guns, is that right?"

"Yes."

"And was there a .22 caliber bullet in that investigation file that was recovered from Mrs. Kincaid's body during the autopsy?"

"No."

"There wasn't?"

"No."

"And the reason for that would be?"

"There are two reasons for that. The first would be there wasn't an autopsy."

"Even though in cases of violent death, it's been a legal requirement in the state of Georgia for some time that autopsies be performed. Was that the law at the time of Mrs. Kincaid's death?"

"Yes, it was."

"And what does the file show as the reason for the omission of an autopsy?"

"That it was so obviously a suicide there was no reason to put the family through any further suffering."

"I see. And the second reason for there being no bullet in the file would be?"

"An autopsy wouldn't have recovered a bullet."

"Why not?"

"Because the bullet shattered bone both on entry and exit, falling somewhere on the ground. Or possibly lodging in a tree, depending on the growth there at the time. Apparently, no one looked."

"And following the logic of the investigating officers on this case that it was so obviously a suicide as to necessitate no follow-up checks, no investigator looked for a bullet— or a casing, since that bullet—or casing—would be the .22 caliber bullet that caused her death. Would that be why there's no .22 caliber bullet in the file?"

"No, that wouldn't be why."

"Then please tell us why there isn't."

"Objection, calls for an opinion."

"Your Honor, that's why it's called an expert opinion."

"Overruled. But move this line of questioning on, Mr. Whittaker."

"Yes, Your Honor. Mr. Atkins, why would no .22 caliber bullet be found?"

"Because she wasn't killed with a .22 caliber revolver."

The murmurs reverberated throughout the rows of benches.

"She wasn't?"

"No, she wasn't."

"And without the bullet how do you know this?"

"Because a .22 wouldn't have caused that kind of damage. It wouldn't have shattered the skull, the bullet wouldn't have exited. Suicides attempted by head shots with a .22 don't, in fact, always succeed."

"Really?"

"Really."

"And from the GBI's examination of the exhumed body, what gun did kill Mrs. Kincaid?"

"A .38 or a .357 Magnum. Either one at that range would be consistent with the damage."

"And were there any extenuating circumstances which might have reasonably caused this misconception by the investigating officers?"

"I can't think of any. I've never known an experienced lawman who didn't know the difference between the damage a .22 and a .38'll do."

"And that's your expert opinion?"

"No, that's a fact."

"And this investigation was conducted by experienced lawmen?"

"I would hope so. Bo Franklin'd been the sheriff almost thirty years at the time."

* * *

Thursday's menu at the Scales of Justice Cafe: Fried chicken, turkey, dressing, sweet potato soufflé, macaroni & cheese, broccoli casserole, peas, collard greens, banana pudding.

Junie Bug mixed the secret ingredients of the cornbread dressing everybody loved. Leola measured the vanilla that gave the sweet potato soufflé an extra dash of sweetness. Lord knows, they'd tried every summer to change the Thursday menu to something lighter than a Thanksgiving feast, but the regulars threw a fit. So Thursday's menu was eternal. Just like every day's menu at the Scales of Justice Cafe.

Across the street in the courtroom, the prosecution put the first of its two star witnesses on the stand.

"State your name, please."

"Lamar Simpson."

"And your occupation?"

"Have two of 'em. Far as most folks know, I'm Major Lamar Simpson, Supervising Officer, Crime Prevention/Swat Team, Rockland County Sheriff's Department."

"And the other?"

"Special Agent Lamar Simpson, Georgia Bureau of Investigation, specially assigned to the Rockland County Sheriff's Department."

"On one particular assignment?"

"Yes."

"Which would be?"

"To work the Kincaid Cartel."

"Why's the Kincaid Cartel important?"

"It's a major mid-state link in the drug traffic up from Florida for distribution up the east coast."

Murmurs resounded throughout the courtroom. Of course, everybody knew that already. No way to keep that under wraps in Turkey Creek during the intervening time from the take-down at Clayton Chapel till trial time, but it just sounded so—dramatic—when actually admitted by the man many in the room had watched grow up.

"To work? Not shut down?"

"Oh no, we could have shut it down a long time ago. But that would have killed our link to the current cartels on the coast and the northern cartels they supply. The Kincaid operation was much more valuable left in place."

"And do you know who the head of the Kincaid Cartel is?"

Lamar smiled.

"Oh, yes."

"And that would be?"

"John Kincaid."

"And do you have any relationship with John Kincaid other than through your undercover work?"

"Well, I sure hate to admit it, but yes, I do."

"And what would that be?"

"He's my father. But I don't want any of y'all holdin' that against my mama. Wasn't her idea at all to get that up close and personal with the man."

"Objection!"

The courtroom went wild. The judge pounded for order.

"Agent Simpson, watch your comments," the Judge ordered.

"Yes sir."

"But the drug charges aren't the only thing John Kincaid's on trial for here, is it?"

"No sir."

"He's on trial for the murder of Magdalene Kincaid. So would you tell the jury why you're a witness on that aspect of the charges?"

"I was there. I saw it. I saw John Kincaid hold a .38 Special to Magdalene Kincaid's head and pull the trigger."

Waves of shock rippled across the courtroom. Lamar had waited years to tell this story publicly. He did it justice.

The defense counsel approached cautiously.

"And you were how old when Magdalene Kincaid committed suicide?"

"She didn't commit suicide."

"But that's the official ruling, isn't it?"

"It's wrong."

"Major—"

"Special Agent."

"I apologize. Special Agent Simpson, you didn't answer my question. How old were you at the time of Magdalene Kincaid's death?"

"Five."

"Five-year-olds aren't generally considered reliable witnesses, wouldn't you say?"

"Depends on what they're witnesses to. Murder has a way of imprintin' itself in the brain, know what I'm saying? Makes kind of a lastin' impression."

The prosecution fired the second barrel of its smoking gun.

"Now, would you state your name for the Court, ma'am?"

"Luellen Simpson."

"And are you Special Agent Lamar Simpson's mother?"

"I am."

"Did you know your son's true job here in Rockland County?"

"No, I spent all those years worried to death he was his daddy made over in black skin."

"Objection!"

"And I'm ashamed." Aunt Lulu waved at her son from the stand. "Love you, baby. And I'm *so proud*!"

"Mrs. Simpson, please—"

"Yes sir. Watch the comments."

The district attorney smiled.

"And how much can you tell us about John Kincaid's business dealings over the years, Mrs. Simpson?"

"How much you wanta know?"

* * *

Big John Kincaid sat in his study after the day's Courtroom drama concluded. That bitch Luellen had put a hurting on him, for sure. After all he'd done for her, given her a home all those years, the job that let her raise her brats in a good home. Her other brats, that is. Lamar was his and blood was blood and she couldn't ever say he hadn't helped her take care of the boy, even if he wasn't about to acknowledge it publicly. And look what she'd done to him today. Her and Lamar both.

He was tired. Tired of being cooped up in a courtroom, tired of being a virtual prisoner in his own house. He hadn't been in a jail cell these past months, because money was good for bail if nothing else. He didn't want to run, even if he had anywhere to run, which he didn't, and even if he could, which he couldn't. Some member of the Rockland County Sheriff's Department followed him everywhere. Brayton made sure of that. And if that wasn't a kick in the ass, he didn't know what was. Bo Franklin must be rolling in his grave, that white trash wearing the Sheriff's badge. John guessed he'd find out whether folks really rolled in their grave sooner rather than later. He still didn't think he'd be convicted, but even if he was, no way he wouldn't be dead of natural causes long before any execution ever took place. Yeah, his grave wasn't that far out in the future. He knew that.

He was seventy-five years old, in bad health, betrayed by the two children who'd been his private pride and joy. He'd never told them that, of course, and was really glad he hadn't. Fruit wasn't supposed to fall far from the tree, but his sure had. They'd played him like a fool and that had aged him years overnight, aged him far quicker than diabetes or heart disease or high blood pressure ever had.

But these walls—they'd gotten awful old, awful quick. He laughed and picked his car keys up from his desk. Time to let those damn deputies earn a little of their paychecks. He'd give 'em a game of follow the leader. Too bad he wasn't heading down a dirt road so they could eat his dust.

Dusk settled in as he parked. Hazy mist rose from the ground, born of humidity trapped during the heat of the day. He got out and walked toward Clayton Chapel's cemetery. Toward Magdalene's grave. He didn't believe in any afterlife, not really, but if there was one, that bitch must be ecstatic. She was still dead, though. And he wanted one last spit on her grave. Just one.

The mist was thicker by her headstone, almost solid. A figure swirled and condensed into solid form. It didn't bother to reform the features shattered so many years ago by a .38 bullet.

He grabbed his chest. Shooting spasms of electric shocks exploded outward from his heart. He dropped to the ground. The figure spoke.

"Hello, John. I've been waiting for you."

* * *

Friday's menu at the Scales of Justice Café: Hamburger steak, catfish, baked beans, coleslaw, fried okra, baked potato, hushpuppies, cook's choice of dessert.

The early crowd gathering at the café was as large as it had been during the prior days of Big John Kincaid's trial, but for a different reason. Court wasn't in session today. Things had changed since court adjourned the evening before.

"I declare, did you ever?"

"What you think possessed John to go out there?"

"Makes you think, don't it? I mean, if he killed her, why'd he want to go out to the grave?"

"Ever hear of a guilty conscience?"

"Ever hear of true love? You could give the man the benefit of a doubt!"

"Why the hell would I give Big John any benefit? He damn sure never gave anybody else any benefits, not less'n it got him something he wanted, anyway!"

Gail Roughton

The town buzzed, but no one knew what happened last night. No one ever would. No one had been there. Nobody but Big John and his wife. No witnesses except the graves of Clayton Chapel.

The End.

Gail Roughton Books Published by Books We Love

The Witch - War-N-Wit, Inc., Book 1
Resurrection - War-N-Wit, Inc., Book 2
The Coven - War-N-Wit, Inc., Book 3
Meanstreet – War-N-Wit, Inc., Book 4
Vanished
The Color of Seven

About the Author

Gail Roughton's spent close to forty years in a law office as a legal secretary/paralegal. During those years, she's raised three children and quite a few attorneys. She kept herself sane by writing books, tossing each completed novel in her closet. A cross-genre writer, her work spans the spectrum from humor to horror and even she never knows what to expect next. She sends special thanks to her son-in-law for allowing her to pick his brain unmercifully throughout the writing of this book, a book written with love and dedicated in part to the small towns of the South. She knows them intimately. She lives in one.

http://bookswelove.com